Maud closed her eyes again, too weak even to voice agreement with Diana. At that moment she would have given every penny that she'd managed to save since September to turn the clock back two years. She wanted to be fourteen again. Curled up in her big, warm, comfortable, flannel-sheeted double bed, a stone footwarmer at her feet, and her big sister Bethan to soothe and cuddle her.

But Bethan wasn't home, and before she'd be allowed to go to bed she'd have to face her mother. One glance at the apprehension on Diana's face was enough to tell her that she wasn't the only one dreading the encounter.

Catrin Collier was born and brought up in Pontypridd. She lives in Swansea with her husband, three cats and whichever of her children choose to visit. Her latest novel in Orion paperback is *Finders & Keepers*, and her latest novel in hardback, *Tiger Bay Blues*, is also available from Orion. Visit her website at www.catrincollier.co.uk.

By Catrin Collier

HISTORICAL

Hearts of Gold
One Blue Moon
A Silver Lining
All That Glitters
Such Sweet Sorrow
Past Remembering
Broken Rainbows
Spoils of War
Swansea Girls
Swansea Summer
Homecoming
Beggars & Choosers
Winners & Losers
Sinners & Shadows
Finders & Keepers
Tiger Bay Blues

CRIME (*as Katherine John*)

Without Trace
Midnight Murders
Murder of a Dead Man
By Any Other Name

MODERN FICTION (*as Caro French*)

The Farcreek Trilogy

One Blue Moon

CATRIN COLLIER

An Orion paperback

First published in Great Britain in 1993
by Century
First published in paperback in Great Britain in 1994
by Arrow
This paperback edition published in 2006
by Orion Books Ltd,
Orion House, 5 Upper St Martin's Lane,
London WC2H 9EA

A CIP catalogue record for this book is available from the British Library.

ISBN-13 978-1-4072-0688-2

Printed and bound in the EU

The Orion Publishing Group's policy is to use papers that
are natural, renewable and recyclable products and made
from wood grown in sustainable forests. The logging and
manufacturing processes are expected to conform to the
environmental regulations of the country of origin.

www.orionbooks.co.uk

For my cousin Marion Goodwin and all those who
have fought the illnesses associated with
the Welsh valleys armed with nothing more
than patience, courage and the
indomitable Welsh sense of humour

Acknowledgements

The 'research' (if you can grace it by that name, for I was totally unaware that I was doing anything so grand) for this book began years ago, when as a schoolgirl anxious to earn pocket money, I took a Saturday job in Pontypridd, in where else but an Italian owned and run café. I very quickly discovered that the Italian race are warm, generous (dare I say soft) hearted and, like the Welsh, ever ready to help anyone in genuine need. My employers and my co-workers taught me a great deal, and not just about the café and restaurant business.

I also owe a great debt of gratitude to Mr Romeo Basini of Treorchy, who is every bit as wonderful as his name, for his inexhaustible fund of knowledge both about the Welsh/Italian cafés, and about rural life in Bardi in the 1930s. He very kindly allowed me to monopolise many of his lunch hours when I am sure he would have been far happier taking his customary walk and breath of fresh air.

I would also like to thank my parents Glyn and Gerda Jones, for their love, and the continual help they both give me with my research.

Mid-Glamorgan County Library Service, the County Librarian Mr J. I. Davies, and all the staff of Pontypridd Library, especially Mr Adrian Burton and Mrs Penny Pughe for their constant ongoing assistance and support in ways far too numerous to mention.

My husband John and my children Ralph, Sophie and Ross, for only moaning 'a little bit' when I took this unfinished book on our annual holiday.

Jennifer Price and Margaret Bloomfield without whose friendship and practical help I would cease to function.

And above all my editor Jo Frank, who was always on the end of the telephone when I needed a sympathetic ear, and who kept the book firmly on course, and my agent Michael Thomas for his help and many kindnesses.

Thank you.

I have again taken the liberty of mixing real people with my fictional ones, particularly theatrical artistes, such as Willi Pantzer who actually toured South Wales in the 1930s. However, I would like to stress that all my main characters, although firmly rooted in the Welsh and Italian Welsh communities of the valleys in the thirties are entirely fictional and creations of my imagination. And while gratefully acknowledging all the help I have received with my research I would also like to say that any errors in *One Blue Moon* are entirely mine.

Catrin Collier, August 1992

Chapter One

Most people, especially men, thought of Diana Powell as pretty. She was, in a fresh, youthful, plump kind of a way. Red, rosy cheeks highlighted flawless, creamy skin, her brown eyes sparkled with vitality, and as she travelled towards Pontypridd in the train with her cousin Maud, her lips were as perfect, pouting, expressive and red as Carole Lombard's on the poster for her latest film *Lady by Choice*. A poster that had been plastered over every available inch of hoarding heading out of Cardiff station, thus giving Diana ample time to study and imitate. Even the curls that escaped from beneath Diana's market stall version of the current fashionable cloche hat bounced shining and wavy, despite the damp, heavy atmosphere.

Maud Powell didn't resent her cousin Diana's attractive looks. Envy had never been a part of Maud's nature, and her naturally sunny disposition was the one constant that remained, even now, with her body weak and devastated by sickness. But occasionally, she wished – and dreamed herself into health every bit as exuberant and vigorous as Diana's. Slumped back against the grimy upholstery of the sagging railway carriage bench seat, she closed her eyes and indulged in what had rapidly become her favourite occupation – daydreaming.

She was in danger, terrible danger, but the peril wasn't great enough to interfere with her grooming. A long, creamy satin gown clung to her figure, suddenly, miraculously transformed from scrawny to curvaceous in all the right places. Swirls of ostrich feathers swanned around her ankles in a fashion reminiscent of Ginger Rogers. White kid gloves clad her arms to the elbow, her blonde hair was immaculately waved and gleaming. Her face, no longer pale and haggard, was stunningly, heart-stoppingly beautiful. And every time she moved, the perfume of magnolia blossom wafted from her skin, scenting the atmosphere. (She didn't have a clue what magnolia blossom smelt like, but she'd liked the sound of the name when Robert Taylor had praised it in one of his films.)

1

She was running – running along an upstairs corridor in a Hollywood version of the English country manor (the only version she'd ever seen) that was filled with acrid smoke. Flames licked at her heels as she stood, alone and vulnerable at the top of a magnificent burning staircase. She cried out, and there walking towards her through the smoke and the fire, arms outstretched waiting to carry her away, was – was . . . this posed the most difficult question in any daydream. She hated having to choose between tall, elegant, aesthetic, poetic Leslie Howard, and robust, cynical, darkly handsome Clark Gable.

A coughing fit shook her thin frame, jolting her sharply back into the present. Lifting her sodden handkerchief to her stained lips, she looked around the railway carriage in bewilderment.

'Off on a fancy again? With Robert Donat instead of that porter, I hope,' Diana said caustically. 'Here, you're hopeless.' Seeing the state of Maud's handkerchief she pulled a crumpled white cotton square out of her coat pocket.

'I can't take yours. I'll stain it, and it won't wash out,' Maud gasped breathlessly.

'Then I'll just have to bleach it before I put it in the wash, won't I?' Diana thrust the handkerchief impatiently into Maud's hand. 'Here. Yours is soaking.' She rummaged in her coat pocket, found an empty triangular sweet bag and held it out.

'Thanks.' Maud dropped her bloodstained handkerchief into the bag as she turned to stare out of the rain-spattered window. All her carefully nurtured romantic images had fled. Unable to rekindle the sense of exoticism, she despised herself for her foolish fancies. Looking the way she did, a tramp wouldn't waste time on a second glance, let alone Clark Gable.

As she closed her eyes again, another, darker image came to mind. A winter's scene. Cold, dismal. Rain noisily spattering the bark and dead leaves of the skeletal trees that laced the grey skies above Glyntaff cemetery. On the ground, vibrant splashes of white and red flowers piled next to a mound of freshly dug earth – would they have to be wax flowers if it was winter? The headstone in the mason's yard close to the gate, already chiselled and embossed with shiny new black Gothic lettering

Here lies Maud Powell
Cut down in the full flush of youth
aged 16 in 193—

Nineteen thirty what? Would it be this year's date, or next? Would she live to see the New Year in? If she did there'd be Christmas to look forward to. Her father nearly always managed to get a chicken, and she could hang up her stocking . . .

'Almost there,' Diana observed briskly, shattering Maud's lachrymose thoughts as moss-green hills crowned by precarious pyramids of black slag began to roll sedately past.

'Unfortunately,' Maud snapped with unintentional harshness as she was prised from the tragic scenario of her own funeral.

'Well, it might not be the homecoming we dreamed of when we left for Cardiff, but at least it is a homecoming,' Diana commented philosophically, buttoning the old red wool coat that she'd 'turned' at the beginning of winter.

'I'm dreading telling everyone that Matron asked me to leave.'

'You won't have to say a word,' Diana reassured her bleakly. 'One look at you will be enough. You're in no fit state to be a patient in the Royal Infirmary, let alone a ward maid.'

'If I get better, they will take me back, won't they?' Maud demanded, struggling for breath.

'If you've any sense left, you won't ask,' Diana retorted. 'No one with a brain in their head would want to work as a skivvy in that place.'

'It wasn't that bad,' Maud protested. 'And they would have taken us on as trainee nurses when we were seventeen.'

'You, perhaps, Miss Goody Two-Shoes, not me.' Seeing despondency surface in Maud's face yet again, Diana reached out and touched her cousin's hand. 'A couple of months' rest at home, in the warm, in front of the fire, and you'll be right as rain,' she asserted boldly, hoping she sounded more convincing than she felt. 'Then if you really want to carry on scrubbing floors, emptying bedpans and cleaning lavatories for the rest of your life, I'm sure they'll welcome you back with open arms.'

'I didn't like that side of it, any more than you did,' Maud countered irritably. 'But it was a way into nursing, and all I've wanted since Bethan passed her exams was to be a nurse like her.'

3

'Little sister, big sister! Well thank God I've no one's footsteps to follow in except dear brother William's, and as he's an absolute waster, that leaves the coast clear for me to do as I like.' Diana deliberately chose not to mention her mother, Megan, who was in jail for handling stolen goods. 'And before you go all noble, sacrificial and Florence Nightingale on me, remember, even Bethan got out of it as soon as she could.'

'After she qualified, and only when she married,' Maud remonstrated.

'Aha! So that's it. You want to marry a doctor. Well it beats me how Bethan managed to hook one. The nearest I ever got to the almighty breed was to scrub their dirty bootmarks off the floor after they'd passed by. A long time after they'd passed by,' she qualified sourly.

'I do hope Bethan's taking care of herself,' Maud murmured absently. 'It's bad enough having to live amongst strangers in London, but being pregnant as well must be horrible.'

'She's better off than most with a doctor for a husband.' Diana rose to her feet and lifted down their shabby and threadbare gladstones from the knotted string rack above their heads. 'He'll bring home enough to keep her in the lap of luxury. Bet he even buys her roses and chocolates on pay night, which is more than you and me'll ever have if we don't pull our fingers out and start looking for something better than that porter you got mixed up with in the Infirmary,' she added practically.

'I wasn't mixed up with him!'

'No, you only held his hand every time you thought no one was looking.'

'He was so far from home, and lonely.'

'And you're a sucker for a corny line.'

'I am not!' Maud gasped indignantly.

'Jock Maitlin was a self-righteous, self-seeking, selfish clot, who wanted someone to wash his dirty socks, and you didn't even wait for him to ask.'

'Diana, everyone knows how helpless men are.'

'And helpless they'll remain while there are idiots like you willing to run after them. Look, we're here.' Diana turned away from Maud and gathered up her handbag.

Maud rose unsteadily to her feet, succumbed to yet another

4

vicious coughing fit that lent unhealthy colour to her face, and sank weakly down on the seat again. Diana flung open the door, threw out their bags and looked back at her cousin.

'Here, grab my arm!' she commanded ungraciously. 'The guard's about to blow the whistle, and I've no intention of carrying on up to Trehafod.'

'I'm sorry,' Maud whispered hoarsely, as she clutched Diana's sleeve and stumbled out on to the platform.

'Oh God, what am I going to do with you?' Diana griped as, ignoring their bags, she struggled to dump Maud on a bench set against the wall of the refreshment bar. Maud had no voice left to apologise a second time. She fell on to the grubby seat and continued to cough into Diana's now bloody handkerchief.

'Damn! There's not a soul around we know,' Diana cursed, as she scanned the crowds that were leaving the train and pushing their way past the ticket collector's booth at the top of the wide, steep stone flight of stairs that led down into the station yard. 'And it's raining cats and dogs,' she continued to moan, brushing away the raindrops that were falling on to her head from the high roof of the open platform. 'Well you'll just have to jolly well sit there while I carry the bags,' she asserted forcefully, abandoning Maud and picking up their luggage. 'I'll leave them downstairs, and come back up for you.'

'I'll take your bags, Miss.'

Diana stared coolly at the young, scrawny, ginger-haired porter.

'I haven't any money to tip you,' she said bluntly.

'I'd settle for a kiss,' he grinned cheekily.

'Chance would be a fine thing,' Diana retorted.

'Visit to the pictures tonight, then? Dutch treat.'

'I'd sooner go out with . . .' The whistle blew and the sound of the steam engine drowned out the rest of Diana's words, which was probably just as well.

'Why don't you stick to old ladies, Pugh, and leave the young ones to those experienced enough to deal with them?' A square-built, thickset porter elbowed Pugh aside and swept Diana's bags from her hands.

'Here, where do you think you're going?' she shouted furiously.

'Station yard,' he called back glibly, running smartly down the stone steps.

'Men!' Diana gripped her handbag firmly in her left hand, and offered her right to Maud.

'I'm sorry for being such a trouble,' Maud wheezed from behind the handkerchief she still clutched to her mouth.

'For pity's sake stop apologising,' Diana snapped.

'Diana . . . I . . .' Black mists swirled upwards from Maud's feet. The grey stone platform spotted with black coal smuts, the mass of ill-dressed women and damp, red-nosed children revolved headily around her. She slumped forward.

'She's in a bad way,' the young porter observed tactlessly as he struggled to catch Maud's head before it hit the flagstones. 'Consumption, is it?'

'Of course it's bloody consumption,' Diana raged as the anger she'd barely managed to hold in check all morning finally erupted. 'Any fool can see that.'

'She looks just like my older sister did before she went.' For all of his slender build, the boy scooped Maud high into his arms. 'She died last year,' he added forlornly.

Diana heard what he said, but her temper had risen too high for her to think of commiserating on his loss.

'Is there anyone meeting you?' he asked, as he carried Maud down the steps.

'No one,' Diana said flatly. 'Our family don't even know we're on our way home.'

'There's usually a taxi waiting in the yard.'

'Do we look as though we've money to pay for a taxi?' she demanded hotly.

'Have you far to go?'

'The top of the Graig hill.'

'I could always carry her to the Graig hospital. It's only around the corner.'

'I *do* know where the Graig hospital is. I've lived here all my life, and I'm not putting her' – she pointed at Maud – 'in any TB ward. There's only one way they come out of there, and that's feet first, in a box.'

The boy turned white; Diana's bluntness conjured up painful images of his sister's death and funeral. Images that constantly hovered too close to consciousness for peace of mind.

'She needs help,' he emphasised bitterly. Turning left at the foot

6

of the steps he walked swiftly through the rain into the shelter of the booking hall.

'What do you think you're doing, Pugh?' the porter who'd carried Diana's bags down demanded.

'Young lady passed out cold.'

'Yes well, that's as may be. But now you'd better leave her to me and get back on to the platform before you're missed. I'll call you a taxi, Miss,' he smirked at Diana.

'You most certainly won't,' Diana said fiercely. She thought quickly. If her brother William's friend Giacomo 'Ronnie' Ronconi was working in his family's café on the Tumble, his Trojan van wouldn't be far, and once he saw the state Maud was in he could hardly refuse to drive them up the hill. 'Carry her across to Ronconi's café,' she ordered Pugh, as she picked up her bags from the older porter's feet. 'Ronnie's a friend of ours. He'll see us home.'

'Pugh, you know you're not allowed to leave station yard during working hours,' the older porter lectured, ruffled by Diana's offhand dismissal of his services.

'That's all right. I'll take the lady from here.' A tall thickset man with light brown curly hair, who for all of his size, weight and athletic build had a soft feminine look about him, lifted Maud from Pugh's arms.

'Wyn Rees!' Forgetting her brother's antipathy to Rees the sweetshop's son, who was more commonly known in the town as 'Rees the queer', Diana hugged him out of sheer joy at seeing a familiar face. 'Where did you spring from?'

'Saw the commotion as I was on my way back to the shop from the post office,' Wyn explained. 'Dear God, Maud's lost weight!' he exclaimed, shifting her to a more comfortable position. 'What have you two been doing to yourselves in Cardiff?'

'Working ourselves to the bone.'

'So I see. Did I hear you say you wanted to go to Ronnie's?' Diana nodded.

Tenting his coat over Maud's head, he walked out of station yard and crossed the road quickly, avoiding a milk cart laden with churns that came rattling down the Graig hill at full tilt. Sidestepping a couple of boys on delivery bicycles, he pushed through a gawping group of gossiping women, and into the café.

Struggling with the two gladstones, Diana failed to keep up with him. By the time she'd opened the café door, Tina Ronconi, Ronnie's sister, had taken Maud from Wyn, uprooted two customers, stretched Maud out across their chairs and was bathing her temples with cold water.

Hot, steamy air, and mouthwatering warm aromas of freshly ground coffee and savoury frying, blasted welcomingly into Diana's face as she dropped her bags and closed the door. The interior of the café was dark, gloomy and blessedly, marvellously, familiar. A long mahogany counter dominated the left-hand side of the room, with matching shelves behind it, backed by an enormous mirror that reflected the rear of the huge mock-marble soda foundtain, and stone lemon, lime and sarsaprilla cordial jars. A crammed conglomeration of glass sweet jars, open boxes of chocolate bars, carefully piled packets of cigarettes, cups, saucers and glass cases of iced and cream cakes filled every available inch of space on the wooden shelves.

She paused and listened for a moment, making out the distinctive voice of her old schoolfriend, Tony Ronconi, as it drifted noisily above the din of café conversation from behind the curtained doorway that led into the unseen recesses of the kitchen. All the tables she could see were taken. They were every Saturday morning, especially those around the stove that belched warmth into the 'front' room of the café. Through the arched alcove she could see a tram crew huddled round the open fire in the back area, shoes off, feet on fender drying their soaking socks.

'I see you looked after Maud all right?' Ronnie, the eldest and most cynical of the second generation of Ronconis, called from behind the counter where he was pouring six mugs of tea simultaneously.

'I'd like to see you look after anyone where we've come from, Ronnie Ronconi,' Diana scowled, moving the bags out of the doorway and closer to the chairs Maud was lying on.

'Here,' Ronnie pushed a cup of tea and the sugar shaker across the counter towards her. 'Tony?' he called out to the brother next in line to him, who was working in the kitchen. 'Take over for me.'

'Who's going to do the vegetables for the dinners if I have to work behind the counter?' Tony asked indignantly as he appeared from behind the curtain. 'Angelo can't. He's still washing

8

breakfast dishes. At half speed,' he added. Noticing Diana for the first time, he smiled and nodded to her.

'It's only ten o'clock,' Ronnie countered, quashing his brother's complaints. 'Papa and I used to get out seventy dinners in two and half hours on a Saturday in High Street with no help, and only an hour's preparation. Time you learnt to do the same, my boy.'

Maud began to cough.

'Prop her up, you stupid girls,' Ronnie shouted at his sister and Diana. 'Can't you see she's choking?' Lifting himself on the flat of his hands he swung his long, lithe body easily over the high counter. He pushed his hand beneath Maud's back and eased her into a sitting position. Startled by how light she was, he failed to stop the shock from registering on his face. He looked up. Diana was watching him. 'I've seen more meat on picked chicken bones,' he commented. 'Didn't they feed you in the Infirmary?'

'Slops and leftovers, and not enough of those,' Diana said harshly.

'You back for the weekend, Diana?' Tina asked brightly in a clumsy effort to lighten the atmosphere generated by Ronnie's insensitive questioning.

'No, back for good,' Diana said flatly.

'Job didn't work out then?' Tina asked.

'They gave us all a medical yesterday. Afterwards they told Maud she was too ill to work. Swines handed over her wages along with her cards. I could hardly let her come home on her own.'

'Language!' Ronnie reprimanded. 'If you were my sister I'd drag you into the kitchen and scrub your mouth out with washing soda.'

'Then it's just as well I'm not your sister.'

'One more word from you, young lady, and I'll put you outside the door.'

Diana fell silent. Although Ronnie was eleven years older than her, and more her brother's friend than hers, she knew him well enough. He wasn't one for making idle threats, and she was too worried about Maud to risk being parted from her now, when they were so close to home.

'They only told Maud to leave yesterday?' Ronnie demanded incredulously as he brushed Maud's fair curls away from her face with a gesture that was uncommonly tender, for him.

'It was as much as they could do to let us sleep in our beds in the hostel last night. New girls took over from us today.'

'Maud didn't get like this in a day or two, I know.'

'She never was very strong,' Diana insisted defensively. 'And as soon as the weather turned really cold, she got worse.'

'Stop talking about me as if I wasn't here,' Maud murmured, consciousness coinciding with yet another coughing fit.

'See what you get for trying to talk?' Ronnie unpinned the corners of the tea towel he was wearing round his waist and flung it at Tony. 'I'm going to get the Trojan out of the White Hart yard. You'll have to hurry the dishes and do the vegetables as well Angelo,' he ordered his fifteen-year-old brother, who was peeking out from behind the kitchen curtain to find out what all the commotion was about.

'I was going to the penny rush in the White Palace. Why should I do Tony's jobs as well as my own?' he complained.

'Because Tony's needed behind the counter, and because I'm telling you to,' Ronnie said forcefully.

'Well I'm not doing the cooking as well.' Angelo slammed the pile of tea plates he was holding on to the counter. 'And that's final.'

'I wouldn't trust you to,' Ronnie rejoined.

'Then who is?' Angelo demanded.

'Tina, and before you say another word, think of Tony. He'll have to manage both the counter and the tables for half an hour.'

'But Ronnie, you promised I could go to the penny rush this week. You promised.'

'Just stop your griping and get on with it, will you? It's time all three of you learned to cope on your own for five minutes.'

'Ronnie . . .'

'One more word out of you, Angelo, and you'll be working every night next week.' He looked at the girls. 'When you hear the horn, get Maud ready. I'll come in and carry her outside.'

'Thanks, Ronnie.' Diana was grateful to him for not making her beg for the lift. She finally picked up her tea from the counter and sugared it.

'There's no need to thank me. I owe Will a favour. And you,' he glared at Tina. 'Take a good look at these two and think twice before you try to nag Papa or me into letting you leave home again.'

10

'See what you've done, Diana,' Tina hissed as Ronnie went out. 'Now they'll never let any of us leave home.'

'Except to visit our grandmother in the back end of Italy,' Angelo crowed. He'd never had any desire to leave Pontypridd.

'Don't you dare go rubbing it in, Angelo Ronconi,' Tina snapped.

'Leaving home's not all it's cracked up to be. Is it kid?' Diana helped Maud to sit up while looking around for Wyn. She wanted to thank him. The first familiar face in Pontypridd had shown her that she no longer had to shoulder the problem of Maud's illness alone. But she couldn't see him anywhere.

Maud closed her eyes again, too weak even to voice agreement with Diana. At that moment she would have given every penny that she'd managed to save since September to turn the clock back two years. She wanted to be fourteen again. Curled up in her big, warm, comfortable, flannel-sheeted double bed, a stone foot-warmer at her feet, and her big sister Bethan to soothe and cuddle her.

But Bethan wasn't home, and before she'd be allowed go to bed she'd have to face her mother. One glance at the apprehension on Diana's face was enough to tell her that she wasn't the only one dreading the encounter.

Chapter Two

'You're going the wrong way,' Diana protested, struggling to prevent Maud from falling on to Ronnie as he swung the Trojan around a sharp left turn a third of the way up the Graig hill. Ronnie had insisted on sandwiching Maud on the bench seat between them, but with Maud still teetering on the point of collapse, Diana was finding the drive up the hill more of a strain than the train journey.

'I'm stopping off at Laura and Trevor's,' Ronnie announced. 'What's the point in having a sister married to a doctor if you don't make use of him occasionally?' The eldest of eleven children, he was accustomed to making decisions and assuming authority. Authority strengthened by the business responsibilities his father had thrust upon him at an early age, and his mother's habit of deferring to him almost as much as she deferred to her husband.

'I think Maud should go straight home to bed,' Diana said forcefully.

'And I think she needs to see a doctor,' Ronnie countermanded, swinging the van round to the right and pulling up outside a low terrace of stone houses that fronted directly on to the pavement. 'And if you're worrying about Trevor's bill, don't. Your uncle pays Trevor his penny a week same as all the other families on the Graig. Trevor won't charge him any more for looking at Maud now.'

'I didn't think he would.' Diana flung open the door of the van and turned to help Maud, but Ronnie had already lifted her cousin from the van. Cradling Maud in one arm, he opened the front door of one of the houses with his free hand.

'Laura!' he shouted, walking straight past the parlour, down the narrow passage and into the back kitchen.

'Ronnie?' Laura answered from the range where she was stirring a pot of stew. 'I am honoured,' she said sarcastically. 'What brings you here in the middle of the day, and a market day at that . . . Dear God!' She stepped back, dropping the spoon to the floor as

12

Ronnie carried Maud into the tiny room and set her down in an easy chair comfortably placed in front of the fire.

'She's ill,' Ronnie announced somewhat superfluously as Laura, still very much the nurse despite her new status of housewife, loosened the collar of Maud's coat and checked her temperature by laying her cool hand against Maud's flushed cheek. She looked up and nodded to Diana, who was hovering awkwardly in the passageway just outside the kitchen door. Seeing condemnation where none was intended in Laura's glance, Diana forced back the tears that were stinging the back of her eyes.

'The Infirmary didn't work out then?' Laura asked.

Diana shook her head.

'They've just come in on the Cardiff train,' Ronnie explained briefly. 'Maud fainted in the station so I thought it might be as well if Trevor took a look at her before I take her home.'

'He's in the Central Homes.' Laura glanced up at a smart black modern clock on the wall. 'I'll telephone and see if I can get hold of him. Morning ward rounds should be about finishing by now. I'm sure he'll be able to spare a few minutes.'

'I'm fine,' Maud murmured faintly.

'I can see just how fine you are my girl,' Laura said in a calm voice that reminded Maud of her sister Bethan. 'I'll telephone. Diana, get your hat and coat off and make us all some tea.'

Diana did as she was asked, while Laura went into the hall. Ronnie sat in the easy chair at the opposite end of the range to Maud's. He pulled the *Pontypridd Observer* out from behind the cushion at his back, propped his feet up on a kitchen chair, and began to read.

Diana bustled around, checking the kettle was full, lifting cups down from the dresser, all the while marvelling that Laura – the Laura she'd known ever since she could remember – had a telephone in her house, and a doctor for a husband.

'Trevor will be here in five minutes.' Laura wiped her hands on her overall and checked her reflection in the bevel-edged mirror that hung above the table. She had to lean over the table in order to do so: there wasn't much free space to move around in between the range, easy chairs, dresser, table and kitchen chairs.

'Bride primping for hubby?' Ronnie teased, peering over the top of the paper.

'Just checking to see I don't look as scruffy as you.' Laura kicked the chair out from under Ronnie's feet. 'And don't treat my home like a dosshouse,' she ordered.

'Tea's poured,' Diana interrupted. The fights between the Ronconis, particularly the two eldest, were legendary on the Graig.

'Is it sugared and stirred?' Ronnie extended his hand from behind his paper.

'You paralysed, or what?' Diana retorted.

'Just looking after my driving arm.'

Conscious that Ronnie had only ferried them half-way up the hill, Diana heaped three sugars into the tea, stirred it and handed it to him.

'Maud, do you want some tea?' Laura asked in the slightly loud voice that nurses on public wards usually adopt when talking to their patients.

Heaving for breath, Maud shook her head.

'Laura, I'm home.' The door banged and Trevor strode into the house. Not quite up to Ronnie's six-foot mark, he was dark and slightly built. His thin face flushed with pride as he looked briefly at his wife before turning to Diana and Maud.

'Back already from the Infirmary?'

'It didn't work out,' Diana muttered, embarrassed by the constant repetition of her and Maud's failure.

'The Infirmary's hard on junior doctors,' Trevor said kindly, 'but I've heard it's even harder on ward maids.' He glanced at Ronnie. 'It's good to see you, Ronnie, you should come down more often.'

'I would if dear sister didn't live here.' Ronnie finished his tea, stood up and stretched. 'I've been meaning to check the oil in the van for days. Give me a shout when you're ready to go, Diana. See you Trevor, Laura.' He closed the door behind him.

Trevor took Maud's pulse while Diana squeezed another cup of tea out of the pot for him.

'Looks like you've had too much work, not enough food and nowhere near enough rest.' Trevor released his hold on Maud's wrist.

'They said it was consumption,' she said flatly, taking deep breaths in an effort to stop coughing.

14

'Did they take an X-ray?' he asked.

'They X-rayed all of us twice. Once when we started in September, and again last week,' Diana answered for her.

'And they asked you to go after they had the results of last week's tests?'

'Yes,' Maud whispered.

'How long have you been coughing like this?'

'For a couple of weeks,' Maud mumbled vaguely.

He wrapped his hand around her fist, and forced her fingers open. Diana's sodden and bloody handkerchief lay in her palm.

'And how long have you been coughing up blood?' he asked quietly.

'A week, perhaps two,' she replied reluctantly.

'Home for you, young lady,' Trevor decreed. 'Warm room, warm bed, and plenty of rest. Tell your mother I'll be up as soon as I've finished in the hospital for the day.'

'I'll be fine.'

'Who's the doctor here, me or you?' He looked at Diana. 'You'll see she behaves herself?'

'I tried my best the whole time we were in the Infirmary. I'm not likely to stop now,' Diana replied. She felt as though the whole world were blaming her for the state Maud was in.

'I'll give Ronnie a shout.' Laura opened the door. 'Tell Mrs Powell I'll call in and see her when I come up to visit Mama.'

'I'll do that,' Diana said dully, picking up her coat and handbag.

'They'll all be glad to see you safely back home.' Laura smiled brightly as she helped Maud button her coat.

'I'm not too sure of that,' Diana answered as she walked down the passageway. Her Aunt Elizabeth had never attempted to hide her dislike of her, her brother Will or their widowed mother Megan, and after her mother had been arrested Aunt Elizabeth had publicly announced that none of Evan's dead brother's family would ever set foot in her house again. Diana had nearly collapsed when she'd received a letter from Will two weeks after she and Maud had started work in the Infirmary telling her that both he and their mother's Russian lodger, Charlie Raschenko, had moved in with their uncle and aunt, after he'd been forced to sell their house to pay off their mother's fines. But for all of Will's cheery determination to make the best of a bad situation, and

15

Laura's sentimental forecast of a warm welcome, she rather suspected that the atmosphere in Graig Avenue would be strained enough, without her and Maud adding to the already overcrowded household.

Elizabeth was alone in the house, dredging sugar over the pastry top of an enormous bread pudding, when Diana and Ronnie walked into the back kitchen, half carrying, half dragging an exhausted Maud between them. Ronnie took one look at the deserted room and remained only as long as it took him to exchange pleasantries with Elizabeth before returning to the van for Maud and Diana's bags. He left them in the passageway, shutting the front door behind him.

'What's this, then?' Elizabeth demanded, although a look at Maud had been sufficient for her to sum up the situation.

'They wouldn't let me stay on in the Infirmary,' Maud began to explain in a cracked whisper.

'They gave Maud her cards yesterday,' Diana interrupted. 'I couldn't let her go home by herself.'

'Then you'll be wanting a bed tonight too,' Elizabeth sighed in a martyred voice.

'Diana's come home for good. Same as me Mam,' Maud broke in quickly.

'And pray tell, what are the pair of you going to live on?'

'I'm sure I'll find something soon.' Diana knew full well that the question had been directed more at her than Maud. 'I promise I won't be any trouble, Aunt Elizabeth.'

'And I know you won't, my girl!' Elizabeth echoed harshly. 'First sign of any nonsense and you'll be out through that door quicker than you walked in. That's something I'm promising you.'

Taking Elizabeth's idea of 'nonsense' as a veiled reference to her mother's transgressions, Diana found it difficult to hold her tongue.

'Heaven only knows where I'm going to put you,' Elizabeth complained, crashing open the oven door and thrusting the bread pudding inside. 'The house is full to bursting with William and Charlie lodging here as it is.'

'Diana can share with me,' Maud said faintly from the depths of her father's easy chair, where Ronnie had left her.

16

'I think not,' Elizabeth contradicted. 'Not with that cold. If Diana shares a bed with you, like as not she'll catch it, and the last thing I need is two of you to nurse.'

'Diana and I have been sharing a room for months, and it's not a cold . . .'

'Of course it is, girl,' Elizabeth broke in too quickly. 'You obviously haven't been looking after yourself the way I taught you to. I don't expect you've been airing your clothes properly, or wearing the warm flannel underwear I stitched for you.' She shook her head briskly. 'It was the same with Bethan. She wouldn't listen, and look where that got her. And when she was ill, what did she do? Expected me to drop everything and nurse her, same as you do now.'

'I don't expect anything, Mam,' Maud croaked.

'She has been wearing her warm underwear, Aunt Elizabeth,' Diana protested, angered by her aunt's lack of sympathy.

'Seeing is believing,' Elizabeth chanted smugly. 'She wouldn't be lying there like that if she had. Neglect! Pure neglect and selfishness, that's what this is.'

'I think Maud ought to go to bed, Aunt Elizabeth,' Diana suggested. 'She fainted twice on the journey here and the doctor said . . .'

'What doctor?' Elizabeth commanded, instantly on the alert.

'Doctor Lewis. Ronnie stopped off at Laura's house on the way up the hill, so Maud could see him, and Doctor Lewis said Maud should be put to bed in a warm room right away, and he'd call in tonight after he finished in the hospital.'

'And just what did Ronnie Ronconi think he was doing, taking my daughter to a doctor when he wasn't asked?' Elizabeth ranted. 'Is his brother-in-law so short of work now that he has to tout for trade for him? And I suppose Trevor Lewis suggested that we go and buy some expensive concoction or other in the chemist's, when any fool can see all that's wrong with Maud is a common cold.'

'He didn't prescribe anything,' Diana said coldly, before Maud, who was struggling for breath, managed to speak. 'All he said was that Maud should go to bed.'

'As if I need a doctor to tell me to put my own daughter to bed when she's in that condition,' Elizabeth sneered. 'Well, doctor or

17

not Maud, I'm afraid you're going to have to make do in your father's easy chair with a stool at your feet for an hour or two while I make up and air your bed. It will do more harm than good for you to go upstairs the way it is now. I don't think your bedroom door's been opened more than once or twice since Bethan left. And seeing as how you're here,' she turned to Diana, 'you may as well make yourself useful. You can bring up some sticks and half a bucketful of coals, and lay a fire to chase the damp out of the room. And don't go thinking that you can have a fire in there every day either,' she cautioned her daughter. 'We haven't money to waste on coal for anyone's bedroom, ill or not. We're hard pushed to keep the kitchen stove going, even in this weather, on what little your father and Eddie bring in. This will be a one-off treat because the room's not been used since the cold weather started.'

'Don't put yourself out on my account,' Maud bit back, her eyes heavy with anger and exhaustion.

'Looks like I'm going to have to, whether you want me to or not.' Elizabeth opened the washhouse door and lifted out her brushes and dusters.

'Won't take long, Maud.' Diana lifted Maud's feet on to a kitchen chair. Taking her coat off, she draped it over Maud, who was still wearing hers.

'There's spare blankets in the ottoman at the foot of my bed,' Elizabeth said. 'You can bring one down. It will be a sight more serviceable than your damp coat.'

'Yes, aunt.' Inwardly seething, Diana left the room. She brought down a thick grey blanket that smelt of moth-balls and folded it around Maud. Her cousin was already asleep. Slumped sideways in the chair, her fair hair was plastered close to her head in tendrils that had been curled into tight ringlets by the rain. Her face was flushed with illness and the heat of the fire. An overwhelming sense of guilt washed over Diana as she tucked the blanket around Maud's emaciated figure. She should have done something weeks ago: persuaded Maud to leave the Infirmary when the signs of tuberculosis had become increasingly apparent; rushed her home when she had first coughed up blood, not a couple of weeks ago as Maud had told Trevor, but months back. During the first week they'd spent in Cardiff.

It was four o'clock in the afternoon before Elizabeth had organised Maud's bedroom to her satisfaction. Spotlessly clean furniture had been dusted and polished unnecessarily. The immaculate linoleum had been scrubbed with a bucket of warm water, lye soap and a well-worn scrubbing brush. The fire had been laid, lit, and the grate cleaned and blackleaded – by Diana. As soon as she'd finished, Elizabeth propped the double mattress against the dressing-table stool in front of the flames for airing, and it was two hours to the minute before she allowed Diana to lift it back on to the bed. The sheets, blankets and pillowcases that Elizabeth had removed from her ottoman were carried downstairs and hung over the wooden airing rack and hoisted above the range for the same magical two hours before they too were allowed on the bed.

When the bed was finally made up to Elizabeth's exacting requirements, she and Diana woke Maud from her unnaturally deep sleep and helped her upstairs. Elizabeth undressed her while Diana unpacked Maud's bag. Diana's own bag still stood ostentatiously alone and abandoned in the hall.

'I suppose you'll be wanting something to eat,' Elizabeth muttered as she pulled the curtains against the light. Maud didn't reply. Worn out, she was asleep again, curled comfortably into the depths of the great bed.

'I'm not hungry,' Diana answered curtly. She would have died rather than admit she was starving.

'If you want a cup of tea, I'll make you one,' Elizabeth offered brusquely. The bread pudding was cooked, but she wouldn't have dreamed of cutting into it before the men came home.

'I'll wash and change, and go into town.' Diana glanced at the clock as they returned to the kitchen. 'I need a job and the sooner I start looking, the sooner I'll find one.'

'There's plenty of advertisements in the *Observer* for live-in kitchen and parlour maids in England,' Elizabeth suggested in a marginally lighter tone. 'There's an agency opened in Mill Street. You can find out more there.'

'One stint in the Infirmary was enough,' Diana insisted. 'I don't intend to go back into service. Besides, I really would like to stay in Pontypridd close to Will.'

'Beggars can't be choosers,' Elizabeth recited in a schoolmarm voice. 'I didn't say too much in front of Maud because I didn't want to risk upsetting her, but we've no room for you here. Your brother and your lodger Charlie are sharing the downstairs front room as it is. Haydn and Eddie are in one bedroom, your uncle and I in the other and there's no way Maud can share a room in her condition. The box room as you well know isn't even furnished, and we've no way of furnishing it. Not with the way things are at the moment.'

'In that case I'd better see if I can find somewhere else.' Diana concealed the pain of her aunt's rejection beneath the façade of belligerent abrasiveness she had adopted as both shield and defence mechanism since the day her mother had been wrenched out of her life.

'Your Uncle Huw is still living in Bonvilston Road,' Elizabeth reminded her. Huw, Megan's bachelor brother, was a policeman in the town and worked all kinds of unsocial shifts.

'Perhaps I'll go and see him. Is Will still working on Charlie's stall?'

'He was when he left this morning.'

'As soon as I've washed I'll go down and see him.'

'I've cleaned all the bedrooms I intend to for today, and I'm certainly not going to traipse up and downstairs with any more buckets. If you want to wash you can use the washhouse. There's no one to disturb you. You'll find soap in the dish, and a towel on the top shelf.'

'Thank you.' Diana didn't even attempt to keep the sarcasm from her voice.

It was a long, cold walk down the Graig hill, made all the more unbearable by a cordial greeting from the Reverend Mark Price and his pretty young wife, who assumed that Elizabeth would be ecstatic to have her daughter and niece back home again. Pulling the collar of her sodden red coat high around her ears, Diana struggled to make civil replies to their polite enquiries after her own and Maud's health, before trekking on, past the rows of dripping stone cottages. The downpour turned into a drenching torrent. Twilight became a dark and early night, but sentiment took precedence over reason, and she paused for a few moments at the junction of Llantrisant Road and Leyshon Street.

She'd known it would hurt, and it did – more than she would have believed possible – but she couldn't stop herself from looking down the narrow terraced road towards the tiny house that her parents had bought when they'd married. She and William had both been born there in the front bedroom, where, as her mother had told them with brimming eyes glittering with happy memories, they'd also been conceived. She'd never known her father. He'd died in the mud of the Western Front six months before she'd been born. Her mother had hung his photograph on the wall of the kitchen so she and William would at least know what he'd looked like, but the photograph had faded with time, until there was only a blurred face that looked remarkably like her Uncle Evan. Quiet, kind Uncle Evan who'd been led a dog's life by Aunt Elizabeth for as long as she could remember.

Tears mingled with the rain on her cheeks as she stared at the house that had once been her home. She closed her eyes, wishing with all her might that she could walk down the street, turn the key that protruded from the lock, and enter the house. But then it wouldn't be the same. She didn't even know who lived there now. William had written to say that he and Charlie had taken the best of their mother's furniture across town to their Uncle Huw's before the bailiffs had moved in, but that was all. Perhaps it was just as well. If it was an old friend or a neighbour she'd have an excuse to call, and the sight of unfamiliar objects within the familiar walls would be more than she could bear right now. Even from where she stood she could see strange curtains hanging limply at the windows. Made of green and gold artificial silk, they sagged a little lopsidedly. The front door had been given a new coat of paint as well. A grim, unwelcoming shade of dark brown so different from the vibrant sapphire blue Will had painted it at her mother's instigation.

'Lost your way, Diana?' Glan Richards, a porter in the Graig Hospital, and the next-door neighbour of her Uncle Evan and Aunt Elizabeth, stood before her.

'Glan! How are you?' she cried out eagerly, sentiment causing her to forget the antagonism that had once existed – and for all she knew, still did exist – between him and her brother.

'Better than you by the look of it.' He thumbed the lapel of the new raincoat that he'd bought in Leslie's stores on a sixpence-a-week card. 'Lost a bob and found a farthing?'

21

'I'm great,' she smiled through her tears. 'It's just this damned cold and wet.'

'Back for the weekend?'

'No, for good,' she said, forgetting for an instant that she had nowhere to sleep that night.

'Couldn't stand the pace?' he asked snidely.

'No, the wages,' she said cuttingly. 'I've had enough of hospital slave labour. I'm off to town to look for something better.'

'If you find it, let me know. I've had about enough of hospital slave labour too, but then, whenever I've looked I've never found anything better. There's a depression on, or so they tell me.'

'Could be that you're not looking in the right places, and then again could be that you haven't the talent I've got on offer,' she retorted, regaining some of her old spirit as she lifted the hem of her coat provocatively to her knees. 'See you around.'

'In the Palladium, six o'clock tonight?' he asked hopefully.

'With an old man like you?' she laughed. 'I'm kind to the elderly, but not that kind.'

'Since when has twenty-two been old?'

'Twenty-three,' she corrected. 'You're four years older than Will and that makes you *ancient*!' She stuck her tongue out cheekily. 'See you around, Grandad.'

Glan laughed in spite of the brush-off as she walked away. He'd forgotten what a Tartar Diana was. Life was certainly going to perk up with her living next door.

22

Chapter Three

'I hate Saturdays,' Tina moaned to her younger sister Gina who'd been ordered into the café by Ronnie to put in an hour's practice in the cashier's chair. 'Here, move over.' She nudged her sister from the edge of her seat, unlaced her shoes and rubbed her aching feet through her thick, cable-knit stockings. 'And I hate waitressing,' she added emphatically. She affected a whining voice: ' "Miss . . . Miss, I ordered two teas, not coffee . . . Miss there's only butter on one side of this Chelsea. It costs a penny farthing you know . . ." Never mind that the lump of butter I slapped on the other side of the bun is big enough for four. Next week I'm sitting on the till, dear sister. It's time you got blisters on your feet.'

'I'm too young to wait tables,' Gina said. 'Too much exercise stunts growing bones.'

'In that case you'll grow into a ruddy giant.'

'I'll have none of that language in here, Tina,' Ronnie reprimanded her. 'And get your shoes on – sharpish. You're putting the customers off their food.'

'Slave driver.' Her voice pitched high as her temper flared. 'I must have walked twenty miles today around these tables . . .'

'And you can walk twenty more. With your shoes on,' he added loudly, slapping the ice cream and coffee she'd ordered on to the marble-topped section of the counter. 'Serve these. After you've washed your hands.'

'He's getting far too big for his boots,' Tina hissed at her sister as she laced her shoes back on and fired mutinous glances in Ronnie's direction. 'Sometimes I think he's in training to become another Papa.'

'He's ten times worse than Papa ever was,' Gina answered, smiling as one of the market boys approached the till with a sixpence in his hand. 'Mama can always soften Papa.'

'It'll take a blue moon for a woman to want to stand close enough to Ronnie to soften him.'

'Tina!' Ronnie snarled.

'I'm going. I'm going,' she shouted irritably. Pushing her way around the counter she threw back the curtain and stormed into the kitchen, where she washed her hands with as much fuss and splashing of water as she could manage.

A pretty girl with unfashionably long fair hair and soft grey eyes opened the café door, folded her umbrella, shook the rain from her coat and walked up to the counter.

'Seen Haydn Powell, Ronnie?' she asked quietly as she looked shyly around the room.

'No but he'll be here in – ' Ronnie glanced at the clock ' – five minutes. Usual?'

'Yes please.' She rummaged in her handbag and pulled out a well-worn leather purse. 'And . . .' she peered through the steamed-up glass on the cases that held the cakes. 'One of those custard slices, please Ronnie, and a . . .'

'Knife and two plates. I know,' he grumbled good-naturedly. 'With customers like you and Haydn Powell I'll be in the bankruptcy court next week.'

'Better half a sale than none. Leastways, that's what's my dad always says.'

'Your father has a thriving shop and the whole of the Graig to sell to.'

'And you have an enormous café and the whole of the town to peddle to,' she smiled. She pulled a chair out from a table crammed into a corner between the counter and the till. It was the only free table in the café but precious few meals were being eaten. A couple of customers had plates in front of them that held buns, cold pancakes or sandwiches, but most were nursing tepid cups of tea or Oxo.

'Here you are. One tea, once iced custard slice, a knife and two plates.' Ronnie left the counter and laid them on her table himself. 'How's that for service?'

'Wonderful.' She smiled at Gina. 'Does he do this for all the girls?'

'Only other people's girlfriends,' Gina said mildly. 'That way he knows he can stay safely married to Papa and the business.'

'Time you started bagging some of that change in the till, Gina,' Ronnie ordered.

'You know I hate doing that. My fingers get filthy and my nails break . . .'

'Gina!' Ronnie warned in a voice that was used to being obeyed.

'People are saying that you're thinking of opening another café in that vacant shop opposite the fountain,' Jenny interrupted tactfully.

'Are they now?' Ronnie murmured as he returned behind the counter.

'Well are you?'

'Better go and ask whoever told you. Seems they know more about my business than I do.'

'Make way for two drowned rats,' William shouted as he and Haydn burst, dripping and cold, into the café.

'Hello sweetheart,' Haydn ruffled Jenny's curls with a damp hand.

'I've got us a custard slice,' she beamed, her face lighting up.

'Can I take your order?' Tina sidled close to William, pouted her well-formed lips, hitched her skirt up slightly, and stood in what she hoped was a fair imitation of the Jean Harlow pose.

'Two teas, is it?' Ronnie shouted from behind the counter.

'And a couple of Welsh cakes,' William replied, winking at Tina. 'I'm starving.'

'Aren't you always?' Haydn commented scathingly.

'I haven't a Jenny to take my mind off food.' William stared at Tina. 'Corner of Griffiths' shop, ten o'clock tonight,' he whispered teasingly. 'I'll walk you home if you spend the evening with Jenny. Sorry I can't make it any earlier, but you know the market on Saturday nights.'

'Tina, those back tables need clearing, and wiping down,' Ronnie directed. He was too far away to hear what William was saying but he knew William -- and Tina. They'd had a soft spot for one another ever since they'd been classmates in Maesycoed primary school. A soft spot that had led his father to decree that Tina could only talk to William in the presence of himself or one of her grown-up brothers. It was a rule that Tina made a point of breaking wherever and whenever she could.

Ronnie watched as Tina reluctantly dragged herself off to the back of the café. They stared belligerently at one another through the thick, smoky atmosphere as she began to heap dirty dishes into a pile. Finally her temper flared up again, to the delight of all the customers except William.

'I *am* eighteen,' she snapped.

'And when you're twenty-one you can do as you like,' Ronnie said softly. 'Until then you do as Papa and I say.'

Ronnie took his duties as older brother seriously, very seriously indeed. It had hurt when his father had blamed his lax attitude for Laura finding time to fall in love with an Irish Catholic doctor, as opposed to the nice Italian boy he'd wanted for his eldest daughter. Trevor had eventually gained acceptance, but not before Papa Ronconi had told his other five daughters, including little Theresa who was barely eight years of age, that when the time came they would be introduced to nice Italian or Italian Welsh boys who met with *his* approval. Apart from William's wholly Welsh antecedents, there were other drawbacks. His wheeler-dealing, both on and off the market, coupled with the receiving charge that had led to his mother's imprisonment, had given him a not entirely undeserved shady reputation. And Ronnie, who'd always had a discreet eye for the ladies, was beginning to see a far more reckless philanderer than himself in William, that made him all the more determined to keep William as far away from Tina as possible.

'Bad luck about your sister, Haydn, I'm sorry,' Ronnie sympathised.

'Bethan?' Haydn asked quickly, wondering what gossip had found its way to the café via the maids who worked for Doctor John senior, Andrew's father, in his house on the Common. It still grieved him that the Johns had found out about Bethan and Andrew's marriage (via the telephone) before any of her own family.

'Not Bethan, Maud,' Ronnie corrected. 'I'm sorry, I thought someone would have gone to the market to tell you. She came in this morning on the Cardiff train.'

'Maud's home?' Haydn asked in bewilderment.

'She's ill,' Tina announced thoughtlessly, relishing the importance that the imparting of the news gave her. 'She collapsed in the station. Wyn Rees carried her over here, then Ronnie had to drive her and Diana home.'

'Diana's home too?' William interrupted.

26

'They've left the Infirmary. Maud was told she was too ill to work . . .'

'Tina, you'd better finish clearing those tables before they're needed for another customer,' Ronnie broke in, silencing her. He poured himself a tea and looked around the café. Seeing no one clamouring for anything, he shouted to Tony, who was washing dishes in the kitchen, to take over the counter, then carried his tea to Haydn and William's table.

'I thought you would have heard,' he explained as he sat down. 'Half of Pontypridd saw Maud being carried out of the station.'

'It obviously wasn't the same half that's been hanging around Charlie's meat stall all day,' William said caustically.

'Or Horton's second-hand stall.' Haydn cupped his hands tightly around his tea. 'What's wrong with Maud?' he asked Ronnie.

'I took her to Trevor's. He had a quick look at her before I drove her and Diana up to Graig Avenue,' Ronnie murmured, wanting to delay the moment when he'd have to tell Haydn the truth. Then he looked into Haydn's eyes and saw that he already knew. 'It's TB,' he admitted bluntly, not knowing how else to phrase it. 'Your mother and Diana were putting her to bed when I left.'

Haydn didn't say anything, but his hand shook as he reached for the sugar bowl. Jenny fumbled for his other hand beneath the tablecloth. There were tears in the corners of her eyes.

'How's Diana?' William demanded.

'Diana's Diana,' Ronnie replied. 'Cheeky as ever.'

'Did she say if she's staying?'

'She said she had no intention of going back.'

'Then she's going to need a job.'

'And a place to live.' Diana closed the door behind her and shrugged her arms out of her sodden coat.

'Long time no see, sis,' William said unemotionally, moving his chair so she could fit another one in beside him.

'My gain, your loss,' she sang out as she hung her coat and scarf on the hat stand behind the till.

'Didn't expect to see you back in here today.' Tina paused in between clearing tables. 'How's Maud?'

'In bed asleep when I left.'

'Best place for her,' Ronnie said authoritatively.

27

Diana went to the counter. 'I'll have a tea and a hot pie, please Tony,' she said. He poured the tea and gave it to her.

'I'll bring the pie when it's ready,' he smiled.

'Surely you're going to stay with us, Diana,' Haydn said as she moved a chair between him and William.

'Your mother says there's no room.'

At the mention of Elizabeth everyone fell silent. Haydn could almost taste the air of oppression his mother carried with her whenever she walked into a room.

'If Maud is ill you can't share with her, that's for certain.' Haydn replaced his cup on his saucer. 'But there's always the box room. We can squeeze a single bed in there – just.'

'But there is no single bed,' Diana protested feebly, not wanting to tell her brother and Haydn about Elizabeth's decisive pronouncement on her presence in the house.

'You took your furniture over to your Uncle Huw's, Will. Was there a bed?' Haydn asked.

'Five.' William finished his tea. 'Three single and two doubles. I saved all of Mam's bedroom suites, bedding, rugs and china, as well as all the downstairs furniture. Uncle Huw threatened to hold an auction there when I left.'

'That's settled then.' Haydn rose from his seat and reached for his coat and muffler. 'Soon as you finish on the stall you can go over and get whatever Diana needs to furnish the box room. Dad can take it up on the horse and cart.'

'Your father and Eddie will be calling in here before they finish for the day,' Ronnie shouted above the hissing of the steamer. 'They're bringing my flour over from the canal wharf.'

'In that case nothing could be simpler. You stay and wait for them, Di,' Haydn suggested, 'then you can go over to Bonvilston Road, pick out whatever you want, and they can take it up.'

'Wouldn't it be easier if I just moved in with Uncle Huw for a bit?' Diana pleaded.

Haydn looked at her and instinctively knew where the problem lay.

'Not with Will living the other end of town. It would look funny.'

'Come on, Di, you don't need me to tell you what a tip Uncle

Huw's house is. I don't think he's cleaned it since the Great War,' William said drily.

'Open horse and cart isn't ideal in this weather,' Ronnie commented practically. 'The Trojan's empty at the moment. There's more than enough room for a bed and bedding in the back.'

Diana squirmed uncomfortably. 'Aunt Elizabeth isn't expecting me back,' she said slowly.

'Dad's got a tarpaulin,' Haydn said tactfully. 'And the yard doesn't close until late on a Saturday, so he won't be in a hurry to take the horse and cart back. Best to leave it to him.' Everyone took that to mean leaving Elizabeth to him, not the moving of the furniture.

'If he needs a hand between six and seven, come and get me,' Will offered. 'There's usually a slack time then. It picks up around eight o'clock, because people know Charlie cuts the price of any joints that are left, rather than see them get knocked down in the nine o'clock bell when the leftovers are auctioned. But if it's not between six and seven, it'll have to wait until after nine.'

'I doubt there'll be anything that Dad and Eddie won't be able to handle between them.' Haydn squeezed Jenny's hand and whispered in her ear. She smiled and clung to him.

'Walk me over to the Town Hall?' he asked her.

'It's a hard life being a callboy,' Will joked. 'Nothing but pretty chorus girls, chocolates and nips of whisky backstage.'

'I'd swap jobs with you any day!'

'Need muscles to hump meat around, not pretty-boy looks,' Will teased, flexing his biceps and wrapping his arm round his sister. 'See you later, sis.'

'Thanks, Will. Haydn.' She wiped her eyes hoping that everyone would think she was still rubbing raindrops from her face.

'One pie.' Tony laid it on the table in front of her.

'Before you go,' she called out to William, Jenny and Haydn as they opened the door. 'Any of you know of a job that's going?'

'No, but I'll keep an eye open,' Haydn shouted as he left.

'Two, even,' Will grinned as he followed Haydn.

'What about you?' Diana pressed Ronnie as he rose from his seat and cleared the dishes from the table.

'With two sisters and two brothers over fifteen out of work, I always live in hope of hearing something, but at the moment there's nothing about.' Ronnie stacked the dishes on the edge of the counter.

'Your family all work here!' Diana remonstrated.

'Work? Call that work?' Ronnie pointed to where Tina was sitting perched on the back of a chair, deep in conversation with a couple of chorus girls from the show that was currently playing in the New Theatre. 'My family visit here every day. They eat and drink the profits of the place, but they don't work. They don't know the meaning of the word.'

'It's that bad around here?' Ignoring his grumbles, Diana stared glumly at her pie.

'I'd start eating that while it's hot,' Ronnie advised. 'The situation's bad,' he modified his opinion a little, 'but it's not that bad. Not for a smart girl. Pity I can't call either of my sisters that.'

Diana cut the pie and began to chew it slowly, savouring its rich meaty taste. She made a mental list of places she could try for vacancies. If there had been anything going on the market or in the Town Hall, William or Haydn would have known about it, but then the market was only open on Wednesdays and Saturdays. A few of the food stalls, like Charlie's, opened on Fridays too, but it was hard going, trying to keep yourself on three days' pay a week. The only places that were open five and a half days were the big shops like Wien's, Rivelins, Gwilym Evans and the Co-op, the three cinemas, and the theatres. If the New Theatre had needed help, Ronnie would have known about it with half the company eating in the café. As she scraped the last of her pie from her plate she decided to start on the big shops first.

'Will you be working very late?' Jenny asked Haydn as they pushed and jostled their way through the miserable, wet crowd of evening shoppers in the glistening, black and gold lamplit market square.

'You know Saturday nights.' He shrugged his shoulders. 'One company moves out, another in. They'll want a hand to move their costumes, props and scenery into the vans.'

'And with their last-night party.' Her voice held a bitterness she couldn't have concealed, even if she'd wanted to.

30

'Jenny,' he pulled her into the brightly lit shelter of the Co-op Arcade. 'Don't let Will's teasing upset you. You know they never invite the likes of the callboy to the after-show party.'

'I know no such thing. I saw the way that – that – chorus girl', she almost exploded in indignation, 'ogled you when we were sitting in the café yesterday afternoon.'

'The girls do that to everyone,' he said wearily, already tired of the conversation. It was one she insisted on having at least twice a week. 'It's habit. Nothing more. They're so used to making eyes and smiling on stage, they don't know when to stop. Half the time they don't even realise they're doing it. Will you wait up for me?' he pleaded, grasping her hand.

'That depends on what time you walk past the shop.' Her voice was brittle. 'I'll be in bed by twelve.'

'As I'm not likely to be walking up the hill much before one, I'll not bother to call in.'

Devastated by the news about Maud, up at five to help set up and work on Horton's stall, cold, tired, wet through and dreading the prospect of coping with keyed-up comics and chorus girls during an exhausting, final double house of revue which would last at least another seven hours, he was too numb to rise to Jenny's bait. At that moment he decided if that was the way she wanted to play their relationship, she could play alone. Pulling down his cap, and turning up the collar of his good, partly worn overcoat that had come courtesy of Horton's stall in lieu of wages, he stepped out into the rain-soaked throng milling around the stalls. Too proud to follow, Jenny continued to wander up the arcade towards Gelliwastad Road.

Inwardly she burned with righteous indignation, but the display windows either side of her grew misty as her eyes clouded with unshed tears. She loved Haydn with all her heart, but she felt threatened by the facets of his life that took him away from her. His job as callboy swallowed every night of the week except Sunday, and that meant they could never spend an ordinary night when the cinemas or theatres were open 'courting', like every other young couple on the Graig. Even the busiest and best market mornings were out, because he helped out on Horton's second-hand clothes stall. She had to count herself lucky if he stole enough time, as he had today, to grab a quick cup of tea in

Ronnie's before going to the Town Hall to begin his shift there. She knew his family needed the money, but she only wished he could earn it somewhere alone, in isolation, not in the Town Hall which was full of half-naked, predatory chorus girls, or Horton's stall which acted like a magnet to all the would-be maneaters and vamps in the town.

Whenever she saw him standing beneath the canvas that covered Horton's trestles, he was surrounded by admiring and giggling groups of females, and whether they were twelve years old or pushing thirty, they all looked at him with blatantly plaintive and adoring eyes. 'Cow's eyes', she'd called them the last time she and Haydn had rowed. Every word he exchanged with them, every smile he sent their way, sliced agonisingly through her heart.

She'd frequently crept away from Horton's stall before he'd noticed her presence. Running home where she could assuage her wounded pride by indulging in mild flirtations with the boys who picked up their mother's groceries or bought odd cigarettes from her father's shop. But no matter how late the shop closed, Haydn was inevitably still at work, and she was left with the dreary routine of supper eaten in a grim, oppressive silence with her mentally, if not physically, estranged parents. Followed by the door closing on her father as he left for the Morning Star to drown his sorrows over the loss of his one true love, Megan.

Her mother was no comfort. She lived out her life in a sweetly smiling torpor which enabled her, outwardly at least, to ignore most of the unpleasant aspects of her life, including and especially her husband. Desperate for conversation and companionship, some nights Jenny walked up the Graig hill and called in on the Ronconi girls. The large, warm family overflowed into every corner of their double-bayed terraced house on Danycoedcae Road, but their company, pleasant and amusing as it was, only seemed to accentuate her evening loneliness; and when she'd tried to discuss her problems with Tina Ronconi, Tina had laughed, telling her frankly that if she was tired of Haydn there were plenty of others, herself included, willing to take him off her hands.

What made her present row with Haydn all the more unpalatable was that she'd seen it coming. For weeks now her jealousy had simmered dangerously close to the surface. Lying in bed at night she'd rehearsed the scene a hundred times over. Even down to the final bitter words she'd flung at Haydn. Only in her imaginings he had always apologised, reaching to her with outstretched arms and tears of contrition in his eyes. If only she'd known that he would walk away . . . Would he come back? Or was this the end?

Last night she'd dared to interrupt the Mother Riley show in an attempt to discuss her confused feelings with her mam. Her mother had merely smiled wanly as she'd strained to catch the punch line of a joke. During the subsequent laughter of the radio audience, she'd murmured that she simply couldn't understand why Jenny should want a boyfriend at all. Jenny had dropped the subject. At eight years old she'd caused great amusement in the playground of Maesycoed junior school by innocently mentioning her parents' separate bedrooms. That casual remark had made her the laughing stock of the girls' yard. Glan Richards' sister Annie had taken her to one side and told her in graphic and fearsome detail exactly what married men and women did when they went to bed together, and as if that wasn't enough, Annie had concluded by telling Jenny that her own father didn't want to do it to her mother because he did it every night to Megan Powell, William and Diana Powell's widowed mother.

She'd called Annie a liar and hit her, but Annie was bigger than her, and pushed her over. She went home that day with a bloodied nose and a torn pinafore, but when she answered her mother's probing questions, telling her precisely and truthfully what had happened, her mother slapped her legs hard and told her never to repeat such wicked stories again. And she'd learned to do just that.

Five years later she'd noticed Haydn Powell. All the girls had, with his handsome regular features, shining blond hair and piercingly blue eyes. The miracle was, he'd noticed her right back. When she knew him well enough, she told him the story and he laughed. But her mother hadn't laughed when she found out that Haydn was 'walking out' with her daughter. Instead she'd taken Jenny into her own prim, virginal bedroom, shut the door, sat with her back to it, and told her in words every bit as cold, clinical and sordidly detailed as the ones Annie Richards had used, what marriage and lovemaking really meant.

Only by then Jenny knew better. She'd spied on her father, peeping through her bedroom curtains as he stepped lightly along the street and in through the door late at night. She'd heard him whistling as he walked up the stairs after his evening visits to Megan Powell's house, and she'd seen Megan. A happy, plump, good-humoured woman who had a hug and a kiss for everyone. So different from her mother, who for all of her smiles, flinched from physical contact even with her own daughter, and especially with her husband.

So Jenny had watched, listened, learned how to return Haydn's kisses, and drew her own conclusions about the way relationships should progress. Most nights she stole downstairs after her parents went to their separate rooms. Slipping the latch against a piece of woollen cloth to muffle the click, she sat on the boxes of tinned sardines, cocoa and tomatoes in the back storeroom, and waited for Haydn to call in on his way home. And when the months of their courtship turned into years, she allowed him a few 'liberties' as befitting his status of long standing boyfriend. Afterwards she lay on the boxes of canned and dried goods and revelled in his whispered protestations of true, single-minded and everlasting devotion. But now . . . now had she had destroyed all that?

But while Haydn worked endless evening shifts, it was what she wanted, wasn't it? The freedom to find a real and devoted boyfriend who could be by her side all the time.

She tried to remember if she had ever been happy with the situation. In the beginning perhaps, before Haydn had begun to work in the Town Hall. Even later it hadn't been so bad, not just after he had got the job. The worm of discontent had only really begun to gnaw when Laura Ronconi had married Doctor Trevor Lewis, and Bethan, Haydn's sister, had run away to London with a posh doctor. Laura and Bethan were only two years older than her. And after Laura's wedding it hadn't been enough for Haydn to tell her that he loved her. She'd wanted him to declare it publicly, and she'd told him so. She wanted to wear his ring, to be with him all the time. By his side where she could keep him away from all the other girls who made eyes at him.

Why had he allowed a simple thing like lack of money to come between them? Why wouldn't he change his job for a daytime one and marry her? They'd find somewhere to live even if it was only a rented room. Then she'd cook and clean for him. Be there whenever he came home. Why couldn't he realise that she needed him all to herself? That every time he talked to, or smiled at another girl it hurt. Enough for her to create the scene that had driven them apart.

Chapter Four

Evan and Eddie hadn't had a bad day. Leaving home at half-past five, they'd paid their sixpence to hire a shire horse and cart for the day from the yard down Factory Lane. It had become easier since they'd been counted as regulars. They no longer had to fight their way into the stalls to get one of the better horses or sounder carts. Ianto Watkins kept back one of the best rigs for them, and Goliath, a huge shire whose ferocious appearance and rolling eyes belied his sleepy nature.

By eleven they'd unloaded and sold two cartloads of rags to the pickers' yards. Rags that they'd called in on the streets of Cilfynydd. But it had cost them. Eddie'd had to hand over every last farthing, halfpenny and penny of the three shillings' worth of change Evan had set aside to tempt the women into selling their family's worn clothes; clothes that of choice they would have kept until the cold weather had abated. But then, Saturday mornings were special. Good days for the rag and bone men with every household trying to scrape together the ten pennies they needed to buy a beef heart for Sunday's roast.

Between eleven and three they'd delivered goods to customers of Bown's second-hand furniture shop, one of the few that was surviving the recession comparatively unscathed. Evan was proud of his Bown's contract, and justifiably so. It didn't bring in much – seven shillings a week at most – but as he pointed out to an unimpressed, scornful Elizabeth, it paid for the cart rental.

It wasn't easy trying to make a living out of rags. Evan hadn't been the only unemployed miner to think of the idea, and there were far too many carts on the streets for comfort. It had taken Evan eight weeks just to pay back the pound he'd borrowed off their lodger Charlie to set up in the trade, but now he and Eddie were clearing a steady pound a week during the bad weeks, and as much as thirty shillings in the better ones. It wasn't good money by pre-pit-closure days, just enough to pay the bills and the mortgage. But as Elizabeth frequently and sourly pointed out, there wouldn't be much in the way of food on the table if it wasn't for the seven and six a week Charlie and William each paid to lodge with them, and the twelve shillings a week Haydn handed over out of the twelve and six he earned in the Town Hall, as well as the six shillings he picked up for his three short days on Horton's stall.

They were surviving. 'Getting by', as his mother used to say, Evan mused as he wearily flicked the reins in an effort to keep a tired Goliath plodding on. And surviving was more than some of their neighbours were doing. Bobby Jones, whose wife was in the same jail for the same offence as Megan, had taken his five children to the workhouse and abandoned them there. An hour later the bailiffs had moved into his house, carried out the furniture, loaded it into their van and driven off. No one knew where Bobby had gone. Rumour had it he was on the 'tramp'. And Bobby's family weren't the only ones who had ended up in the workhouse or were heading that way. The Richards next door would be out on the street if it wasn't for the eighteen shillings and sixpence their son Glan earned as a porter in the Central Homes, and the five shillings Mrs Richards made scrubbing out the Graig Hotel every morning.

What worried Evan the most was having no savings to fall back on. As soon as he managed to put a few shillings aside in the hope they'd grow into pounds, they slipped through his fingers. Either his or Elizabeth's shoes finally gave out, or a saucepan had to be replaced because it had gone too far for patching, or the price of coal went up, and rags down. There was always something. . .

'You're quiet, Dad,' Eddie commented, biting into a wrinkled winter apple the manager of the canal warehouse had thrown him when they'd picked up Ronnie's flour.

'Thinking how we can do better than we are.'

'Give me a cart of my own,' Eddie said impatiently.

'There's too many calling the streets as it is. If you go out on your own, all we'll do is double our outlay to a bob a day for two carts, instead of a tanner for one. We'll have no more rags to show for it at the end of the day.'

'Don't know unless we try,' Eddie insisted optimistically. 'I could always get up earlier and try further afield. The Rhondda, or down Cardiff way perhaps.'

'There's plenty working the trade down there without you adding to their number. There's got to be more ways to make a living around here if only we knew where to look.'

'I don't see how,' Eddie snapped. 'We're carting all the furniture and rags we can now, and since Fred Davies switched to lorries there's precious little removal work going on.'

'That's what we need,' Evan said decisively. 'A lorry.'

'Joe Craggs bought one off the Post Office last month for twenty-five pounds,' Eddie said eagerly. 'It only cost him ten pounds to get it ready for the road . . .' He fell silent. From what they made on the cart last month, thirty-five pounds might as well be three hundred and fifty.

Evan heaved on the reins, and slowed Goliath to a halt outside Ronconi's café.

'Don't pull back the tarpaulin. Ease the flour bags out from under it,' he cautioned Eddie, 'or you'll soak the whole load.' Eddie jammed his sodden cap further down on his head, leaped off the side of the cart, and pulled the first of the flour sacks from under the tarpaulin. He manoeuvred carefully, but not carefully enough. A puddle of standing water slithered off the cart and drenched his trousers. Cursing under his breath he heaved the sack on to his shoulders and pushed open the door of the café. Evan tied the reins to a lamp-post and climbed awkwardly off the cart. His joints were stiff after sitting in the cold and damp all day, but it had been worth a little discomfort. Between them he and Eddie had made eighteen shillings: a nice little cushion to set against the two bob they'd made last Monday, the quietest day they'd ever had.

He pulled out the second sack, took the weight on his bowed shoulders and staggered into the café.

'Wet enough for you, Mr Powell?' Ronnie called from behind the counter where he was sitting on a stool, watching his brothers and sisters work.

'Could be worse, Ronnie. Could be snow.' Evan carried the flour behind the counter and into the kitchen where Eddie was standing, wringing the water out of his cap into the square stone sink.

'Tea, Mr Powell?' Tony offered politely.

'Thanks, but Eddie and I'd better move on.' Evan thought of

the Cross Keys pub a few yards up the road. A dram of brandy was what he needed before they took the cart back.

'Tea's no good on its own in this weather, Tony.' Ronnie walked into the kitchen behind Evan. 'Take over the counter for me Angelo, and bring in three teas.' He pulled his watch chain out of his waistcoat pocket, picked out a key from amongst the fobs and inserted it into the lock of a cabinet the size of a wardrobe set discreetly behind the door. It swung open to reveal rows of bottles. Some fruit essence, some ice cream flavourings, a few wines and spirits and, at the bottom, half a dozen bottles of beer.

'Café stock for cooking,' Ronnie explained nonchalantly, amused by the amazement on Eddie's face. 'Diana and Maud are home,' he murmured, pouring a generous measure of brandy into two of the three-quarter-full cups of tea Angelo carried in. He handed one to Evan and took the other himself. 'Boxer indulging?' he enquired, holding the bottle poised above Eddie's cup.

Eddie shook his head. 'Hope to be fighting next week,' he explained defensively.

'The girls back for the weekend?' Evan took the cup into his freezing hands.

'No, for good. Maud's ill.'

'TB.' It was a statement, not a question. Evan had read the signs when he and Eddie had taken the cart down Cardiff way a month ago and called into the Infirmary. The only reason he hadn't dragged Maud home with him then was the hope that she'd be better off working in a hospital than anywhere else.

'I took her to see Trevor. He said he'd call in your house after he finished in the hospital for the day.'

'That's good of him.'

'It's what you pay him for,' Ronnie said casually. 'Diana went to your house with Maud, but she came back down this afternoon. She's looking for a job and – ' Ronnie took a packet of cigarettes out of his top pocket and handed them round. Evan took one but Eddie didn't ' – she said, a place to stay. Apparently the only empty room in your house is unfurnished.'

'We'll manage to put her up somehow.' Ronnie didn't have to say any more. Evan knew precisely what had gone on between his wife and his niece.

'William said he put all his mother's furniture in Huw Davies' place. Even if Huw's on duty the key'll be in the door. I offered to go over in the Trojan and get whatever Diana wanted, but Haydn thought it might be better if we waited for you. You know the size of the room, what it will take, and what it won't,' he added diplomatically.

'Is Diana here now?'

'She was until half an hour ago. Then she got edgy. She went to Rivelin's with Tina to see if there's any jobs going. Not that they've a snowball in hell's chance of finding anything.'

Evan stared down at the dregs in his cup. Just when he'd been congratulating himself on keeping his head above water, two more mouths had appeared who'd need feeding. And not only feeding. Illness meant bills for medicine and extra, invalid's food. He stubbed his cigarette out in the sink. Ronnie looked into the teacups. The tea had gone, but that didn't prevent him from pouring more brandy into his own cup, and Evan's.

'Sure you don't want a hand to shift the furniture, Mr Powell?' he offered, raising his cup to Evan's.

'Sure, thank you,' Evan echoed hollowly, downing the contents of his cup in one gulp. 'Tell Diana to go home when she gets back. I'll fetch what's needed for tonight. If she wants more it will have to wait until Monday.' He turned to Eddie. 'We'd best be off, boy, if we want to finish before midnight.'

'I'll pass that message on to Diana.' Ignoring the covetous looks that Tony and Angelo were bestowing on the brandy bottle, Ronnie corked it and returned it to the cupboard. 'But don't expect her back too early,' he warned. 'I know Tina and her idea of job hunting. She'll do all she can to inveigle Diana into the pictures. I bet you a pound to a penny they're sitting in the back row of the Palladium this very minute on the strength of a rumour, which Tina alone has heard, that an usherette is about to hand in her notice.'

'I just hope she doesn't raise Diana's expectations too high.' Evan laid his cup down on the edge of the stove. 'Sounds to me as though the poor girl has had enough knocks for one day.'

'Nothing in Rivelin's, nothing in Wien's, nothing in Leslie's,' Tina opened her umbrella and held it more over her own head than Diana's as they stepped out of Rivelin's doorway into the street.

'And none of the other shops are big enough to take on staff. God, what wouldn't I give to escape Ronnie's clutches and work for someone decent, and human!' she swore daringly. 'He's a swine of a brother, but he's an even worse boss. He never lifts a finger himself. Just stands behind the counter all day shouting orders. "Do this! Do that! And do it quicker while you're at it." He's ten times worse than Papa ever was. You're lucky to have William for a brother.'

'I'd be luckier still if William were able to give me paid work,' Diana snapped, irritated by Tina's grumblings. From where Diana was standing, Tina had everything a girl could possibly want: paid work; money in her pocket; a settled home, with a mother and father waiting. It was bad enough to be unemployed, but to be unemployed without a home to fall back on was infinitely worse. She would have given her eye teeth at that moment for one of her mother's cuddles, and a bowl of home-made cawl eaten in the warmth of the back kitchen of her old home.

She looked down, pretending to study her worn shoes. The soles were leaking. She could feel water, icy and damp, soaking through her woollen stockings, freezing her toes. She had to stop thinking about the past. It only made her cry. And crying made her weak when she had to be strong. The old days had gone. Her mother wouldn't be released for another nine years eight months and four days, and already the woman she visited in Cardiff prison didn't look like her mother any more. The last time she'd seen her, Megan had been pale and drawn. A painfully thin shadow of the vivacious, loving woman who'd steered her and Will through baby and childhood.

She hesitated for a moment. Glancing under the overhanging shade of the umbrella, she looked up and down Taff Street. The shop windows shone, bright golden beacons that illuminated tempting displays of the new season's flared skirts, long jumpers and shiny glass and brass jewellery. All well beyond her pocket. Away from the pools of light, a patchwork of dismal grey and black shadows blanketed the rain-burnished flag and cobble-stones. Too early for the nine o'clock market bargain rush and too late for the day shoppers, the crowds had thinned from the torrent that had flooded the street at midday, to a trickling stream. Women in cheap coats that had shrunk in the rain dumped their

41

string and brown paper carrier bags at their feet, while they waited for trams. Men and older children, who'd escaped the discomfort of their homes by lingering in the light and warmth of the shops and cafés, were buttoning their shabby jackets in preparation for long, cold and wet walks home. The last time she was home she'd noticed that more and more people were behaving as though they didn't have homes to go to. When she'd mentioned this to Will and Charlie they told her that most families had taken to lighting their kitchen stoves only two days a week. The price of coal being what it was, they had no choice. It was either freeze and eat bread and jam, or be warm and go hungry.

Pulling her collar higher to avoid the rain that poured down her neck from a bent spoke in the umbrella, she stepped decisively forward.

'I'll try Springer's shoe shop,' she said briskly, wanting to delay the moment when she'd have to return to the café. She knew her uncle would probably be waiting for her, but she was gripped by an overwhelming sense of urgency. It was already half-past five. She had to – simply had to find a job before the shops closed at six so that when she walked back into her uncle's house she could look her aunt squarely in the eye and say, 'I won't be a burden to you. I have a job. I can pay my own way.'

'There's no point in trying there. They laid off Ginny Jones last week.' Tina dampened Diana's hopes before they'd even begun to smoulder, let alone flame. 'You'd stand a better chance in one of the pictures. Why don't we walk up to the Palladium?' she suggested artfully. 'If there's nothing going there, we could try the Park and the White Palace on the way back.'

'I'd rather work in a shop,' Diana protested, remembering Haydn's complaint that his mother never saw his evening job in the Town Hall as a 'proper job'.

'Beggars can't be choosers,' Tina said cruelly.

'I'm not a beggar.'

'Not yet, but it can be arranged,' Tina said, annoyed by Diana's refusal to go to the Palladium.

Tina was wrong, Ginny Jones hadn't been laid off in Springer's. That was Ginny's and the Springers' story, concocted so neither party would lose face. Ginny had been fired by Beatrice Springer, the wife of the owner, Ben. Beatrice had visited the shop unexpectedly in the middle of the day and caught her husband looking up Ginny's skirt, while Ginny was perched on a ladder lifting down a stock of miners' boots that hadn't shifted in months, and wasn't likely to while the pits remained closed. Ginny had been sent packing with a week's wages in her pocket, but Mrs Springer's indignation at the sight of Ginny 'leading a respectable married man on' hadn't extended as far as volunteering to work in the shop herself. She had four children and an unmodernised house with a Victorian range and no indoor plumbing to look after, with only one 'skivvy' to help. Ben had been left to fend for himself in the shop all week. Not over-fond of hard work, he'd resented having to do all the humping of stock himself. With no minion to order around, he'd also had to climb the ladder and wait on the ladies of the crache, who were unbelievably finicky and thought nothing of surrounding themselves with twenty pairs of shoes only to buy the first pair he'd brought out, if any at all. So when Diana walked in with her damp clothes clinging to her well-developed figure, her cheeks and lips rosy from the cold and her brown eyes sparkling with raindrops, he saw her as something of a godsend. He looked, he stared, he coveted, licked his lips and uttered a silent, grateful prayer that his wife wasn't around to vet Diana's request for a job. Beatrice had turned down five girls in a row last Monday morning, and the news travelled. Enough to put off any other girl who'd thought of applying for the vacancy Ginny's leaving had created.

'So you're looking for work?' he said somewhat superfluously, nodding enthusiastically, more at the sight of Diana's breasts outlined beneath the tight bodice of her outgrown coat than at the prospect of having someone to order around again.

'I've good references,' Diana said eagerly, her heart pounding with excitement. He was talking to her. He hadn't sent her on her way. That had to mean something.

'Well there's no denying I need help,' he mused. 'But I'd have to see those references.'

'I have them here.' Diana opened her handbag and pulled out the envelope they'd given her when she'd handed in her notice. 'They're from the Royal Infirmary,' she said proudly, thrusting the papers into his hands. 'In Cardiff.'

'What were you doing there?' he asked as he opened the envelope.

'Working as a ward maid.'

'And before that?'

'I was in school.'

'Then you've no experience of shop work?'

'Not in an actual shop,' Diana admitted reluctantly, 'but I'm keen, and quick to learn. It says so in there.' She indicated her references.

'All ward maids do is scrubbing and cleaning. There's some of that here, but not much,' he shook his head. 'I don't know if you'll suit. I need someone who's good with customers. Particularly the crache. The wrong girl will put them off. I've found that out to my cost before now, and whoever I take on will have to be quick on their feet, and ac-cur-ate', he articulated the word slowly, mulling over each syllable, 'with figures,' he finished as he studied Diana's legs.

'I came top of my class in Maesycoed seniors in arithmetic,' she interrupted brightly.

'You'd have to dress the part.'

'I have a white blouse and black skirt.' She crossed her fingers behind her back, hoping she could squeeze herself into Maud's blouse.

'I suppose I could give you a try.' He scratched the top of his balding head doubtfully.

'I promise you won't be sorry, Mr Springer.'

He looked hard at Tina, who was standing next to the counter studying the pictures of shoes drawn on the side of the boxes.

'I only came back to Pontypridd today,' Diana explained, following his glance. 'My friend offered to help me look for a job.'

'She's not looking for work herself, then?'

'She works in Ronconi's café.' Diana didn't elaborate on Tina's family connections.

'I'll give you a trial. One week, starting Monday morning. Seven sharp,' he warned. 'I like the shop clean and tidy before it opens.'

'And the wages?' she ventured boldly.

'Six shillings a week.'

Diana swallowed hard, only just managing to contain her

44

indignation. 'That won't even pay for my board and lodging,' she said quietly.

'Then your mam will have to cut corners.'

'I don't live with my mam. I have lodgings to pay for.'

'And I have overheads. I can get any number of girls to work for that money,' he replied testily.

She hesitated.

'Tell you what,' he said airily. 'We'll leave it at that for the week's trial. If it works out, we'll talk about your wages again.'

'I was getting seven and six and my keep in the Infirmary,' Diana protested.

'I might go as high as seven shillings, if you prove to me that you're worth it.'

'It's a long way short of seven and six and my keep.'

'If you liked the Infirmary so much, why did you leave?'

'You will discuss a pay rise at the end of the week?'

'Are you going to turn up on Monday morning or not?' He was beginning to regret talking to this girl. Her outward appearance of youth and naivety had proved deceptive, and the last thing he needed was another forceful woman in his life. One Beatrice was enough.

Diana took a deep breath. She knew she wasn't going to find anything better, at least not before Monday morning.

'I'll be here,' she conceded with as good a grace as she could muster.

'Six days a week. Seven to half-past six, except Thursdays. It's half-day and we close at one, but sometimes I'll need you for stocktaking. There's no dinner break, but if you bring sandwiches you can eat them in the back when it's quiet.'

'Thank you.' She wasn't quite sure what she was thanking him for.

'Black skirt and white blouse, mind you!'

'Yes sir,' Diana replied meekly. She had a feeling that her training in the shop business had just begun.

Chapter Five

'You're not really going to work for him, are you?' Tina asked as they picked their way through the gritty puddles that filled the pot-holes in Taff Street. 'He's an old lech.'

'Beggars can't be choosers.' Diana tossed back Tina's own words. Not even the prospect of being closeted in Springer's shop with Ben Springer and his funny looks could dampen her spirits. Monday morning was the whole of Sunday away. And there was nothing to stop her from continuing to look for something better. It would turn up. She had succeeded in finding one job when she'd been assured there was nothing about. And everyone knew it was easier to get a position when you were already in work. She'd ask Will, Charlie, Haydn and Ronnie to keep a look-out. Between them they virtually covered the whole town. Somewhere there'd be work that paid more. There had to be. The sum total of her savings amounted to just over five pounds, and that wouldn't last long with her aunt wanting at least seven shillings and sixpence a week to cover her keep. But she had a foot in the commercial door of Pontypridd. It was a start. The only way forward was up.

'Me, Gina, Tony and Angelo are going to the pictures. It's a good one,' Tina wheedled. 'Want to come?'

'No thanks. Not tonight. I'll come to the café with you and see if my uncle's there, then I'd better get going. I want to see how Maud is.'

'Do you think her mother would mind if Gina and I called in tomorrow to see how's she's doing?'

'Maud would like to see you,' Diana answered evasively.

'What will you do, Di?' Tina asked, with her hand on the café door. 'I mean if he . . . if he . . .'

'Tries anything?' Diana supplied the words for her.

Tina nodded.

'Deal with him,' Diana said flatly. 'I've eaten his sort for breakfast before now.'

46

'Have you really?' Tina's eyes were enormous.

'A girl has to know how to take care of herself. Especially when she leaves home,' Diana said airily.

'Well I wouldn't like to be alone in that shop all day with Ben Springer.' Tina pushed the door open. 'Hey, guess what?' she shouted, stealing Diana's thunder. 'Diana's got a job.'

'Six o'clock, Ronnie.' Gina shut the till with a bang and left her chair.

'You know the rules. No leaving until the next shift comes in.' Ronnie picked up a rag and began idly to polish the steam off the tea urn.

'Come on, have a heart.'

'Off to the pictures, are we?' He looked from Gina and Tina to his brothers, who were hovering behind the curtain that covered the kitchen door.

'There's a musical on in the White Palace,' Tina bubbled, showing more enthusiasm than she had done all day. '*The Lady of the Rose*. It has a full soundtrack. Vivienne Segielle and Walter Pidgeon are in it. Vivienne plays a bride and Alma said her wedding dress is simply stunning. Gorgeous! The best she's ever seen . . .' Tina's voice trailed off as she saw a strange glint in Ronnie's eyes.

'If the main picture is so good, you won't mind missing the second feature, or the cartoon, or even the Pathé newsreel,' he said heartlessly.

'Come on, Ronnie,' Tony pleaded. 'It's quiet now, and we've all worked . . .'

'Worked! Worked!' Ronnie repeated incredulously. 'Not one of you knows the meaning of the word.'

'Ronnie, Papa said if we put in a full day we could finish at six,' Angelo interrupted.

'Don't see me finishing at six, do you?' Ronnie crossed his arms and glared at them.

'You're different.' Tina's temper flared.

'May I ask how, little sister?' Ronnie demanded. 'Pray tell me, are there new rules governing the eldest in the family now?'

'This is your business, not ours. Papa gave it to you . . .'

'Papa gave it to me? Gave it to me?' he repeated as though he

47

couldn't believe what he was hearing. 'Let me tell you something Miss Knowitall. I built this café up from nothing, by sheer hard work. By working seventeen-hour days when I was a damned sight younger than you . . .'

'And you've a lot more to show for it than the rest of us,' Tony intervened, elbowing Tina out of the way before the argument grew uglier.

'I suppose you're going to the pictures too?' Ronnie asked Tony belligerently.

'Papa said the girls could go, if Angelo and I went with them.'

'The sooner you go to the seminary the better.'

Tony was about to retort that he didn't want to go to the seminary at all, but managed to bite his tongue.

'If you and Angelo both go, who's going to work in the kitchen tonight?' Ronnie asked softly.

'You've got help coming in.' Angelo untied his apron.

'Only Alma, and she's a waitress. What happens if we get busy?'

'You were the one who told Papa that you didn't want to replace Bruno when he went to Italy.'

'Only because the fool will want a job when he comes back.'

'He said he wasn't coming back,' Tina chimed in irritatingly.

'One month in that backwater of Bardi is more than any man can stand,' Ronnie insisted feelingly.

'You left there when you were five. It could have changed since then,' Gina said.

'Places like Bardi never change,' Ronnie replied firmly. 'If you're going, you'd better move,' he shouted angrily, irked by the lot of them.

'Oh God, Ronnie, I'm awfully sorry.' Alma Moore ran in breathlessly, her red hair soaking wet, plastered to her beautifully shaped head, and her coat flapping, open to the cold wind and the rain. 'I didn't want to walk through town in this downpour, but all the trams were running late,' she explained. 'And then the one I was on was held up by a brewery cart that had pulled up all skewwhiff opposite the fountain.'

'I must remember to complain to the tram company for delaying my staff,' Ronnie snapped humourlessly. He stared at his brothers and sisters. 'Well, what are you waiting for? Off with the lot of you,' he commanded. 'There's no point in my trying to keep you here. I won't get another ounce of work out of any of you with your heads stuffed full of Hollywood nonsense.'

'Thanks, Ronnie,' Tina said heavily.

Tony hung his apron behind the door, then as he passed the counter on the way out, he reached towards a box of P.K. chewing gum. Ronnie grabbed his wrist before his fingers could close over a packet.

'Not until you give me a penny.' Ronnie held out his hand.

'Ronnie, come on. . . .'

'Come on nothing! I'll not have anyone, especially family, eating my profits.'

Tony fumbled in his pocket and handed over a penny.

'Bye, Ronnie. Hurry up, Tony.' Angelo, Tina and Gina had their coats on and were holding open the door.

'Have a good time,' Alma called after them. 'I know you'll enjoy the film.'

'They'll enjoy anything that involves sitting on their arses and doing no work,' Ronnie commented scathingly.

'Just us tonight, then.' Ignoring his griping Alma glanced around the café. Apart from a couple of market boys on tea break the place was empty.

'Just us.' Ronnie carried a tray of pies out from the kitchen and heaved them on to the shelf next to the steamer.

'What happens if it gets busy?'

'We've plenty of pies, and Tony's left some cooked dinners that can be heated up.'

'And if the customers want egg, bacon and chips?'

'You'll have to watch the front while I make them. It's never that busy when the weather's like this. We'll manage.' He pushed a cigarette between his lips and lit it with a silver lighter. She smiled at him and he gave her a scarcely perceptible wink, as he turned to one of the market traders.

'A tea, a pie and a Chelsea?'

'That's right Ronnie.'

'Seeing as how it's you, we'll call it ninepence. And cheap at half the price,' he mocked in market-style patter.

Diana had plenty of time to think over her day as she walked up the Graig hill towards Graig Avenue. Darkness had settled over the mountain, black, glittering with silver raindrops caught in the glow of the street lamps. The slate roofs of the terraced houses shone, slabs of polished jet. The blank, staring front windows reminding her of the sightless eyes of the blind in the Infirmary. Occasionally an odd square of etched glass above a front door shone with a dim, subdued passage light. No one on the Graig lived in their front parlour. Even the cold, laid fires of coal and sticks traditionally set up in the grates of the front rooms against celebration or trouble times had been raided in most homes. Every stick and lump of coal was needed for the kitchen range.

Slowing her steps, she walked beneath the shadow of the high wall of the workhouse. She jumped in shock as a basket appeared from nowhere and hit her on the head as it was lowered none too gently over the wall.

'Psst! Psst!' A harsh, cracked, disembodied voice grated through the darkness. 'Psst!'

'I've got it,' she whispered. Catching the string, she pulled the basket into her hands.

'There's twopence in there, love. Get me two fags and an apple over the road,' the voice pleaded.

'OK. Hang on.'

'For pity's sake be quick, love. If the master's around he'll have my guts for garters. I'm in enough stick as it is.'

'I'll be as quick as I can,' she called back touchily. It was one thing to agree to do a favour, quite another to be told how to do it. She took the twopence and crossed the road to the corner shop, smiling, despite the cold and the rain, at the memory of an awful fight she'd had with her brother Will, when she'd found out that he and Eddie had once stood under the wall collecting the pennies and pocketing them. After half an hour the inmates had become suspicious, but not before the pair of them had collected one and a penny. They'd spent the entire haul on penny dabs, farthing sherbets, sweet tobacco and Thomas and Evans pop. And what was even worse, they'd refused to give her or her cousin Maud a single lick of their ill-gotten gains.

Burning with temper, an unassuaged sweet tooth and self-righteous indignation, she'd run home and told her mam. Megan had hurtled down the hill to replace the money from her own meagre stock, making both boys stand in the cold for a further two hours until someone found the courage to lower another basket. But they'd never been sure that the inmates who'd paid over the pennies had been the same inmates who'd got the goods. The best part about the escapade was that William had been denied sweets for an entire month afterwards. How she'd enjoyed licking all her lollies and toffees, slowly . . . very slowly . . . in front of him during that month.

Still smiling, she pushed open the door of the shop. The swollen wood grated over the uneven red quarry-tiled floor, accompanying the shrill clang of the bell with a deeper resonance.

'Diana, it's lovely to see you back home love,' Mr Rees, Wyn's father, chirped cheerfully from behind his counter.

'It's good to be back home,' Diana replied, feeling happy for the first time since her train had pulled into Pontypridd that morning. 'I'll have an apple and two cigarettes please, Mr Rees.'

'Basket across the road?' he wheezed as he took the coins.

'You guessed.'

'They're starting early tonight. The master caught them at it a couple of weeks back and threatened to put out all the casuals.'

'And himself out of a job?'

'Fat chance,' Mr Rees laughed.

'Tell you what,' Diana produced another penny from the depths of her damp handbag. 'I'll take another two Woodbines please, Mr Rees.'

'Taken up smoking have you, love?'

'Something like that,' Diana said lightly. 'Oh and by the way, will you please thank your Wyn for me? I meant to do it myself but he disappeared before I had a chance to. He carried our Maud out of station yard over to Ronnie's café this morning, when she fainted. I don't know what I would have done without him.'

'I won't forget, love,' he smiled with an odd expression on his sickly yellow face.

'Thanks.' Diana smiled as she shut the shop door behind her.

'That one's as soft as her mam ever was,' Mr Rees told his next customer fondly, as he watched Diana cross the road clutching her apple and cigarettes. 'And Megan was one in a million,' he murmured, remembering a courtship he had begun two years after his wife's death; it had come to an untimely end, with the appearance of Harry Griffiths on the scene.

As Diana put the apple and four cigarettes into the basket and gave it a tug, an illogical, superstitious, almost prayer-like hope crossed her mind. Perhaps the fates – and her Aunt Elizabeth – would be kinder to her for sharing what little she had with those who had even less.

'Haydn, fasten this for me, will you?' Tessie Clark, one of the more 'forward' girls, stepped out of the grubby, sweet-smelling, communal dressing room that the female chorus shared. Her silver, sequined shorts snaked over her hips like a second skin, but the back of the matching bra flapped provocatively as she held the cups loosely over her ample bosom.

'All the girls' hands full in there, are they Tess?' Haydn enquired caustically.

'You know how it is, Haydn.' She wriggled past him in the narrow corridor, brushing the front of his trousers with her buttocks and allowing the cups of the bra to slip below her nipples. 'Women simply don't have the strength to pull the edges together and button the back.' Her warm breath wafted headily over his right ear.

'Is that right now?' Dropping the *South Wales Echo* that he'd bought for the lead comic, he gripped the edges of her bra between his forefingers and thumbs. Heaving with all his might, he pulled the straps back.

'Ow, that hurt!' Tessie complained playfully, wiggling her hips and batting her eyelashes coyly.

'Women have to suffer to be beautiful, or so my girlfriend's always telling me. There, all done. Can I get on with what I was doing now?' he asked wearily.

'Sneaking a whisky with Ambrose?' she said loudly, piqued by the reference to his girlfriend.

'Not before the show.'

'Goody Two-shoes.'

'Only where maneating vampires are concerned,' he countered, remembering this was the revue's last night, and that if he were fortunate he'd never see Tessie again.

'Not queer, are you?' she taunted.

'My girlfriend doesn't seem to think so,' he replied softly as he went on his way.

52

'No luck, Tessie?' One of the girls' mocking laughter followed him along the narrow corridor.

'Boys, they're all the bloody same!' Tessie muttered savagely. 'Don't know what to do with it.'

Haydn heard the remark as he banged on Ambrose's door. It slid away like jelly from a spoon. None of it stuck, or hurt. Not any more. The manager of the Town Hall had warned him when he'd taken him on that the first six months would be the worst. They had been: crawling past in red-faced embarrassment, he'd answered cries for help from the girls' dressing room, only to walk in on crowds of half-naked, giggling girls, who had nothing better to do than torment him by drumming the tips of their fingers on his flies. More than once he'd found himself running messages along the corridors with vital buttons undone. His boss had said nothing. He'd seen it all before.

And there was more than just teasing. Offers of intimacy had come thick and fast, and not only from the girls. Naturally easygoing, he'd made an effort to remain pleasant and friendly while turning them down, but his refusals hadn't always been well received. The kinder ones gave up when they realised that they could neither embarrass nor use him; others went out of their way to humiliate him.

When he got to know variety girls better, he began to understand them. Every revue carried about four times as many girls as men. Moving to a new town every week, or at best fortnight, they spent their days bored out of their skulls, and their evenings prancing around with next to nothing on, while strange men ogled every inch of flesh that the Lord Chamberlain allowed them to bare. And no matter how they tried to live their private lives they were regarded – and treated by the locals of the towns they played – as little better than prostitutes. It wasn't a lifestyle that allowed for sanity, or morality, but he could honestly say he'd never been tempted. Not with Jenny to go back to. Jenny who – he slammed the door shut on the painful memories of that afternoon, valiantly suppressing the urge to try to leave the theatre early so he could go knocking on her door.

As Will would say, there were plenty of other fish in the sea. And not all of them were like Tessie.

For once he wouldn't rush home. He'd go to the last-night

party, that's if he was invited. Take a good look round. Watch the girls; not Tessie – perhaps one of the quiet ones like small, dark-haired Betty. If he was lucky, word would get back to Jenny. Then she'd realise he could survive without her.

Yes that was it. He'd really give her something to think about. And for once perhaps her nagging would be justified.

Diana walked the long way round to Graig Avenue. She didn't want to take the short cut up past Leyshon Street, and through Rhiannon Pugh's house. One look at her old home had been enough for one day, and she'd met too many old friends and neighbours as it was. She was tired of telling people why she and Maud had left Cardiff. She couldn't take any more sympathetic, knowing nods from women who'd soon be baking for Maud's funeral. And it would be even worse if her aunt didn't listen to the boys and her Uncle Evan, and threw her out. The disgrace of trying to explain why she'd moved away from Will, across town to Bonvilston Road to live with her bachelor uncle, would be the final, bitter straw.

The first thing she saw when she walked over the rise past the vicarage was her uncle's horse and cart. He and Eddie were struggling up the steps with the spring base of Will's old bed.

'It seems you're moving in then?' Elizabeth said acidly, as Diana walked slowly up the steps behind them.

'I told Diana she had no choice in the matter. It would look bloody funny, a girl of her age moving in with her bachelor uncle when her brother and married uncle are living here,' Evan panted as he and Eddie hauled the bedstead on to the doorstep.

'I've a job, Aunt Elizabeth,' Diana announced proudly, too excited to wait for a more propitious time to announce her news.

'You've a *what*?' Evan dropped the bedsprings on to the hall floor.

'Don't you dare scuff that lino, Evan Powell!' Elizabeth shouted angrily. 'Lino doesn't grow on trees. And with what you bring in we'll never be able to replace it.'

'It's resting on my foot, woman,' Evan snarled. 'Where are you working?' he asked Diana in a gentler tone, as he turned his back on Elizabeth.

'Ben Springer's.'

'Oh! Oh! Oh! You'd better watch that one.' Eddie forgot Elizabeth's presence for a moment. 'We may have to punch him on the nose.'

'What do you mean?' Diana asked, knowing full well what he meant.

'If you don't know, I'm not going to tell you,' Eddie mumbled, looking at the floor as his mother cast her disapproving eye on him.

'And I'll have none of that filthy double talk in my house, Edward Powell,' Elizabeth ordered.

'I can look after myself,' Diana asserted, lifting her chin defiantly.

'If you get any trouble from him, love, just tell me.' Evan picked up the bed again. 'How much is he paying you?'

'Six bob for the moment, but he said he'd review it if I suited the job.'

'That's bloody slave labour,' Eddie cursed.

'And how much do you intend paying me out of six shillings a week?' Elizabeth demanded, too concerned with the changes in the family's income to chastise Eddie for swearing.

'Whatever Will and Charlie are paying you,' Diana said boldly. 'I can afford to make it up until I get a pay rise. I've got savings,' she said boldly.

'They're paying seven and six a week. Each.' Elizabeth folded her arms and stepped aside so Evan and Eddie could move the bed on to the stairs.

'There's no way a slip of a girl like Diana will eat the same as those two great hulking men,' Evan protested. 'Four bob a week is more than fair.'

'Evan!' Elizabeth exclaimed.

'I've spoken, Elizabeth,' he said decisively. 'Right, Eddie?'

Carefully, so as not to tear the twenty-year-old jute carpet on the stairs, they manhandled the bedstead into the hall and over the banisters. It was tricky manoeuvring it through the narrow passageway and into the box room, but eventually they managed it, and laid it on its side beneath the window opposite the door.

'I don't know where you think you're going with all that furniture,' Elizabeth said as she peered through the darkness at the lumpy tarpaulin on the cart. 'That box room is full as it is.'

'Eddie and I will empty what's there into the attic,' Evan said calmly, refusing to allow himself to be rattled.

'Like as not, on top of the plasterboards, so you'll bring the ceiling down.'

'I hope tea is about ready, Elizabeth,' Evan reminded her. 'As soon as we've finished here, Eddie and I'll be wanting to eat.'

Elizabeth knew when she was beaten. Muttering under her breath, she retreated to the back kitchen.

'This room could do with a bit of a sweep out.' Evan brushed aside the dust as he handed Eddie the first of the boxes.

'I'll do it,' Diana called out from the hall, smiling in response to Eddie's wink, as he walked along the landing. Happy at the thought of making herself useful, she took off her wet coat and hung it on one of the hooks behind the front door, then rushed through to the washhouse to get a duster and a broom.

'As you're intent on staying here, you may as well know first as last that I'll have no barging around in this house,' Elizabeth shouted, stepping out of the way as Diana entered the kitchen.

'Sorry, Aunt Elizabeth,' Diana murmured. But she wasn't really downcast. She'd forgotten just how nice her Uncle Evan could be. And Eddie. She glanced at the clock. It was past seven. Another couple of hours and Will and Charlie would be home. Maud might wake up at any minute. Living in Graig Avenue wasn't going to be so bad after all.

Chapter Six

'We closing early tonight then, Ronnie?' Alma asked as Ronnie switched off the electric lights in the front of the café, and locked the door after the shop's last customers left.

'Hardly early, that was the last bus down from Ferndale.' He pulled a cigarette out of the top pocket of the boiled white shirt he was wearing beneath his jacket, and pushed it into his mouth. 'Rake the coals out of the fire on to the hearth and douse them, there's a good girl,' he ordered absently. 'I'll sort out the kitchen.'

Alma topped up the salt, pepper and vinegar bottles on the tables while Ronnie did what little had to be done in the kitchen. She wiped down the tables and chairs and swept the floor, as he opened the till and counted the money. It was their normal routine, and had been for two years.

Papa Ronconi had never liked any of his own girls to work the evening shifts, and as his wife was kept busy taking care of the younger children, he and Ronnie had been forced to employ part-timers in the family's two cafés. Evening hours suited Alma. Every morning she helped out in the tailor's shop lower down Taff Street. Work was slack because of the depression, so they could only afford to pay for her services two and a half days a week. The six nights a week she worked for Ronnie made all the difference. Apart from a small widow's pension her wage was all the money she and her mother had to live on.

A slim, green-eyed redhead, Alma had the kind of looks that turned men's heads, and she wasn't unaware of the fact; but she'd set her sights high – on Ronnie. She knew she was fighting fierce competition. Tall, dark, handsome, in a typically warm-blooded Latin way, with craggy, masculine rather than Hollywood good looks, Ronnie attracted women like syrup attracted flies. And most of them came to the same sticky end. It was probably true that Ronnie's attractions lay as much in his flourishing business as his looks. Security was a luxury few women had been able to aspire to since the pit closures.

But whatever good points Ronnie possessed, charm was most definitely not one of them. Lazy to the point of lethargy socially, when it came to wooing women he merely sat back and waited for them to come to him. Even when his friends or sisters dragged him to a late-night dance he never graced the floor. His forte seemed to be leaning on the bar, glass in hand, watching the world go by. Alma didn't mind. Not even when he refused to take her to the few annual dances that still went on after the café closed for the evening. When all was said and done, they saw one another six nights a week. What other couple could say that? And if he hadn't publicly acknowledged their relationship, so what? It would only be a matter of time. He simply wasn't given to gushing displays of sentimentality or affection, that was all. Besides, the words 'I love you' were the most overworked in the English language. They didn't mean anything: not when glib, flashy Romeos who fancied themselves as ladykillers used them over and over again. Men like Glan Richards, who murmured them to any girl foolish enough to go to the pictures with him, only to use the same phrase the next night, when he moved on to the next gullible female. She didn't need Ronnie to make any declarations of love to her. He showed her in so many ways other than words. Besides, what more could she ask of him? When they were alone . . .

'Ready then?'

She looked up and smiled. 'Ready for what?' she asked innocently, knowing full well what was coming.

'Upstairs, woman. Now!' He patted her behind. 'Then if you're good I just might take you home.'

'Via the mountain?' she asked hopefully.

'What for?'

'Look at the scenery?'

'It's raining. There's nothing to see.'

'It might clear up.'

'Even if it does, there'll only be slagheaps lit by the moon and the stars,' he teased, a deadpan expression on his face.

'Men!' she exclaimed disparagingly. But his lack of romance didn't prevent her from running up the back stairs to the small bedroom that he'd furnished for the nights when he told his parents he was too tired, or as they privately believed, too drunk to drive the Trojan home.

Ronnie ran his hand through his Vaselined, slicked-back hair and glanced at his profile in the huge mirror that hung on the back wall behind the counter. Smiling broadly, he studied his teeth. Satisfied with what he saw, he checked around the café one last time before stuffing the contents of the till into a cloth cash bag. He pushed it into one of the capacious pockets of the loose-cut khaki jacket he kept for work. Pulling down the door blind, he tried the lock on the front door to make sure it was fastened, switched out the back lights and followed Alma.

He knew she would be undressed, ready and waiting for him between the sheets of the small single bed. If he'd ever stopped to think about their relationship he might have realised just how much he took her for granted. Almost as much as he took every other female in his life for granted, including his mother and his sisters. Used to being one of the family's breadwinners from an early age, the responsibility had made him, if not callous, then at least indifferent to their needs and desires. Without thinking, he tended to treat those dependent on him like children. Beings to be petted when they were good, chastised when they were not, and to be kept in the dark about his private thoughts and any problems he might have, lest the need to confide in someone be misinterpreted as weakness.

Alma was undoubtedly the prettiest, brightest and longest-lasting of his many girlfriends, but he had never allowed her to be the only woman in his life. Their physical relationship, satisfying as he found it, didn't prevent him from paying regular visits to a shy little widow in Rickards Street. Not to mention Molly the flower and peg seller who had a stall on the market, Lucy the usherette who worked in the New Theatre . . . Ronnie, like all Italian men of his class, saw unblemished virtue, abstinence and chastity as an integral part of the make-up of every decent woman. A vital and essential attribute in his sisters, his mother, and the woman he would eventually marry; but something he, his father and his brothers could comfortably ignore when it came to their own affairs.

'You took your time coming upstairs,' Alma complained, wriggling between the sheets as he walked into the bedroom and shrugged his arms out of his jacket.

'Just checking around.' He felt in his shirt pocket for his cigarettes, and lit one. Throwing his coat on the only chair in the room, he sat on the bed, rested his ankle on his knee and pulled his shoe off. He glanced across at Alma. She was lying on her back, the sheet tucked demurely beneath her chin. He reached over and yanked it down.

'Ronnie!' she cried out angrily. Blushing, she grabbed the top blanket and hastily covered herself.

'Can't see any point in you doing that.' He took off his socks and tossed them on top of his shoes. 'Not when you consider what we're going to be up to in five minutes.'

'I don't like it,' she said petulantly.

'Only when I can see, and the lamp is lit.' He slid his hand beneath the sheet, and reached for her breast. 'You never object to this when I do it in the dark,' he whispered, as he fondled her.

'Come to bed,' she snapped touchily.

'Is that an order, Miss?'

She tried and failed to suppress a smile.

'That's better,' he laughed. Turning his back on her, he pulled the collar and tie from his neck and began to unbutton his shirt.

'Ronnie?' Alma asked hesitantly, wondering if she dare mention Liz Williams and Dickie Shales' engagement, or if that might be a bit obvious. She knew he reacted angrily when she talked about anything that could be remotely construed as 'pressurising', and it wasn't as if she was unhappy with their relationship. Last month he'd even asked her to stay on in the café after hours, so she could attend his parents' wedding anniversary celebrations. Granted she'd ended up by acting as waitress and helping Tina and Gina clear up, but the invitation was more than any other girl had received from him. She knew that for a fact, because Tina, fishing for gossip about her brother, had told her so.

That marvellous, wonderful evening, all the Ronconis, senior as well as junior, had been incredibly kind to her. So much so, she'd wondered if any of them other than Tina had their suspicions about her and Ronnie. She wasn't quite sure where she stood with him. From the moment she had allowed him to make love to her she had considered herself engaged, assuming that he would take their relationship as seriously as she did. That eventually it would lead somewhere, hopefully marriage. But occasionally, like now, she felt that their unspoken understanding was something that was understood only on her side.

'Yes?' he threw his shirt on to the chair.

'Are you staying here tonight?' she asked, losing courage and saying the first thing that came to mind.

'That's a strange question.' He unbuttoned his vest.

'Well, it's just that if you are, I could always walk home. It's not far.'

'It won't kill me to take the van as far as Morgan Street,' he murmured carelessly. He took the burning cigarette from his mouth and handed it to her to hold, as he heaved his vest over his head. Unbuckling his belt, and unbuttoning his braces and fly, he pulled off his trousers, took the cigarette and climbed into bed beside her.

'Ow, you're bloody freezing!' he complained as his legs met her feet between the sheets.

'It's this bed. It's not aired properly.'

'That's because it's not slept in enough.' He set his cigarette down carefully in an ashtray placed strategically at the side of the bed. 'Here,' he pulled her close. 'May as well get it over with.' He held her close, rubbing his hands over her shivering body, lingering over her breasts and thighs. She knew him too well to expect words of endearment.

'Ronnie?'

'Yes.'

'Turn down the lamp.'

'I want to see you.'

'Please, just for me.'

'Two years of this, and you're still shy?' Despite his grumbling, he leaned over and turned down the wick on the oil lamp. Some time he'd have to see about running electricity cables up here, but it would be difficult to justify the expense to his father. As he turned, she lifted her face to his so he could kiss her. He did so, thoroughly and expertly. He also knew her well. He may have been an inarticulate lover when it came to words, but he was anything but inarticulate when it came to the physical side of their relationship.

Afterwards there was no teasing, only quiet, relaxed fulfilment, and the sound of their breathing, muted, soft as Alma lay with her head on Ronnie's shoulder. Outside the street was still. The second houses in the New Theatre and the Town Hall had long since ended. Even the staff in the cinemas had gone home, and those who had the money and the inclination to spend the early hours drinking in pubs where the landlords were brave, or foolhardy enough to defy the licensing hours, were already there.

'Happy, Ronnie?' she asked, satisfaction and contentment making her bold.

'No.' He paused for a moment, watching her eyes cloud over. 'But I will be once I have a cigarette.'

'You're impossible,' she laughed, tickling his armpits.

'Here watch out, I might burn you.' He struck his lighter.

'Have you thought about the future?' she asked, wrapping her arms around his chest.

'Nothing but.' He inhaled deeply. 'How do you feel about giving up your job in the tailor's?'

'Giving up?' Her eyes glittered with dreams poised on the brink of transformation into reality. Of course, he wouldn't want his wife working. At least, not for anyone else.

'My father has just bought the lease on the empty shop in the centre of town. You know, the one by the fountain.'

'I know.' Her green eyes grew large, almost luminous in the soft glow of the lamp.

'It's huge,' he mused thoughtfully, flicking ash into the ashtray. 'You've never seen anything like the size of the basement.'

'Then it's big enough to set some rooms aside for living quarters?' Of course it wouldn't be ideal. Living in the middle of town. There'd be nowhere to hang washing. But then, if they were both working, and making enough money, they could send their linen out to the Chinese laundry in Mill Street. Her mother would be close: Morgan Street was no distance at all from the fountain. And the park would be just around the corner. Handy when they had children. She'd never spoken to him about children, but she was sure that he'd want lots. Just like his parents. When the time was right he'd put away the ghastly, thick, rubber French letter he used when they made love and . . .

'Not living quarters,' he laughed, 'a restaurant. A big one. Enormous, even. We're turning the basement into a kitchen the like of which this town has never seen before. Half of it will be used to turn out cooked meals, the other half will be a first-class confectioner's kitchen. I'm going into cakes and confectionery in a big way. There's a hell of a market there, and St Catherine's café in the Arcade hasn't even scratched the surface. When you consider it, it's amazing no one's thought of it before. Everyone in this town has a birthday, and not everyone's on the breadline.'

'Only about half the population,' she interrupted bitterly.

'Exactly,' he enthused. Carried away by his grand scheme, he failed to pick up the acid tone of sarcasm in her voice. 'And we'll cater for the other half. We'll make cakes for every occasion. Weddings, christenings, to celebrate someone in the family getting a job – and the bakery will be only part of it. There's two windows at street level. We'll fill one with pastries, the other savouries. Pies, pasties, faggots, pease puddings – you know the sort of thing. We're knocking all the ground floor rooms into one. Putting counters and four tables in the front to cater for tea and snacks, and behind those there'll be an archway that will lead into the main restaurant. More upmarket than this. It'll specialise in cooked dinners and set teas. The second floor is big enough to house a function room. You wait until you see it, it's as big as the silver and blue ballroom in the New Inn. Not that we'll be anywhere near as pricey, because all our profit will be made on the food. I think we'll aim for the club dinners. The Tennis Club, the Golliwog club. The store do's like Rivelin's . . .'

'And where exactly do I fit into all this?' she asked icily, moving as far away from him as the small bed would allow.

'I'll need a head waitress.'

'What about your sisters?'

'Too young, too inexperienced. They haven't the staying power. I need to put someone who's hard-working and knows what they're about in charge, to set them a good example. It'll be worth . . .' he thought carefully for a moment, weighing up all of Alma's pluses. She certainly knew how to work, and there was no shirking of unpleasant tasks with her. The first thing she did when she started a shift was to look around and set about what needed to be done, whether it was scrubbing the floor or serving one of the town councillors. On the minus side, he realised that once he set her wages he'd have to pitch everyone else's to them, including the cook's, and that could prove expensive.

'How does twelve shillings a week plus tips sound to you?' he asked, running his fingers through her red curls.

'Sounds like more than I'm getting now.' She struggled to feign gratitude. After all, a job and a pay rise had to be worth something, even if it wasn't the engagement ring she'd hoped for.

'Then you'll give it a try.' He fumbled in the bedclothes at the bottom of the bed for the underpants he'd kicked off earlier.

'I'll give it a try.'

'Good, that's settled then. Come on girl,' he threw back the sheet. 'If you make a move, we'll go through the back door of the Horse and Groom for a quick one.'

'Looking like this?'

He jumped out of bed.

'You don't need to dress, not on my account, but your lipstick has wandered up as far as your nose, and your hair needs a good combing.'

'Why you – ' she threw the pillow at him.

'Come on, woman. It's good drinking time you're wasting,' he grumbled irritably as he pulled on his trousers.

'Here's to the next town, and the next audience.' Ambrose, the producer cum comic of the revue shouted as he held up a bottle of champagne. 'May they be as kind, welcoming and, God willing, a little more forthcoming and richer than the audiences here.' He looked around, gauging the reaction to his poor joke. 'Is everyone's glass full?' he asked abruptly.

'Not mine,' Tessie giggled.

'Yours is never full, Tessie,' he reprimanded humourlessly.

'Never,' she simpered in a voice that squeaked from too much cheap sherry.

'And here's to the best callboy in the business.' Ambrose touched his glass to Haydn's and winked. Haydn pretended not to see the wink. He'd been careful to leave Ambrose's dressing-room door open all week when he'd delivered the evening *Echo*.

'If the oldest,' Tessie sniped.

'Leave it off, Tess,' Patsy the head chorus girl muttered through clenched teeth.

'Right then, where are we going to carry on?' Ambrose slurred.

'Depends on what you mean by "carry on",' Tessie giggled archly.

'Two foot nine I think,' the manager suggested, pointedly ignoring Tessie. 'They're not too particular there about closing hours.' He had the urge to add, 'or clientele'. Some of the girls had a disconcerting habit of dressing for the stage, off it. Half a dozen looked modest enough. They could have sat in the New Inn and passed unnoticed, but a few, Tessie included, could have lost themselves amongst the ladies of the town who were touting for trade in station yard.

'Everyone game?' Ambrose downed the last of his champagne. When his glass was empty he looked around the stage. 'Everything packed here?' he demanded imperiously of the stagehands.

'Did you doubt it, sir?' one of the hands answered in a wounded voice.

'Just checking, dear boy. Just checking. It's all right for you people, you have no idea what it's like to sit on a filthy train all night, only to arrive in the back end of Aber-cwm-llan-snot with half your bloody props missing, and what's worse, no spirit gum to stick the stars and spangles on the girls. They don't look very alluring performing in their shimmys and knickers, believe you me,' he whispered conidentially, wrinkling his nose.

'Shut up, Ambrose,' Patsy snarled, pushing her status as head girl to the absolute limit.

'You sound just like a mother hen, darling,' Ambrose cooed patronisingly. 'Come on then girls and boys. Are we all ready?'

'I'm glad you're coming with us Haydn,' Betty whispered, tottering precariously on her high heels over the littered cobblestones of Market Square as she struggled to keep up with his long-legged stride.

'Why's that?' he asked vacantly, his thoughts still preoccupied with Jenny.

'Because you're sane and normal,' she murmured in a voice that sounded incredibly old and tired for one so young.

'That's a funny thing to say.' He ushered her around a pile of soggy newspapers heaped high on the spot where the china stall had stood.

'It's true. You've no idea what this life is really like.'

'It can't be any worse than life around here.'

'Don't you believe it. My mother warned me not to go on stage,' she confessed tremulously, sliding her fingers surreptitiously into his as they followed the others round the corner into Taff Street. He didn't like the touch of her skin very much. It felt damp and greasy, not at all like Jenny's cool, dry hand. 'But I wouldn't listen,' she continued. 'Thought I knew everything, didn't I? Two of my aunties were in variety, and they got me an audition. It all seemed so glamorous. Whenever I saw them they were smothered in furs and jewellery, and they spent hours telling me about the famous people they knew, and the places they'd seen. It all sounded absolutely heavenly.'

'Will I have heard of them?' Haydn asked quickly, knowing full well just how many doors one famous name could open for a beginner.

'No, of course no,' Betty answered scornfully. 'Aunt Edie is running a boarding house in Blackpool now, with a comedian turned to drink. He's horrid, and the house is disgusting. Not even clean. I stayed there last summer. She keeps it "exclusive".' Betty adopted what she considered a 'posh voice'. 'Theatricals only darling,' she purred. 'It has to be, because no tripper would look twice at the dump. And Auntie Rita ended up in the workhouse,' she said coldly. 'She's a live-in cook.'

'That's not so bad,' Haydn smiled, seeing the irony in the story. 'At least she has enough to eat, and a captive audience to practise on.'

'Perhaps I should join her,' Betty whined.

'Come on,' Haydn said. 'Pontypridd on a Saturday night, or should I say early Sunday morning, isn't that bad.'

'It's not the place, or rather places,' she said hastily, wary of offending him. The one thing she had learned about the Welsh was that they could be touchy about Wales, especially their home towns, which were inevitably coated with a thick, filthy layer of coal-dust and crumbling around the edges from the worst effects of the depression. 'It's the other girls,' she moaned. 'They're so bitchy. I have to share a bedroom with four of them, and because I'm the youngest and last in, I've no choice as to who I share a bed with. And Tessie . . .' she hesitated for a moment.

'If you're homesick why don't you go home?' he suggested

66

brutally. Any well of sympathy he might have felt for the ego-induced traumas of theatrical life had been sucked dry by a succession of chorus girls who had sobbed out the most horrendous stories on his shoulder, only to switch to smiles and laughter when someone better heeled had come along and offered to buy them a drink or a meal.

'Pride, I suppose,' she intoned dramatically. 'Besides,' she curled her damp sweaty fingers around his, 'there's nine of us kids in a two-bedroomed house in Bermondsey. It's so bloody full. You can have no idea what it's like . . .'

'You can't tell me anything about overcrowding,' he said shortly. 'As of today there's eight of us living in our house.'

'Then you *do* know what it's like.' She fluttered her lashes in the direction of his blue eyes.

'Not really,' he dismissed her attempt to steer the conversation into intimacy. 'We all get on pretty well.'

He thought of William, Charlie, his father, Diana and now Maud. If she was as ill as Ronnie had hinted, God only knew how much longer they'd have her with them.

He already missed his older sister Bethan more than he would have thought possible. He hadn't realised just how much he'd talked to her, or relied on her judgement, until she was in London and out of everyday reach. Maud was no Bethan. She'd always been the baby of the family: the one who needed protecting and keeping safe from the harsher realities of life. He shuddered, hating himself for even thinking of a time when Maud would no longer be in the house. As though he were precipitating tragedy by giving free rein to such thoughts.

'We all get on very well,' he murmured again, superstitiously crossing his fingers and hoping that his home and house as it stood now, full of family and cousins, would remain exactly as it was that night. He wished with all his might that he could make it last for ever. But even as he formulated intense wishes into silent prayers he knew it wouldn't. Because change, whether welcome or not, was inevitable.

Chapter Seven

'Here we are,' Ambrose announced loudly, halting outside the entrance to the pub. 'In you go, girls and boys.'

'If he calls us "girls and boys" once more I'm going to thump him right where it hurts with my handbag,' Betty whispered in Haydn's ear.

They filed down the tiled passageway and into the long, narrow back room that had been named after the length of the bar. Ambrose clicked his fingers and shouted for the head barman in a voice calculated to be heard in every nook and cranny of the building. He pulled a five-pound note out of his wallet and held it upright between his thumb and forefinger.

'Drinks for the entire cast, and all the stage crew of the Town Hall,' he ordered flamboyantly. 'No doubles or trebles,' he muttered confidentially into the barman's ear. 'And just so you can't say you haven't been warned, these are coming out of the profits of the tour,' he explained to his fellow artistes. 'You'll be drinking your bonus.'

'Old fart,' Patsy griped. 'Has to hold centre stage, even when he's out of the theatre.'

'What's yours, Patsy?' Haydn asked, looking for an excuse to move away from Betty.

'Gin and T, darling,' she called out as she sank into the sagging plush upholstery of a couch pushed against the back wall. 'Treble,' she added defiantly, eyeing Ambrose.

'Seeing as how it's you darling, I'll make an exception.' Ambrose mouthed an OK to the barman.

'Same for me, Haydn,' Betty demanded, pouting because he'd left her side.

'And me,' Tessie cried out.

Before Haydn knew what was happening, he was acting as waiter, ferrying gin and tonics, whisky-and-its, and brandy and sodas between the bar and the seats. A good quarter of an hour elapsed before he was free to look for a seat for himself. Clutching a full pint he rested his heel on the brass rail, turned his back on the bar and looked around.

'Haydn!' Betty patted a stool she'd commandeered. Puckering her lips, she blew him a kiss. Seeing no other seat he reluctantly moved towards it.

'And I'm telling you now, Myra won't make it. There's a world of difference between the chorus in the London Pavilion and the real big time,' Patsy lectured a young and astonishingly pretty blonde who was sitting next to her.

'But she's got talent,' Alice protested vehemently.

'Talent on its own is never enough. Haydn?' Patsy smiled, showing two rows of large, improbably white teeth as he shifted his stool as far away from Betty as space would allow. 'Be an angel and find me a light,' she pleaded, jamming a cigarette into an extremely long, mother-of-pearl-handled holder.

'My pleasure.' He produced a box of matches and struck one.

'Of course I'm not saying you can get anywhere without talent,' Patsy qualified, 'but it's not enough. Not on its own. And a break that takes you as far as the Pavilion chorus –'

'And what would you know about the Pavilion, Patsy?' Tessie sniped bitchily.

'I've covered five seasons there, and ten in the Adelphi,' Patsy countered brusquely, 'which is more than you'll ever do. And I could have stayed in both.'

'If you were so great, what are you doing in the sticks with Ambrose now?' Tessie enquired nastily.

'If you must know, paying back a favour to an old friend.'

'Sure it wasn't because your face was beginning to look like an old prune?'

'Tessie!' Alice hissed angrily.

Haydn stared down at the table, twirling his empty glass in his hand. He was waiting for the eruption that generally splintered a group when one of the chorus took on the head girl.

'I retired five years ago,' Patsy's voice was ominously calm, 'after I'd had more than my fair share of moments of glory. Unlike you, I've realised all my ambitions. I've enough money stowed away in the bank for a rainy day or two, and a man waiting for me in Brighton when this revue finishes. And I can't wait, because when it does, it'll be "bye, bye" touring for good.'

'You're giving up the stage?' Haydn asked incredulously.

'I've had a good run.' Patsy flicked the ash from her cigarette delicately into the ashtray on the table. 'I lasted until, as Tessie just so tactfully pointed out, "the wrinkles came", which is a darned sight longer than most. I wouldn't have come out of retirement if it had been anyone other than Joe Carver who'd asked. The head girl for this tour took up an American offer a month before it was due to start. Joe's done a lot for me over the years. I felt I couldn't really refuse him.'

'How long have you been in retirement?' Alice asked.

'Two years.'

'I would never have thought so from your dancing, and those damned rehearsals you put us through,' Betty complained.

'I keep telling you,' Patsy finished her drink and put her glass down on the table. 'Constant rehearsing is the secret of a successful show. And then again, a dancer can never retire. That's if she wants to keep her body from seizing up like a rusty piece of old machinery. I've kept my hand in. My sister and I run a dancing school in Brighton, and that's where I'll be a week from now. For good! Joe Carver can shout till he's blue in the face next time. He's called in every favour I owe him with this one. Sixteen years on the road is long enough.'

'I wonder if I'll last as long,' Alice murmured.

'You won't.' Patsy crunched her cigarette out, and telescoped her holder to flick out the end. 'The chorus is not for you, my girl. You're headed for the big time. You listening?' She dug Haydn in the ribs. 'Watch out for this one. You'll be seeing her up on the silver screen one day. She may look quiet, but she has more talent in her little finger than the rest of this troupe put together. Not only can she dance and act, but she can sing as well. Like an angel. And she has plenty of what counts most in this rotten business. Ambition.'

'I wish Ambrose thought as highly of me as you do,' Alice said between clenched teeth.

'You won't always be working with an egotistical comic who tries to dominate the whole show.' Patsy smiled insincerely at Ambrose, who was holding forth at the bar.

'How about giving us a song now?' Haydn suggested to Alice in an attempt to dispel the clouds of last-night gloom that were gathering in the atmosphere. 'There's a piano in the corner.'

70

'I've met pub pianos before,' she replied derisively.

'So have I, and that one's not too bad. Come on, I'll play for you.'

'Can you?'

'Try me and you'll find out.' He left his stool and Betty, who was beginning to annoy him with her games of footsie under the table.

'Hey everyone!' Viv the barman shouted when he saw Haydn heading for the piano. 'Quiet! Haydn's going to sing.'

'You sing?' Alice asked as she perched on a high stool next to the piano.

'Only for pints on Saturday nights,' he laughed. 'Nothing like you, and certainly not professionally. What do you want me to play?'

'Do you know "If I Should Fall in Love Again?" '

Although Alice had danced, kicked and sung her way through the chorus routines of a matinée and two shows, she threw all she had into her performance. Haydn sensed that it wouldn't have been any different if she'd been playing centre stage at His Majesty's Theatre in London. The hubbub of conversation died in the hot, smoky bar as the customers turned their attention to the corner where Alice sat, legs demurely crossed at the ankles, singing her heart out. Soon only the clean, clear, pure notes of her music filled the air.

'That's some voice the little lady's got, Haydn. Why don't you sing alongside her?' Viv asked when the applause finally died down.

'And show myself up? Not likely. I'm not in her league.'

'Says who? Have you heard him sing?' the barman demanded of Ambrose and the Town Hall manager.

'Haven't had the pleasure, old boy,' Ambrose replied in a bored voice.

'What about you?' Viv demanded of the manager.

'Only when he's sweeping the floor of the stage,' the manager replied flippantly.

'Give the lad a chance,' Viv said sternly.

'I'm game for anything at this time of night,' Ambrose grinned superciliously.

'Go on, Haydn. This is my pub. You won't drink here again if you don't.'

71

'I can't. Not in this company, Viv,' Haydn pleaded. 'It's different when there's only the boys around.' He fumbled in his pocket for change, and asked for another half, all he had money for.

'Come on, Haydn.' Freda the barmaid took up the chorus. 'Please, just for me. "Heart and Soul". '

'An artiste never disappoints his public. First lesson a trouper has to learn.' Ambrose slapped Haydn heartily across the shoulders, splashing most of his precious beer down his shirt front. 'Besides, I've always been one for giving the hired help a chance. Come on, we'll turn this into a talent contest,' he shouted, putting himself centre stage yet again. 'Don't be shy, lad. I'll play for you myself.'

'I only sing for pints,' Haydn said firmly. 'I'm not a professional.'

'You told me when I took you on that you wanted to go on stage some day,' the manager said insensitively. 'How are you going to manage that if you won't even stand up and sing in a bar?'

'A bar full of professionals,' Haydn thought angrily. People who were used to hearing top names perform, not the dregs of raw talent like him. He held no illusions about his voice. It wasn't trained. It was reasonable, good even, for the chapel choir and Saturday nights in the pubs of Ponty, but it wasn't up to Adelphi standard.

He downed what little remained of his half-pint. Ambrose was already sitting at the piano.

'Come on, Haydn. I'll sing with you if you want,' Alice offered sympathetically, hating the way he'd been pressurised into performing.

'What's is to be then, old boy?' Ambrose shouted above the noise of the bar.

' "Heart and Soul",' Freda called out.

' "Heart and Soul" it is.' Ambrose flourished his hands over the keys and began to play. Haydn dumped his empty glass on the bar and walked over to where Alice was still sitting on her stool. He'd sung in pubs, including this one, many times but the audience of professionals totally unnerved him. He opened his mouth and the first note that issued forth fell cracked and discordant into the atmosphere. Tessie tittered. He glared at her and stiffened his

72

back as Ambrose began to play the introduction again. Alice took his hands in hers, looked into his eyes and lent her voice as backing to his for the first line.

'Heart and Soul, I fell in love with you. Heart and Soul the way a fool would do . . . Madly . . .'

Staring into the depths of her eyes, seeing nothing else, he took his cue from her and sang. The third line went well. The fourth better. When Ambrose began to play the second verse, Alice fell silent. Haydn didn't need her any more. He was singing to the bar as he'd done so many nights before.

Freda stood, tea towel in hand, tears flowing down her withered cheeks, rapt, lost in emotion. Even the manager of the Town Hall left his drink untouched on the bar.

'Good Lord, he's good. Really good,' he uttered in amazement when Haydn had finished, and the applause had begun.

'Pretty, too.' Patsy cast a critical eye over Haydn's smooth blond hair, blue eyes and six-foot, slim frame. 'Given the right break he could do well,' she mused critically, taking another cigarette.

Ambrose looked at Haydn and mouthed, 'Another?' Haydn nodded, and went into his standard repertoire of, 'I'll take you home again Kathleen', 'Goodnight, my love', and 'Just let me look at you'. Alice joined in the last one, and it was evident that the two of them were lost in their own enjoyment, singing only for one another. Patsy fumbled for a light as she watched them, her thoughts racing. They made a very good couple. Two blonde angels together. Given the right lighting, the right costumes, the right parts . . .

'You want a job, just say the word. Three pounds a week, boy in the chorus, with a chance of solo spots whenever they can be fitted in,' Ambrose offered expansively. Haydn looked Ambrose in the eye; saw the way the comedian ran his tongue over his fat, wet lips as he looked him up and down.

'No thanks,' he said quickly. Too quickly. 'I can't tour, I've too many commitments that keep me here.'

'Good boy,' the manager enthused, thinking of all the slots he could ask Haydn to fill at minimum payment.

'Never look a gift horse in the mouth, old boy.' Ambrose laid his arm across Haydn's shoulders and pinched his cheek. 'Think about it, and while you're thinking I'll buy you and Alice another drink. Gin and T?'

'I only drink beer,' Haydn replied ungratefully. 'And Viv's just poured me one.'

'There's worse than Ambrose around in this business,' Alice commented after Ambrose had left them for the bar. 'Much worse. All you have to do is say no to the man, and he'll back off.'

'Is that the voice of experience talking?' Haydn asked, studying Ambrose's fleshy back.

'As you're asking, yes. I mentioned my steady boyfriend and he apologised, handsomely.'

'And have you a steady boyfriend?' Haydn asked, wondering why he'd never noticed Alice before.

'Oh yes.' Alice picked up her handbag and took out a packet of Du Mauriers. 'And a good-looking boy like you must have a steady girlfriend.'

'I did until this afternoon.'

There was something so comically mournful about his expression that Alice laughed out loud.

'If the spat had been serious, you wouldn't have just thrown Ambrose's offer back in his face.'

'It's not Jenny that's keeping me here,' he explained. 'It's my family. They rely on what I bring home.'

'Your parents.'

'And my kid brother. My youngest sister came home today as well, from a live-in job in a hospital. She has consumption,' he added bitterly, suddenly ashamed of himself for pouring out his troubles to her. He wondered why he was doing it. Perhaps it was the beer on top of an empty stomach.

'That's tough. Consumption, I mean. My mother died of it when I was two. Ciggie?' she offered him the packet, and he took one. 'Look Haydn, that is your name isn't it? Haydn?'

He nodded.

'If anyone makes you an offer like Ambrose's again, grab it with both hands,' she advised seriously. 'That's if you really want to go on stage.'

'I've never wanted anything else.'

'Offers like that aren't two a penny. I don't know if you've got what it takes to make it. I don't mean talent,' she added, sensitive to the hurt look in his eyes. 'Despite what Patsy said earlier, I don't think anyone can predict who's going to make it in this business. It's nothing as simple as ambition or talent. It's luck, being in the right place at the right time . . .'

'And this tour could have been that?'

'Don't knock the provinces. Word gets around, and every audience you play teaches you something.'

'Thanks for the tip.'

'Well, I'm for bed.' She knocked back the last of her gin. 'Two gins and one cigarette is enough for me after a show, and we still have to be on the early train for Swansea tomorrow.'

'I'll walk you home if you like.'

'As long as you realise that it will be just that. A walk.' She raised her enormous blue eyes until they were level with his.

'I wouldn't dream of trying to turn it into anything else.' He picked up his cap and coat from the top of the piano.

'See you, Haydn,' Viv shouted from behind the bar.

'In work bright and early Monday morning, Haydn. New scenery to set up, and calls to check,' the manager warned.

'I'll be there. Goodnight.'

'Good luck, boy,' Patsy called out. 'Look after that talent of yours.'

Ambrose turned his back as Alice and Haydn walked out of the door. He was too angry with Haydn's refusal even to say goodbye.

'Where are you staying?' Haydn asked as he and Alice left the shelter of the tiled doorway.

'Lodgings on Broadway.'

'At least it's not far to go.' He fastened the collar of his coat. The early evening rain had turned to pounding hailstones, and the street was covered with a fine layer of slippery ice. Alice put up her umbrella and held it over both their heads.

'Take my arm.' He held out his left arm. 'Or is that going too far?'

She laughed as she hooked her hand into the crook of his elbow. 'I was wrong about you, Haydn. You shouldn't take up the next offer an Ambrose makes you.'

'Why?' he demanded innocently.

'Because you're far too nice for the theatre,' she teased. 'You take a girl at her word.'

*

Jenny Griffiths sat on an empty, upturned pop crate and huddled into her thick, red Welsh flannel dressing gown. She was freezing. Not wanting to go upstairs for a blanket in case she missed the all-important footstep on the hill, or the hand on the latch, she looked around the storeroom for something she could use to warm herself. A couple of empty sacks lay in the corner. Shivering, she pulled them towards her. Two were potato sacks, one had held carrots. Plumping for the cleanest, she took the carrot sack. She wrapped it around her shoulders on top of her dressing gown. Both her parents had been snoring when she'd crept silently down the stairs, so she'd risked leaving the door between the storeroom and the shop open in the hope of siphoning off any warmth that remained in the shop from the paraffin heater that had burnt there all day. Crouching on the crate, she stared up at the back door. Her eyes had become accustomed to the darkness. She could see the bolt that she had drawn back earlier. Her gaze flickered from the bolt to the latch. She concentrated with all her might, willing the metal bar to lift.

Haydn had to come! He simply had to! He'd been tired that afternoon. That was all. He'd been tired, and she'd been miserable at the thought of spending one more Saturday night alone. That was why they'd had that stupid row. He, like her, would have calmed down by now. He wouldn't pass the shop, not without testing the latch to see if she'd left the door open. She wondered if it was one o'clock yet. She'd left her room at twelve. It seemed like she'd been sitting here for hours, but she'd spent enough early mornings waiting for Haydn in the storeroom to know that the passage of time could be deceptive. She'd probably only been here for half an hour, and if Haydn was loading scenery into the back of a van . . .

Steps echoed along the pavement in front of the shop. She jerked upright and ran stiffly to the shop window, hovering just behind the counter. She saw the back of a constable's broad figure, lamplight burnishing the buttons on the shoulders of his overcoat. Disconsolate, she checked the clock on the wall behind the counter. Its hands pointed to five to one. Haydn couldn't be much longer now – unless he'd gone to the last-night party with the chorus girls. Jealousy began to bubble violently inside her as she returned to the storeroom. Curling her feet beneath her, she clutched the sack across her shoulders and waited, her stomach kneading itself into tight little knots that were half fear, half anticipation. What if – what if Haydn had thought she meant what she said? What if he'd taken her seriously? What if he never spoke to her again?

She'd been such a fool. She couldn't survive without Haydn. If he came back she'd never allow her jealousy to surface so destructively again. Never speak sharply. Never . . . Even as she made heady promises to herself, and to whatever peculiar deity she believed presided over lovers blighted by misery, her eyelids grew heavy. She curled herself tightly into the corner. The walls at her back and side were cold, but just about bearable. The sacking helped to insulate her from the brick's freezing temperature.

Haydn dragged himself wearily up the hill. Every step took an enormous effort that drained his strength even further, but in spite of his exhaustion he was restless and on edge. His throat burned full of indigestible remorse. What insane impulse of self-destruction had led him to give Ambrose the wrong answer when he'd invited him to join the revue? He'd never get another offer like that. Not in a million years. He'd allowed his dislike of Ambrose and what he was to ruin his whole life.

How often had he told his sister Bethan that all he wanted was to go on stage? Now his bluff had been called. At the slightest suggestion that his lifelong ambition might be realised, he'd turned chicken and run. Flung an offer that any aspiring chorus boy in the country would have sold his soul to get, back in Ambrose's indignant face. As Alice had said, if Ambrose or anyone else for that matter had made overtures to him, he could always have said no. He'd been a fool. A stupid fool. And for what? To turn up at the Town Hall again at eight o'clock on Monday morning to begin another fourteen-hour day. Three pounds a week Ambrose had offered! He could have lived like a king on two, and sent a pound home. Eight shillings more than he paid his mother now, and he wouldn't have been eating any of her food. But it was too late. He'd seen the look on Ambrose's face after he rejected the offer. If he went crawling back now Ambrose would kick him in the teeth, and quite rightly so. He'd been too stupid to recognise a golden egg when it had been laid in front of him.

He flung the cold cigarette butt that he held clamped between his lips to the ground. He was too upset and too angry to think any more about the implications of what he'd done. He paused to get his breath. Fury had turned his walk up the Graig hill into a run, and the Graig hill wasn't built for speed. He looked around, taking his bearings. He was standing in the road in front of the fish shop. Opposite, a street lamp shed a benign yellow glow over the front of Griffiths' shop, highlighting the displays of tins of tomatoes, polish and sardines. To the left he could see the sweets: as mouthwateringly tormenting as they'd been during his childhood and, since the shop was closed, just as unattainable. Everlasting strips, Five Boys chocolate, pear drops – he remembered their sharp acidic taste and suddenly craved it. It was comforting to think of childhood. The only problems he'd had then were connected with money. Finding enough pennies to go to the Saturday morning rush in the White Palace, and to buy his liquorice sticks and 'jelly comforters'. He'd had no regrets then, made no wrong decisions to beat himself over the head with. He hadn't even really known Jenny.

He walked closer to the shop on his toes, taking care to keep his steps silent. Fumbling in his pocket he took out the last of the two cigarettes he'd bought earlier in the kiosk in the Town Hall. He struck a match and lit it before walking softly round to the back of the shop. Lifting the latch on the gate set into the wall of the yard he stepped up to the back door. Hand on the leaf of the latch he paused. What would he do if it was locked? She could be on the other side of the door, waiting, ready to laugh at him as the door failed to give. She might even wake her father, and what on earth could he say to Harry Griffiths if he were caught here, skulking like a burglar?

Turning on his heel, he walked quickly away. Retracing his steps he continued his journey up the hill.

Still lying on the upturned crate with the sack wrapped round her, Jenny didn't hear a sound. Head slumped forward she slept on, oblivious to everything. Even Haydn's absence from her life.

Chapter Eight

'You feeling any better this morning?' Diana walked into Maud's bedroom, set the tray she was carrying down on the empty half of the bed, and drew the curtains.

'I feel fine,' Maud lied.

'You look better,' Diana agreed. 'But not better enough. You know what Doctor Lewis said last night. Plenty of rest and – '

'Good food, warmth and plenty of doing nothing. Come on, Di, don't put me in a box before my time,' Maud snapped, regaining, along with her strength, some of the rage against being singled out for tuberculosis.

'I'm not putting you anywhere before your time,' Diana retorted, her hackles rising at the hint of self-pity in Maud's voice. Maud had tuberculosis, but tuberculosis could be fought, especially by people who had a family to look after them and a home to call their own. 'Are you going to eat that salt fish I cooked with my own fair hand or not?'

'I am,' Maud took the cup of tea from the tray and placed it on the bedside cabinet, then picked up a slice of bread and butter and began to eat. 'What's everyone doing?' she asked.

'Seeing as how it's ten o'clock, their usual Sunday morning business. The boys have gone rabbiting over the mountain with your father, Charlie and the dog. But knowing William and Eddie they'll probably return via the coal tip in the Maritime.'

'They can get done for that.'

'They don't need you to tell them that,' Diana said crossly. Maud could be stupid at times. The boys would never risk going near the guarded dumps of the closed pits if it wasn't for Maud. There'd been quite an argument over breakfast about whether enough coal could be spared to light a fire in Maud's bedroom, or not. Elizabeth had insisted that they couldn't afford it. Evan had said they had to, and Charlie hadn't helped by offering to pay more for his board and lodging. Diana had seen William nod to Eddie across the table, and she knew precisely what that meant.

They intended to solve the problem in what was rapidly becoming a typical valley way, without any money changing hands.

'Where's Mam?' Maud asked, wondering if Diana was snapping because her mother had upset her more than usual.

'In chapel.'

'So that's how you managed to bring me breakfast in bed,' she smiled, knowing her mother would never willingly have countenanced food, especially fish, being carried upstairs.

'Don't worry, I'll air the bedroom well afterwards.' Diana walked to the narrow sash window and looked down at the street. It was quiet. The children who were used to obeying their parents were in chapel, the others were up the mountain with the men and the dogs. 'Are you coming down today?'

'You bet your life. I don't intend to lie up here all day and play the invalid.'

'I'll bring you warm water to wash.'

'Thanks Di,' Maud said fondly as her cousin opened the door. 'For what?'

'For looking after me,' she said huskily, her voice raw with the cold she'd picked up.

'If I don't, you'll never get well enough for that trip to Spain we promised ourselves. Remember!'

They both laughed. Brought up on their Spanish-born grandmother's tales of her homeland, when they were five they'd decided to go to Spain. William, Haydn and Eddie had teased them unmercifully about it at the time, telling them not to spend any of the pennies they scrounged on sweets, because they'd need them for their boat tickets.

Maud was up, washed, dressed and sitting downstairs by the time Elizabeth returned from chapel. Diana had washed the breakfast dishes, including the ones she'd taken up to the bedroom. She'd also opened Maud's bedroom window, sprinkled precious drops of essence of violets in the air to disguise the smell of fish, and made the bed. And in an effort to please Elizabeth she had the dinner well under way. The potatoes for boiling were peeled, ready in a saucepan of water. She'd cleaned out the two beef hearts and breast of lamb that William had brought home from the stall the night before, stuffed them and put them in the oven, along

80

with a generous portion of second-quality dripping from Elizabeth's pot, and was now cleaning carrots and swedes to go with them.

'Girls,' Elizabeth nodded briefly as she came in. 'Are you well enough to be sitting up, Maud?'

'I think so, Mam,' Maud replied.

'Either you are, or you're not,' Elizabeth countered briskly.

'I don't want to stay in bed all day,' Maud retorted.

'I'll have none of that tone in this house. What you want, or don't want, is immaterial where your health is concerned.' Elizabeth sounded every inch the schoolmarm she'd once been. 'You heard Doctor Lewis last night same as I did. Rest, warmth plenty of good food . . .'

'I'm hardly running a marathon sitting here!' Maud exclaimed indignantly.

'No, but you're exposing yourself to draughts as Diana walks back and for to the pantry.' She looked suspiciously at Maud's hair, clean and fluffed out. The fair curls shone like a halo around her thin, pale face and deep blue eyes. 'You've washed your hair, haven't you?' she asked accusingly.

'It needed it.'

'Not in your condition it didn't.'

'I helped her dry it right away, Aunt Elizabeth,' Diana interrupted, forcing her aunt to acknowledge her presence for the first time since she'd entered the room. 'And I've all of the dinner under way,' she added, hoping to deflect Elizabeth's attention. 'It should be ready by half-past one. That is when you eat on a Sunday, isn't it?'

'It is. I've tried to ensure that this family keeps normal hours,' Elizabeth sniffed, debating whether to make a deprecating comment on the hours Diana was brought up to keep by her jailbird mother.

'The hearts are in and roasting . . .' Diana began defensively.

'Have you basted them well?' Elizabeth opened the oven door and lifted the lids of the two roasting pans sitting on the shelf.

'I think so, Aunt Elizabeth.'

'Think so! What's got into you girls? What have they been teaching you in that hospital? Don't either of you give straight answers to straight questions any more? *I think*', she pronounced decisively, 'that I'd better see what you've done for myself.' With a martyred sigh Elizabeth took down the rag-stuffed stocking potholders and lifted first one pan then the other on to the iron top of the stove. She removed their lids, and poked at the meat. She knew, and Diana knew, there was more than enough fat in the pan, but that didn't prevent her from lifting down her fat jar and adding another dollop to both pans. She turned the potatoes that were sizzling nicely in the molten dripping at the side of the meat. 'Don't you think you put them in a little early?' she criticized.

'They always seem to take hours to brown,' Diana protested, biting back the urge to scream at her aunt.

'They will if you don't baste them regularly.' Elizabeth took a wooden spoon from the kitchen table drawer, and began to spoon fat from the base of the pans over the contents.

'I can do that,' Diana said mutinously.

'And what are we having for dessert, young lady?' Elizabeth enquired, ignoring Diana's offer.

'Dessert?' Diana looked blankly at her aunt.

'Afters,' Maud supplied helpfully.

'You know I hate that word, Maud.'

'Diana and I are both used to hospital language, Mam.'

'Then it's as well you both left when you did.'

'I was going to make an apple crumble with some of the apples from the sack at the back of the pantry,' Diana said, wondering if her aunt would find fault with the suggestion.

'They're windfalls, so be careful to cut out all the bruised bits or the whole crumble will taste rotten, and that would be a waste of good sugar, fat and flour, not to mention apples,' Elizabeth warned.

'I do know how to cut up apples,' Diana said testily.

'You're just like your mother, Diana. She never would take telling either.'

Diana didn't trust herself to answer.

'You'll find custard powder at the back of the top shelf in the pantry,' Elizabeth continued. 'Right-hand side, next to the tins. And in this house it's made with half milk, half water.' She pulled on her gloves.

'You going out, Mam?' there was a hint of relief in Maud's voice.

'Seeing as how Diana's here to help with the cooking, I'll walk back down the hill and check your Uncle John Joseph is all right.'

'I thought he was moving to the Rhondda,' Maud said.

'He is, next week. But that's all the more reason for me to go down there now. I've been working there day and night for the past two weeks, emptying and cleaning the house out for the next minister. You've no idea how much rubbish your Aunt Hetty accumulated. God rest her soul,' Elizabeth added, remembering that it wasn't done to speak ill of the dead.

Diana fell into Elizabeth's chair as soon as Elizabeth shut the front door behind her. She looked across at Maud and smiled. 'If we were back in the hospital, I'd suggest tipping one of the porters to get us a bottle of stout.'

'Mam would die at the very thought of her daughter knocking back beer at home.'

'Chance and money would be a fine thing,' Diana said sourly. 'Never mind, how about a cup of tea?'

Maud smiled at her. 'It'll do until we can afford Champagne.'

'Roll on next week,' Diana laughed.

The front door opened and closed.

'The boys,' Diana said excitedly.

'They'd come the back way,' Maud pointed out. 'More likely Mam forgot something.'

'Hello, it's me,' a familiar drawl echoed down the passage.

'Ronnie?' Maud made a face at Diana. 'What on earth does he want?' she hissed, keeping her voice low and resenting the intrusion.

'Taxi fare for taking us home yesterday?' Diana suggested.

Ronnie opened the kitchen door and walked in.

'All alone?' he asked.

'We did invite Clark Gable and Robert Donat to call in, but they were busy. Said they had more interesting things to do on a Sunday morning than watch a girl slave over housework.' Diana picked up an enamel bowl from the kitchen table and resumed peeling carrots.

'Do you want to see the boys?' Maud asked.

'Not particularly. Is there any tea going?' Ronnie pulled a chair out from under the table, sat on it, and propped his long legs up on the rail in front of the stove. He glanced across at Maud. She looked very different from the girl he had carried into his van yesterday. Her face sparkled with animation despite her emaciated appearance. Her hair shone pale yellow, the same glowing shade as the early daffodils that bloomed for St David's day, and her eyes were blue, so blue they reminded him of the eyes on his little sister Theresa's china doll. Even the vivid colour of her crimson thick-knit woollen suit went some way to disguising her deathly pallor and skeletal figure.

'You're looking a bit more human,' he said flippantly, conscious that he'd been staring at her.

'Thought I was on the way out yesterday, did you?'

'No,' he replied slowly. 'But I didn't expect to see you sitting up in a chair today.'

Diana lifted the cover on the hotplate and set the kettle, which had been warming on the hearth, to boil.

'Take sugar and milk?' she asked curtly, annoyed with herself for forgetting the manners her mother had drilled into her since childhood, and Ronnie for asking for tea before it had been offered.

'Three sugars and a quarter of an inch of milk.'

'If you're that finicky, you can measure it yourself.' She carried the milk jug out of the pantry and set it on the table. Pouring half the contents into a china bowl she picked up an egg and a cupful of flour, and tossed them in on top of the milk.

'Good heavens, don't tell me they taught you to cook in that place as well?' Ronnie laughed as she set about the mixture with a fork. 'I thought I'd never see the day.'

'There's a lot about me you don't know, Ronnie Ronconi,' Diana said brusquely.

'Apron too,' he mocked. 'I take my hat off to them, you really do look the part of the little housewife.'

'Becomes me, doesn't it?' Half flirting, half hoping to annoy, she twirled around in front of him.

'Depends on what you consider becoming,' he said cryptically.

'Did you call in for anything special?' Maud interrupted, tired of listening to their banter.

'Oh yes.' His attention was distracted by Diana, who was spooning tea into the warm teapot. 'No more than four in a pot that size, you stupid girl,' he admonished. 'Don't you know anything?'

'I know a sight more than a man who's only ever made tea in a giant café urn,' Diana bit back.

'*You* know more than *me*?' he asked incredulously. 'You're still wet behind the ears. I can see I'm going to have to give William a lesson or two in keeping little sisters under control.'

'How many sugars did you say you wanted?' Diana asked, holding the bowl just out of reach.

'You said you called in for something?' Maud reminded him tersely.

He turned away from Diana, and faced Maud again. There was something pathetic, disturbing even, in her fever-bright eyes and skeletal hands.

'Do you know Alma?' he asked, turning to Diana again. It was easier to look at Diana, with her healthy, rosy cheeks and robust, firm-breasted figure.

'Yes, we know Alma.' Diana glanced knowingly at Maud. Tina loved to gossip about her speculations on Ronnie's love life.

'She's working in the tailor's at the moment. You know, the one on top of the Express café, but we're opening another place soon. More of a restaurant than either of the places we have now. It'll be smarter, posher and as soon as it does open, Alma'll be working for us full time. I thought, as you were looking for a job, you might like to apply to the tailor's now. Get your name down first before the rush starts. I don't know what it's like in Cardiff, but it's hard here, and with Ben Springer's record of laying off girls, you might be better placed in the tailor's than the shoe shop.'

'Thanks for thinking of me.' Diana took down three cups and saucers from the dresser, picked up the teapot and poured out the tea. She was touched by his concern. Yesterday in the café he'd left her with the distinct impression that he either hadn't heard her talking about her problems, or hadn't cared.

'You know me, your friendly neighbourhood benefactor,' he sipped his tea and winked slyly at Maud. 'Not bad,' he pointed to his cup. 'A few more lessons and it might even be passable.'

'I'm grateful Ronnie, but don't push your luck.' Diana glared at him.

'As soon as the restaurant gets going, you can have Alma's old job in the café if you want it. Saturday nights, Sundays and four nights in the week. Alma has Wednesday off but I might be able to sort out another one if you prefer it.'

'Mam will never stand for anyone in this house working a Sunday,' Maud warned.

'It wouldn't be for long,' Ronnie interrupted. 'As soon as the new place gets going, we may be able to offer you full time in the day. We're going to need a lot of waitresses. I talked it over with Papa. He said someone lively like you might suit us. Full time, six days a week, eight until six pays nine shillings plus tips, but just so there's no misunderstanding, it's hard work. Tina'll confirm that. She's not only the worst waitress I've ever had to cope with, she also loathes the job more than most.'

He was talking to Diana but he couldn't get his eyes – or his mind – off Maud.

'There's nothing for me, is there Ronnie?' Maud asked somewhat poignantly.

'There might be when you're better,' he said with more diplomacy than usual.

'I'm fine now, really. It was just the shock of losing my job on Friday, and then the journey home.'

'That's not what Trevor told me this morning when I asked after you in church.'

An awkward silence fell over the room. Ronnie didn't have to say any more. Maud knew just what a liability people with tuberculosis were, especially in places that sold food.

'We're back, and we're starving.' The door to the washhouse slammed opened and shut, and William, closely followed by Haydn, walked through to the kitchen.

'Good God, look what the wind's blown in. What's up, Ronnie? Lose your way into town?' Will asked.

'He's opening a new café,' Diana explained, 'and when he does there might be a job there for me.'

'It'll beat working for that creep in the shoe shop.' William picked up the teapot and two cups and poured tea for himself and Haydn. 'Better make some more, Di. Uncle Evan, Eddie and Charlie will be in as soon as they've cleaned the rabbits and bedded the dog down.'

'How many did you get?' Maud asked.

'Would you believe four? Genius, that's what I am. Led them

86

straight to the burrow. Up the top, close to the glass tower.' He referred to the remains of a folly that the industrialist Crawshay had built on the summit of the Graig mountain for no good, practical or particular reason.

'Eddie got a fight arranged soon?' Ronnie asked.

'Looking to make some money to set up the new café?' William laughed.

'Not that way.'

'Eddie's always a sure thing,' Haydn asserted defensively.

'Touch wood!' Maud demanded urgently. 'You know you should never say anything like that.'

'Superstitions!' Ronnie scoffed. 'The Welsh are worse than the Italians. Well I'd be better off. Tony'll be screaming for me as it is. Father O'Kelly's been giving me a hard time lately. Tony opened up so I could go to mass. See you down the café later?'

William looked at Haydn, who seemed to be slumped deep in his own thoughts, just as he had been all morning. When Haydn didn't respond, he followed Ronnie to the door.

'I'll see you out,' he offered.

'Bye.' Ronnie smiled at everyone and took his leave, but as he walked through the door his backward glance was for Maud. She was so thin it was difficult to see where the patched cushions of the chair began and she ended. She was a child, and because of her sickness hardly a beautiful one. He told himself that it was the look of death in her eyes that disturbed him. Nothing more.

Every family in Pontypridd, no matter how poor, tried to organise themselves a Sunday dinner. Since the pits had closed it was very often the only hot meal of the week, and after the last slices of bread had mopped the final vestiges of gravy from thick earthenware plates, and the remaining crumbs of pudding had been licked from spoons slippery with watery custard, a quiet peace settled over the terraces that clung to the hillsides. Graig Avenue was no exception.

When Elizabeth rose to clear the table, Diana steeled herself for yet another rebuff, and suggested she do it for her. Before Elizabeth had the chance to either accept or reject Diana's offer, William left his chair and began to ferry the dirty plates into the washhouse. His helpfulness wasn't born out of any finer feelings for his aunt, but from a desire to get her out of the kitchen, and out of the way, as quickly as possible. He knew her Sunday routine well. As soon as the table was cleared and the plates, pots, pans and stove washed and scoured, she liked to 'retire' to the front parlour to read her Bible. Winter or summer, the temperature of the room made no difference. She sat stiffly upright on one of the slippery, Rexine-covered chairs in front of the cold, screened-off fireplace, slowly turning the pages of the heavy, leather-bound Bible that had been treasured by her family for four generations. If Evan made tea, which he sometimes did late in the afternoon, she always refused a cup with a glare that suggested it was sacrilege even to suggest carrying boiling liquid into the hallowed 'best room'.

When William had first moved into his uncle's house he found it peculiar to think that on the one traditional day of rest, his aunt actually preferred the cold, sterile atmosphere of the parlour to the warmth and companionship of the back kitchen. But then there was no accounting for tastes, especially his aunt's. His mother had never had the luxury of a front parlour, at least not within his memory. Megan had been forced to let out the room to lodgers to make ends meet. Perhaps if she'd had one, she might had sat there.

'Seems we have two skivvies to help you now, Elizabeth,' Evan commented as William returned for more dishes.

'Just as well, given the increased workload in this house.' She turned to examine the stove.

'I'll clean that for you,' Diana offered.

'Just be sure you do it properly. Any food left on the hotplates smells the whole house out.'

'I know, we had a stove exactly like it at home,' Diana said in an injured tone.

'What are you going to do, Snookems?' Evan asked Maud, in an attempt to divert his wife's attention from his niece.

'Go dancing,' she suggested mischievously.

He looked at her plate: she'd scarcely touched her meal. Elizabeth, with her customary caution and inbred loathing of waste, had only dished out small portions of meat, stuffing and vegetables on to Maud's plate, consoling herself with the thought that there was always the extra she'd allowed for Monday's fry-up waiting in the pantry if Maud wanted more. But a good half of the meagre portion remained untouched, ineffectually hidden beneath the knife and fork.

'You're not going to have the energy to go dancing on what you've just eaten, love,' Evan reprimanded her mildly.

'No one in this family will go dancing on a Sunday while I have breath in my body!' Elizabeth exclaimed, taking their conversation literally.

'I was joking, Mam,' Maud protested wearily, exhaustion getting the better of her.

'Why don't you sit next to the fire for a bit?' Charlie suggested in his quaint accent. Three years in Wales had left his harsh Russian consonants untouched, while lending the thick, Slavic speech the singsong lilt of the valleys. 'Your father's promised me a game of chess, and you can help me beat him.'

'I never was a good player,' Maud said dully, watching William, Diana, Haydn and Eddie rush around. Saturday nights and Sundays were special in Pontypridd. Nearly all the girls and boys their age dressed up in whatever finery they could beg, borrow or steal, and walked in groups from one end of the town to the other. Crowds passed, the boys catcalling the girls they fancied, the girls returning the smiles of any boys they didn't want to openly discourage, and occasionally, very occasionally, the two very separate groups stopped to talk, but the real talking usually came later when everyone, even the ones without money, went to Ronconi's. The 'Bunny Run' they called it, and at that moment Maud would have given a month of whatever was left of her life to join them.

She watched William rattle the change in his pocket and wink at Haydn. Suddenly she felt angry and restless. Angry because she was going to be left behind, stuck at home while they were all going to town and the café to have a good time. And restless because she knew that even if her mother allowed her to go, she wouldn't be able to manage the walk down, let alone back up the hill. And probably couldn't for some time.

'If you're tired sis I'll help you upstairs.' Stung by the look of sheer misery on Maud's face Haydn held out his arm.

'You will not,' Elizabeth said sharply. She had never allowed the boys to enter the girls' bedroom, and had no intention of changing her notions of propriety now, just because Maud was ill.

89

'It's all right Elizabeth, I'll take her.' Evan rose from his chair.

'I don't want to go to bed,' Maud protested petulantly.

'If you rest now, you'll feel better later on. You can always get up for the evening,' Evan said patiently.

'Gina and Tina want to come and see you,' Diana interrupted. 'If it's all right with you, Aunt Elizabeth, I'll ask them to call in on their way back from the café this afternoon.'

'You going down the café with the boys, Diana?' Elizabeth demanded coldly.

'For a little while,' Diana murmured mildly, reining in her temper. 'Ronnie called earlier and mentioned that he and his father would be looking for more waitresses soon. They're opening a new place, and I thought I'd like to find out a bit more about what jobs they'll have on offer.'

'Ronnie called in when you two girls were alone in the house?'

'We were here,' Haydn broke in not entirely truthfully. 'He wanted to talk to Eddie about some haulage work,' he added, straying into the realms of fiction.

'Then it's a pity you didn't think to discuss whatever jobs he has on offer with him while he was here, Diana,' Elizabeth sniffed.

'Diana was busy cooking the dinner at the time. Besides, the boys commandeered most of his attention,' Maud snapped.

'Come on, Snookems, up the wooden hill.' Evan scooped her into his strong arms. 'A couple of hours' sleep now will do you the world of good. Set you up for when Diana brings the girls back.' He looked at his wife as he helped Maud out of the room, daring her to say anything more.

Chapter Nine

Charlie set up his chessboard on the side of the table closest to the stove, amusing himself by making a few practice moves while he waited patiently for Evan to return from upstairs. The boys and Diana rushed round him as they scurried between the kitchen and washhouse, spending as much time on sprucing themselves up as on clearing the dishes.

'You coming down the caff later, Charlie?' William asked, bending his knees so he could see enough of himself to Vaseline and brush back his hair in the low-hung mirror on the back wall.

'Perhaps,' Charlie replied impassively.

William knew better than to push. Charlie was always polite. Pleasant and helpful when he could be, but eighteen months of living with him, six months in the same room, had taught him that when it came to making plans, Charlie was a law unto himself.

Dishes washed in record time, Diana raced upstairs to the cell that had now become her bedroom. Her uncle had brought a bed, bedclothes, pillows and a chest of drawers from Bonvilston Road. No rug, no pictures, no toilet set and no personal knick-knacks. In the absence of a wardrobe she'd folded her clothes into the drawers. Opening them one after another she dug out a thick, navy-blue, home-knitted sweater that William had grown out of, and pulled it on over her blouse. Tiptoeing out on to the landing she stood silently and listened. She heard the creak of damp, rusting springs as Elizabeth settled on a chair in the front parlour. Picking up her handbag, she crept quietly across to Maud's bedroom and lifted the latch slowly, starting at the loud scraping click the iron bar made when it finally left its rest.

'Who's there?' Maud called out.

'Ssh, it's only me.' Diana stole in, pushing the door to behind her. 'How are you feeling?'

'Fed up and tired,' Maud said irritably.

'You might be well enough to come with us next week.'

'I doubt it.'

91

Diana stood in front of the bed feeling impotent and entirely useless.

'The mirror's over there.' Maud nodded at the dressing table where a shawl lay draped over the top, concealing the glass.

'How did you know what I was after?' Diana asked sheepishly as she lifted the shawl.

'Your hair looks a mess,' Maud smiled, relenting a little. After all it was hardly Diana's fault that she was ill. 'You will bring Gina and Tina back with you, won't you?' she pleaded.

'Even if I have to twist their arms. What time does your mother go to evening service in chapel?'

'It starts at six, but she generally leaves about a quarter-past five to see if she can help the deacons' wives with anything that needs doing.'

'And what time is she back?'

'Never much before half-past eight. After Aunt Hetty died she took over making my uncle's Sunday supper.'

'I'll see if I can get the girls to come about half-past five then. We'll wake you if you're not up. Promise. Sleep tight, don't let the bugs bite,' Diana whispered as she left the room.

Irritation almost abated by the thought of having something to look forward to, Maud snuggled down as she heard the latch drop. The old mattress was soft, the room comfortingly familiar and wonderfully warm from the fire Eddie had banked up with small coals that morning. She listened to the rain patter on the slates that covered the top of the downstairs bays, below her window. The light was grey, dull where it crept through the partly closed red plush curtains. Flickering firelight glowed dimly, its reflection shining in the polished mahogany panels of the wardrobe and dressing table. She plucked at the itchy, scratchy, Welsh flannel blanket with thin fingers, covering herself to the chin with the soft flannelette beneath it.

Downstairs she heard the raised voices of Haydn, Eddie and William as they walked along the passage and slammed the front door behind them. She didn't doubt Diana was with them. Closing her eyes, she allowed her body to relax. It was good to be home, even if she was ill.

The thought of her illness held sway for a moment, carrying with it a chill, icy portent of nothingness, and death. The conception of oblivion worried her more than the imminent prospect of pain. She thrashed desperately in the bed. She had to think of something else, and quickly. And not her own funeral! What about the last film she'd seen in Cardiff with Diana? *Camille*? No, that was no good. *It Happened One Night*. That was better: she would try to imagine what it would be like to share a bedroom with Clark Gable. Pleased with herself for conjuring up the diversion, she fantasised about what Clark Gable's lovemaking was *really* like!

Her imagination was strong enough to drive the spectre of death temporarily from her mind. And for that she was grateful. She didn't want to think about her own end. Not yet. Not until she was old and miserable – like her mother.

Jenny Griffiths prowled restlessly from behind the counter of the shop to the storeroom door and back. She looked out of the shop window, peering over the display of cheap farthing sweets and tins. Wanting a better view she went to the front door and pressed her nose against the dusty glass panel, staring disconsolately at the rain falling into the empty street. The hands of the clock above the counter pointed to a quarter-past three. Usually Haydn was in Ronnie's café by now, and until now he'd *always* called for her on his way down the hill. She'd eaten her Sunday dinner in record time, gulping it down so she could return to the shop. Even her mother had noticed her uncharacteristic haste, threatening her with a tablespoonful of bicarbonate of soda to counteract indigestion.

What if – what if – he was already there? She'd been behind the counter since a quarter to two so he couldn't have passed her, not if he'd stayed at home to eat his own dinner. But then he could have avoided the hill altogether by walking along Leyshon Street and down the steps at the end into Graig Street. That's if he really didn't want to see her.

'Come to take over so you can go down the café, love,' her father said as he opened the door between the shop and the stairs, knocking her into the glass. 'That's a funny place to stand,' he commented, setting down the *News of the World* he was carrying on the counter. 'Haydn late, is he?'

'He's not coming, Dad.'

93

'You two haven't had a spat, have you?'

'No,' she lied quickly.

'There's not a blue moon tonight, is there?'

'He's staying home. Maud came back yesterday.'

'So I heard.' He shook his head sadly. 'Mrs Richards came in yesterday and told me. My heart goes out to Evan Powell. You do know Maud's not expected to last long don't you?'

'Says who?' Jenny demanded, her blood running cold.

'Everyone, love. Come on, I don't have to tell you what a killer consumption is.'

Jenny lowered her head so he wouldn't see the tears, or the fear in her eyes. Five of her schoolfriends had died of it before they'd even tried their school-leaving exam.

'That doesn't mean they can't do anything for Maud,' she said defiantly.

'No, it doesn't. Look, why don't you go on up and see her? Take her a couple of bars of chocolate, and one of those fruit cakes we had in from Hopkin Morgan yesterday.'

'I don't know, Dad,' she murmured doubtfully.

'Go on, love. If you can't call there, no one can. You're practically family.'

'I'll think about it.' She opened the door between the shop and their living quarters. Harry watched her go and wisely said nothing. Lovers' spats, quick to blow up, and just as quick to blow over if his experience with Megan was anything to go by. He gritted his teeth as he visualised Megan. Her absence from his daily life had left an aching void that nothing and no one could fill. And as he couldn't count himself as family he didn't even have visiting rights to see her in prison. He had to rely on William's generosity; but the lad was good enough, allowing him every other monthly visit.

He sat and stared at the blank wall that faced the counter, reliving the past, seeing once again each and every nuance of expression flit across Megan's face. Her quiet, knowing smile, her frowns of annoyance, beams of joy, the slight puckering of the top lip that meant she was bored. She never could keep any emotion from him. What wouldn't he give for one of her hugs right now. Right this minute.

*

'Wet enough for you?' Tina asked Trevor as he walked into the café with an expression on his face that matched the weather.

'Just about. Is Ronnie in the back?'

'Where else on a Sunday afternoon. Laura with you?'

'No.'

'It was a bad row you had then?'

Trevor stopped dead in his tracks.

'How do you know we quarrelled?' he demanded.

'Because it's a wet Sunday afternoon and you're here, not tucked up at home with her. Take your coat off, and go and sit in front of the fire in the back,' she ordered, mothering him with the authority of her status as eldest sister-in-law. 'I'll bring you a hot Oxo.'

'I'd prefer coffee.'

'Oxo is better for you.'

'Who's the doctor here?'

'Doctors know nothing. Here, dry yourself on this.' She handed him a rough glass towel so he could dry his face. Pushing him into the back, she carried his coat into the kitchen and hung it next to the stove.

Ronnie, Haydn, William, Eddie, Tony, Angelo, Glan Richards and an assortment of boys from the Graig were sitting at two tables pulled close to the fire. They were playing brag. Small piles of farthings and halfpennies were heaped in front of them. They all knew they risked a fine or, on a magistrate's off day, a couple of weeks' imprisonment for playing cards for money in a public place, but with Tina, Gina, Alma and Diana watching the front they felt safe enough. Or at least, a whole lot more comfortable and safe than they would have done playing in the rain on a street corner, which was the only alternative to the café on a Sunday.

'Seat, brother-in-law.' Ronnie pushed a spare chair towards Trevor. Rubbing his hair with the towel, Trevor joined him. Tina breezed in carrying Trevor's Oxo and slapped it down in front of him.

'Better be kind to him,' she said in a loud voice to no one in particular. 'Laura's thrown him out.'

'Dear sister performing true to form then?' Ronnie queried as he laid out his cards. 'Well you can't say I didn't warn you what she was like before the wedding.'

Acutely embarrassed, Trevor remained silent.

'Anything else?' Tina demanded.

'This will do fine, thank you.' Trevor picked up the cup. It was boiling hot, just what he needed to thaw out his white and frozen fingers.

William managed to catch Tina's eye, as he scooped the winning hand. Shovelling the pile of copper from the table into his trouser pocket, he glanced around. 'Anyone want anything?' he asked as he left his chair.

'I'll have a glass of lemonade,' Glan said. William followed Tina out through the door.

'What time are you leaving tonight?' he whispered as he leant over the counter.

'Five. Gina and I are going up to see Maud with Diana.'

'And when are you going to see me?' he demanded.

'You know it's difficult.'

'Difficult? It's downright bloody impossible!'

'Ssh, Ronnie might hear.'

'What if he does?' he demanded belligerently. 'He can't lock you up for ever.'

'Only till I'm twenty-one,' she said mournfully.

'Look, how about the pictures tomorrow night? White Palace. Six o'clock.'

'Tina, the back tables need clearing and wiping down.' Ronnie appeared in the archway between the back and front rooms.

'I'll be there as soon as I've poured out Glan's lemonade,' she shouted irritably.

'Alma or Gina can do that.' He smiled at William. 'Everything all right?' he asked coldly.

'Fine, Ronnie, what more could a man want than you supply here?' William grinned cheekily. 'Good food, good drink, good surroundings, a warm stove, and – ' he winked at Tina, much to Ronnie's annoyance, ' – beautiful waitresses.'

'Just as long as you remember that the waitresses aren't what's on offer here,' Ronnie said sharply.

'As if I'd ever think that.' William picked up the lemonade that Tina had just poured for Glan. 'Cheers mate!' He raised the glass to Ronnie as he returned to the back room.

'It must be catching then,' Gina whispered to Tina as Ronnie followed William.

'What?' Tina demanded angrily.

'Rows. You told Diana about Jenny Griffiths?'

'What about Jenny Griffiths?' Diana enquired lazily from the corner next to the stove where she was studying magazine fashion plates with Alma.

'She was in her Dad's shop when Tina and I walked down the hill. We saw her through the window, so we called in and asked her to come down with us, but she wouldn't.'

'So?' Diana waited for more.

'So she must have had a row with your Haydn,' Gina crowed.

'Perhaps they just wanted to give one another a day off, for a change,' Diana suggested disinterestedly.

'You think so?' Gina pressed.

'I think it's their business,' Diana replied evenly.

The bell clanged and the café door opened again. Wyn Rees stood on the outside doormat, his coat clinging to his legs like a second, slippery skin. The torrential downpour that was flooding Taff Street had soaked it as thoroughly as if it had just been pulled out of the washtub. He eased the coat off his back, shook himself and finally stepped inside, sliming the floor with a layer of mud from his boots as he did so.

'You're well and truly dripping, and filthy with it,' Tina complained as he lifted off his hat, inadvertently pouring the water that had collected in the brim over the mud on the floor.

'I'm afraid I am.' He shrugged his well-muscled shoulders out of his damp jacket, exposing his fancy Sunday waistcoat and best trousers. 'All right if I hang my jacket and coat here?' he asked, holding them poised next to the rack.

'Don't see what else you can do with them. Just keep them as far away from the others as you can.'

'Wyn?' Diana left the back corner and the fashion plates, and walked to the counter. 'Never seen you in here on a Sunday before.'

'I don't usually come,' Wyn admitted diffidently.

'I wanted to thank you for carrying Maud out of the station yesterday, only you didn't stay around long enough.'

'It was nothing,' he said shyly.

'You want anything?' Tina asked, tired of waiting for him to order.

'Whatever it is it'll have to be warm by the look of you. Tea?' Diana asked.

'Yes please. And something to eat. Whatever's easiest for you,' he said to Tina.

'I can warm you up a dinner in the stove, or a pie in the steamer. Anything else and I'll have to roust Ronnie out of the back.'

'A dinner will do me fine. Thank you.'

'If you sit next to the stove, I'll bring your tea over.' Diana pointed to the tables next to the stove in the front area.

'Taken up waitressing, Diana?' Tina whispered as Diana remained next to the counter waiting for her to produce Wyn's tea.

'If I'm going to work for Ronnie the sooner I start learning the ropes the better.'

'You know he's . . . he's . . .' Tina glanced around furtively. When she was sure no one could overhear them, she continued. 'A queer,' she blurted out.

'That's why I suggested he sit by the stove in here and not next to the fire in the back room with the boys. Will and Haydn can't stand him, and Eddie's always moaning that he shouldn't be allowed in the gym.'

'I didn't know that.'

'Thanks for the tea. Give me a shout when the dinner's ready,' Diana said loudly, cutting Tina short as she took Wyn's tea over to him.

'You always go for long walks through mud on rainy Sundays?' Diana asked tactlessly as she dumped Wyn's tea down in front of him, slopping it in the saucer.

'Only sometimes.'

She sat in the chair next to his. Alma had left the café for the kitchen, probably to see to Wyn's dinner, and Gina had taken herself and her magazine over to the counter where she was whispering and giggling with her sister. 'Something wrong then?' she asked.

Wyn lifted his wet face to hers. 'You don't want to be burdened with my problems,' he said quietly.

'Oh I don't know. They're not my problems, so I won't really feel burdened by them, not enough to cry about them any road. And you'll feel better for talking about them, because by telling someone else your troubles you'll have halved your load.'

'Who says so?'

'My mam for one.'

Diana looked at Wyn and remembered a time when Will had been railing against queers in general, and Wyn in particular, and her mother had looked at him and said, 'Poor dab. You just remember, William Powell, there but for the grace of God goes you or any man. And the world would be a lot poorer place if there was no room for anyone who was a bit different.'

'It's my Dad,' Wyn admitted. 'We had a row.'

'Before you had your Sunday dinner.'

'You've got it in one.'

'That's bad luck. Before dinner I mean, but then most families row from time to time. You should have seen me and my mam.'

'Really?'

'At it hammer and tongs. Next door used to complain like anything.'

'Dad and I have always had trouble getting on, and it's grown a lot worse since Mam died.'

Diana looked at the thick mud on his shoes, and instinctively knew where he'd been.

'You've been to the cemetery, haven't you?'

'Mam's buried in Glyntaff. It's not too far to walk . . .'

'On dry days.'

'I know she's not there,' he smiled self-consciously. 'Not really there, but it helps to go and talk to her as if she could he r me. You think I'm crazy, don't you?'

'No,' Diana said seriously. 'Not in the slightest. Rhiannon Pugh used to spend a lot of time talking to her son and old man after they both got killed in a pit accident. It was only natural really, they were all she had. And it was my mam who suggested she do it. You see my dad got killed in the war before I was born. Mam used to keep two photographs of him, one in the kitchen and one next to her bed, and she used to talk to him every night before she went to sleep, and every morning before she got up. She said it was no different from when he was alive. He never used to listen to her then either. But it helped her to say what she had to say and to get it off her chest.' She looked wryly at Wyn, 'I'm sorry, I know I'm probably not making much sense. Will, that's my brother, he's always telling me off for gabbling. But what I mean is, Mam would have gone to a grave if she'd had one. But she didn't, at least not here. And it's not the same talking to a cenotaph. Although she used to go to the sunken garden in the park a lot. It helped war widows you know, having the Memorial Park dedicated to all those who were killed in the war.'

'Your mother sounds a sensible woman. I was sorry when I heard what happened.'

'Yes well, couldn't be helped I suppose. She broke the law and ended up in clink. Although I still think the sentence she got was a bit much. And I do miss her. Like hell!' she exclaimed feelingly.

'I can see why.' He tried to remember the *Pontypridd Observer* article he'd read on Megan Powell's trial, but he couldn't recall how long she'd been sent down for so he decided against reminding Diana that she was luckier than him, because at least she'd get her mother back some time, whereas he'd never see his again.

'Do you want another cup of tea with your dinner, or after?' she asked.

He looked down at the table and realised that Alma had put his meal in front of him. Two thick slices of breast of lamb, four round ice cream scoops of mashed potato, four roast potatoes, two scoops of stuffing, a pile of mashed swede and sliced carrots, the whole covered with piping hot thick gravy.

'After, please,' he said to Diana. 'Thank you,' he shouted to Alma, who'd retreated behind the counter. 'This looks great.'

'We don't usually do dinners this late in the afternoon, but it should be all right. If you want more, just give me a shout.'

'I'll be doing fine if I manage to eat all this.' He picked up his knife and fork and began.

'If you've anything better to do I won't keep you,' he said between mouthfuls to Diana as he heard a loud burst of masculine laughter coming from the back room. A girl like Diana was bound to have a boy in tow, and the last thing he wanted was to have his quiet talk with Diana Powell misconstrued by an over-protective, jealous boyfriend.

'I've nothing better to do,' Diana replied. 'And I certainly don't want to go and sit in the back with that noisy rabble,' she shouted, trying to make herself heard above another deafening roar.

'If you're sure.'

100

'I'm sure. My cousin Eddie says you train down the gym at the back of the Ruperra. You a boxer too?'

'No, I'm not quick enough on my feet, but I play rugby now and then on a Saturday, when my father can spare me from the shop.'

'Tell me, what's it like running a sweet shop so close to the New Theatre? Do you get to meet the stars?'

'Once in a while.'

'Bet they buy pound boxes of chocolates.'

'Two-pound sometimes,' he grinned. 'Now it's your turn. Tell me about Cardiff and the Royal Infirmary.'

Diana told him, and he listened and commiserated on the hardships she and her cousin Maud had endured at the hands of over-zealous supervisors; as they talked he reflected that he had never found a woman so easy to get on with before, except of course his beloved mother. Not even his older sister Myrtle. He finished his dinner and persuaded Diana to let him buy her a tea and a slice of apple pie, scarcely daring to hope as they ate companionably together that this could be the beginning of a real friendship. He'd never experienced anything that remotely resembled a real, unselfish, disinterested friendship outside of his family, in his entire life.

Chapter Ten

At five o'clock the rain turned to hailstones. Ronnie looked around: the café was relatively quiet, and in this weather nothing was likely to happen that Tony, Angelo and Alma couldn't handle between them.

'If you're going to see Maud I'll run you all up in the Trojan,' he said to his sisters.

'You'll never get all of us in the Trojan,' Haydn protested.

'The back's empty,' Ronnie said carelessly. He felt most peculiar. A strange excitement was curling in the pit of his stomach. He didn't want to analyse the feeling, knowing it was in some way connected with the prospect of seeing Maud, and he wondered if he was turning into a ghoul like Mrs Richards, Glan's mother, who made it her business to visit everyone on the Graig who was in the remotest danger of 'passing on', taking it upon herself to issue bulletins on the patient's progress, or lack of it, right up until the day that Fred the dead, the undertaker, was called in.

Alma touched his arm and smiled at him, breaking into his reverie. 'Are you going to be long?' she asked pleasantly.

'Not long,' he replied irritably, ignoring the touch of her hand as he reached over and took a box of best-quality chocolates from one of the shelves. She said nothing as she moved away, but his curt response hurt. She'd half hoped to be included in the small excursion. They could have driven back down the hill together after leaving everyone in Graig Avenue. Stopped off for a few moments somewhere quiet. It wouldn't have had to be anywhere special. The car park of the closed White Hart provided privacy enough on a Sunday night.

She busied herself clearing away the dishes left on the tables as Tina and Gina fussed around getting their coats and Trevor's from the kitchen. Glan ordered a meat pie, and by the time she'd heated it in the steamer, the girls were shouting goodbye. She looked up, just in time to shout, 'Give Maud my love' as Diana shut the door behind her.

'Three sugars, Ronnie?' Diana asked pointedly as she made tea for everyone in the back kitchen of Graig Avenue.

'You'll have to impress me with more than that if you want me to give you a job,' he mocked, pulling the kitchen chair he was sitting on closer to the stove and, incidentally, closer to the easy chair Maud was half lying, half sitting in. 'Ronconi waitresses have to remember all the customers' likes and dislikes, or they're out of a job, right Tina?'

The Powells' square back kitchen was furnished in old-fashioned, clumsily carved oak furniture. A huge dresser dominated the back wall opposite the oven. A large oak table and dark-stained deal kitchen chairs commandeered what little space was left, which meant that the Ronconis and Powells were squashed into close proximity whether they liked it or not, and it was fairly obvious to anyone who took the trouble to look that Tina and Gina did like it. They sat either side of William on the arms of the easy chair that he, with his innate love of comfort, had organised for himself, shrieking with laughter at his bad jokes. Eddie wasn't so fortunate. He knelt on a chair in front of the dresser, the furthest point in the room from the warmth of the fire, leaning over the table as he watched Charlie and Haydn play chess. Only Diana was moving around, stepping cautiously over William's long, outstretched legs as she set the kettle on to boil.

'Your mam and dad out?' Ronnie asked Maud, for once apparently unconcerned about his sister's flirtation with William.

'Mam's in chapel, Dad could be anywhere,' she said carelessly. 'He has a lot of friends.'

'I've noticed.'

'When do you think you'll be opening your new restaurant?' she asked.

'As soon as we get around to finishing everything that needs doing in the place. It's a tip at the moment.'

'One week? Two?'

'The impatience of youth,' he said in a grand tone more suited to a forty-seven than a twenty-seven-year-old. 'It'll be months not weeks before we open the doors, but don't worry – ' he pulled his cigarettes out of his shirt pocket and offered them to Charlie,

yet another coughing fit. Ronnie sat by, helplessly watching her shoulders shake with the effort. Haydn and Eddie looked across from the table.

'Want me to open the window, Maud?' Diana asked briskly, handing her a clean handkerchief and removing the soiled one. Taking care of Maud in an alien environment for three months had given her the confidence to tackle even the most unpleasant aspects of her illness.

'No! No thank you,' Maud gasped breathlessly, ramming the clean handkerchief into her mouth. Ronnie saw fresh blood stain the cloth. He made tight fists of his hands, butting his knuckles together. He wasn't used to sitting idly by, witnessing things he didn't like. He'd always charged at problems, bull at a gate, demolishing them whenever possible, tackling them head on when he couldn't. He found it intensely difficult to accept anything unpleasant as inevitable, especially the progression of a potentially fatal illness.

'Maud, I think it's time I took you upstairs,' Haydn said with an air of authority he only dared to assume when his father was absent from the house.

'I've been there all afternoon,' Maud snapped.

'You look tired,' he persisted.

'I'm not!' she retorted vehemently. The room fell silent, everyone assuming a sudden interest in Haydn and Charlie's chess game. Charlie brought his rook down with a flourish, displacing Haydn's queen.

'Do you play chess?' Ronnie asked Maud quietly, finally shattering the stillness.

'Check!' Haydn shouted gleefully.

'You fool,' Eddie reprimanded. 'You've walked right into his trap.'

'I'm nowhere near bright enough to play,' Maud murmured in answer to Ronnie's enquiry. 'Bethan and Haydn got all the brains in this family.'

'It doesn't take brains to play chess,' Ronnie mocked. 'At least not the sort that matter.'

'And what sort are those?' Maud asked.

'The brains that enable you to count the money you've earned.'

'And you have those?'

'In vast quantities,' he winked. 'If you're good I'll let you come and watch me bag my gold some time.'

'You're risking it, Ronnie,' Gina crowed from the corner.

'Risking what?' he demanded laconically.

'Leaving Tony and Angelo in charge of the café for so long. They've probably eaten the whole day's profits by now.'

'If they have, you two will be working for nothing next week.'

'You wouldn't dare . . .' Gina began.

'Wouldn't I just? You're only half-trained girls and everyone knows what they're worth,' Ronnie taunted mischievously.

'Papa', Tina asserted haughtily, 'would never stand for it.'

'That's just what I mean,' Ronnie continued. 'Women can never stand on their own two feet, they always have to hide behind a man's coat tails.'

'Why you . . .' Tina didn't know whether to be angrier with Ronnie for his outrageous teasing, or her sister for drawing his attention to them in the first place.

'Time for goodbyes,' Ronnie rose to his feet. 'Please accept my apologies everyone for my ill-mannered sisters. I won't let them out again until they're on their best behaviour,' he joked heavily, blanching at the sight of the high spots of unhealthy colour on Maud's cheeks.

'If you're in a hurry to go back to the café I'll walk the girls home, Ronnie,' William offered lightly.

'There's no need to put yourself out, Will,' Ronnie replied evenly. 'As it's past their bedtime I'll take them up now.'

'Ronnie!' Tina whined.

'It's Sunday night, Tina,' Ronnie smiled condescendingly. 'You know how Papa likes to have all the little ones home and tucked up in bed by seven.' Ronnie put his teacup on the table. 'See you tomorrow, Diana,' he said as he walked towards the door. 'Let me know how Springer's goes.'

'I will, and thanks.'

'For what?' He stepped aside and looked at his sisters pointedly, leaving room for them to walk past him to the door.

'For letting me know about Alma's job.'

'You're not brilliant,' he smiled, 'but there's a lot around who are even more incompetent, and if you work mornings in the tailor's it'll leave your afternoons free for when I need you.'

'Thanks a bundle Ronnie, you really know how to make a girl feel wanted,' she complained.

'Any time. You two moving or not?' he asked in exasperation.

Tina rose clumsily, falling as she tried to rise from the arm of the chair, and landing right in William's lap.

'Tina!' Ronnie snarled.

'Sorry William, sorry Ronnie.' She bit her lower lip hard, to stop herself from laughing.

'See you,' Haydn left his chair and showed them out. When he returned to the kitchen Maud was slumped against the back of the chair.

'Bed for you, my girl.' He wrapped the blanket containing the chocolates around her frail figure and lifted her high into his arms. This time Maud made no protest. Too tired to argue, she allowed him to carry her out of the room and up the stairs.

Ronnie didn't go into his house. He dropped Tina and Gina off in the street and waited only as long as it took to see them safely inside. He'd noticed the way Tina and William had looked at one another, and didn't entirely trust her, even now, believing her quite capable of sneaking back down to Graig Avenue. Once the door had closed on them and the light had dimmed in the passage, he turned the cumbersome vehicle laboriously in the narrow road, pointing it towards the end of the street and town.

He drove slowly down the hill, but he didn't go straight to the café. Instead he turned right, up Graig Street, and drew the van to a halt outside Laura and Trevor's house.

'Mama mia!' Laura exclaimed as he walked through the kitchen door. 'Twice in as many days. You out to set a record?'

Ignoring Laura, Ronnie took one look at Trevor sitting huddled in a red tartan dressing gown and striped pyjamas, his feet soaking in a bowl of hot water and mustard, and burst out laughing.

'Sure you've wrapped him up well enough, Laura?'

'You men,' she burst out angrily. 'You're all the same. Think it's clever to go out and get yourself soaked. Never give a thought to the poor women who have to stay at home and nurse you.'

'No one has to stay at home and nurse me,' Trevor protested mildly.

'And I suppose that *you*, like him, believe that brandy is

the cure for all ills,' Laura continued, this time targeting Ronnie.

'Now that you mention it, that's not a bad idea.' As Ronnie sat in the vacant easy chair he noticed the brandy bottle and glass on the table in front of Trevor. 'Got a spare glass, dear sister?'

Laura stormed across the tiny kitchen and lifted down a small, uncommonly thick glass from the dresser. She almost threw it at Ronnie. He picked it up and held it to the light.

'Wedding present from Tony,' Trevor explained. 'I think he won them on the fair.'

'I hope you make him drink out of them when he comes to visit.'

'Join us?' Trevor smiled lovingly at Laura.

'Some of us', she tossed her head as high as her five-foot-three-inch frame could reach, 'have more important things to do.'

'Like what?' Ronnie sneered, filling both glasses to the tiny brim.

'Mary Price asked if I'd take a look at her baby.'

'Don't you want to eat, woman? You're doing your own husband out of a job.' Ronnie touched his glass to Trevor's and started to drink.

'Alf Price drinks everything the dole gives him, even the penny a week Mary tries to earmark for the doctor. The children only know what breakfast is because the Salvation Army dish it up three days a week in Jubilee Hall before school.'

'I'd look at her baby for nothing,' Trevor protested in a wounded voice.

'I know that, sweetheart,' Laura said gently, ruffling his unruly mop of hair. 'And so does Mary, but like most people around here, having to beg for charity sticks in her craw. It hurts having to rely on handouts to feed and clothe your kids. And then again,' she bent to kiss Trevor's cheek as she lifted her coat down from the peg on the back of the door, 'if it's something serious you know I'll call you. See you, Ronnie.' She pulled the rug a little higher over Trevor's shoulders before she walked out of the door.

'Married bliss,' Ronnie mocked.

'You can't beat it,' Trevor replied gravely.

Ronnie fell silent. He looked around the warm, cosy kitchen. There was nothing worth more than a pound or two in the entire room. Laura, with Tina and Gina's help, had made the rag rugs that lay on the floor. The furniture was pine, second-hand, mellowed and scarred with age. The dishes and saucepans, plain and serviceable, had been donated by his parents as wedding presents. But with the aid of a few beautifully embroidered cloths that his mother and aunts had passed on to Laura for her 'bottom drawer', and a couple of cheap vases filled with dried bulrushes from Shoni's, Laura had contrived to make the room look homely and welcoming. He was suddenly very ashamed of his earlier, derisive comments. Picking up his glass he finished his brandy in one gulp and reached for the bottle.

'Tony and Angelo still minding the shop?' Trevor asked, holding out his own glass for a refill.

'Yes.'

'It's not like you to leave them in charge for so long.'

'It's high time they learned that running a business means more than emptying the till at the end of the day.' Ronnie lifted his feet on to the fender and pulled his cigarettes from his top pocket.

'Abdicating your responsibilities in the Tumble café in readiness to open the new place?'

'No, just trying to get lazy little brothers to do more.' He lit his own and Trevor's cigarette and rested his head on the back of the chair. 'This is the life. People who stay home evenings don't realise how lucky they are.'

'You could be lucky if you'd learn to walk away from work, at least one day a week.'

'Fat chance with Papa wanting the new place open in eight weeks.'

'Anything I can do to help?'

'Persuade the Hospital Board to hold their annual dinners there.'

'It's Doctor John you should be talking to about that, not a mere minion like me.' Trevor sipped his brandy, allowing its heady warmth to percolate through his veins. His body was glowing from the rub-down Laura had insisted on giving him, which had inevitably led to something even more enjoyable. The quarrel of earlier that afternoon forgotten, he felt cosseted, loved and just a little bit smug to have landed a wife as warm and passionate as Laura. He wondered why Ronnie had called, but his curiosity wasn't keen enough for him to disturb the peaceful atmosphere with extraneous talk. If Ronnie wanted anything he would get round to telling him in his own good time. Meanwhile there was his cigarette and glass of brandy to enjoy.

'That William Powell is a menace,' Ronnie said at last.

'William?' Trevor raised his eyebrows.

'He won't leave Tina alone. Encourages her to behave like a fool. Whenever he's around, all she does is gaze at him vacantly, like a stupid kewpie doll.'

Trevor recalled the interference he'd been forced to put up with from his in-laws when he'd been courting Laura, and almost said 'Perhaps they want to stare vacantly at one another', but he managed to keep his opinion to himself. The subject of his beginnings with Laura was still too raw to joke about.

'Has anything new in the way of TB treatments come out lately?' Ronnie asked casually, as he picked up the brandy bottle for the third time.

'You're thinking of Maud Powell?'

'Has she got it bad?'

Trevor looked carefully at Ronnie before he answered. 'If you're worried about Tina or Gina catching it off her, don't,' he reassured. 'Tuberculosis is rife in this town. They're as much at risk from the customers in the café as they are from Maud. The fact that they've reached the age they have without getting it says something. They're healthy girls, and in my opinion likely to remain so.'

'You didn't answer my question,' Ronnie continued impatiently. 'Has Maud Powell got it bad?'

'I've only examined her briefly,' Trevor procrastinated, then looked at Ronnie again and saw that he knew. 'If you want my opinion, very bad,' he admitted finally.

'She told me tonight that you want to put her in the Central Homes.'

'I suggested the idea to her father. It's probably the best place. She's going to need a lot of nursing, and warmth. The Respiratory wards are kept at a constant high temperature. The Powells can barely afford to heat their kitchen.'

'Supposing she did go in. Could you do anything for her once she was there?'

'Difficult to say. We'd have to do a whole lot of tests first, including X-rays. If one lung is more affected than the other it might be possible to deflate it – '

'How?' Ronnie demanded, moving to the edge of his seat.

'Cut through the ribcage, collapse it manually. It sounds much worse than it is. It's a bit like letting air out of a balloon.' Trevor refused to elaborate, or linger over the details.

'That means an operation?'

'Yes, but the technique can only be used on one lung. The idea is to render the most diseased lung useless in order to give the other a chance to work healthily and recover from any contamination it's been exposed to.'

'Does it work?'

'Not often,' Trevor replied brutally, his tongue loosened by brandy. 'But then, she hasn't much chance anyway.' There was a peculiar expression on Ronnie's face that Trevor couldn't quite fathom. 'I know Maud's the same age as Gina, and that must cut deep, but the chances of anyone surviving tuberculosis as bad as she has it aren't good,' he murmured.

'Then it's not simply a question of money?'

Trevor was touched. Most people in Pontypridd looked only as far as the well-stocked shelves in the Italian-owned and run cafés, and the food that came out of the kitchens, and assumed that all the owners were millionaires. They didn't realise just how small the profit margins were, or see the coal and electricity bills that had to be paid in order to keep the places warm and open all hours just to serve a cold bus driver and conductor a cup of tea at a thumping great loss. What little money the Ronconis had made they'd earned the hard way, and there were a lot of them to lay claim to it.

'No, Ronnie,' he said quietly, 'it's not simply a question of money, at least not the kind of money you'd find in this town.'

'Explain that.' Ronnie reached for the brandy again, pouring it out with an unsteady hand.

'If she was the daughter of a rich man, a very rich man,' Trevor qualified, 'there are clinics in Switzerland, set high in the mountains. Fresh air, good diet centred around dairy foods might do the trick, and then again it might not. You could spend hundreds if not thousands of pounds looking for a cure for Maud Powell and still not find one.'

Ronnie stared at him. 'How long do you think she's got?'

'If it doesn't get any colder, and we get a good, early spring and a warm summer, she might live through this winter and see the next,' he predicted harshly. 'But I don't believe she'll see more than one more spring in. It's a pity,' he continued, unnerved by Ronnie's silence. 'She's a pretty little thing, or she would be if she wasn't ill. Her spirit and character remind me a lot of Bethan. Not her looks, of course, they couldn't be more unalike.'

He lifted the bottle of brandy. It was empty. Ronnie took it from his hand and carried it out to the back. Trevor heard it smash as Ronnie threw it into the ash bin.

'I'll go down the café, hand over the keys to Tony, pick up another bottle and drop it in on the way back,' Ronnie said.

'How about we open that one too?' Trevor suggested.

'Developed a taste for it?'

'Sometimes, just sometimes I hate my job!' Trevor exclaimed savagely. 'Every time I come across someone in Maud's state I feel so bloody, pathetically useless,' he explained in answer to Ronnie's enquiring look.

'You and me both, mate. You and me both,' Ronnie replied as he walked unsteadily through the door.

Diana stood washed, hair pristinely waved and combed, and as neatly dressed as the combined contents of her own and Maud's wardrobes would allow, on the doorstep of Springer's shoeshop at precisely ten minutes to seven on Monday morning. Terrified of being late, she'd run the last two hundred yards down Taff Street. She felt breathless and, for all her show of bravado in front of the boys in Graig Avenue earlier that morning, apprehensive.

She tugged down the old school skirt that had been made when her figure was straighter and skinnier, removed the home-knitted, grey woollen glove from her right hand, and slipped her numb and frozen fingers beneath her coat. She pulled the edges of Maud's white cotton blouse together, hoping it had somehow miraculously stretched since she had last looked at it in Maud's dressing-table mirror. It gaped a good half-inch across her bust, straining the buttonholes to their utmost. There was no getting away from the fact: Maud was at least four inches narrower across the chest than her, if not more. Perhaps if she stitched the plackets together it wouldn't gape. On the other hand it might be better if she went to the post office and broke into the five pounds she'd saved. She'd get a good white blouse for half a crown in Leslie's, only then she wouldn't have five pounds any more, she'd have four pounds seventeen shillings and sixpence. And once she went down that road it would be easier to draw money out the next time she needed it – and the next; and before she knew it the five pounds would be four pounds, or even less.

It was simple to break into savings, and an uphill struggle to replace them when you were earning reasonable money. Impossible on the pittance that Mr Springer was paying her. The five pounds was all the cushion she had against having to take live-in domestic work. It was enough money to keep her for ten weeks or more, and it could take that, or even longer, to find another job in Pontypridd if she lost this one. A new blouse would have to wait until Ronnie found her some part-time work. She'd sew up the placket on this one tonight. That would stop Ben Springer ogling her the way he had last Saturday.

The clock struck seven and still she waited in the cold, dark, inadequate shelter of Springer's doorway. At least the rain had stopped, although a keen wind blew, freezing her ankles even through her thick lisle stockings. Heads down, coats buttoned to their chins, shop workers scurried around her. Shop doorways opened and closed, lights flickered on above counters. Gwilym Evans' display windows grew brighter as the shop lights went on behind them. A brewer's dray thundered down the street, pulling back sharply as a tram raced forward. She stamped her feet and swung her arms. Her coat still felt damp from the drenching it had got when she'd walked down the Graig hill to the café yesterday afternoon. She'd hung it in the passage overnight, but as the passage was never heated it was hardly surprising that it hadn't dried out. But then, that was where the boys had hung theirs. Aunt Elizabeth might be a great believer in 'airing' but she obviously wasn't a believer in drying wet coats, especially those belonging to lodgers.

'Glad to see you on time.' Ben Springer walked up to the door as the clock on St Catherine's church spire struck a quarter-past seven, and just as the final vestiges of feeling were leaving Diana's lips and nose.

'Good morning, Mr Springer,' she mumbled politely through chattering teeth.

'I'd prefer "sir" if you don't mind, Diana,' he corrected her curtly. Unlocking the door, he preceded her into the shop and switched on the lights. 'Hang your coat in the back, then you can

113

start by picking up and putting away any stock that's lying around. I'll tell you where. Every box has its allotted place in this shop and it has to go there. If it doesn't, we'll soon be in a pretty pickle, ordering stock when it's not needed, and running short of good selling lines. As soon as the general tidying's done, I want every surface in the shop dusted and polished until you can see your face in them. You'll find beeswax and dusters in the stockroom. When you've finished the polishing, you can do the floor. Well what are you waiting for, girl? Move!'

The stockroom door was in the centre of the back wall of the shop.

'Light to the left of the door,' he shouted as she went in.

She found the switch without any trouble. The room was really a narrow cupboard, running the entire length of the shop. It was about fourteen feet wide, but no more than five feet deep. Shoe boxes were stacked on foot-wide shelves from floor to ceiling. Bewildered by the vast array of boxes, she blinked dully, then after a few moments realised that the narrow wall on her far right sported a few hooks and two shelves that held cleaning materials and shoe polish. There was also a stiff broom, propped head upright in the corner.

'What are you doing, girl?' Ben appeared alongside her in the cramped doorway. 'Come on, we haven't got all day. Coat off, make a start.' She took her coat off reluctantly, walked deep into the cupboard and hung it on one of the pegs.

'Turn round,' he barked. 'Let's see if you'll do.' She did as he asked. 'Your shoes could be cleaner,' he commented, studying the shabby navy lace-ups that she'd cleaned that morning.

'I'm afraid there were a lot of puddles on the hill this morning after the rain, Mr Springer.'

'I would have thought it might have been possible for you to avoid at least some of them. There's a rag, brushes and shoe cream behind the furniture polish, you'd better use it. But in future you'll have to bring clean shoes with you. The one thing I will not abide in this shop is an assistant wearing dirty, shabby shoes.'

'I only have the one pair,' Diana confessed.

'In that case I'll have to give you a pair,' he said irritably, rummaging through the boxes. 'But I won't allow you to take them out of the shop until they're paid for.'

'I don't have the money – '

'And I just told you that I can't have an assistant in this shop with shabby shoes. Wear those in here and there'll be no point in you cleaning the place. You'll be tramping mud all over everything. Leave them with your coat.'

She slipped her shoes off obediently and stood them neatly beneath her coat. When she turned, Ben was watching her. He held out a pair of sturdy black lace-ups. Strong, unattractive walking shoes of the ilk that Diana instinctively knew Elizabeth would approve of, and Ben would have trouble selling.

'Try these,' he barked. Facing him, she crouched down so she wouldn't expose any length of leg, slipped them on, and tied the laces. Unfortunately they fitted perfectly.

'They'll do.' He peered at the side of the box. 'Twenty-one shillings . . .'

'I haven't any money, Mr Springer.'

'Seeing as how you need them to work here, I'll sell them to you for eighteen.'

'I can't afford that,' she protested.

'Course you can, girl. Sixpence a week.'

Diana's heart sank to her boots. With her wages knocked down to five shillings and sixpence a week, she'd only have one and sixpence for herself. And knowing her aunt, she'd have to buy all her own soap, for washing her clothes as well as herself. By the time she bought bread for her lunch out of what was left over she wouldn't be able to afford a Sunday cup of tea in Ronnie's, let alone a weekly visit to the pictures.

'Now let me see,' Ben pondered slow-wittedly. 'That's sixpence a week for thirty-six weeks. I'll just make out a card.' He reached past her to where a stack of 'tally' cards was piled up and as he did so his hand brushed against her breast. She moved back quickly, unsure whether his touch was calculated or inadvertent.

'Well now that I've provided you with shoes, you've no excuse to dally,' he said, apparently unaware of her unease. 'Come on, get a move on. There's an apron next to the polish, you'd better make sure you keep your skirt clean.'

'Yes, Mr Springer.'

'I told you "sir" once. I'll not remind you again.'

'Yes, sir.' She picked up the polish and a rag and left the

stockroom for the front of the shop. She wasn't sorry to move. She'd felt extremely uneasy, confined in such a small space with Ben Springer.

By half-past seven she'd polished every inch of dark oak wood that was on view. Her arm ached, and her fingers were bright red from the effort it had taken to keep a grip on the slimy rag. She paused for a moment, standing back to admire the long run of gleaming counter and dust-free edges of the shelves. Ben had even made her polish the two wooden shoe-fitting stands.

'The carpet now,' he barked from the stool where he was counting change into the till, 'and tomorrow you'd better work a lot faster. The till should be Brassoed every morning, but there's no time for you to do it now.'

She was sweeping the last of the dust into a cracked and warped metal pan when the door opened and the first customer of the day walked in.

'So this is what you've hired, Ben Springer?' An extremely large lady dressed in a navy cape coat, which lay unflatteringly tight over her thick arms and wide shoulders, towered above Diana. Diana's eyes were on a level with the woman's ankles. Wreathed in rolls of flabby fat, they spilled over the top of her elaborately decorated, expensive leather court shoes. 'Well stand up girl, let's take a look at you!'

Diana rose slowly to her feet. The woman's face was puffy, swollen by layers of fat that matched those on her ankles. Her small, greedy eyes darted unnervingly in deep sockets set beneath a low forehead, crowned by a navy felt Tyrolean hat held in place with two enormous, pearl-headed pins.

'Do you think she'll do, Beatrice?' To Diana's amazement her employer was suddenly transformed from shop owner, manager and bully to servile lackey.

'I hope you ascertained that before you took her on.'

'It's not easy to find good help these days.'

'As we've found out to our cost,' Mrs Springer pronounced heavily. It was obvious from the curl of Beatrice Springer's lower lip that Diana did not meet with her approval, but she was totally unprepared for her next question.

'Is that rouge I see on your lips and cheeks, girl?'

'No, Mrs Springer,' Diana faltered, wondering if she should

116

address her as ma'am, as she'd been taught to address the senior female staff in the Infirmary.

'Hmm. Naturally florid complexion then.' Beatrice Springer made it sound like a disease. 'Turn around, girl.'

Feeling intimidated and humiliated, Diana did as Beatrice commanded.

'Your blouse is tight.'

'I've put on weight lately,' Diana lied.

'Comes of being unemployed and idle. Tell me – the truth, mind – when was the last full day of work that you put in?'

'Last Friday,' Diana protested spiritedly. 'I've only just left the Infirmary in Cardiff. I was working as a ward maid – '

'You don't have to tell me any more,' Mrs Springer cut her short. 'When my husband told me that he'd taken on a new girl, I made it my business to find out all I could about you. Diana Powell, isn't it? From Leyshon Street?'

'I live with my uncle and aunt now in Graig Avenue.'

'And I know why.' She glared at Diana. 'Take after your mother?'

Diana felt silent. Experience had taught her that it was the best thing to do whenever anyone brought up the subject of her mother.

'Just as long as you know that I'll be watching you.' Mrs Springer crossed her stubby arms across her ample bosom. 'And to let you know that we – that's both me and Mr Springer – will be a great deal more fussy about someone who works for us than a supervisor in an Infirmary who hasn't got their own place and their own trade to worry about. So before you do anything else, I suggest you sweep out the shop again. There's dust in the corners. Mr Springer, being a man, may not always notice sloppy, half-hearted cleaning, but I warn you I always do.'

'Yes, Mrs Springer. Diana sank to her knees again, wondering if there was a chance that Ronnie would open his restaurant before she answered either of the Springers back. Or if she'd soon find herself unemployed again.

Chapter Eleven

'Hey listen to this, Haydn, Maud,' Eddie held up the copy of the *Pontypridd Observer* that he had found folded behind the cushion of Evan's chair and read out:

' "Do the general public realise the skill, patience and practice necessary to perfect an act like that presented by Mr Willi Pantzer and his wonderful troupe of performing midgets at the New Town Hall, Pontypridd next week? We think not. Willi Pantzer is a lifelong vaudeville artist, he and his little men have been together many years, and his search for midgets is never ending." What do you think, Haydn? Worth shrinking for, eh? He may even offer you a contract,' Eddie mocked.

Haydn had burned in a fever of ambition ever since he had turned down Ambrose's offer to join his revue, and Jenny's absence from his life hadn't helped one bit. He'd bored William, Eddie, Maud and Diana to screaming pitch with extrapolations of 'might have beens' until Eddie was ready to seize any opportunity to get his own back.

'Don't be cruel, Eddie,' Maud said primly from the depths of her mother's chair. Her bedroom and the easy chairs in the kitchen still encompassed her entire world. But like wishful children, her family clung to the entirely irrational hope that the excitement of Christmas, followed by a warm spring, would bring a visible improvement to her health.

'I'm not being cruel,' Eddie insisted, a mischievous glint in his eyes. 'Who knows where an opportunity like this could lead?' He rustled the paper ostentatiously and continued to read. ' "His present company includes midgets of all nationalities," – there's your big chance now, Haydn,' he suggested gravely. 'He may not have a Welsh one.'

Haydn picked up the cat that was sleeping peacefully on one of the wooden chairs and threw it at him.

'Haydn, you'll hurt it!' Maud protested, as the cat sank its claws into Eddie's trouser legs and scrammed him.

persuaded her. I sometimes wonder if those two have anything on their minds other than what they read in Hollywood star magazines. Where's William?' he asked suspiciously.

'You know Will?' she answered carelessly.

'Yes I do,' he frowned, thinking how often Tina had gone to the pictures with Diana lately. 'Want some tea?' He held up the cold teapot.

'No thank you,' Maud refused primly, suddenly conscious of being totally alone in the house with him. Her mother's warnings about placing herself in a vulnerable position with a man, any man, rang clearly through her mind. Then she remembered how long Ronnie had been a friend to her family, and the vast difference in their ages. Sickness was making her paranoid. The problem was she'd never really had a boyfriend, only dreams. She couldn't even count Jock Maitlin, they'd never actually gone anywhere together. Diana was right: doing a man's washing and darning his socks was no substitute for romance.

She allowed herself to drift into a cold, comfortless tide of self-pity. Looking the way she did now, she'd never experience love first-hand. And unless she made a remarkable recovery she wouldn't even be seeing it on a cinema screen again.

The sound of Ronnie replacing the teapot on the shelf above the range jolted her back to the present. She watched him as he settled into the easy chair opposite her own.

'Don't you ever get fed up of the same four walls?' he asked, tapping a cigarette out of a packet he'd removed from his shirt pocket.

'A little,' she admitted reluctantly.

'The Trojan's outside. It's not the most comfortable of rides, but I could take you down to the café for an hour or two. Gina and Angelo are there, and Alma,' he added as an afterthought.

'I don't know,' she murmured hesitantly. The prospect excited her, but she knew her mother, and probably her father, would quite rightly be furious when they found out what she'd done. As they undoubtedly would. Pontypridd was no place for secrets.

'Come on,' Ronnie coaxed, 'I'll have you down and back before half-past seven. No one will be any the wiser,' he smiled.

The smile decided the matter for her. 'All right,' she said resolutely.

childhood. The dull tick of the kitchen clock that had been a wedding present to her mother from her Uncle John Joseph. A soft hiss, as a damp piece of coal crumbled into the flames in the stove, probably one of the pieces that Eddie or Will had risked prosecution over on one of their scavenging trips to the Maritime tip. She'd seen their blackened hands and faces when they'd sneaked in over the back wall after adding their ill-gotten spoils to the meagre stock in the coalhouse when her mother wasn't looking.

'Hello, anyone in?' The front door slammed and footsteps echoed on the lino in the passage.

'Ronnie?' Half asleep, Maud peered through the gloom as Ronnie's tall figure emerged from the shadows that lay thickly in the corner by the door.

'Just passing, so I thought I'd call in and see how the boys are doing. Haydn must be about ready to walk down the hill.'

'They've already gone to town,' Maud said, expecting him to walk straight back out again. Instead he came closer to the fire and pulled his hat off.

'Leaving you all alone?'

She bristled at the hint of criticism. 'It's nice to be alone sometimes,' she replied tartly.

'I know what you mean.' He took off his rain-spattered coat and hung it over the back of one of the kitchen chairs. Walking over to the range, he placed his hand against the side of the teapot.

'No one will be back for ages.' She resented him intruding into her peace and quiet and wanted him to go so she could sit back and dream. Of Jock Maitlin, the porter in the Infirmary who'd shown more than a passing interest in her. Of the career in nursing that she'd wanted so badly, and now realised she'd never have.

'Not even Diana and your parents?'

'My father and Charlie have gone to a meeting in the Unemployed Club.'

'The anti-Mosley meeting?'

'I really don't know, I don't pay much attention. My mother's gone to Uncle Joe's and won't be back until late. And Diana's – '

'As soon as Diana finishes work she's meeting Tina to go to the pictures,' Ronnie told her. 'When Tina saw Ben Springer walk into the bank this morning, she ran to the shoe shop and

'As I'm working in half an hour I suppose I'd better make a move,' Haydn said miserably.

'Nothing like it, boyo,' William grinned. 'You may have Willi Pantzer and his performing midgets next week, but this week you have some cracking chorus girls. Saw one going through the stage door yesterday that brought tears to my eyes.'

'A red head, wearing a blue, fur-trimmed coat?'

'That's the little beauty.'

'Stuck-up madam, more like it.'

'Enjoyed that, did you?'

'What?' Haydn asked in bewilderment.

'Shattering my dreams.' William pulled a comb out of his pocket and ran it through hair so heavily Vaselined it barely moved. 'You ready or not?' He winked at Maud. 'Tell that sister of mine to catch up on some rest. Shops close on Thursday afternoons for the staff to enjoy time off, not scrub the place out.'

'She's still trying to make a good impression.'

'Nothing would make a good impression on Ben Springer.'

'You be all right if I walk down with them, Maud?' Eddie asked.

'Of course I will,' she retorted. 'I'll enjoy the peace and quiet.'

'That's a nice thing to say to your brother.'

'Fight coming up soon?' William asked.

'Not until the Easter Rattle Fair.'

'Don't expect to clean up this year like you did last,' Haydn warned. 'They know your face now, boy.'

'Just practise for the big time. Joey says that if I do well enough at Easter he'll take me up to Blackpool this summer.'

Maud had to force herself to hold her tongue. She'd never liked Eddie's boxing any more than her mother or sister had. In their opinion the dangers far outweighed any rewards.

'Right, if we're going, we'd better go.' Haydn picked up his cap from the back of the chair where he'd left it to dry, and patted Maud on the head.

'I'm not a dog.'

'No, but you're too big to kiss goodbye.'

William finished lacing on his boots, then with Eddie trailing in the rear the boys left.

The house was remarkably still. Maud lay back in her chair, listening to the quiet sounds she'd associated with home since

'Ow!' Eddie screeched, as the cat fled. Undeterred, he carried on reading. ' "A great little artiste is Willi Pantzer. He creates most of the comedy and enacts the role of Jack Dempsey in the boxing ring" – Hey do you think you could put a word in for me? This could be the start of a whole new career.'

'Only if you allow me to chop your legs off,' Haydn said viciously, furious with Eddie for daring to joke about feelings that were painfully tender.

'I'm sorry for getting your hopes up, Haydn, they wouldn't want you after all. Listen to this: "Willi Pantzer's troupe are all modest, genial little fellows." That leaves all bad-tempered growly bears like you out. "Mr Willi Pantzer is an athlete, boxer and wrestler and in addition he models in papier mâché, wonderful little dolls he uses in the Pantzer Trot." What do you say Will? Worth going to see, just for the dolls?'

'Eddie if you don't shut up, I'll shut you up,' Maud threatened as a thunderous look crossed Haydn's face.

They all fell silent. None of the boys smiled at her ridiculous outburst. Maud's ill-health hung, a dark and gloomy portent of the inevitability of death, over the entire household.

'You walking down the hill, Haydn?' William asked, breaking into the oppressive atmosphere. It was late on a foul and filthy Thursday afternoon. So foul that Eddie and Evan, having nothing to do except call the streets, had packed in their carting at midday. Charlie and William had finished early in the slaughterhouse. Setting up their stall for the Friday trade in record time, they had returned home early, much to Elizabeth's delight. She had tea on the table before five o'clock, and put Diana's meal on top of a saucepan of water on the shelf above the stove so it could be heated up later. Then she'd rushed down the hill to catch the six o'clock bus for her Uncle John Joseph's house in Ton Pentre. She'd organised his move from the Graig; now she was busy organising his furniture in the new house.

Evan and Charlie had left straight after tea for the Institute for the Unemployed in Mill Street. Although neither of them were unemployed in the strict sense of the word, like dozens of others they used the centre as a meeting place, especially on nights when Evan couldn't scrape together the money for a half of mild in any of the pubs.

Haydn and William, ' – there'll be a job for you there when you're up to working again.'

'Do you mean that?' Her eyes glittered with excitement – and fever.

He glanced round the room to make sure no one was listening to their conversation. He knew from signs and symptoms he'd seen in others that it was extremely unlikely that Maud would ever work again, but what use was there in reinforcing her worst nightmares and telling her that? With nothing to look forward to she'd only wither and die all the sooner.

'I'm not in the habit of saying things I don't mean.' He pulled the box of chocolates out from under his coat. 'Here, if you eat all these by yourself you may put some meat on your bones. God knows you could do with some,' he murmured, ashamed of his own generosity.

'Thank you . . .' she gasped, overwhelmed by the quality and size of the box.

'Quick, hide them,' he hissed. 'Before Gina sees them. Another pound around her waist and she'll be fatter than Mama.'

Maud laughed as she pushed them beneath the blanket that covered her, and the laughter brought on a short-lived coughing fit. Ronnie watched helplessly as she spat blood into the handkerchief that had become a permanent fixture in her hand.

'You know what you should do, don't you?' he asked seriously.

'Go into the Graig Hospital?' she answered bitterly.

'No,' he contradicted flatly, disregarding the underlying hint of fear in her voice. 'When the fine weather comes, spend as much time as you can on the mountain. Fresh air is what you need.'

'So they told me in the Infirmary.'

'They were right.' He lit his cigarette and puffed it carefully, blowing the smoke away from her face.

'Trevor said I should go into hospital.'

'What does he know?' Ronnie asked laconically. 'He'll be lucky if he keeps himself out of the place, and I don't mean as a doctor. The fool got soaked earlier, walking down the hill to the café when he's got a car sitting outside his front door. You should have heard Laura shout at the state of him when I dropped him off at Graig Street.'

'I can imagine,' Maud laughed again. Her laughter triggered off

'You'll have to dress up warm,' he commanded in the tone of voice he usually reserved for his eight-year-old sister and six-year-old brother.

'You can't get much warmer than what I've got on,' she protested strongly.

'That's just the problem. You've been sitting in thick clothes in a warm room for weeks. A strong dose of real, fresh air is likely to . . . knock you for six,' he said quickly, almost kicking himself. He'd almost said 'finish you off'.

She threw back the grey rug that covered her legs. He was right about her clothes. She was dressed for a trip to town on a freezing, damp and miserable market day. Thick flannel skirt more serviceable than attractive. Winceyette blouse, topped by the red cable-knit jumper from her suit, and cable-knit lisle stockings.

'I'm not taking you out of here without a cardigan. Where can I find one?' he demanded.

'On top of this, you must be joking. I'd feel like a bundle of laundry.'

'You don't put one on, I don't take you.'

She glared at him, but it had no effect. Used to dealing with the tantrums and vagaries of ten younger brothers and sisters, Ronnie shrugged off her display of temperament without a second thought.

'I'll get one from my room,' she said, suddenly thinking of her hair – her face – she didn't even have a dab of powder on her nose, and if she was going out she really ought to put some scent on. Her spirits suddenly soared at the prospect of sitting in the café. Talking to the girls. Seeing people . . .

'Are you allowed to walk upstairs?' he asked sharply.

'Of course, how do you think I get to bed?' she retorted.

'There's a difference between walking up and down once a day and running up and down for no good reason in between. And before you say another word,' he flicked his lighter on and lit his cigarette, 'I know what's on your mind. You don't want to go upstairs to get a cardigan, you just want to primp in front of the mirror.'

'I do not!' Her voice rose high in indignation.

'Tell me what you want and I'll bring it down,' he interrupted just as she was about to burst into full flow.

123

Gripping the sides of her armchair she levered herself upwards. Ronnie wavered alarmingly within her sight. The room began to sway, and black spots swam before her eyes as they always did whenever she tried to rise.

'You're as weak as a kitten.' He pushed her gently down into the chair and she fell back, grateful for the feel of its solid support beneath her. 'Which is your room?'

'Right at the top of the stairs.' She felt a draught of cold air as he opened the kitchen door. 'The grey cardigan,' she called after him. 'It's on the stool in front of the dressing table.' She blessed her mother's rigid housekeeping. Her bedroom would be immaculate, just as it always was when she returned upstairs after a day in the kitchen. 'And bring my handbag as well,' she shouted, hearing his step on the stairs. 'It's next to the bed.'

'Women!' he moaned when he returned a few moments later with her handbag and the cardigan. 'They've always got to primp themselves up, even for a trip out the back.'

He watched her as she squinted into the mirror. She'd washed her hands and face after tea, so comforting herself with the thought that she was at least clean, and very conscious of him watching her, she ran a comb through her hair, holding the mirror up in an effort to get a better view.

'Your hair's fine,' he reassured her. It was, she noted with relief. Diana had helped her wash it yesterday evening when her mother had left to go to a chapel committee meeting. It had always been her best feature, and since she'd been ill she'd tried to make the most of what her father called her 'crowning glory', torturing her sleeping hours by wearing metal grippers in an effort to tame the unruly curls into fashionable waves. The only problem was, since her illness the contrast between the rich golden colour of her hair and the deathly pallor of her skin had become even more noticeable. Putting away her comb, she pushed up her lipstick with her thumbnail and spread it over her mouth. It was bright red, a colour Diana had assured her, suited her when she'd first gone to the Infirmary. Now it made her mouth look like an ugly red wound against the unnatural whiteness of her face. She lifted the stick, intending to dab some on her cheeks.

Stung by the pathos of what she was doing to herself, Ronnie turned away. Maud painting her thin, sickly face for her first outing in weeks reminded him of an incident he'd witnessed as a child. The curtains had been drawn in the house next door to theirs. He'd asked his heavily pregnant mother if he should go next door and tell Mrs Brown that it was daytime. She'd warned him tersely not to go near the house. It was the lack of explanation that intrigued him: he'd sensed that something secret, something forbidden, was going on behind those closed drapes. When his mother had called him for dinner he'd scoffed it in record time. Then sneaking out into the deserted street, he'd crept up the short flight of steps to next door's front door. The curtains were still drawn, but there was a crack at the side where they didn't quite cover the edge of the bay. He'd crouched down and looked through the small gap. Mr Brown was lying on the table in the parlour. Mrs Brown was bending over him, tenderly washing a thick layer of coal dust from his grey, dead face.

He rubbed his eyes. Why had he thought of that incident now? He hadn't called it to mind for years.

'I'm ready.'

Maud had put away her lipstick and powder and closed her handbag. She was sitting forward on the edge of her chair, the grey cardigan round her shoulders. The air was sweet, redolent with essence of violets, but he noticed, thankfully, she'd decided against reddening her cheeks.

'Your hat and coat by the front door?'

'They are.'

'Green coat, isn't it?'

'Yes,' she was surprised he'd remembered. 'And the black tam's mine.'

He fetched them. She rose somewhat unsteadily from the chair. He caught her shoulder as she staggered. Slipping her arms quickly into the sleeves of her coat, he lowered her back into her chair.

'Stay there for a minute,' he ordered, unnerved by her fragility. She looked down at her feet and saw the old slippers she'd inherited from Bethan. Tartan with red pom-poms, their ugliness hurt.

'Shoes?' Ronnie asked abruptly.

'They're in the washhouse on the shelf. Plain black with a bar.'

He found them and brought them out. She kicked off the

slippers, but when she bent to do up the buckles, she almost fell head first on to the floor. Ronnie knelt and fastened the buckles for her. Embarrassed, she made a bad joke.

'Does your girlfriend know you play Prince Charming with other girls?' She didn't dare mention Alma's name.

'You're not a girl, you're a baby,' he contradicted her. 'Right, blanket around your shoulders.'

'Ronnie . . .'

'It's not up for discussion. Either you do it or you don't go. I've left an umbrella by the door. It'll keep off the worst of the rain, but not all of it. Right, can you walk by yourself or do I carry you?' he asked, looking at her critically.

'I can walk,' she asserted forcefully, swaying precariously.

He put his arm round her waist and pulled her close to him, steadying her. 'One slip and I'm carrying you.'

He helped her as far as the door, then opened his umbrella and gave it to her to hold. Stepping outside, he swung her up into his arms. 'Don't argue,' he ordered, silencing her protests. 'It's too damned wet to hang around here quarrelling.' He carried her down the steps and set her on her feet by the side of the van. Pulling open the door, he lifted her on to the bench seat inside. He ran around to his side of the van, took the starting handle from beneath his seat and swung the engine into life, before climbing in. 'Right, first stop the café.' He looked across at her and smiled. The smile froze on his lips. She was lying back against the seat, her thin face grey in the watery lamplight. Perhaps this had been a crazy idea after all. What right did he have to come in and sweep her off to the café for some social life just because her family had left her alone for the evening? Then he remembered what Trevor had said: this was her last year. She deserved every minute of animation and life he, or anyone else, could give her.

'I would much rather have gone to the pictures,' Diana moaned to Tina as they queued outside the Town Hall.

'I would have gone with you if the boys hadn't hogged the only decent talkie in town.'

'It's the pictures, for pity's sake. Half the town would have been there, as well as my brother and Glan Richards. Just what are you afraid of?'

'Being seen sitting too close to Will by someone who'd carry tales back to Papa or Ronnie.'

'It's not as if you don't like my brother . . .'

'That's just it. I like him, and Ronnie and Papa know it.'

'And just what could they do to you if they did find out that you were going out with Will?' Diana demanded testily, convinced that Tina was making a melodrama out of absolutely nothing.

'Send me to Italy,' Tina said flatly.

Diana stared at her incredulously. 'They wouldn't.'

'They would,' Tina assured her.

'But you've never been there, it'd be . . .' The queue shuffled forward and Tina grabbed her arm and pulled her up the line. 'You're serious, aren't you?'

'I'm serious,' Tina whispered. 'Didn't Bethan ever tell you what Laura had to put up with when Papa found out about her and Trevor Lewis? My father wants – no, *expects* – all of us to marry Italians, or at the very least, Welsh Italians. I think secretly he still regards Laura's marriage as a disgrace to the name of Ronconi, and he certainly doesn't intend to stand by and do nothing while any of the rest of us dishonour it any more than Laura already has.'

'But he seems to get on all right with Trevor Lewis,' Diana protested, trying to recall the few times she'd seen Mr Ronconi senior and Doctor Lewis together.

'Get on with has nothing to do with it. He *gets on* with Trevor, likes him even for being a doctor, and a Catholic. What he doesn't like is Trevor being Irish/Welsh instead of Italian.'

'But isn't Ronnie keen on Alma Moore?' Diana persisted.

'Perhaps,' Tina said darkly. 'And then again perhaps not. Ronnie's made sure that no one really knows, not even Alma. But believe you me, even if he is keen on Alma, "keen on" is nowhere near marrying.' The queue surged forward again, and this time Diana pulled Tina on. 'Ronnie'll never marry a Welsh girl,' Tina pronounced decisively. 'Take my word for it, even if he loves Alma Moore, he'll walk up the aisle with Papa's choice. For the last four Mondays Mama's invited Maria Pauli to tea. She was born in Wales, but Papa's prepared to overlook that, as both her parents are from Bardi and like us they speak Italian at home. Her father has a café in Ferndale,' she informed Diana matter-of-factly. 'And I think both Papa and Mama are expecting Ronnie to succumb to her charms any day now. I overheard Papa tell Ronnie three times last week that a man should be married before his twenty-fifth birthday. Ronnie was twenty-seven last month.'

'Does Alma know any of this?' Diana demanded.

'If she doesn't she's a fool,' Tina said. 'She's been mooning around after Ronnie for years. If she can't read the writing on the wall by now, she never will.'

Diana remembered the blatant adoration on Alma's face every time she looked at Ronnie. 'Knowing someone and being in love with them are two different things,' she sighed theatrically, recalling the plot of a Claudette Colbert film she and Maud had seen in Cardiff. 'I think when you love someone you can forgive them anything, and overlook everything.'

'If Ronnie was anywhere near serious about her, he would have married her years ago,' Tina said impatiently. 'If you want my opinion, I think she's just someone he's passing the time of day with,' she continued airily with all the worldliness of her sixteen years.

'Well I'm sorry, but I think that's a foul way for Ronnie to behave towards any girl, let alone one as nice as Alma.'

'He wouldn't go out with Alma if she wasn't nice.'

'I don't think I like your brother very much!' Diana pronounced resolutely, already half-way into weaving a tragic romance in which Alma was the wronged, doomed heroine.

'All the years you've known him, and you've never come to that conclusion before? I'll let you into a secret. I've never liked him,' Tina grinned. 'Two sixpences please,' she said to the girl in the cashier's kiosk, as they reached the box office.

'I would have rather had fourpenny seats.' Diana rummaged in her handbag for her purse. Tonight was a real extravagance. Tina had caught her at a low ebb when she'd come into the shop mid-morning. After four stern dressing-downs from Ben Springer, and three from his wife, she hadn't needed much persuading to agree to an outing, although she knew perfectly well there was no way she could really afford it. Despite Ben Springer's assertion that he'd review her pay at the end of the week, she knew now that she wouldn't dare bring up the subject of her wages again. Not after seeing so many girls her age walking the shops in Taff Street every day in a last-ditch attempt to find local work before resorting to the domestic agencies that trained women for service in England.

'This one's on me,' Tina insisted, pushing the change she'd received from half a crown into her handbag. 'I'm rich. Ronnie actually paid me this week.'

'Don't be silly,' Diana scolded. 'You can't afford to treat me.'

'Tell you what, you buy ice-cream wafers in the interval and we'll call it quits.'

'They're only twopence . . .'

'And cornets are a penny. Look, we can swap over next time if it makes you feel any better. Give us a good excuse to go out together again.' She ran up the steep flight of steps into the hall.

'I don't like owing money.' Diana reluctantly returned her purse to her handbag. Like all people living close to the bone, she resented taking 'charity' from anyone.

Tina led the way down the long corridor to the usherette, who guided them to the rear of the stalls.

'At least they're right at the back,' she said cheerfully. 'We can put our seats up if we have to, and sit on them. Chewing gum?' she flipped open a packet of P.K. and flicked one into Diana's hand.

'Did you pay for these?' Diana asked.

'They fell on the floor when I was opening a new box. Can't sell spoiled goods to the customers,' she grinned.

The orchestra began to tune up, scratchily and noisily. Diana settled back in her seat. The manager walked out in front of the curtain and held up his hand.

'Oh, oh, here comes a programme change,' Tina moaned. 'What's the betting that the leading lady and all the chorus girls are sick and they're bringing on the Dan-y-Lan Coons instead.'

'Ssh!' Diana hissed as heads turned towards them.

'Ladies and Gentlemen,' the words fell unheard into the auditorium. He lifted the microphone stand towards him and tapped it. A hollow boom echoed around the theatre.

'Something you ate, Dai,' a wag shouted from the front row. A gale of laughter drowned out the manager's words.

'Ladies and Gentlemen . . . Ladies and Gentlemen . . .' It took a full minute of stammering repetition for him to regain the attention of the restless audience. When hush finally descended he continued, 'I regret to inform you . . .'

'Told you,' Tina crowed.

'Ssh!' Diana commanded as she tried to listen.

'. . . is ill. To take his place we have a local boy, who works here, and I want all of you to give him a chance,' he shouted above the cat-calls and jeers. Someone offstage pushed Haydn in front of the curtain. He bowed quickly and dashed off, but not before the audience had dissolved into mirth at the costume he was wearing. A ruffled matador shirt strained tightly across his broad shoulders and gaped across his chest where the buttons refused to meet the buttonholes. A short cloak hung half-way up his back and a ridiculously small tricorn was perched on the crown of his head.

'The hat looks like a pimple on a haystack,' Tina giggled helplessly. 'And I would have loved to see him in the trousers that went with that outfit. He looks like Gulliver dressed by the Lilliputians.'

Diana alone out of all the people packed into the auditorium kept a straight face.

'I wonder what he's going to do?' Tina wiped tears of laughter from the corners of her eyes with the back of her hand.

'Something good, I hope,' Diana murmured, crossing her fingers and hoping against hope that Haydn wasn't about to make a fool of himself.

Chapter Twelve

When Haydn was told that the head chorus boy was sick, and was asked to stand in for him, his spirits soared. The head chorus boy had two duets with the head chorus girl, one of which contained three precious solo verses. He felt that the gods had smiled on him – forgiving him for rejecting Ambrose's offer after all. Who knows, when the revue moved on he might be taken with it. To big cities – exotic places he'd only read about and heard of, never visited – Birmingham, Manchester, Bristol. Perhaps the biggest prize of all – London. But even as he built his towering, glittering castles of success in the air, the bombshell struck.

The manager had handed him the head boy's costume, which was at least five inches too narrow and a good six inches too short for him, with the news that he was going to fill in for the newest and least important chorus boy in the line-up. His presence was only needed to even numbers up in the dance routines, and provide another male voice in the background. All of the boys in the chorus had been understudying the head boy and praying for this moment. He watched them practise the solo verses and fight over the role while he struggled into the matador's shirt (he failed even to pull the satin trousers over his thighs). In vain he protested to the show's director and the manager that he couldn't dance.

'You don't have to dance, boy, just be there,' the director boomed in his best Shakespearean voice.

'You've seen the routine often enough, Haydn. It's not much to ask,' the manager snapped. Ice cold and paralysed with fear, Haydn watched while Dolly, a charming little teaser on stage and an absolute bitch off, executed a complicated tap step in the corridor.

'Got it now?' she asked briskly.

Haydn tried to copy her fancy footwork but his feet simply failed to respond to the directives he sent them. Tripping over his ankle, he fell flat on his face.

'He'll never do,' Dolly complained loudly, making Haydn feel about two inches high. 'He's got two left feet.'

131

'It's only for tonight, darling,' the director said soothingly. 'Right, everybody ready?'

'Just one more thing, hot shot,' one of the boys whispered to Haydn as he followed them up the steps to the wings. 'Don't try to drown us out with your singing. We've all heard you backstage. You haven't got a bad voice, for an amateur,' he added deprecatingly. 'But like all amateurs you obviously think the louder you sing, the better it is.'

'Mime, sweetheart.' Dolly pinched his arm viciously as she walked past him on her way to the stage. 'Just open and shut your mouth like a goldfish, stand still and you can't go wrong.'

'I hope so,' Haydn muttered fervently as he followed the others out on to the darkened, curtained stage. 'I really hope so.'

'You tired yet?' Ronnie asked Maud solicitously as she sat in front of the fire in the back room of the café with Gina on one side, Angelo on the other and him opposite her.

'A little,' she admitted reluctantly.

'How about I make you one of Papa's special ice creams to perk you up?' Angelo offered. Tony had only just taught him how to make the raspberry delights, banana splits and knickerbocker glories that formed the backbone of Ronconi's dessert menus, but so few customers could afford to order fancy ice creams that he grasped every opportunity to air his new-found skills.

'No thank you,' Maud smiled. Ronnie had whisked her off in such a rush she hadn't even thought to bring her purse with her, and even if she had, she doubted she had enough to cover the sixpence that a knickerbocker glory cost. Besides, Gina had already given her a hot chocolate on the house.

'Angelo will be so upset if you don't let him make one of his ice creams,' Ronnie coaxed. 'Go on, be reckless for once. There's nothing in this world like the taste of Ronconi's ice cream smothered in raspberry sauce.'

'I know, I've eaten it,' Maud laughed.

'Well then, you can eat one again.' Ronnie nodded to Angelo. 'Go and make her one,' he ordered.

'A very small one,' Maud pleaded. 'I really couldn't eat a lot.'

'And one for me, Angelo,' Gina shouted. 'An extremely large one. With nuts, and a cherry on top,' she added as an afterthought.

'No work, no eating,' Ronnie said briskly. 'Clear and clean down those tables.' He pointed to four tables covered in cigarette ash and sandwich crumbs that the evening tram crews had just vacated. 'When that's done, you can finish for the day. I'll take you home when I take Maud back.'

'No peace for the wicked,' Gina sighed as she rose reluctantly from the table.

'Or the idle,' Ronnie emphasised. 'Alma, I'll have a coffee,' he shouted, clicking his fingers to gain her attention.

Alma was accustomed to Ronnie's imperious ways, but familiarity with his behaviour didn't make it any easier to bear. She marched furiously to the metal coffee jug which was kept on a low oil burner behind the counter. She poured out Ronnie's coffee just the way he liked it, thick and strong, with no extra water. Adding three sugars and a dash of milk she stirred it, then carried it over to the table where he was sitting with Maud.

Gina was busy clearing the tables, and Angelo hadn't yet returned from the kitchen with the ice creams, so Ronnie and Maud were alone. A warm wave of sympathy washed over Alma as she looked at Maud. The young girl was sitting, head in hands, slumped over the table, her face pale with exhaustion, her lips bloodless. The thin veneer of cheap lipstick had worn off on the warm rim of her cup of chocolate. She seemed to be listening intently to something Ronnie was saying. Alma looked instinctively from Maud to Ronnie, and all her feelings of sympathy were washed away on a floodtide of acutely painful suspicion.

For the first time since she'd known him, Ronnie had lowered the defensive shield of cynicism he habitually used to camouflage his finer feelings. His eyes were naked, mirroring his thoughts. And she didn't like what she saw in them. Not one little bit.

A benign expression softened his features as he gazed at Maud. He was speaking too low for Alma to catch his words, but judging from the lack of response from Maud he wasn't telling her anything of vital importance. Only his eyes betrayed his feelings: speaking with an eloquence she had never suspected him of possessing.

'Your coffee, Ronnie,' she said spikily, slamming the cup on to the table and slopping the hot liquid into the saucer.

'Remind me to give you a refresher course in waitressing some time, Alma,' he reprimanded her icily.

133

She glared at him as she walked away.

'Two knickerbocker glories,' Angelo announced grandly, bearing his creations proudly into the back room of the café. Pink and white scoops of ice cream were piled high in silver fluted goblets, the whole creation topped with whirls of whipped cream, glazed with rivulets of raspberry sauce and sprinkled with fine layers of crumbs of toasted nuts.

'Not bad,' Gina said condescendingly as she walked over to the table. 'Not bad at all. Not as perfectly symmetrical as Ronnie's or Tony's, of course. But passable.'

'What do you mean not as symmetrical as Ronnie's or Tony's?' Angelo demanded touchily.

'Well there's more nuts on this side than the other,' she teased. 'And the sauce?' she raised her eyebrows. 'You really should have put on more sauce.'

Ronnie stared at the creations critically. 'Did you put sauce in the bottom of the dish?' he demanded.

'Yes,' Angelo answered belligerently.

'And half-way up?'

Angelo stuttered, then faltered.

'You left it out!' Ronnie exclaimed. 'What on earth do you expect it to taste like with no sauce running through the lower scoops of ice cream and chopped tinned fruit? Really, Angelo . . .'

'I put a double helping on the top,' Angelo protested strongly.

'It should have gone under the cream, Angelo, not on top,' Ronnie said heavily. 'You sour the taste of the cream by putting it on top – '

'It's delicious,' Maud interrupted, scooping a spoonful into her mouth. 'Absolutely delicious,' she smiled at Angelo.

'Thank you for saying so,' Angelo replied sullenly, glaring at Ronnie.

'Each to their own,' Alma interposed from the front of the café. 'Just because you and your father have done it one way for years, Ronnie, it doesn't mean that it's the right way.'

Ronnie stared at the counter, ignoring her comments. 'Couldn't that do with a wipe-down, Alma?' he said curtly.

She picked up a cloth and did as he asked, burning with indignation and damning him for trying to keep her out of his public life. But despite her anger she sensed he was slipping through her fingers: she felt as though she were trying with her bare hands to stem water that was pouring from a fall. Ronnie was leaving her, and she didn't know how to hold him.

She only knew that she couldn't imagine living any kind of a life without him.

'Well, boyo.' The director of the show, a fat, cigar-smoking lecher who dived into the chorus girls' dressing room on each and every pretext, eyed Haydn over the top of his rimless spectacles. 'That was a bloody disaster, wasn't it?'

Haydn stared down at his feet, encased like bursting chrysalides in a pair of varnished leather tap shoes that he had borrowed from the show's dresser. They were two sizes too small for him, and he could already feel the raw skin and blisters that had formed on his heels and toes after only an hour of wear.

'It was,' he acknowledged miserably. Pressing the front of one shoe against the back of the other, he kicked it off. A blissful, soothing feeling of ease and comfort seeped up through his body, to be superseded moments later by intense, mind-blowing, agonising pain as his battered feet stung alarmingly back to life.

'Well?' the director urged. 'Do you mind telling me why you didn't do as you were told? Hell's bells, man, you only had to stand at the back of the stage and let the girls dance around you. A tailor's dummy could have done as much. What are you? An imbecile?'

Too mortified to attempt an explanation, Haydn remained silent while the director's face turned purple with rage. He could have protested that the other members of the chorus had, for reasons of their own, resented his presence on stage and set out to deliberately make things difficult for him, but the director wasn't in a listening mood.

He'd begun the routine well enough, standing on the chalk marks that the director had drawn for him at the very back of stage left, only to be sent flying by Tom, the youngest and greenest of the chorus boys, who was ecstatic at his elevation to the third row. Mesmerised by the lights, the colour, the music, the movement, but most of all by the dark void that hid the audience, he hadn't even seen Tom coming. It was as if the boy had materialised out of

135

nowhere. Unable to prevent himself from stumbling forward, Haydn found himself centre stage, blocking everyone's path. His size hadn't helped. He'd felt like a huge, clumsy giant in a light, flitting fairyland. Stepping back quickly he'd knocked Dolly flying. Totally disorientated, he then committed the cardinal sin of continuing to move forwards not backwards, fouling the movements of the newly elevated head chorus boy Sean, an Irish lad, who had, as the director put it, 'a beautiful turn of step'. His step was anything but beautiful after Haydn had lumbered in front of him. It had been up to Dolly to rescue what was left of the number. Pushing Sean forward and Haydn backwards, she'd managed to retrieve centre stage for herself and Sean, earning herself a cheer from the restless first-house audience, whose gales of laughter at Haydn's antics had unnerved him all the more.

Mortified, Haydn had remained glued to the backdrop until the time came for the chorus to sing. Feeling that this at least was something he could do well, he ignored Sean's advice to mime the words, and added his deep, rich baritone to the chorus's efforts. Riding high on a crest of emotion and music, a good minute passed before he became aware of his fellow performers.

Dolly and Sean were both firing furious glares his way, interspersing them with the bright, brittle, artificial stage smiles they reserved for the audience. He paused, faltered, listened for the first time to the others and in a single, tingling moment of utter embarrassment and mortification, realised he'd been singing in the wrong key.

'Ah manager, there you are.' The director waylaid the manager as he walked towards them in his boiled shirt, black bow tie and evening suit. 'I was just telling this boy that we'll have to drop one and a half couples from the chorus for the next house,' he said bitterly. 'Needs must,' he boomed as he flicked a disparaging glance at Haydn. 'After all we can't really call *this* – ' he jabbed his forefinger painfully into Haydn's arm, '– half of any couple.'

'The others might be safer without his presence on stage,' the manager agreed drily.

'A whole lot safer,' the director concurred sharply.

'Do you really need to drop one and a half couples?' the manager ventured. 'Why not put Dolly and her partner centre stage and allow the others to dance around them?'

'Good idea, old man! Good idea, I'll get the boys and girls together to talk about it.' He immediately banged on the door of the girls' dressing room. 'Girlies!' he shouted in a sickly voice, his small piggy eyes gleaming at the thought of catching a glimpse of one of them in a state of semi-undress.

'We'll be out in a minute,' Dolly's nasal voice echoed through the door.

The manager was fond of Haydn. He'd watched him grow in confidence and competence during the months that he'd worked in the Town Hall, and he'd already marked him down for promotion to assistant manager when George Bassett, the old man who held the post at present, retired. But he was also aware of what a fiasco like this could do to the Town Hall's and his reputation when the story got back to the booking agents in London. With the coal pits closed and money a scarce commodity in the valleys, it had become almost impossible to induce good-quality acts to visit South Wales. And the few people who still had money in Pontypridd wouldn't patronise shows that weren't top drawer. Every week he and the manager of the New Theatre fought for better shows and a bigger share of diminishing audiences. And it wasn't just the New Theatre. Since the talkies had hit town, they'd had the cinemas to contend with as well.

He felt sorry for Haydn, read the misery of shattered dreams in the boy's face, but with the director's furious gaze upon both of them he didn't feel disposed to openly sympathise with him.

'The sooner you get out of that ridiculous outfit and back to work, the better,' he said frostily. 'There's a mess waiting to be cleared up in the boys' dressing room. Once you've changed, deal with it. Then come to the office. I've a list of errands for you to run between houses. Well, what are you waiting for?' he demanded. 'Get on with it. There's still the calling to be done, you know. You can't expect Judy to do your job for you just because you went out on stage for five minutes. She has her tray to set up and take out in the interval.'

'Yes sir,' Haydn mumbled. He was having a hard time grappling with mixed emotions that were half shame, half mutinous. He didn't know what he wanted to do most urgently: sock the manager and the director on the nose, or break down and cry.

'Oh, and Haydn?'

'Sir?' Haydn paused with his hand on the door of the boys' changing room.

'After tonight's little fiasco I don't want to hear any more from you about going on stage. That offer Ambrose made to you when he was drunk seems to have gone to your head. You've been fit for nothing since. Even if you hadn't refused, he would have retracted it in the morning. You *do* know that, don't you?'

'I never said I was a dancer, sir . . .'

'If you ask me you're not much of anything. Not even a callboy. Perhaps now that you've finally been given the "break" you've been whining for, you'll understand that it takes good all-round talent to get anywhere in variety. It's a tough world, and there's any amount of idiots around who can sing a few notes. Most of them even manage the right key,' the manager added sadistically, convinced he was doing the right thing in trying to keep Haydn's feet firmly on the ground. 'Believe me, boy, you need a lot more than just a pleasant voice. Talent, looks, ability to dance . . .'

Haydn couldn't listen any more. 'Sir,' he muttered dejectedly as he opened the dressing-room door and stepped inside. Feeling sick and faint he breathed in the oppressive stench of stale male sweat and greasepaint. Clothes were strewn from one end of the bench that traversed the centre of the room to the other. He nodded to the boys. They stared at him before continuing to change in silence. He knew they'd heard every word the manager had said to him. And revelled in it.

Steeling himself, he entered the room and closed the door behind him. With his back to the door he unfastened the only button of the shirt he had managed to do up, the last one, closest to the tails.

'Careful you don't rip it, callboy,' one of the boys jeered in a derisory tone. 'It's worth more than your week's wages.' Haydn stripped it off in silence, folding it meticulously, collar up, sleeves neatly tucked in behind the front. He looked around for somewhere to put it.

'You're not going to give it back to us like that, are you?' Tom, the youngest of the chorus boys and the butt of all their jokes was only too delighted to give a little of what he had to take. 'Phew!' he moved near the shirt and staggered around with his fingers over his nose in a parody of a man fainting. 'Phew! Phew!'

'Knock it off, Tom,' Sean shouted irritably, succumbing to a sudden empathy for Haydn. He'd had a rotten break on his first job too. It had been so bad his career had almost ended before it had begun, and he knew exactly what Haydn was feeling right now.

'I'll take it home and wash it,' Haydn murmured, looking around for his own shirt. He saw it, lying on the floor in the corner of the room. It was only when his fingers closed over the cloth that he realised it had been used to mop up the mess that the manager had told him about.

'What's the matter, Taffy?' Tom laughed. 'Something on your shirt?'

Dropping the shirt, Haydn looked around the room.

'Which one of you jokers did this?' he asked quietly. Only Tom, who was as insensitive as he was naive, continued to laugh.

'Can't the Welsh take a joke?' he sneered. 'Do you think that's lemonade on your shirt, Taffy?' He looked to the others for support. 'We all know different, don't we boys? That's – ' he pointed to the floor where Haydn's soiled and sodden shirt lay, a limp, discarded rag ' – that's what you get for trying to climb into boots that are too big for you, or,' he grinned as he saw the shoes that Haydn was carrying, 'in your case, too small.'

'Shut your mouth before I shut it for you,' Haydn hissed, focusing all his embarrassment, disappointment and anger on Tom.

'Ooh, masterful,' Tom pranced around in front of Haydn. Once Haydn saw Tom move he realised that he was a queer, like Wyn Rees. His emotions clarified, converging into cold, murderous rage. No one in the mining community liked queers. They were strange, unnatural . . . his hand closed into a hard, tight ball of a fist. Lashing out, he hit Tom squarely on the jaw. The boy flew backwards. The last thing Haydn saw before Tom lay, a crumpled heap on the floor, was the startled expression as Tom's eyes blinked open when the back of his head connected with the painted brickwork on the wall.

'You've killed him,' one of the boys wailed.

'Don't be so bloody soft,' Sean exclaimed, hiding his own fear behind a thin veneer of irritation. He moved before anyone else. Kneeling at Tom's side, he laid his hand over where he thought Tom's heart should be. 'He's just out cold.'

Haydn's knees gave way as a surge of relief rushed through his veins. He almost fell to the floor. Sitting there with his head resting on his knees and his back to the cold brick wall, he trembled uselessly while Sean assumed absolute control.

'We need a doctor. Haydn?' He turned and saw that Haydn was on the point of passing out himself.

'I'll get one,' Haydn breathed faintly, hoping his legs would carry him as far as Trevor's house.

'Now listen, all of you.' The note of authority in Sean's voice was unmistakable. 'Tom slipped on the metal tap of his shoe while he was trying to take it off. Does everyone understand what I'm saying here?'

The entire chorus nodded dully and in unison, as though practising a routine.

'You don't have to do that,' Haydn whispered hoarsely, finally finding his own voice.

'We're not doing it for you, but for Tom,' Sean said scornfully, looking pointedly at Haydn's shirt. 'If half of what happens in this dressing room ever got out, the gossip could kill the show dead, not to mention our careers. Particularly in one or two of the towns we've been playing in lately.'

Chapter Thirteen

It was closer to eleven than ten o'clock when Ronnie drove back down the Graig hill. He and Gina had gone into the Powells' house to sit with Maud until someone came home. They had a long wait. William and Diana didn't walk in until nearly ten o'clock, and meanwhile Maud's face grew paler, and her thin frame slumped further and further in the chair until she looked on the point of collapse.

Ronnie hadn't seen the animation in her face, or the glow in her eyes as she'd talked to Gina. Only the gaunt, grey sickness that was eating her alive. He'd wanted to kick himself for his stupidity. Only an idiot would have taken a girl as frail and ill as Maud out on a cold, rainy winter's night.

He'd sat in silence, drinking the weak tea Gina had made for them, without tasting it. He hadn't even heard a word they'd said. For once the cynicism he habitually adopted to buoy him through life had deserted him. Instead he'd visualised Maud, dead. He found himself picturing the misery of her funeral, the gap her death would create in the lives of his sisters . . . and perhaps not only his sisters. He could actually hear the awed whispers in which they would speak her name. See the babies that would be named after her.

Distraught at his own imaginings, the moment William and Diana walked into the back kitchen he'd dragged a protesting Gina out. Left to her own devices she would have gossiped with Maud and Diana all night. He drove up to Danycoedcae Road and dropped Gina off, stopping only as long as it took him to shout a quick hello and goodbye to his parents.

A pang of conscience niggled at the back of his mind. He should never have left Alma to cope for so long alone. He comforted himself with the thought that she'd had Angelo in the kitchen, but then he remembered just how useless Angelo was as soon as he was put under any pressure. But perhaps Angelo was entitled to be useless. After all he was only fifteen, no more than a kid. He scrutinised his thoughts and wondered if he was going soft in the head. He'd done as much work as Angelo – and a great deal more – when he'd been only twelve.

He drove his Trojan under the archway that led into the back yard of the White Hart, and pulled into the car park. He nodded to, but didn't dare stop to pass the time of night with the landlord who was putting out a crate of empties. Hurrying around the corner it only took a few steps for him to realise his worst fears. The windows of the café were misted up, but inside he could make out the dark, shadowy shapes of blurred figures at virtually every table.

He thrust open the door. Alma glanced up from an order she was taking, and he thought he saw a fleeting look of annoyance cross her face as she pushed her hair back from her forehead. She picked up a tray from the table behind her; it was loaded with dirty dishes. Turning her back on him, she carried them out to the kitchen. He smiled thinly, acknowledging the customers he knew and checking the dirty plates to see what had been ordered. He recognised the swirls of grease and thin vestiges of egg yolk which meant the bus crews had been in, in force. They always mopped up the last traces of egg, beans and chips with double orders of bread and butter. An endless array of empty cups covered with a fine sprinkling of sugar and cigarette ash lay strewn across the tables in the back. He didn't have to ask Alma anything. He could see that she'd coped. Just!

Without waiting to don his khaki work jacket, he stacked a pile of dirty cups and saucers and carried them into the kitchen.

'Boy, did this place turn into a madhouse after you left,' Angelo grumbled loudly as soon as he caught sight of him. 'Sixteen orders of egg and chips, seven of beans and chips. Five pie and chips. The fat hasn't been off the gas ring in the last hour, and my hands are covered with spit burns . . .'

'Well, I'm here now.' Ronnie dumped his load into a sink that was already overflowing with dirty dishes, before taking his jacket down from the hook behind the door.

'What took you so long?'

'I stayed with Maud. She wasn't well, certainly not well enough to be left alone,' he explained abruptly.

'Gina could have stayed with her.'

'By herself?' Ronnie retorted derisively.

'You could have got Mama,' Angelo suggested in exasperation as he lifted yet another load of chips out of the fry basket.

'I could have, but I didn't,' Ronnie snapped, wondering why he hadn't thought of getting his mother. Angelo was right: it would have made more sense for her to have sat with Maud, than him and Gina.

'Two toasts, two boiled eggs and a pie, Angelo,' Alma shouted through the counter door.

'Damn,' Angelo swore. 'Just when I thought I could go home.'

'Finish that order and you can,' Ronnie conceded.

'Ronnie?'

'Yes?' Ronnie thrust his arms into the sleeves of his khaki coat. He could see a queue waiting to pay at the till. And the first rule of business that his father had hammered home to him was: *never* keep a man waiting when he wants to pay his dues.

'You will get a replacement cook as soon as you can, won't you?' Angelo pleaded. 'I don't mind helping out – '

'I'll start looking tomorrow,' Ronnie shouted testily as he went to the till.

Alma called off the orders of the customers as they reached him. 'One egg and chips – two eggs, beans and chips and extra bread and butter' – that one had to be a bachelor, but then who was complaining – 'one tea and a pie – one Oxo and a ham sandwich . . .' He found difficulty in adding up the money. Maud's face kept intruding into his mind: drained of all colour, like the clear lard they used for frying. He remembered her racking cough, wondered if she was coughing up shreds of her lungs along with the blood he had seen her spit into her handkerchief . . .'

'Ronnie!' Alma stared angrily at him, her temper rising precariously at his lack of response. 'Ronnie!' She repeated furiously.

He looked up blankly. The last man in the queue had gone. He glanced around the café: there were only a few late stragglers finishing their teas and Oxos. Without acknowledging that she'd spoken he picked up a damp rag and wiped down the counter, paying special attention to the area around the coffee machine. When he'd finished he lifted down a tin of coffee beans from a high

143

shelf, tipped half a handful into a small wooden grinder, and turned the handle. He refilled the coffee jug, setting it on the small oil burner to warm, making it as much for himself as for any customer. Then he took his rag and went to the tables to give Alma a hand. She'd piled a tray high with dishes and was carrying them into the kitchen. He wiped down the tables and chairs, setting them all back carefully into their allotted positions. No sooner had he finished than a dozen people walked in from the New Theatre across the road. Five minutes later they were joined by a small crowd who'd been to the Town Hall. Unlike the bus crews, they didn't buy much in the way of food. They wanted to linger in the warmth and light of the café, delaying for as long as possible the moment when they'd have to leave town for their homes, using the time they should have spent sleeping to relive the magic they had seen on stage.

Ronnie and Alma were kept busy making and serving coffee, teas, chocolates, Oxos, but mercifully few time-consuming titbits like toast. Just after the clock struck half-past eleven the door closed on the last customer.

'I think it's over,' Alma breathed heavily.

'Did you say something?'

'I was talking about the rush.' She dropped a tray piled high with cups and saucers noisily on to the counter.

'Yes, I suppose you're right,' he agreed absently. He took the dishes into the back. Angelo had tidied up before he left, but hadn't pulled the plug on the washing-up water. Ronnie tossed the cups and saucers into the sink and left them there to soak. Gina and Tina could do them in the morning. By the time he returned to the café Alma had upturned the chairs on to the tables and was sweeping the floor. He blew out the light beneath the coffee burner, and took down two cups from the shelf.

'Want a coffee?'

She shook her head. 'It'll keep me awake.'

'Chocolate, then?' he asked pleasantly, trying to make amends for his absence.

'Nothing. Thank you,' she snapped.

'Damn it all, Alma, I've said I'm sorry, what more do you want me to do?' he demanded, concealing the guilt he felt at leaving her and Angelo alone at the busiest time of the evening, behind a screen of anger.

144

'You know what more you can do!'

'No I bloody well don't. I've never seen you like this before. You're behaving like . . . like . . .'

'Like what?'

'Like a typical bloody woman,' he answered hotly. 'Like one of my sisters, if you must know,' he shouted. He felt betrayed by her mood. Other women threw tantrums or fell into black sulks, but not Alma. Never Alma. Good old reliable Alma. He propped his elbows on the counter, and sipped his coffee slowly in a determined effort to calm himself.

Keeping her back to him, Alma swept the dirt from the floor into a neat little pile.

'You still haven't told me what's the matter,' he ventured, struggling to keep his voice even.

Alma didn't reply. Picking up a tin dustpan, she swept the mess of crumbs and dirt into it. Holding it carefully aloft, she made her way through the kitchen and out to the dustbin in the back yard.

'Hello Alma,' Ronnie shouted sarcastically. 'Can you hear me? Can you see me? Am I invisible?'

She slammed the back door behind her, locking it ostentatiously, then glared at him, eyes blazing. 'You disappear for the busiest part of the evening leaving me and Angelo to work our fingers to the bone. Then you swan in two and a half hours later and casually ask me what's the matter?'

'I wasn't away for two and a half hours,' he protested mildly, picking on the one thing he could contest. He abandoned his coffee and walked over to her, settling his arm around her waist.

'You're quite right, it wasn't two and a half,' she retorted, stepping out of his reach. 'It was nearer three,' she said caustically, borrowing his habitual attitude.

'Alma, I'm sorry,' he repeated abjectly. 'I didn't realise the time . . .'

'You're so damned besotted with that . . . that girl,' she spat out the last word as though it left a foul taste in her mouth, 'you don't even know what time of year it is, let alone what time of day.'

'What girl?' he asked in genuine bewilderment.

'Ronnie Ronconi, you're the dumbest, stupidest man I've ever come across . . .'

145

'What girl?' he repeated, grabbing her wrist across the counter as she tried to pass in front of him.

'What girl?' she mocked, temper making her bold. For once she didn't care about security, or her job. 'What girl?' she asked incredulously. She attempted to pull her wrist away but he hung on to it, holding it tight. 'There is only one girl. The one you drive up and down the Graig hill every half-hour in your van for. The one you give all the best-quality chocolates and cream cakes in the café to, the one you wrap up in a blanket and bring down here "for a change of scenery",' she sneered.

He released her arm in disgust. 'You're being totally ridiculous. Maud's a child. She's Gina's age . . .'

'She may be a child, and she may be the same age as Gina, but neither of those facts have stopped you from falling head over heels in love with her,' Alma countered.

'You're crazy. She's ill. She's . . . she's . . .'

'Dying!' Alma supplied the word he couldn't bring himself to say. 'She's dying, it's eating you alive, and you can't even see it. Well I'm not going to stay around doing your dirty work and watching you cry for the moon. I've a life of my own to live . . .'

'Alma you're insane!' he cried out in exasperation.

'Have you fallen in love with her because she's dying, Ronnie? Is that it?' she taunted. 'Don't you trust yourself with a healthy girl because she might actually demand something of you, and stay around long enough to see that you give it to her? It's useful to fall in love with a girl who has one foot in the grave, isn't it? You can martyr yourself while she's alive, and mourn her forever more when she's dead, effectively keeping me and the rest of the world at bay.'

'I don't know what brought this on . . .' Ronnie began in disgust.

'Perhaps I just don't like the way you make me feel,' Alma interrupted. 'I look at Maud, and I look at you mooning over her like a lovesick dog, and I find myself wishing her dead. As if she won't be dead soon enough . . .' she burst into tears. 'Damn and blast you, Ronnie Ronconi!' She fumbled her way into the kitchen and grabbed her hat and coat. 'Damn you to hell!'

'Wait, Alma, you can't go out like that. I'll take you home.'

She ran headlong out of the café. By the time Ronnie reached the door she was half-way up Taff Street. He called her name just once, feeling foolish when Constable Huw Griffiths answered his cry from the doorway of the New Theatre, asking if there was anything wrong. Shaking his head, he retreated into the café and locked the door. Feeling restless, he went into the kitchen and heated fresh water to wash the cups and saucers he had dumped in the sink earlier. Alma had wound him up too much to sleep, so he decided he might as well work off his mood. There was certainly more than enough to do. When he finished the dishes, he scoured the pots and pans; afterwards he set about the gas stove, and the kitchen floor. Then it was the turn of the café. First the floor. He noticed a few spots on the walls, so he scrubbed those. When he couldn't find any more work to do he looked at the clock: its hands pointed to a quarter to three. He could hardly go home now. It simply wasn't worth it. Besides, he didn't want to go home. He wanted peace and quiet, one commodity that was always in short supply in Danycoedcae Road.

Freeing the key from his watch chain, he opened the cupboard at the back of the kitchen, took out a bottle of brandy, and relocked the cupboard. Picking up a glass, he struck a match and lit a stub of candle that swam in a saucer of congealed wax on the windowsill above the sink. Candle in one hand, bottle and glass in the other, he ascended the creaking staircase. The room he used as a bedroom was freezing cold and smelt of damp. He laid the saucer down next to the oil lamp. There was no oil in the reservoir, it must have burnt out the last time he and Alma had used the room.

Stripping off to his underpants, he flung back the sheets. They too felt cold and damp to the touch. He would have given a great deal to have had . . . have had who? Alma next to him? In her present mood?

For the first time he thought, really thought about what she had said. The woman was truly mad. It simply wasn't possible. He couldn't love Maud. Little skinny Maud, the baby he had warmed milk for when Bethan Powell had carried her into their High Street café after school. Bethan and his sister Laura, and Maud and Gina, two little girls playing with babies instead of real dolls. There had to be eleven years between him and Maud. Almost half his lifetime. He'd never thought of Maud as anything other than a kid. Sick as she was, she was still annoying and irritating, like . . . Gina and Tina. Surely he couldn't be in *love* with her?

Love was something else he'd hardly ever thought about. On the few occasions circumstances had forced him to consider it, he'd decided it was faintly ridiculous, and embarrassing. Something that affected others. Fools like Trevor Lewis and his half-baked sister Laura, who'd fussed and fretted for months before they finally managed to organise themselves a wedding. A wedding . . . was that what Alma wanted? Was that what all this fuss and emotion had really been about?

He shook a packet of cigarettes out of his shirt pocket and lit one on the flame of the candle. If she was unhappy with their 'arrangement' as it stood, all she had to do was say. He'd assumed that she was as content as he was. But for her to be jealous of Maud . . .

He puffed a smoke ring and watched it rise gently in the candlelight. The problem undoubtedly lay between him and Alma. The question was, did he want to marry her? Now marriage was something he *had* thought about. Even if he'd wanted to, he couldn't have avoided it, when his father brought up the subject every time they spent more than ten consecutive minutes together. And he only had to hint that he'd be home at a mealtime for his mother to invite one of the daughters of a fellow café owner. Italian, of course. Not that they'd ever made Alma feel less than welcome on the rare occasions she had attended any of their family gatherings. But then perhaps they'd never realised that Alma meant more to him than any other waitress they'd employed. Why should they, when he hadn't taken the time or trouble to explain his relationship with Alma to them? Possibly because both parents, Papa especially, had said enough to Laura when she'd brought home a non-Italian boy. Poor Trevor.

He wondered if he wanted Alma enough to go through what Laura had gone through to marry Trevor. Then he thought beyond the ceremony. Marrying Alma would mean settling down with her; living in a small house like Laura's; being with her all the time, in and out of the café; having no time to himself. And with his luck there'd soon be a parade of squalling babies who would grow into kids every bit as obnoxious and demanding as his

148

younger brothers and sisters. If that's what marriage to Alma meant, he definitely preferred his present life.

But then, what was his present life? Work, more work, followed by the occasional foray into this bed with Alma, or a sneaky visit to one of his other 'ladies'. He had a sudden, incredibly vivid and real image of Maud. They were sitting side by side next to the fireplace in her back kitchen. She was smiling at him, and he could feel the weight of her hand in his. Only something was wrong. He sat up, almost dropping the cigarette when he realised what it was. The Maud in his vision had been plump, well; her cheeks bright with the warm glow of health, not the sickly spots of tuberculosis. The concept of Maud well elated him. Then it hit him. Alma was right. He did love her.

He was in love with a girl eleven years younger than him who had terminal tuberculosis. The thought wasn't a pleasant one. He'd always assumed that love would be something he'd be able to control, subjugate to his will. Maud was hardly the robust beauty he pictured whenever he'd thought of his future wife.

In a sudden, inspirational flash of self-knowledge, he realised why he'd never asked Alma to marry him. He didn't love her. Had never loved her. Instead he was in love with a scrawny kid who was going to die. He stubbed out his cigarette and lit another, staring up at the ceiling until the light from the candle flickered out.

He continued staring and smoking all through the night, watching the shadows move on the ceiling as Huw Griffiths paced at hourly intervals past the lamppost outside the window. He listened to the creaks and groans of the building, and heard the thunder of the milk train as it rattled noisily over the rails and out of the station. He didn't close his eyes once. And in the morning when the first customer tried the door of the café, he left the bed and dressed next to the untouched bottle of brandy.

He'd decided one thing and one thing only during his long vigil. He couldn't let Maud die. Not without putting up a damned good fight.

Chapter Fourteen

'Were you very late last night?' Laura asked as she lifted two pieces of bacon and an egg out of the frying pan on to Trevor's plate

'Not very.' Struggling to push his collar studs through both his collar and his shirt, he leant across the table and kissed her. 'I was back in bed by twelve.'

'Sorry I wasn't awake.'

'I didn't want you awake. Just warm. And you were exactly what a poor fellow needed after an hour spent in a freezing dressing room.'

'Dressing room?' Laura's eyes shone as she nosed out potential gossip. 'Anyone exciting?' she asked, taking the last piece of bacon for herself and sitting across the table from him.

'One of the chorus boys,' Trevor answered, through a mouthful of bacon and bread. 'The others insisted that he knocked himself out. Slipped while changing.'

'But you don't believe that?'

'Good God, woman, I can't keep anything from you, can I?'

'Don't blaspheme,' Laura lectured. 'And no, you can't. I know you too well. Tea?' she asked, picking up the pot.

He nodded, his mouth still full.

'What happened then?' she persisted, ferreting out the story with the dogged determination of a terrier in a rabbit burrow.

'Put it this way, he had one hell of a bruise on his chin. It almost matched the one I noticed on Haydn's fist.'

'Not Haydn Powell?'

'I don't know of any other Haydn who works in the Town Hall, do you?'

'You've got to be wrong on that score,' Laura remonstrated. 'Haydn wouldn't hurt a fly.'

'A fly maybe. After last night, I'm not so sure about chorus boys. The whole time I was there, he hung back in a corner, looking incredibly sheepish. And that's not Haydn.'

'Well?' She stared at him, an uneaten bacon sandwich in her hand.

'Well what?' he asked blankly.

'What did the chorus boy do to deserve it?' she demanded in exasperation.

'How should I know?'

'You were there,' she grumbled. 'If it had been me, I'd have found out a whole lot more.'

'I don't doubt that you would have,' he murmured drily.

A frown marred Laura's smooth forehead as a loud banging at the front door interrupted them. 'Oh heavens above, not again!' she said peevishly.

'Now who's blaspheming?' Trevor cut an enormous piece of bacon. Holding it poised only as long as it took him to shout, 'Come in', he shovelled it into his mouth.

'I hardly ever get to see you. We can't even eat a meal in peace . . .'

'You should have thought of that before you married me,' he broke in, taken aback by the vehement tone in Laura's voice.

'I did, I just assumed people would have the common courtesy to get taken ill outside of mealtimes, especially breakfast. And you're going to get indigestion eating like that. *Do* come in,' she shouted with exaggerated politeness, just as Charlie burst through the door.

'Sorry Doctor Lewis, Mrs Lewis,' Charlie apologised in his heavy Slavic accent. Not even an emergency could make inroads into Charlie's formal, courteous way of speaking.

'It's Maud.' Trevor rose from the table without waiting for Charlie to confirm his suspicions. 'My bag's in the front room,' he said as he picked up his coat from the back of the chair and disappeared into the passage.

'I'm sorry for disturbing your breakfast, Mrs Lewis,' Charlie apologised again as Laura made another sandwich of the remaining bacon on Trevor's plate.

'Can't be helped.' She gave him a tight little smile. 'How are they all coping?'

Charlie shrugged his massive, heavily muscled shoulders.

'They're coping,' he repeated unconvincingly.

'I know, they're coping because there's nothing else for them to do,' she murmured sympathetically.

'Charlie, if you're going back up, I'll give you a lift,' Trevor shouted from the hall. Charlie hung back as Laura preceded him. She thrust the sandwich she'd made into Trevor's hand.

'Give them all my love, especially Diana,' she said quietly. 'And tell Mrs Powell I'll be up to see her later.'

Trevor kissed her cheek as he opened the front door. Charlie followed him out on to the pavement.

'Jump in,' Trevor said to Charlie as he removed the starting handle from beneath the front seat. Charlie needed no second bidding.

'Don't forget to tell Mrs Powell I'll be up just as soon as I've washed the breakfast things,' Laura shouted to Trevor above the noise of the firing engine. He nodded to show he'd understood.

'How bad is it?' he asked Charlie as he steered the car up the Graig hill.

Charlie turned away from Trevor and stared out of the car window. As far as Trevor could see there was little except early morning workers and shoppers to hold Charlie's interest, but he seemed to find them fascinating.

'I'm sorry, did you say something?' Trevor asked. Between the noise of the engine, the accent and the distance, Trevor wasn't certain whether Charlie had answered or not.

'I didn't say anything,' Charlie replied flatly.

'She's haemorrhaging, isn't she?' Trevor said, hoping for a contradiction.

'It started when Diana took her breakfast up.' Charlie finally turned his head and faced Trevor. 'Diana has taken her breakfast up every morning since they've come back from Cardiff.'

'It's what I've been afraid of all along,' Trevor muttered.

Charlie was out of the car before Trevor parked it. He ran up the steps and opened the front door, slamming it straight into Evan who was sitting, head in hands, on the bottom stair.

Haydn and William, not knowing what else to do, were hovering in the passageway, effectively blocking the way into the kitchen. Eddie, anxious to be of help, had valiantly fought back his tears, and made tea in Elizabeth's chipped and cracked everyday cups. Because everyone had congregated at the foot of the stairs he'd carried a tray into the front parlour, laying it out on

152

top of the dustcloth that covered Elizabeth's treasured mahogany octagonal table. He'd filled the teacups so much they'd slopped over into the spoons and saucers. The messy parody of a formal tea party was the first thing Trevor saw when he pushed his way into the house. He couldn't help thinking that it looked totally incongruous. Like a miner sitting in working clothes in the lounge bar of a pub.

He avoided meeting Evan's eyes as he asked, 'Upstairs?'

Evan rose silently and made room for him to pass. Trevor ran up the stairs two at a time. Diana was waiting for him in the doorway of Maud's bedroom. He felt as though he were walking into a hothouse. The atmosphere was stuffy, unpleasantly warm after the sharp freshness of the winter morning. He looked from Diana to the fire-grate, where lumps of coke still smouldered among the ashes. The Powells had evidently taken to heart his advice about keeping Maud warm. He recalled Elizabeth's moans about the cost and wondered if Evan had swallowed his pride and gone to the parish for help. Then he remembered the boys. They wouldn't have allowed Evan to succumb to the final indignity of the unemployed. There'd be no means test conducted on the Powell household while there was coal on the Maritime tip free for the thieving.

Elizabeth moved back, away from the bed, allowing Trevor his first glimpse of the unconscious Maud. She lay pale and still, like one of the waxwork effigies of murder victims in Louis Tussaud's in Porthcawl fair.

'There's nothing you can help with here, Diana,' Elizabeth voiced a harsh practicality Diana didn't want to hear. 'The best thing you can do is go to work. You don't want to lose your job now, do you?'

'I thought . . . I thought . . .'

Trevor sensed Diana's reluctance to leave Maud while her cousin's immediate future was so uncertain. 'I'll get Laura to call in the shoe shop and let you know how she gets on,' he promised quietly.

'Just go, Diana,' Elizabeth said brutally. 'You're holding up the doctor.'

Diana finally did as Elizabeth asked, closing the door behind her. But she didn't go downstairs. Instead she sat on the step outside Maud's bedroom, shivering, cold and clammy from the fear that crawled insidiously over her skin and invaded her mouth. She heard Trevor's footsteps echoing across the linoleum. There was a faint murmur of voices, but the thunder of her own heartbeat drowned out any intelligible sounds. One phrase kept repeating itself over and over again in her head. She mouthed the words, whispering them, not really knowing what she was saying: 'Please God, don't let her die. Please God, don't let her die. Please God . . .'

Trevor folded back the bedclothes; they were clean and fresh. He glanced around the room hoping to catch a glimpse of the soiled linen. He couldn't see anything.

'You changed the sheets?' he asked Elizabeth.

'I could hardly leave her lying in a pool of blood,' she retorted defensively. 'It was all over the sheets, the bedcover and the blankets,' she explained.

'Was it dark or bright blood?' He picked up Maud's wrist and checked her pulse. It was barely perceptible.

'Bright, I think,' Elizabeth faltered, suddenly unsure of her facts and wondering how much depended on the accuracy of her answer.

Trevor saw her uncertainty and didn't press her. Most of the mothers he'd seen in similar circumstances had succcumbed to hysteria when they'd faced what Elizabeth had faced that morning.

'How long has she been like this?' He replaced Maud's wrist gently on the bed.

'Since she stopped haemorrhaging,' Elizabeth's voice was brittle with emotion. He looked at her, wondering how much more she could take before she broke down. Removing his stethoscope from his bag, he unbuttoned the top of Maud's nightdress. She didn't even move when he examined her.

'I'm sorry, Mrs Powell,' he said as he finished. 'There's nothing more I can do for her here. She'll have to go into the hospital.'

'The Graig?'

The mixture of fear and condemnation in her voice struck a chord, making him effusive, almost garrulous in his defence of the hospital cum workhouse.

'The isolation ward is quite separate from the workhouse,' he explained, with all the emphasis on the word 'separate'. 'It's on the top floor, there's a fine view over the Maritime pit . . .' he hesitated as he realised what he'd said. An abandoned pit was hardly the view to cheer a sick young girl. 'You can see as far as the fields in Maesycoed,' he added with a forced heartiness. The fields of the farm above Maesycoed were the closest thing to countryside that could be seen from the windows of the hospital. He looked at Elizabeth. She was staring at him. He sensed that she could see beyond his pathetic attempts at bluster, read the damning, tragic diagnosis that he was struggling so hard to soften, if not conceal.

'How long has she got left, Doctor Lewis?' Elizabeth asked. She might have been enquiring about a train timetable. Unused to such direct questioning from the relatives of his patients, Trevor remained silent.

'How long?' she repeated flatly.

'I don't know,' he said slowly. 'I'm not lying,' he protested in the face of her obvious scepticism. 'I really don't know,' he insisted. 'It depends on how much damage has been done by the haemorrhage. On whether or not both lungs are affected . . . we might be able to collapse one if the other's healthy . . .' his voice trailed miserably. 'The sooner we get into the Graig and do some tests, the sooner I'll be able to give you a fuller diagnosis,' he finished on a more decisive note.

'I'll pack her things.'

'I'll go downstairs and send one of the boys for an ambulance. You do pay your extra penny a week for the use of one?'

'We do,' Elizabeth affirmed as she lifted Maud's suitcase down from the top of the wardrobe.

Diana was still sitting on the top step of the landing when Trevor emerged from Maud's bedroom. She looked up at him.

'How about you go downstairs and make a pot of tea for Mrs Powell,' he said kindly, recognising the girl's need to do something. 'I think she could do with one.'

'Maud?' she asked.

Trevor turned away from her. 'She's going into hospital,' he murmured. He could see Evan waiting for him at the foot of the stairs. He gritted his teeth, preparing to repeat the whole heart-rending, unpleasant process he'd just gone through with Elizabeth.

'There really isn't anything else left for us to do except go to work.' Charlie wrapped his arm round Diana's shoulders as they watched the ambulance bump its way over the rough, unmade road, down the incline, past the vicarage, and around the corner into Llantrisant Road.

'Come on, Di, cheer up,' William ordered, putting on a brave face.

'I'll get my coat.' Diana turned and walked back into the passage. She could hear Elizabeth already filling the wash boiler. Her aunt was obviously of the same opinion as Charlie. But then perhaps they were right, work might be the best antidote. Anything had to be better than moping around here thinking of Maud, and what she was going through right now.

'It's too late for me and Eddie to take out a cart now, Elizabeth,' Evan called into the washhouse from the back kitchen. 'I think I'll go to town and get a bucket of whitewash to do out the *ty bach*. Can you think of anything else that wants doing while I'm at it?'

'The front door could do with a coat of paint,' Elizabeth said sharply.

'Same green as before?'

'Of course. There's half a tin going to waste in the shed.'

'In that case I'll make a start and Eddie can get the whitewash.'

Eddie picked up his working and only coat from the row of pegs behind the door. Shiny with age and wear, it was a hand-me-down from Haydn, and as he was now outstripping Haydn in height, if not width, it was far too short for him. He stood next to Diana in the open doorway of the passage as he put it on.

'Beats me how they can think of things like that at a time like this,' he said sullenly.

'What else are they going to think about?' Charlie reprimanded gently. 'No one can even visit Maud until Sunday.'

'Well, they can still think of something other than the walls of the bloody *ty bach*!' he exclaimed savagely.

'Why don't you come down the market with Will and me today?' Charlie put on his own rough tweed jacket.

'And I don't want no bloody charity either,' Eddie retorted moodily.

'Not charity,' Charlie said evenly, making Diana wonder if

anything ever rattled him. 'It's gone nine o'clock. I'll be way behind with cutting up the small joints that the old people are always after. You can help Will serve, while I see to the butchery side. All right?' His ice-blue eyes focused confidently on Eddie.

'All right,' Eddie agreed, all belligerence and fight subsiding at the thought of spending what was left of the day on the market. His sister had been rushed to hospital. Was probably dying, if not already dead. And life was going on as though nothing had happened. Nothing at all.

The hands on St Catherine's church clock were pointing to a little after nine-thirty when Diana walked into Ben Springer's. She looked around, and her heart sank into her boots. She'd been so busy thinking of Maud that she'd forgotten about work, and Friday was the busiest day of the week next to Saturday. When the pits had been open, Thursday night was pay night, and the wives had got used to going into town to buy their dry goods and any bits and pieces they needed for the week, saving Saturday for fresh vegetable and Sunday joint shopping. There were no longer any pay packets given out in the closed and derelict pits on Thursday nights, neither was there enough money to stretch to buying all the necessities a family needed, but old habits died hard, and people still came into town in droves. And some of them even ended up in Ben Springer's. Not many: most children in the town went barefoot, even in winter. A few of the lucky ones – whose parents had succumbed to the demands of the parish and sold off everything they had that was worth selling in order to claim parish relief – were wearing boots that had been provided by the 'Miners Children's Boot Fund', a charity Ben had campaigned vigorously against, until he had been awarded the contract to supply them.

But that Friday morning Ben's shop looked as though the depression had ended. The tiny area that served as both shop and fitting room was packed. Ben Springer was bending over the shapely, elegant foot of Anthea Llewellyn Jones. He was crouched at just the right angle to look up her skirt, Diana noticed cynically as she surveyed the array of expensive gold leather spangled sandals laid out on the floor around them.

'You're late,' he barked as soon as he caught sight of her.

'I'm sorry, Mr Springer,' she apologised quickly. 'My cousin was rushed into hospital. She . . .'

'I'm sure no one here is the slightest bit interested in the comings and goings of your family,' he sneered, still smiling up at Anthea Llewellyn Jones. 'Get your coat off and start work.'

'Yes, sir.' Diana ran out to the back and tore off her coat. Hanging it and her handbag on a hook in the storeroom, she tucked in her blouse, pulled down her skirt and tried her best to smile. After all, she had something to smile about. She still had a job, and that job meant she could stay in the same town as Maud – and William. Anything had to be better than going into service. Even working for Ben Springer.

The first thing Maud saw when she opened her eyes was a shaft of brilliant sunlight cutting diagonally across the room. It illuminated a fairy world of gently swirling dust particles. Baby fairies waiting to be born, her sister Bethan had once called them. Overhead was a high, high ceiling. Far higher than anything she had ever slept under before. Green-painted metal rods stretched across it, locked into place three or more feet below the cracked plaster. She moved her chin down and saw dark green painted walls, the iron headboards of the bed opposite. Then, she realised where she was.

Tears escaped from beneath her eyelids as she closed her eyes and stretched out her body. She moved cautiously, feeling stiff, strange and awkward. But for all of that she was warm and reasonably comfortable. Crisp cotton sheets brushed against her skin, so different from the warm fleecy flannelette sheets that her mother insisted on using until the end of May. She could almost hear her lecturing, hectoring voice . . .

'Don't cast a clout until May's out.'

A rough, hollow coughing shook her back into harsh reality. She opened her eyes again and looked at the bed next to her own, where a painfully thin, dark-haired girl was sitting up, spitting into a jar that she held cradled in her hands. Seeing Maud, she smiled weakly in embarrassment as she closed the lid on the jar and returned it to the top of her locker.

'I hate doing it, but they make you,' she explained as she plucked at her bedcover with a clawlike hand and fell back on to her pillows.

'No one can make you do anything,' Maud retorted, unthinkingly voicing one of Eddie's favourite opinions.

'They can here. You'll see.'

'Our new arrival is awake, I see.' A sister, resplendent in dark blue uniform, the long sleeves finished with a set of immaculate stiffly starched cuffs, walked over to Maud's bed, a trainee nurse trailing in her wake. Maud categorised her as a trainee from the uniform. She knew it well: her sister Bethan had worn it, and not that long ago.

She had often wished for her sister's presence since Bethan had gone to London, but never more so than at that moment. If only Bethan could walk into the ward right now. Down the central aisle, pause at the foot of her bed . . .

'Turn back the sheets, Jones,' the sister demanded. The trainee speedily did as the sister asked. The sister retrieved Maud's wrist and proceeded to take her pulse.

'Am I in the Graig Hospital?' Maud asked, already knowing the answer, although she'd never been inside the place before.

'You are.'

'How soon can I go home?' Maud ventured timorously, remembering all the times she'd heard people say, 'It's easy enough to go into the Graig, plenty do it. But precious few ever come out other than feet first.'

'You've only just been admitted, my girl,' the sister said curtly. 'We'll have no talk of going home from you. Not yet.' She dropped Maud's hand abruptly, and went to the bottom of the bed where she picked up a clipboard that hung from the foot-rail. She scribbled something on it then peered at Maud over the top of her thick-lensed, metal-rimmed spectacles.

'You ever been in hospital before?' she demanded.

'No,' Maud faltered, debating whether to tell her that her sister Bethan had nursed on the maternity ward. Then she remembered all the gossip generated by Bethan's elopement and pregnancy, and decided against it.

'Well the rules here are simple and few,' the sister lectured in a voice that boomed down the long ward and back. 'If you need anything, anything vital like a bedpan that is, you call out loud and clear for a nurse. Understand?'

'Yes sister,' Maud squirmed in embarrassment.

159

'And give yourself, and us, plenty of time. My nurses and ward maids have more than enough to do without clearing up unnecessary messes. Understand?' she repeated.

'Yes sister,' Maud whispered, thoroughly humiliated.

'Just as long as you realise that you're only to call us when it's really essential. If you do that we'll come running when you shout. If you start calling us for any trivial reason we'll soon slow our pace. It's as simple as that. And you'll be the loser, because you, young lady, on doctor's orders are not allowed out of bed at all. Not to wash, not to toilet, not to anything. Your foot is not to touch the floor, under any circumstances. Am I making myself clear?'

'For how long?' Maud asked, horrified by the thought of doing absolutely everything – washing, eating, sleeping, even 'toileting' as the sister put it – within the confines of this one narrow bed.

'Until the doctor says otherwise. Are you comfortable now or do you want a bedpan?' the sister asked insensitively.

'I'm fine,' Maud lied wretchedly, fighting back the tears that were pricking at the backs of her eyes.

'When you cough, spit out whatever you bring up into the sputum jar on your locker. And mind you do just that. Don't try to swallow it. It will only contaminate your stomach. And then you'll have a sick stomach as well as sick lungs.'

'My father and mother?' Maud ventured.

'Your family know where you are.' The sister tucked in the sheet the trainee had wrenched out in order for her to take Maud's pulse, effectively sealing Maud back into her bed again. 'Visiting is for one hour every Sunday afternoon from two to three, and on Wednesdays from six to seven at doctor's discretion. If you get over-excited, you risk what little health you have, and that could result in doctor being forced to cancel your visiting.'

When Maud didn't reply to this standard conclusion to her pep talk, the sister actually wondered if she'd been too hard on the poor girl. She brushed aside the thought almost as soon as it entered her head. With only two qualified nurses, three trainees and two ward maids to see to the needs of thirty-five female patients in the various, but invariably messy, terminal stages of tuberculosis, it was probably just as well that the girl knew the full facts of her position from the outset.

Chapter Fifteen

Jenny knew that Maud had been taken into the Graig Hospital less than ten minutes after the ambulance had left the street. Glan's mother had waited only as long as it took her to check with Haydn (the politest and therefore the least likely of the Powell clan to tell her to mind her own business) that it was the Graig that Maud was being taken to, before walking into her back kitchen to take off her apron and put on her coat. As an afterthought she tied a scarf over her metal wavers, and picked up the worn and string-mended wicker basket that had held her shopping for the entire thirty-two years of her married life. Then she hurried down the Avenue (she hadn't used the short cut through Rhiannon Pugh's house since Rhiannon's lodger, Phyllis Harry, had given birth to an illegitimate child a few months before) and headed for Griffiths' shop, confident in the knowledge that *she'd* be the first one to impart the news to whoever was gathered there.

Jenny was serving old Mrs Evans who lived above the fish and chip shop opposite, with her daily ration of four Woodbines, two ounces of cheese and half a loaf of bread when Mrs Richards bustled in. Without pausing for breath, Mrs Richards interrupted the story that Mrs Evans was telling Jenny, about the boys that had taken to knocking her door after tying jam jars of unmentionable substances to her doorknob.

'You can just imagine,' Mrs Evans wailed dolefully, wringing her hands. 'It flew all over me. Soaking and sticking to my skirt and jumper, and the stink . . . you wouldn't believe the stink!'

'I would,' Jenny enthused, before she realised what she'd said. Hopefully Mrs Evans had changed her clothes and washed, but the odour of the *ty bach* still clung to her frail and aged frame.

'Maud Powell's in hospital!' Arms folded across her inadequate bosom, Mrs Richards stood back, waiting smugly for the impact of her news to hit her audience, but Mrs Evans continued to witter on about 'filthy boys' and 'foul stinks', oblivious to Mrs Richards' presence, let alone her gossip. 'Maud Powell's been rushed into hospital. The Graig,' Mrs Richards embellished her first revelation, but still failed to gain Jenny or Mrs Evans' attention. 'Maud Powell's in hospital,' she shouted at the top of her voice, yet she had to repeat herself twice before Jenny, odd cigarettes and triangular sweet bag in hand, turned to face her.

'She haemorrhaged,' she said proudly, airing her knowledge of the word. 'Haydn told me all about it,' she announced, heavily embroidering the truth. At the mention of Haydn, Jenny turned pale.

'Mind you,' Mrs Richards slammed a red, work-roughened hand down on the counter, 'I said when that one came home from Cardiff – I said to my Viv and my Glan – she's done for. They've worked her to death, that's what they've done. You could see it in her eyes. And her mouth. It always goes to the eyes and mouth first,' she asserted knowledgeably. 'The eyes go sort of dead looking, and the teeth – well they suddenly seem too big for the mouth, if you know what I mean.'

'The . . . the Powells. How are they?' Jenny stammered, concern for Haydn's family giving her the courage to interrupt Mrs Richards in full flow.

'They're how you'd expect them to be,' Mrs Richards side-stepped the question. 'Haydn's the one I talked to.' She gave Jenny a knowing look that set the girl's teeth on edge. 'But then, he stays calm no matter what. A born gentleman, that's what he is. Like his grandfather before him,' she asserted fondly, referring to Evan's father, not Elizabeth's. The Baptist clergy might command her respect, but never her regard.

'But what about the others?' Jenny persisted. 'Diana – '

'Now there's a baggage for you,' Mrs Richards pursed her lips, as though she'd just tasted a sour apple. 'She paints her cheeks and lips bright red. Curls her hair, even to go to work. After all the men. Just like her mother. And everyone knows what became of *that* one.'

'What's that you said, Mrs Richards?' Harry Griffiths appeared from the musty depths of the storeroom. Mrs Richards had grace enough to blush to the roots of her tightly pulled hair.

'Nothing, Mr Griffiths,' she said loudly. 'Nothing at all. Just called in to pick up a tin of tomatoes and a half-ounce of baccy for Viv's pipe.'

Harry reached down to one of the bottom shelves and picked up a small tin of tomatoes. He didn't have to ask what size she wanted; Mrs Richards never bought large tins. The Richards family always had toast for supper. The only one who ever had anything on it was her husband. He pushed the tin across the counter as he passed behind Jenny, who was engrossed in marking out a small portion of cheese to Mrs Evans' exacting requirements.

'The usual?' he asked Mrs Richards, as he rested his hand on the shelf where he kept cigarettes and tobacco.

'Please.' Mrs Richards' colour hadn't subsided at all.

'On the slate, I take it?' Harry demanded coldly.

'Only until Friday.' Mrs Richards tossed her head and turned her back on them. 'Good-day,' she murmured almost inaudibly as she went out through the door.

Jenny finished serving Mrs Evans. She felt sick and dizzy, and it wasn't just the smell of Mrs Evans. As soon as the door clanged behind the old woman she went into the storeroom and sank down on a pile of empy Corona crates.

'Shouldn't you go up there, love?' Harry asked solicitously.

'They won't be wanting me there, Dad. Not now. Not at a time like this.'

'You've got every right. You're practically family. You and Haydn . . .' he looked at her closely. 'There's nothing wrong, is there love?' he probed gently. 'You and Haydn have patched up that silly row, haven't you?'

'Oh Dad,' the single tear turned into a damburst. All the emotion she had pent up since their quarrel erupted into a paroxysm of hysterical weeping.

He knelt beside her. Wrapping his arms awkwardly around her, he tried to comfort her as he had done when she'd been a small child. Only this time, his hugs and murmurs of 'It'll be all right, love. You'll see, it'll all come right in the end' rang false, even to his own ears.

'We had such a stupid, stupid argument,' she sobbed. 'I haven't even seen him to talk to. And I don't know what to do. I love him Dad,' she pulled away from her father and wiped her eyes with the back of her hand. 'I love so much, it hurts,' she cried poignantly.

'I know,' he stroked the back of her head with his hand. 'I know,' he repeated softly, his heart twelve miles away in Cardiff prison.

'I didn't want you hearing it from anyone else.' Trevor heaped two sugars into the tea Ronnie had brought him and stirred it. 'Not after last night.'

'Last night?' Ronnie looked up warily from the stone-cold cup of tea he was hunched over.

'Gina stopped off to see Laura on her way down to town this morning,' Trevor said baldly. 'I saw her when I called back to finish my breakfast after I'd settled Maud in the ward. She told us that you'd taken Maud to the café last night.'

'The girl was all alone in the house,' Ronnie protested.

'And the girl should have been left all alone in the house!' Trevor exclaimed furiously. 'For heaven's sake, she has terminal tuberculosis. Do you know what that means? It means she can die at any moment. She could have died here, in the café last night,' he stressed, trying to bring home to Ronnie the enormity of what he'd done. 'And when her family find out that she haemorrhaged the morning after you took her out on a cold, miserable night . . .'

'I made her worse?' Ronnie looked so grief-stricken that Trevor relented, but only slightly.

'It's impossible to say what brought it on,' he conceded irritably. 'But it's fair to say that last night didn't help. What on earth possessed you to behave like an irresponsible lunatic? You of all people . . .'

'I love her.'

Trevor was so taken aback by the calm, matter-of-fact declaration that he dropped his cup. Tea spilled over the table and dripped down on to his trousers.

'Gina, cloth!' Ronnie shouted in an unnaturally flat voice for a man who had just made an earth-shattering announcement.

'But she's a child, she's a . . .' Lost for words, Trevor's splutterings ceased as Gina wiped his tea-stained trousers, and then the table.

'And I suppose you want me to bring you more tea,' she grumbled, picking up Ronnie's cold cup as well as Trevor's empty one.

'There's no hurry,' Ronnie said sharply. Gina knew when to leave her eldest brother alone. She retreated quickly to the front counter.

'I didn't exactly go looking for this,' Ronnie muttered as soon as Gina was out of earshot. 'It just – well it just happened,' he finished shortly, daring Trevor to reproach him.

'Does Maud know how you feel?' Trevor ventured.

'I don't think so.'

'You mean, you haven't said anything to her?' Trevor breathed a sigh of relief.

'Hardly. I only realised myself last night.' Ronnie looked around the café. It was half-past ten. Too early for the 'elevenses' rush of the market traders and bus conductors, and too late for the breakfasts of the council labourers. He and Trevor were sitting at a table for two, placed in the darkest corner of the back room. Too far away from the stove to be popular, its only advantage lay in the privacy it commanded.

'Alma and I had a row last night,' he explained briefly. After his sleepless, solitary night it was an incredible relief to talk to someone. And while he felt that Trevor might not understand him, he sensed that, being a doctor, Trevor was used to being entrusted with confidences and, unlike some people, would know how to keep them. 'The last thing Alma accused me of, before she flounced out of here in a foul temper, was being in love with Maud. I told her she was being ridiculous. That I couldn't possibly love Maud. I listed all the reasons why I couldn't. Her age, her illness. Then I thought about it . . .'

'All night, judging by the bags under your eyes,' Trevor commented cuttingly. He couldn't resist adding, 'Tina told Laura you didn't go home last night.'

'I slept – ' Ronnie grinned ruefully as he ran his hands through his hair, which for once wasn't smoothly slicked back. 'Or should I say, stayed here last night.'

'You do know she's going to die, don't you?' Trevor said brutally. 'The only question is when.'

'Can you get me in to see her?'

'Are you mad?'

'Come on, Trevor, you're a doctor in the Graig. That position must be good for something.'

'Visiting on the TB ward is strictly limited to Sunday afternoons and sometimes, at ward sister's discretion, Wednesday evenings. No more than two visitors to a patient, and anyone young, or deemed at risk, has to stay in the visitors' room behind a glass screen. Even if I managed to get you into the ward I doubt that her family would look kindly enough on you to allow you to take one of their precious places.'

'Then get me in outside of visiting,' he pleaded.

'It would be easier to get you into the vaults of the Bank of England. She's on an isolation ward, Ronnie. That means she's highly infectious – '

'There has to be a way. If I took a porter's job . . .'

'Now you're being ridiculous,' Trevor said in exasperation. 'Have you any idea of the number of applications we get for every job that comes up in the hospital?'

'Then at least take a letter to her for me?'

'Ronnie.' Trevor slowed his voice as though he were explaining complicated surgical techniques to a two-year-old child. 'She's seriously ill. When I saw her this morning she was in a coma. God knows what a letter out of the blue from you, telling her that you love her, could do to her at this point in her illness.'

'If you won't help me, then I'll find someone who will.' Ronnie turned away from him and pulled a loose cigarette from the top pocket of his jacket.

'Ronnie, be realistic,' Trevor pleaded, slightly alarmed by this strange, passionate man who had sprung from his usually laconic, always sarcastic, and generally easygoing brother-in-law.

'I am,' Ronnie stared intently at Trevor. 'Totally and utterly realistic. For the first time in my life I'm facing facts as they are, not as I'd like them to be. I'm in love. I know what I want. I want Maud. And if she hasn't got long to live, then the sooner we get together to spend whatever time she's got left with one another the better.' He rose from the table.

'I'll try to talk to her,' Trevor conceded at last. 'I can't do any more.'

'You'll find out how she is? Come back and tell me?'

There was such a look of anguish on Ronnie's face, all Trevor could do was nod.

Diana was still in Ben Springer's at eight o'clock that night. He had her humping boxes from the back of the shop to the front; stacking the shelves, rotating stock that wasn't selling to the top

166

shelves and filling the prime positions with new stock. And while she lifted, strained and struggled to carry heavy boxes of boots up and down ladders, he delicately arranged men's patent evening shoes next to gold and silver leather dancing slippers on the display stands in the window.

Hot, sweaty, tired, and worried because so little had been said about her late arrival that morning, Diana was too afraid to utter a single word of protest. What if he decided to dock her a day's pay? She'd already borrowed money off William against this week's wages. Money she knew he wouldn't ask for, but money she also knew he could ill afford to spare.

'Did you hear what I said?'

'Pardon, sir?' Jerking out of her reverie, she almost fell off the top rung of the ladder.

'I was talking to you, girl.' Ben had the till open, and was holding out his hand. 'Four shillings and sixpence. A week's wages less your shoe club money, and less tomorrow's shilling. Not that you deserve that much.'

'I'm happy to wait until tomorrow as usual, Mr Springer,' Diana protested mildly, her arms strained and aching as she descended the ladder with a full load of boxes. She tried, and failed, to stop herself from shaking. The last time she'd been offered money before the end of the week had been in the Infirmary. He couldn't be thinking of giving her notice. He simply couldn't be!

'Take it, girl,' he commanded tersely. She piled the boxes on a fitting stool and reached out nervously, delicately removing a sticky two-shilling piece and a half-crown from the sweaty palm of his hand.

'Thank you,' her voice dulled to a cracked whisper.

'And don't bother to come in tomorrow.'

'Don't . . .' her heart beat unnaturally quickly, and her throat went tight.

'I get girls in here every day looking for a job. The likes of you are ten a penny. This afternoon on my way to the bank, I called into the Labour Exchange.' He smiled maliciously, savouring the power he wielded over her. 'There was a girl there,' he continued gloatingly, 'just sitting, waiting for something to come along. Sharp young thing. Prepared to work five and half days a week for five shillings. And turn up on time every morning,' he finished pointedly.

167

'Mr Springer, I'm sorry,' Diana was too panic-stricken to cry. If she lost her job she wouldn't be able to pay Aunt Elizabeth her lodging money for more than a few weeks. And she wouldn't get any help from the parish. All they'd see was a young, single girl without ties who could take a domestic job anywhere in the country. They wouldn't take into account her need to be near Will, or Cardiff prison. 'Please Mr Springer. Please, it won't happen again I promise you,' she begged abjectly. 'Please. I'll make the hours up I missed. Give the shop a good going through on Sunday . . .' Her voice faded to a whisper as she tried to think of other ways – any ways – to make him change his mind and keep her on. He studied her for a moment. There was a peculiar smile hovering at the corners of the mouth, and she smiled weakly too, hoping against hope that the smile meant he was considering her offer. That she'd touched his pocket and instinct for a bargain, if not his heart.

'I'll work for five shillings a week, Mr Springer,' she begged swiftly, all sense of pride evaporating as the spectre of unemployment, real and terrifying, hovered at her elbow.

Ben continued to smile. He was wondering just how far she would go to keep her job. He eyed her up and down, noticing how the buttons of her tight cotton blouse strained over her bust. She was what he termed a 'ripe piece'. Plump in all the right places, a nice change from most of the scrawny, scarecrow women around town. And a lot more attractive than his wife, who had left plumpness behind for obesity more years ago than he cared to remember.

Diana realised he was eyeing her, and swallowed hard. She knew exactly what that look meant. When she'd left Pontypridd for Cardiff she'd hoped to put her mother's tarnished reputation, and the kind of advances it encouraged from men and boys, behind her. But events had soon led her to the conclusion that it must be something within herself that attracted the wrong sort of attentions, and made men see her as a loose woman, who was good for one thing, and one thing only.

Ben took a step towards her. Lifting his hand, he reached out, slowly, deliberately, and squeezed her left breast hard. She backed away, knocking over the pile of boxes that she'd heaped on the stool.

'I'll just pick these up.' Taking care to keep him within her sight, she crouched down and began to pick up the boxes. He squatted beside her. Sliding his hand up her skirt, he rested his damp fingers on the welt of her stocking top. His touch burnt through the lisle to her leg. She could smell his sweat, feel the unhealthy sexual excitement rising within him.

'Just a little touch . . .' His hand slid higher.

'No.' The voice was so resolute, so loud, Diana barely recognised it as her own.

'You *do* want to keep your job, don't you?' he leered as he moved his hand higher. Pushing up the elastic on the legs of her bloomers he stroked her naked thigh. 'Have you ever had it?' he murmured, lifting her skirt to her waist with his free hand.

'Mr Springer, please!' She jerked awkwardly to her feet, dropping the boot box she was holding on to his toe.

'That hurt,' he protested, rubbing his foot.

'It was meant to.'

She tugged down her skirt. Forgetting about her job, forgetting everything except the need to get out of the shop and away from Ben Springer as soon as possible, she ran into the stockroom to get her coat and bag.

'That's clever of you, Diana.' He followed her into the long, thin, windowless cupboard, and slammed the door hard behind him. She heard a dull thud as he leant heavily against it. 'It *was* too public out there. Where are you?' He clicked on the electric light. She was holding on to her coat and bag, gripping them as though they were lifelines. 'Don't stay all the way over there,' he murmured. 'Come closer.'

'No!' Panic set in as she realised she'd boxed herself in with no avenue of escape. He was leaning against the only exit. There was nowhere for her to run.

'Still pouting,' he laughed, displaying two rows of chipped, yellow and brown stained teeth. 'I'm not going to hurt you, only give you what you want. What you've been after ever since you walked through that door.'

'I'm leaving!' she announced, fear lending her false courage, but her bravado didn't extend to walking as far as the door. After what had happened in the shop she was afraid to move close to him.

'You do want to hang on to your job, don't you Diana?' he cooed softly. 'The six shillings a week that keeps body and soul together.'

'Not any more!' Terror heightened her voice to a screech.

'Such temper.' He stepped away from the door and swung round in front of her, trapping her in a blind cul-de-sac. The coat hooks were at her back, and shelves ranged either side of her. They lined the entire storeroom, even running above the door, narrowing the free space to a corridor of little more than two feet. Diana backed away, still holding her coat and handbag like a shield in front of her. He stepped closer and she cracked her back painfully aginst a hook.

'All I want is a good look,' he murmured thickly.

'Please Mr Springer, let me out,' she pleaded, more terrified than she'd ever been in her life before.

'Please Mr Springer,' he mocked cruelly. 'That's all you've said for the past ten minutes, girl. Please Mr Springer,' he repeated in a strained, high-pitched voice. 'Well now it's my turn to *please* you. Come on, you want it, you know you do. If you didn't you wouldn't have worn that tight skirt and blouse every day, or looked at me as coyly as you did, every chance you got. You would have sewn that button on tighter.' His hand darted across the front of her blouse, flicking open a button, exposing the valley of her breasts above her bust shaper. She lashed out and hit him, but her arms were hampered by her coat and handbag. He responded, slapping her soundly and squarely across the face and sending her reeling sideways into the shelves. The sharp edges bit into her forehead and cheekbones, she crumpled. Sliding down towards the floor, she fought frantically to remain upright. She opened her mouth, tried to scream, but terror muted her voice to a pathetic whimper. He laughed.

'If you find your voice, go ahead, scream,' he taunted. 'There's no one out there to hear you. You wouldn't be heard in the shop, let alone the street.' Releasing her hold on her coat and bag, she summoned all the strength she possessed. Heaving herself to her full height, she grabbed the bottom box of a pile, and tugged at it, meaning to throw it at him. But so little stock had moved out of the shop since the closure of the pits that the boxes were jammed tight against the ceiling. She screamed again, loudly this time, but her voice echoed hollowly around her, muffled by the layers of boxes. He laughed, and she went beserk, fighting and spitting like a cornered alleycat.

'Let me out, let me out of here you . . .' she lashed out with her nails, ripping the skin off his right cheek. He lifted his hand, saw blood on his fingers, and his smile dropped as fury burnt in his eyes.

'Why you little bitch.' He clamped his hand over her mouth and, using his body as a weight, pressed her down on to her back. Her abdomen and limbs were crushed by the weight of him, her nostrils full of the rancid smell of his unwashed body. She tugged his hair, twisting the thin, greasy strands around her fingers in an attempt to get a tight grip. He heaved himself upwards, she took a deep breath as the pressure on her chest relaxed slightly, but the respite didn't last long.

He made a fist with his right hand, and using all the momentum he could gain in such a confined space, slammed it hard into the side of her head.

She was aware only of a wavering black smoke that blotted out most of the glow from the naked light bulb. Then the blackness was superseded by a crimson mist that carried with it an agonising awareness of pain. Bile rose on a turgid tide out of her stomach, but as she hadn't eaten anything that day, not even breakfast, there was nothing for her to bring up.

She lay back, stunned and sickened, her head and face burning with pain, utterly helpless as he plundered her body. The sharp sound of tearing cloth resounded in her ears as he caught the neck of her blouse and ripped it downwards, exposing her underclothes.

'Don't,' she mumbled weakly, through bruised and battered lips, as she felt his fingers clawing at her bust shaper. 'Don't!'

'You little slut, you're enjoying every minute of this. Girls like you enjoy it day and night. You can't get enough of it, you fuck because . . .'

She tried to close her ears to the string of obscenities that poured from his mouth. He was kneeling astride her, pinning her arms down with his massive calves. She struggled, succeeded in lifting her legs – a little. He used the opportunity to pull her skirt to her waist. Gripping the elasticated waist of her bloomers he

171

heaved on them until she screamed from the force of the elastic cutting into her back. Finally it snapped. He thrust his hand between her legs, making her squirm.

'That's it, go on,' he slavered, saliva drooling from his mouth on to her naked breasts as he played with them. 'Struggle, fight, go on girl, move . . .' Tears fell from her eyes as she realised he had her trapped. She wasn't going to escape. And her pitiful attempts to defend herself were only exciting him further. Crying at her own feebleness, vulnerability and impotence, she finally closed her eyes and fell still.

His hands sought and gripped hers. Pulling them above her head, he pinned them down together using only his left hand. He stretched out on top of her. Sliding his right hand between them he undid the buttons on his fly. She screamed as he thrust himself into her. Continued to scream the whole time he violated her. Until in the end she almost believed that she only existed as an extension of the pain, degradation and misery that he was inflicting on her.

Chapter Sixteen

Diana lay on the floor of the stockroom and cried. Her tears weren't slight or silent ones, but great racking sobs that threatened to tear her lungs apart. Even Ben, who had retreated to the far side of the stockroom to button his fly and tuck in his shirt, was unnerved by the primitive, bestial sounds she was making. He combed his hair back from his face with his fingers, staring in horror when he saw blood on them. He touched his cheek tentatively. It was wet. Was the blood his or hers? He yelped as he found a scratch she'd given him.

He looked at her, disgusted with what he saw. A weak, sordid, crumpled heap of flesh. There were great rents in her blouse, blood on the bloomers that lay, torn and discarded, beneath her.

'Stop whining, you stupid cow,' he demanded, using the adjective he applied to his wife when they had one of their frequent rows. 'Pull yourself together. You know you wanted it.'

Diana felt too used, too broken and too dirty to contradict him. She even began to wonder if she had wanted 'it', as he called the eternity of rough, banging, bruising and degrading violation. She'd wondered and dreamed about love and marriage for so long. Well now she knew exactly where all the sweet songs, tender words and poetry led.

Laying her head down on the musty-smelling floor, she closed her eyes. How could any woman want to do anything like that willingly? How did married women cope? Did they have to put up with it night after night or only sometimes?

'Cover yourself, girl,' Ben commanded abruptly as he opened the door into the shop. She heard him leave the cupboard. The noise diminished; she didn't even realise she'd been making it. Tugging down her skirt, and clutching the tattered remnants of her blouse in her fist, she curled into a ball, faced the floor, and wished herself dead.

The pain between her legs was agonising. His sweat, now cold and damp, clung to her bare skin. The stench and the brutality of

173

him permeated every inch of her. She heard the stockroom door open again, but she kept her face turned to the floor. It didn't matter whether he was there or not. Nothing mattered any more. She just wanted to die where she lay. It would be bliss to sink into nothingness, not to feel anything, not ever again.

'Here.' He leant over her and she screamed. It did matter after all! She might not die quickly, and she couldn't bear to repeat what he'd put her through. She wouldn't be able to stand it . . .

'It's your coat,' he announced irritably, dropping it on top of her. 'For God's sake girl, you can't lie around naked. Put it on.' She struggled to her knees. Careful to keep her face averted from his, she did as he asked. He caught her roughly by the elbow and yanked her to her feet. She stared down at the floor. Her bloomers lay there, torn and stained. He picked them up and tried to ram them into the pocket of her coat, but she screamed again when he stepped near her. Only this time she didn't stop. She just kept on screaming and screaming, until the noise in her head blotted out everything else. Even his presence beside her.

He slapped her across the face. Hard. Her cheek stung. The imprint of his hand stood proud and crimson on her skin, but he failed to silence her. He lashed out repeatedly. She went crashing into the shelves again, hitting her head where she'd hit it earlier. He grabbed her arm and propelled her out through the door before she had time to fall to the floor.

She was aware of a cold draught. Looking down, she realised that the front of her coat was open, exposing her breasts. Her thighs were cold, wet and naked beneath her skirt. Her stockings were damp, stained with sweat and blood. Turning her back to the window, she hit away his hand. Trembling like a leaf she began to fasten her coat buttons, slowly, one at a time. Her fingers were huge and swollen; stiff and suddenly arthritic, they refused to obey her commands.

The huge brass till clanged open. Ben walked towards her. 'Here – ' he held out a five-pound note – 'Here, take it,' he commanded impatiently, thrusting it at her. 'After all, you earned it,' he jeered.

'You . . . you . . .' finding her voice at last, Diana could not find adjectives foul enough to express her opinion of him.

'See you, same time tomorrow?' he asked calmly.

'I'll never set foot over this doorstep again as long as I live,' she hissed. 'But you'll see me in court. I'm going to the police. I'll tell your wife. I'll tell – '

He threw back his head and roared with laughter. Diana hadn't been the first assistant he'd had in the stockroom, and in his, granted somewhat limited, experience, he'd learned that they were generally all right when they got to the threatening stage. And experience had also taught him how to handle the threats.

'Tell them what, dear?' he taunted. 'That you stole five pounds out of the till, and when I asked you about it you tore your clothes and threatened to cry rape? Your word against mine, and we all know whose word everyone will believe.'

'You hurt me,' she whispered hoarsely. 'I'm bleeding.' She looked down at her stained stockings.

'Everyone knows that a girl like you has a different boy every night. I've seen you myself in the café talking to the Italian boys. Not to mention Wyn Rees from the sweet shop. Now there's an odd one for you to make a beeline for,' he taunted. 'More woman than man. One word about him will be enough to set the magistrate thinking about your tastes in the bedroom department. And then there's that fair boy you wave to whenever he passes.'

'He's my cousin!'

'There's cousins and cousins. And things are not always what they seem.'

'You swine. You bastard . . .' the words she couldn't think of earlier tumbled out one after another.

He caught hold of her wrists and twisted them painfully.

'One more sound out of you and I'll spread it from the Graig end of town to the Common that you're nothing but a common prostitute. Only being your mother's daughter, you fancy yourself. Set your price higher than the vulgar herd who pick up their customers in station yard. A fiver as opposed to the bob they charge for a quickie in a shop doorway.'

'I suppose that's why I work here for six bob a week . . .'

'A girl without visible means of support soon gets picked up by the police. Your mother would tell you that if she was around,' he sneered. 'But then she didn't get it right either, did she? It wasn't enough that she was Harry Griffiths' whore. She had to steal as well. Like mother, like daughter. Thief and whore, just like Mam.

175

That's what you are, a thief and a whore,' he spat the words at her. 'And there's no one who'll see you otherwise, Diana Powell. Not when I've finished talking to them. No one.'

His laughter and his threats followed her as she ran sobbing out of the shop and down Taff Street clutching her coat over her naked bosom. A couple walking towards her stopped and stared. She ducked into the doorway of an empty shop. There were no lights there, so she felt safe, hidden by the darkness. She took a deep breath, made an effort to still the tremblings of her body, and smoothed back her hair.

As soon as she was able, she walked on, checking her reflection in the shop windows as she passed. She couldn't catch a bus or a tram. Not looking like this. If she walked up the Graig hill slowly, sticking to the shadows and the side-streets, it would give her time to calm down. Maud wouldn't be needing her blouse for a while. She could dump it together with the rest of her clothes over the mountain. If she was quick and careful she could run into the house and straight up the stairs. Change into her nightie before her aunt had a chance to see her. Whatever happened, she daren't let any one, especially Will, find out about this. He was hot-headed at the best of times. He'd give Ben a good hiding, and then Ben would see him put in jail too. Better she go into service and away from Pontypridd than that. Better anything than that.

'I didn't know you came down here.' Eddie rolled around to the side of the rink where Jenny was sitting talking to Tina, Gina and Will – who had mysteriously disappeared ten minutes after inveigling him into spending sixpence of the money Charlie had paid him for working on his meat stall – in the roller-skating rink in Mill Street.

'First time I've been here,' Jenny smiled, taking the opportunity to move away from the others. Will and Tina were getting on her nerves these days. Always flirting with one another every opportunity they got.

'Haydn picking you up?' Eddie asked.

'No,' she said quickly. Too quickly.

'No, of course not,' Eddie murmured. 'This place must close a lot earlier than the Town Hall.'

'I thought you went training every night,' she said, changing the subject.

'I do. I'll probably go down the gym later. I just came with Will after we'd finished on the market.'

'You working on the market now, then?'

'No. Only today. After . . . after . . . well it was too late to take the cart out,' he finished tersely.

'I heard about Maud. I'm sorry Eddie,' she said softly. 'But as my mother said over tea tonight, you can never tell with lung disease. The doctor told my Aunt Phoebe she wouldn't live to see her eighteenth birthday,' she smiled impishly, and Eddie noticed, not for the first time, what a beautiful smile she had. 'Well Dad says that he's sure my Uncle Arthur wishes Aunt Phoebe never proved the doctor wrong. According to Dad, he only married her because his family was nagging him to find a wife, and he finally settled on Aunt Phoebe because he didn't think she was long for this world. They've been married thirty years this year, and now she's twenty stone, and – ' she lowered her voice and put her mouth close to Eddie's ear, '– a right old nag,' she confided secretively.

'I hope Maud lives to see herself married for thirty years,' Eddie said sombrely. 'You're not having me on, are you?' he demanded suspiciously, always on the lookout for people making fun of him.

'I wouldn't, Eddie,' Jenny protested seriously. 'Not about something like that.'

'Want an orange juice?' he asked, looking longingly at the wooden trestle table set out against the back wall where a woman was dispensing drinks into small glasses, and selling bars of Five Boys chocolate from a cardboard box.

'I've used my free ticket,' she said shyly, referring to the one that was handed over for the sixpence that also bought entrance and boot hire.

'So have I, but Charlie paid me today. I'll treat you,' he offered generously.

'All right, if you let me buy the chocolate.' They sat side by side on the fringe of the area set aside for roller-skating, and took off the skates they'd hired.

'My feet feel wonderful,' Jenny beamed as they walked over to the counter. 'Like I'm walking on air.'

'I know just what you mean.' He pulled two pennies out of his pocket. 'Two glasses of orange juice please, Mrs Williams.'

'And two bars of Five Boys,' Jenny added, digging into her own purse.

Eddie dumped his skates under one of the small card tables dotted around the room and went back for the orange juices. He'd expected Jenny to sit opposite, but she sat beside him. Resting her elbows on the rickety table, she wrapped her long, thin fingers round the glass. Her perfume was the same one Maud and Diana used. He found himself staring at her hair. It was blonde, lighter than Maud's, almost white in colour.

'So?' Jenny questioned tremulously. 'What's big brother doing these days?'

'Haydn?' Eddie looked at her in surprise. 'You'd be better placed than me to answer that question.'

'Not any more.' She unwrapped first the paper, then the silver paper from her bar. Staring at the faces stamped on the squares, she concentrated on the boy who was crying. He looked as miserable as she felt.

'You saying, you and our Haydn aren't courting any more?' Eddie stared at her, dumbfounded.

'Haven't seen him in a week,' she said with a studied carelessness that she hoped concealed her pain.

'Oh I know you two,' Eddie coloured in embarrassment. 'You'll soon get back together again.'

'Not this time.' She snapped the miserable boy off the chocolate bar and ate him. It was most peculiar: she felt happier as soon as she'd swallowed the last trace of chocolate in her mouth. 'But then,' she gave Eddie a totally artificial smile, 'there's plenty of other fish in the sea.'

'So they say,' he muttered, thinking of the chorus girl Daisy, and the romp they'd enjoyed in Pontypridd Park. Pity there weren't more around like her, but then, he didn't often have the kind of money in his pocket that he'd spent on her, and he had the feeling that the likes of Daisy wouldn't be interested in a man with only two bob. He looked at Jenny's empty glass, remembered the orange juices and amended two bob to one shilling and ten pence. What the hell, may as well make it one and nine. 'Want another drink?' he asked, nursing his remaining half-glass of juice.

'Only if you take me home afterwards. I promised my mother I'd be in by nine.' She hadn't realised just how handsome Haydn's brother was until now. He was still young, a whole year younger than her, but he'd lost the scrawny boyish look that a lot of boys carried, even into their twenties. She noticed his muscles rippling under the patched jacket he was wearing. And in contrast to Haydn he was so dark. At that moment she felt his deep brown eyes and black hair would outshine the looks of any number of blonde Adonises.

'Are you sure I should?' Eddie asked earnestly. 'It's not that I don't want to,' he added quickly as an odd expression crossed her face. 'It's just that if Haydn should find out . . .'

'Even if he did find out, it's nothing to do with him any more. I told you. Haydn and I are finished. He doesn't want me.' Jenny fumbled in her pocket for a handkerchief, and dabbed her eyes with it. 'He doesn't even talk to me any more. If he sees me he crosses the street. And I swear he walks down the hill along Leyshon Street and the steps into Graig Street rather than pass the shop.'

'I can't see our Haydn doing that,' Eddie protested half-heartedly, suddenly remembering his brother's recent sullen moods.

'Look, the last thing I want to do is come between brothers, Eddie,' Jenny said quietly. 'It's just that . . . that . . .'

'What?' he demanded curiously.

'Oh nothing.' She put away her handkerchief and broke off another piece of chocolate.

'Go on, tell me.'

'No you'll laugh.'

'I promise I won't.'

'You'll think I'm silly, but,' she looked at him and he felt himself drowning in the clear liquid blue of her eyes, 'I've always liked you, Eddie. But then, what girl wouldn't? You're good-looking, and so strong.' She fingered the muscles on his arm playfully, taking care that William should see her. What she was doing was awful, but then she had to get Haydn to talk to her somehow. Even if she only succeeded in making him shout at her for playing around with his brother.

*

179

Diana kept to the shadows as she made her way through the town. Shoulders hunched, shivering as the cold artificial silk lining of her coat brushed against her naked skin, she walked quickly and purposefully. Like a wounded animal returning to its lair, she headed towards the Graig, and subconsciously to a home in Leyshon Street that no longer existed. At painful, spasmodic intervals the enormity of what Ben Springer had done to her hit her anew, and she choked back a sob.

Occasionally she heard footsteps ringing on the pavement. Whenever that happened, she slowed her step and lowered her head, staring down at her feet until the sound died away, either ahead of or behind her.

She couldn't help feeling that people were hiding behind the windows and in the shadows, watching her, laughing, knowing that she was practically naked underneath her coat. That they'd heard and approved of the names Ben Springer had called her. Hating herself, loathing what Ben had turned her into, she felt that she deserved to be stared at contemptuously, just as the old couple had done earlier. That the unspeakable things Ben Springer had done to her in that back room somehow made her less than human, that she really was the whore he'd have her believe she was.

'Diana?'

She heard someone call her name, but she kept her head down. When the cry was repeated she quickened her step, put her collar up and hid her face from view. She couldn't bear to look at or talk to anyone she knew. Not now. All she wanted was to get home . . . home! That was a joke! Home was her mam's warm, cosy, comfortable back kitchen. Her tears flowed faster as she realised the only place she had to go to was her Aunt Elizabeth's house. What if her aunt came out of the kitchen and walked into the passage before she managed to reach the safety of her box room? Aunt Elizabeth never missed the slightest thing. It was too much to hope that she wouldn't notice her filthy, bloodstained stockings, or her torn blouse.

Her fingers closed reluctantly around the ragged and damp bloomers that Ben had stuffed into her pocket. They were the most damning piece of evidence. Even if she threw them away, Elizabeth would miss them in the wash. After all, she only had three pairs. . .

'Diana! Diana!' The voice grew louder. She heard the light patter of footsteps running after her. 'Diana, what have I done?' Wyn's soft feminine drawl wafted towards her through an all-enveloping mist of misery and shame. 'Diana?' He grabbed her shoulder, and she broke away from his grasp. 'My God!' He was staring at her, horror at what he was looking at etched into his shocked and startled face.

Tears were streaming down her cheeks, mingling with the rainwater and blood that oozed persistently from a cut on her temple.

'Dear God, what happened to you?' he demanded. Gripping her hand tightly he pulled her into the shelter of the entrance to Woolworth's store. She tried to slip away from him, but his fingers banded like an iron cuff on her wrist. The light from the windows cast a yellow glow over her strained and terrified face. She turned aside so he couldn't look at her.

'Leave me alone.' She struggled to escape his hold on her. 'Please just leave me alone,' she repeated dully.

'That's just what I'm not going to do,' he said determinedly. 'You can't walk around the streets looking like this. God alone knows what could happen to you.'

'Nothing worse than what already has!' The tears started again. Hot, scalding and bitter.

'Come on.' Still holding her wrist, he put his arm round her shoulders.

'Don't touch me!' she screamed as hysteria threatened to take over once again. 'Don't you *dare* touch me. Don't you dare . . .'

'I'll let you go if you promise to come home with me,' he said in a voice full of concern. It didn't take a genius to look at the state of her, put it together with her insistence on not being touched and guess what had happened. 'Come on, you'll be safe enough,' he coaxed gently. 'My sister will be at home.'

She looked at him, and he shivered. Her eyes were cold, dead. He felt as though she were looking right through him. Then suddenly, without warning, she uttered a dry, choking cry and stretched out her arms. He gathered her close to him. Caressing the back of her head with his fingertips, he pulled her head down on to his shoulder.

'Come on, Diana.' He wrapped his arm round her waist, as

much to support as comfort her. 'Someone's coming,' he murmured. 'Let's go before they get here.'

The silence between them was terrible. The only sounds in the street were her occasional, quiet choking sobs and the patter of the rain falling into the dark, slimy pools of water that had gathered in the cracks of the broken slabs in the pavement. 'My father forgot to take his pills to work with him tonight,' he explained matter-of-factly as he turned left, guiding her into Market Square. He felt he had to talk about something – anything to break the harsh, rasping monotony of her sobs. 'He always calls into the shop I run next to the New Theatre on his way home from his High Street shop,' he continued conversationally. 'He insisted he couldn't walk another step without them, so he's looking after my shop for me while I go to the house to get them. But there's no hurry for me to rush back. I can always get little George next door to run down with them. It'll take half an hour for them to work, and George can stay with him just in case there's a surge of unexpected customers. We can have a cup of tea together . . .'

'I don't want to be any trouble.' She fought, and failed, to keep her voice steady.

'Dad really will be all right for a while. The rush rarely starts in the shop until the end of the second house in the theatre, and that's not for another hour and a half. You've given me a good excuse to skive off.' He smiled at her, and she felt safe. It was ironical. The very reason that made most men, including William, Haydn and Eddie, dislike Wyn so much was at that moment Wyn's main and only attraction. If he preferred men to women, he was about the only man in Pontypridd who wouldn't want to do the disgusting things to her that Ben had done. And the one thing she was sure of at that moment was that she didn't want another man to touch her in that way again – ever.

Chapter Seventeen

Wyn hesitated at the entrance to the Co-op Arcade. It was the way he usually walked home from the New Theatre, but the display lamps that blazed brightly in the windows illuminated the covered walkway with a light as bright and harsh as daylight. And he didn't want to risk Diana catching sight of her reflection. She couldn't possibly realise just how filthy and dishevelled she looked. He glanced sideways at her, hoping to avoid catching her eye. She looked sad, lost and incredibly pathetic. Embarrassed by his indecision, he walked on briskly, leading her up Penuel Lane. It was in darkness. He held her elbow as they crossed Gelliwastad Road, and began the climb up the hill to Tyfica Road.

Diana allowed him to drag her on. Her earlier hysteria had given way to a cold, anaesthetising numbness. It was easier to walk alongside Wyn than think of reasons why she shouldn't. To protest would have meant expending effort and energy, and she had neither. Supporting her lightly, he helped her up a short, steep flight of steps to the front door of a huge semi-detached house. A light shone through the stained-glass panel that decorated the front door, puddling the black and white tiles on the porch floor with pools of brilliant blue and crimson.

'I'm sorry,' he apologised as he turned the key that was protruding from the front-door lock. 'It looks like my sister is out. She always leaves the hall light on when she goes to chapel meetings.'

'It's probably as well.' Diana had just caught sight of herself in the hall mirror as she stepped aside. 'I look like something dead that the cat dragged in.'

'Let me take your coat.'

'No!' her voice rose precariously again.

'Look, you're in such a state, why don't you have a bath,' he offered tactfully. 'You don't have to worry about clothes. I'll get some of Myrtle's.'

'Myrtle's?' She looked at him with large, frightened eyes.

'My sister,' he explained patiently. 'There's plenty of hot water,' he added persuasively. 'We never let the kitchen range go out, and it heats the water in the boiler upstairs.'

The thought of washing away the taint of what had happened to her – the smell of Ben, her blood, his sweat – of soaking her bruised and battered body in a bath was like being shown a glimpse of heaven.

'The bathroom's the first door opposite the top of the stairs.'

She halted indecisively. 'Are you sure your father and sister won't mind? I'm in such a mess.' The tears began to fall again. Quietly this time, Wyn noted gratefully.

'No one is here to mind,' he reassured her. 'And even if they were they'd be saying the same as me. There's no way you can go home as you are. I'll get Dad's pills and give them to George. Then I'll dig out some clothes for you.' He walked down the passage towards the back of the house. She panicked.

'Don't leave me,' she shouted.

He stopped and looked back at her. 'Come with me if you like.' He tried to keep his voice calm, neither insistent nor offhand. He went into the kitchen and switched on the light. There was a bottle of pills on the windowsill in front of the sink. Large blue and red ones. He picked them up and put them in his pocket. 'Here, sit down,' he suggested. She took one look at the highly polished wooden chairs and shook her head.

'I'm too dirty,' she murmured shamefacedly.

He filled the kettle and put it on the range to boil. 'You'd like a cup of tea wouldn't you?' he asked.

She studied the shining, polished brass rail on the range, the ironwork newly blackleaded, the copper saucepans polished and set out on the rack to dry, the huge dresser filled with gleaming china. It all looked so affluent, so calm, so sane, and so ordinary. She broke down again. A single glimpse of normality was too much for her after the madness of the storeroom.

'Do you want to talk about it, Diana?' Wyn asked quietly. She shook her head mutely.

'Then I'll show you where everything is upstairs.' He walked ahead of her, and she followed. Gripping the smooth, dark, mahogany banister rail, she ascended the stairs slowly. It was strange. She'd never thought of Wyn as being either 'crache' or rich, yet living in a house like this, he was obviously both. The hall was tiled to a point half-way up the wall, with beautifully designed squares in a multicoloured dark flower pattern, topped by a shining dado of deep-blue and brown tiles. She touched the dado with her fingertips. It felt cold. She looked down: her feet were sinking into the deep pile of the carpet. It was wool, not jute, brown like the tiles.

The bathroom door was open. Wyn sat on the edge of the bath, put the plug in and turned on both taps. A cloud of steam wafted into the air.

'You don't even have to carry water!' she exclaimed.

'Carry water?' he looked at her uncomprehendingly for a moment, then he coloured, ashamed of his insensitivity. 'Sorry, I suppose I'm so used to this I tend to forget that not many people have plumbed-in baths. Check the temperature's all right for you.' He brushed past her, embarrassed by the intimacy of their situation. 'I'll get you clean towels and some clothes.'

He returned with a large, thick, white fluffy towel, and a smaller one. 'For your hair,' he explained as he handed it to her. 'These were Myrtle's, she's put on a lot of weight lately. Middle-age spread,' he grinned wryly as he held out a neat pile of beautifully pressed and folded clothes. 'She put them into the rag-bag last week. Lucky for you the ragman hasn't called.'

'My uncle's a ragman.'

'Here, take them,' he thrust them at her. 'Myrtle will be happy to know they've been put to good use.' She flicked through the pile. There was a good blue serge skirt, a pair of long, thick woollen socks, a white starched cotton petticoat and a pair of pink silk bloomers.

'I can't take these, they're all brand new,' she protested.

'You can't go home as you are,' he said practically. 'I couldn't find a white blouse so this is one of my shirts.'

'I can't possibly . . .'

He was staring at her. She looked down and saw that although the top buttons of her coat were firmly fastened, the bottom ones weren't. For the first time she noticed that her skirt was as heavily bloodstained as her stockings.

'I'm sure young George next door will be only too happy to give Dad a hand in the shop until I get back. So I'll wait for you to finish. Lock the door behind me. I'll have the tea brewed by the time you've finished and dressed. And if you hear the back door opening and closing, don't worry. It'll only be me going next door. I promise I won't be gone for more than a minute or two.' He patted the pocket he'd slipped the pills into. 'Help yourself to soap, eau-de-Cologne and talcum powder. It's on the washstand.' He closed the door behind him.

She listened. When she heard the creak of the stairs, she turned the key. Safely locked in, she walked over to the bath and turned the taps off. She pulled her bloomers out of her coat pocket and threw them on to a wooden drip tray. Then she stripped off her skirt, stockings and petticoat. She tossed the rags – all that was left of her blouse, bust shaper and liberty bodice – on top of the pile.

She looked around for soap. The washstand was crammed with bottles and tins. In the centre of the display that reminded her of Boots the chemist's window, was a straw basket, packed with small, heavily perfumed bars. She'd never seen such small soaps before. Taking one, she lowered herself into the water. A wooden scrubbing brush lay in the steel bath-rack. She picked it up and began to scrub, and scrub. And scrub!

For a Friday night, the café was relatively quiet. Alma had clearly thought better of her outburst. She had walked in at her usual time, murmured a barely audible 'good-evening' to the café in general and nobody in particular, put on her apron, and began work on clearing the tables. Ronnie nodded to her absently, as he paced uneasily between the kitchen, where Tony was heating pies and frying chips, and the café, where Angelo was serving. He was barely aware of Alma's presence. All he could think of was Maud. He'd been such a fool. Wasted so much time. He could have told her last night – any night – that he loved her. But like an idiot he'd waited until she was incarcerated in the Central Homes, totally beyond his, or anyone except a doctor's reach. If only he was Trevor . . .

He racked his brains coming up with plans, each more ridiculous and outrageous than the last. If he tried to climb the ten-foot-high walls, he'd be seen. Not to mention hurt. There were precious few toeholds in the well constructed stonework. If he went through the main gate the porter would challenge him.

The side gate in Albert Street was only used for delivery vans. He could try taking the Trojan through, but he didn't have anything to deliver; besides, it was locked at night.

Thoughts writhed and slithered through his mind until he felt as though he would go mad from too much thinking. As soon as he conjured up one idea that he felt might work, he lost it, forgetting half of it before it was even conceived. Eventually his restlessness got the better of him. Putting on his street coat, he announced he was slipping out for a while.

He stood on the pavement outside the café, breathing in the damp, cold night air. He had to do something positive about Maud. He simply had to.

He debated whether or not to go and see Evan Powell and announce that he was in love with his daughter. But then what if Evan should talk to Maud, and Maud deny all knowledge of his affection? It would be better to break into the Graig Hospital and see her first. If only – if – a smile brought a strange animated light into his eyes.

He turned on his heel and returned to the café. Heading straight for the kitchen, he opened the pantry door.

'Forgotten something?' Tony asked as he lowered a full basket of newly chipped potatoes into the overflowing fat fryer.

'Yes,' Ronnie snapped enigmatically. He studied the trays of eggs ranged on the slate shelves. There were close on two dozen there. He could always go to the market early and buy some more. Taking one of the small cardboard boxes they used to put cakes in, he carefully lowered all the eggs into it. Then he looked at the cake shelf. There was only a fruit cake left; there wouldn't be fresh cream cakes until the morning. He lifted it gently into another box, then as an afterthought he pulled out his watch chain and opened the cupboard where he kept the alcohol. Looking along the shelves he found what he was looking for: a bottle of sweet Spanish sherry. He closed and locked the door, picked up the boxes and hurried out. Tony heard the clang of the front door banging behind him. It crashed even above the sizzling hiss of the fryer.

Alma walked into the kitchen with a tray of dirty dishes. 'Where's he off to?' Tony asked, pointing to the door.

'How in hell should I know?' she bit back furiously. She crashed

187

the tray down on the wooden table next to the sink. 'And even if I did know I wouldn't give a single, sweet, damn,' she shouted as she stormed out. Tony shrugged as he ladled chips out of the fat with a slatted spoon. Perhaps his father was right, he mused. The priesthood was a good life. If nothing else it would at least be quiet.

Ronnie crossed the road, walked under the railway bridge and up the Graig hill towards the Central Homes. He'd thought of taking the Trojan, but someone might see it parked close to the hospital and wonder what it was doing there. This way, all he had to worry about was getting through the gate, and what he was going to say once he was inside the building, always assuming he got that far.

The porter eyed him suspiciously as he walked along Court-house Street and up to the lodge gate. Pretending he hadn't noticed the man, he went directly to the gate and banged hard on it before the porter had an opportunity to confront him.

'Eggs for the TB ward,' he announced in a loud voice.

'At this time of night?' the porter peered at him suspiciously. 'It's after eight o'clock.'

'Donation from the Catholic Mothers' Union,' Ronnie explained. 'My mother promised to deliver them this afternoon but her rhematism played up. This is the first chance I've had to leave the café all day.'

The man squinted through the gloom, eyeing Ronnie suspiciously. 'Oh, it's you, Mr Ronconi.' He shuffled forward to open the gate. 'You should have said so in the first place.'

'Sorry, haven't deliverd anything for the Mother's Union before,' he replied brusquely.

'And God bless them, that's what I say,' the porter mumbled. 'Even if they are Catholics. Want to leave the boxes with me?' he asked, wondering just how many eggs were inside and if one or two would be missed.

'Better not,' Ronnie said easily. 'There's something else here that my mother promised the ward sister yesterday. She made me swear that I'd take it to the ward office myself.'

'Know your way to the TB ward?'

Ronnie shook his head.

The porter leant against the gate as Ronnie walked through.

'Turn left here, and walk across the female exercise yard. Left is the female side of the Homes,' he explained laboriously. 'Men are on the right, away from the main road, less chance of them escaping that way. The first blocks you come to are the casual wards and the workhouse wards. Then you come to the un-marrieds ward. TB patients are in the end block against the wall, you can't miss it, it's the last block opposite the boiler house. The only blocks ahead of you are maternity, male acute, and J wards and they're not against the wall,' he rambled. 'TB's on the top floor,' he shouted as Ronnie walked away.

Securing the bottle of sherry in the crook of his elbow and balancing the boxes in one hand, Ronnie touched his cap as he continued on his way. The yard was an incredibly depressing place. Hemmed in on one side by a ten-foot-high stone wall, and on the other by a massive stone block that housed the dining room and kitchens, it gave Ronnie the impression that he was travelling through a long, dark, roofless tunnel. If it wasn't for the rain that dripped down on to his hat he could have sworn it had a ceiling. The towering walls and the feeling of claustrophobia fostered the effect of being trapped in a massive, damp, cellar.

Lights glimmered faintly, illuminating the cross-bars of ward windows, but they did nothing to brighten his path. He stepped ankle deep into a puddle of freezing rainwater. Shaking his foot irritably in an effort to get rid of the worst of the water, he kept going. At the end of the dining-room block he passed the kitchens. He recognised them by the smell: an overwhelming stench of rotting vegetables and cabbage water assailed his nostrils. Then he heard the hum of the boiler house. He looked around: to his left was the block he'd been looking for. Balancing the boxes on one arm, he turned the doorknob and stole inside. He found himself in a white-tiled vestibule. A naked light bulb hung from the ceiling, its low wattage tingeing the atmosphere with a gloomy, dark gold light. Everything around him was tiled – the floor, half the walls, even the stairs. The distant sounds of hospital-trolleys rattling over hard floors, and clashings of china against metal echoed towards him. He tiptoed quietly towards the stairs. Holding the boxes out carefully in front of him he climbed up the steps, taking them two at a time. At the top was a closed door, adorned with a large red and white sign.

He knocked softly at the door. He waited a few moments, then pushed it open.

'Do you mind telling me what you think you're doing, sir?'

Ronnie was not normally of a nervous disposition, but because the voice came from behind him, and not in front as he'd expected, he jumped, almost dropping the eggs.

'I'm looking for the sister in charge of the TB ward,' he explained briefly.

'Looks like you found her,' the middle-aged woman said stiffly.

Ronnie had learned enough from Laura to tell the difference between a staff nurse's uniform and a sister's. 'God bless the shortage of nurses,' he thought irreverently, hoping it would be easier to get round the junior hospital hierarchy.

'I've come to deliver eggs, from the Catholic Mothers' Union.'

The stern expression on her face lifted, as what might have been the beginnings of a smile played at the corners of her mouth.

'How thoughtful. I'll take them off you.'

That wasn't what he'd intended at all.

'Let me carry them into the ward kitchen for you.' He gave her his most winning smile, a smile that had melted hearts even harder than hers. 'I've put a little something for the staff in there as well,' he winked. 'Something that will probably be a bit rich for the patients' taste.' He flipped open the top of the box, so she could see and smell the fruit cake, then he removed the bottle of sherry that he had tucked under his arm and waved it under her nose.

'That's very good of you Mr . . .'

'Ronconi,' he said quickly.

'Ronconi,' the smile finally broke through her frosty interior. 'But you still can't go through that door. Can't you read?' She pointed to the sign. 'Do you want to risk getting tuberculosis?'

'I rather think I already have,' he said shortly. 'You see my – my – my – ' he almost said sister, but no one would believe that he and Maud were brother and sister, particularly now he had been idiotic enough to tell the woman his real name. But then again, what was the point in lying? He was too well known in the town as a Ronconi.

'My fiancée is in here,' he blurted out in desperation. 'I was hoping to have a word,' he pleaded, reading suspicion all over her face. 'You see we had the most awful row the night before she came in here – '

'What's her name?' the nurse demanded coldly.

'Maud. Maud Powell. We were to have been married next month.'

'This is the first I've heard of it.'

'There's problems.' This time he wasn't lying. If he was ever lucky enough to get as far as making the kind of plans with Maud that he dreamed about, there would be problems. Serious ones! 'You see my family are Catholics and – '

'And she's Chapel,' the sister finished for him. 'You really are a Ronconi, aren't you?' she said, studying his dark, foreign appearance. 'I've seen you in your café. You have lovely cream cakes . . .'

'I'll bring you a box of them tomorrow,' he promised rashly. 'Please,' he begged. 'There's so much I want to say to her.'

'This isn't the time or place.' Her voice wasn't as firm as it had been.

'Doctor Trevor Lewis is my brother-in-law.' He played his last card desperately. Now he'd got this far he wasn't going to be put off. 'He promised to get me in to see her tomorrow, but I just couldn't wait.'

'Then your sister is Laura – '

'Lewis, who was Ronconi,' he broke in eagerly. 'Please,' he implored. 'No one will ever find out. I promise. Please . . .'

'Everyone on the ward is sleeping.'

'I'll be as quiet as a mouse. Just a minute.'

'She's very ill, you know.'

'I know she haemorrhaged this morning, and that she was brought in, in a coma. Her father told me,' he lied, struggling to contain his irritation with the woman.

'The kitchen's along there.' The nurse finally pushed open the door. 'You can drop your eggs and cake off there. I'll go and see if she's awake. *If*,' she stressed the 'if', 'If she's awake, you can see her for a second. Just a quick peek through the door and a smile. No more, mark you.'

Ronnie felt as though he were floating on air as he watched her broad back disappear through the door marked 'ward'. He rushed down the corridor to the kitchen. The atmosphere was close and unpleasantly warm. Foul and heavy with the mixed odours of stale urine, cheap disinfectant and the strange sour-sweet smell peculiar to all hospitals. But as he left the bottle and the boxes on the kitchen sideboard the only perfume he was aware of was that of blooming roses. Outside was miserable wet winter and he was lost in the wonders of a beautiful summer that he was confident was heading his way.

Chapter Eighteen

It was a long, long time before Diana felt clean enough to stop scrubbing herself. When she finally, reluctantly returned the brush to the bath-rack she noticed her naked body. It wasn't a sight she was accustomed to, simply because she either washed in a bowl in her bedroom or the sink in the washhouse when the boys were out. And neither room had a mirror.

She shuddered, disgusted and revolted by the sight of her own nudity. She closed her eyes against the image of her full, round breasts topped by the soft, pink aureoles of her nipples. But even with her eyes closed she could still see the flat, white plain of her stomach leading down to the triangle of dark hair that lay between her scrubbed red thighs. Feeling nauseous she screwed up her face in self-loathing. She was in pain. Hurting! Not from the tingling left by the vigorous pounding she had subjected her skin to, but something more, something deeper.

Keeping her eyes closed, she ducked her head beneath the water, washing off the soap lather she'd massaged into her hair. When it was clean, she pulled the bath plug with her toe. Crouching forward, she turned on the cold tap and held her head under its steady flow, rinsing away the last vestiges of bath water from her hair. Afterwards she splashed cold water over the rest of her body. Freezing cold and shivering, she finally stood up and wrapped the larger of the two towels Wyn had left around herself. She dried her skin thoroughly, wiping all the scratched areas first with swabs of cotton wool that she found on the washstand, lest she stain the towel with blood.

Tucking the top of the towel in, she decided to clean the bathroom thoroughly, leaving it exactly as she'd found it. She was more than a little overawed by its magnificence, but then it was the first plumbed-in bathroom she'd seen in a private house. The nearest she'd ever got to an indoor bathroom before now were the spartan utility ones she'd cleaned on the wards in the Royal Infirmary, and the bleak communal wash areas she'd been allowed to use in the hostel for ward maids.

She found a cleaning cloth on the side of the slop bucket beneath the washstand. Filling the bucket with warm water and, in the absence of anything better, the remains of the soap she'd washed herself with, she wiped down the huge clawfoot bath, inside and out. Then she washed the floor, taking care to mop up every single drop of water that she'd dripped outside the bath.

She hadn't touched the massive stone sink in the corner, or its ornate, wrought-iron supports, but she cleaned them all the same. The last thing she turned her attention to was the toilet. When she lifted the dark wooden seat, she stared in disbelief. The inside was decorated with circles of beautifully painted daisies. She washed out the bucket and the cloth last of all. Lingering next to the washstand, she admired and envied the range of toiletries. The last time she'd seen a display as lavish was in Norma Shearer's bedroom in a film.

She reached out hesitantly and picked up a bowl of pearl talcum powder. The bowl was beautiful, porcelain china, decorated with a finely drawn design of white, lily-like flowers. She climbed into the bath and gingerly lifted the lid lest she spill a drop, reasoning that it would be easier to wash the powder down the plughole than wipe it off the floor. A circle of white swansdown floated on top of the deliciously perfumed fine dusting powder. She sprinkled a little sparingly over her neck and shoulders. Glancing down at the bath, she noticed with satisfaction that she hadn't wasted a single speck.

She replaced the bowl on the exact spot where it had rested before. She studied the rows of boxes, bowls and bottles, breathing in the mixture of heady perfumes and allowing them to assail her senses. Lavender water, Pears and Kay's soaps. Men's mint Cologne, bottles of Evening in Paris, 4711 eau-de-Cologne and Essence of Violets. Shaving soaps and antiseptic shaving blades. Tubes of cherry toothpaste and small tins of Erasmus tooth-powder, and at the practical end of the table, a massive jar of petroleum jelly and a large bottle of liniment rub.

Feeling like a thief despite Wyn's generous directive that she help herself, she closed her fingers around the beautiful green and gold bottle of eau-de-Cologne. Unscrewing the top, she dabbed a little sparingly behind her ears. She knew what bottles like this cost. Her mother had sold them for a few pence a year ago, but in the shops they were priced at more than she could hope to earn in a month.

At the thought of earnings she shuddered. She tried to marshal her thoughts and concentrate on replacing everything exactly as she'd found it. Even the bucket and cloth.

A man's hairbrush stood on the washstand. Judging by the strands of hair caught up in its bristles, it was Wyn's. She picked it up, automatically pulling out the hairs and preparing to use it. Then she remembered that she'd carried her handbag into the room. She found it, opened it, extracted her own comb and flicked her hair straight back, like a boy's, pushing it behind her ears. Straight hair was unfashionable, unalluring. She made a mental resolution never to wave or curl her hair again.

Using her fingers to wipe away the steam from a mirror that hung on the wall above the sink, she stared at her reflection. Her eyes seemed disproportionately large in comparison with the rest of her face. Her cheeks and lips were white, devoid of even a hint of colour. Only her right temple gleamed red. Angry and swollen where Ben had slammed her into the shelves.

She returned the comb to her handbag. Turning her back on the mirror she removed the towel and dressed quickly. The clothes hung stiff and strange on her, especially Wyn's shirt, which felt peculiar against her bare skin, but he'd been so generous already she felt she could hardly ask him to look for a bust shaper or chemise.

She glanced round the room one last time after she opened the window a crack to let out the steam. She had no more excuse to linger. Gathering up her clothes from the wooden slatted mat, she tied them into a tight little bundle and wrapped the remains of her white blouse round the outside. Only her coat remained. She picked it up, unlocked the door and descended the staircase.

Wyn had made tea. He was sitting at the kitchen table drinking a cup and reading the *South Wales Echo*.

'You look better,' he smiled as she walked through the door. 'Sit down. I'll pour you some tea.'

'I'd like to burn these first.' She dropped her coat on to a chair and held out the bundle of clothes.

'Couldn't they be washed and mended?'

'Even if they could, I'd never wear them again.' Her voice escalated alarmingly. 'Not as long as I live.'

He opened the door to the range. Taking the bundle from her fastidiously with the tongs, he stuffed it on top of the coals, banking it down with a log and a shovelful of small coal.

'That'll soon burn.' He replaced the tongs in the hearth set, and picked up the teapot.

'Shouldn't you be getting back to the shop?' It was warm in the kitchen, and comfortable. She felt like an outsider and, despite the bath, a dirty outsider – a tramp who had no right to sit there.

'I have another ten minutes or so.' He poured out her tea. 'Here, give me your coat.' He took it and carried it over to the sink where he proceeded to brush it down fussily with a damp cloth.

She sat on the edge of the chair, hunched over the table sipping at her tea. 'I don't know how to begin to say thank you,' she murmured in a small voice. 'I'll return the clothes after I've washed them.'

'There's no need. I told you, they don't fit my sister any more.' He dabbed some cold water on to a spot on her coat and rubbed it. 'Do you want to talk about it?' he asked quietly. She stared into her cup. 'You don't have to,' he continued. 'I just thought it might help.'

'You've probably guessed most of it,' she snapped.

'Ben Springer?'

At the mention of Ben's name, it all poured out. The rape, the humiliation, the feeling of complete and utter degradation and worthlessness . . .

He simply stood there, next to the sink, and listened. When she finally ran out of words and into tears, he walked to her and handed over her coat. She delved into the pocket, looking for a handkerchief. When she removed and opened her hand, the five-pound note Ben Springer had thrust upon her fluttered to the floor. Wyn picked it up.

'What do want to do?' he asked quietly, returning the money to her.

She took a deep breath and raised her eyes to meet his steady gaze.

'I don't know,' she admitted brokenly. 'If I tell Will or my cousins or my uncle what Ben did to me, they'd kill him for sure.'

Wyn remembered the beating Eddie Powell had given Bethan Powell's seducer for less, and nodded.

'They'd swing for Ben, that's for certain,' he agreed flatly.

'So what can I do?' she demanded, hysterically.

'You can't be thinking of going back to work there tomorrow?' he asked, genuinely alarmed by the thought.

'No!' her reply was sharp and vehement.

'Then it's obvious, you've got to find a job elsewhere.'

'And what do I tell my aunt, uncle and Will when they ask why I left?'

'Tell them he laid you off. They're hardly likely to go and challenge him about it, are they?'

She realised he was glancing at the clock, and jumped up, upsetting her full cup of tea on the scrubbed wooden table top.

'I'm sorry,' she cried, tears rising to her eyes again.

'For God's sake stop apologising every five minutes. None of this is your fault,' he said curtly, angered by his own inadequacy to deal with the situation. He threw a dishcloth over the mess, deftly mopped it up, put the cup and saucer in the sink, then picked up her coat again and helped her on with it.

'You've been great, Wyn,' she murmured, striving to contain her emotions. 'Really great. I don't know what I would have done without you. Aunt Elizabeth would have killed me if I'd gone home as I was.'

'I doubt she'd have done that.' He took the five pounds from her hand and thrust it deep into her pocket. She immediately pulled it out and walked towards the stove.

'Don't,' he ordered sharply. 'If you don't want the money you can send it back to him any time.'

She pushed it back into her pocket.

'Look,' he conceded, 'you know I work every night, except Sunday. How about I meet you Sunday afternoon? We could go to Ronconi's.'

'I don't know,' she murmured doubtfully.

'You can't let what Ben did to you spoil your life.'

At the mention of Ben's name, she lowered her head and rushed out. He heard her sobbing again, and felt entirely helpless. This was one case where tea and sympathy really weren't enough, and he had nothing else to offer – unless. He remembered something he'd seen and heard when he left the Ruperra after his training sessions. Sunday – all he had to do was wait until Sunday. It would be quiet then. He looked around the kitchen, checked that he'd left it tidy and followed Diana out of the door.

Ronnie hovered impatiently in the corridor outside the isolation area. The night nurse had disappeared what seemed like hours ago. He paced uneasily up and down, diving straight back into the ward kitchen when he heard footsteps echoing towards him from behind the closed doors of the ward, petrified in case it was someone other than the staff nurse that he'd spoken to. Someone with enough authority and acumen to throw him out. He was so close . . . so close . . .

'What are you doing here?'

He whirled around. The nurse was small, plump, dark and, he noticed thankfully, as he whispered a prayer of gratitude to the Virgin Mother – a trainee.

'It's all right, Jones,' the staff nurse he'd spoken to reprimanded sharply. 'He has my permission to wait here.'

'Sorry, staff,' the nurse apologised.

'Now go down to the porters' station as I asked you to five minutes ago,' the staff nurse ordered sharply. 'I want two of them up here with a stretcher in the next five minutes, if not sooner,' she added illogically, knowing full well that the porters' station was a brisk five-minute walk away from the ward for a nurse, and ten for a porter who knew he was wanted to ferry dead, as opposed to live, patients. 'And while you're downstairs you may as well walk across the yard and alert the mortuary that there's a body on its way.'

'Right away, staff.' Looking down at the floor to conceal her red face, the trainee scurried off.

'One of the patients died five minutes ago,' the staff nurse explained briefly to Ronnie. 'The younger nurses often have trouble dealing with the inevitable, especially when the patient is young. It upsets the other inmates too,' she commented drily. 'But then again Jones is hardly the most competent of trainees,' she finished unsympathetically.

Ronnie paled, 'It's not . . . not . . .'

'No, it wasn't your fiancée. But she was only fifteen, and, as it happens, in the next bed. She coughed up an entire lung before she went. Very messy.' She shook her head as though trying to obliterate the image from her mind. 'We had to wheel screens round her bed so none of the others could see what was happening. We've moved the body out now to the treatment room, but the screens are still up. If you promise to be quiet you can have a minute behind them with your fiancée. A minute, mind you. No longer,' she warned.

'Thank you.' Ronnie had to restrain himself from dancing past her and into the ward.

'Oh and by the way,' she gave him a tight little smile as she held the ward door open for him, 'you weren't joking when you said you had problems with her family. It took some time for her even to admit she knew you, let alone was engaged to you.'

He shrugged his shoulders and returned her smile. 'As I said, there's a lot I need to say to her.'

He crept through the door into the silent ward. The nurse didn't follow, merely pointed to the bed immediately behind the door to the left. Because it was next to the wall, the iron and canvas screening that isolated the bed next to it effectively screened it also. Craving privacy, he glanced behind him and saw a tousled, and he sincerely hoped sleeping, head in the bed opposite. The nurse closed the door of the ward softly behind her. She had been kinder than he'd expected: this was as alone as he could reasonably expect to get with Maud while she remained in hospital.

Stepping on tiptoe, lest the rubber soles of his shoes squeak on the highly polished linoleum, he stole behind the screen. For the first time since he'd left school, headmasters and canings behind him, he tasted the cold, metallic tang of fear in his mouth. Wiping his clammy hands on his coat, he swallowed hard.

'Don't forget, one minute,' the nurse warned through the closed doors of the ward, as she made her way back from the kitchen to the treatment room. 'No more.'

The reminder gave him the courage he needed to look at Maud. She was lying, propped up on three pillows, her face as white as the cotton slips behind her head. The gold of her hair and the vivid gem-like blue of her eyes were the only hints of colour in a sea of white sheeting and bedcovers.

'Ronnie?'

Her voice was faint, barely audible. The room faded, until he focused only on her. A pale golden figure shimmering in a fog of grey, wavering darkness. 'The nurse told me that you were here, and you'd asked to see me,' she whispered.

He crept close to the bed and knelt beside it. 'I couldn't rest or settle to anything, not without knowing how you were.' Locking his fingers together he rested his hands on the edge of the bed.

She laid her hand on top of his. It was pale, so white and translucent he could see the pattern of veins beneath the skin, mute evidence of her fragility and mortality. He shuddered, noticing for the first time the mixed odours of decay, disinfectant and death in the atmosphere around him.

'You don't think my being here is your fault, do you?' she asked, giving him a small smile.

'No! Yes . . . I don't know . . .' he stammered like a nervous schoolboy. 'If I hadn't taken you down the café last night . . .'

'I wouldn't have had a good time,' she finished for him. The effort it cost her to talk brought on a coughing fit. He sat helplessly as she clutched the inevitable stained, sodden handkerchief to her mouth. He heard a sound in the corridor, and remembered the nurse's injunction: 'One minute. No more.'

'Maud there's no easy way to say this,' he blurted out uneasily, worried that the nurse would return and throw him out before he had a chance to tell Maud anything important. 'Perhaps if I had more time . . . oh, what the hell. I love you and I want to marry you,' he confessed impatiently, and with a strange lack of eloquence considering the time he'd had to prepare for this momentous occasion in his life. Unnerved by the silence that greeted his outburst, a full minute passed before he dared to raise his eyes to her.

She was staring at him, dumbfounded.

'I love you,' he repeated in a softer tone. 'I've been such a fool. I should have realised sooner. I didn't even think about it until last night. Now I know I want to be with you. Always. I want to marry you . . .'

'Ronnie, I'm ill. The doctor said I'm – '

'I know what the doctor said,' he dismissed scornfully. 'I've spoken to Trevor. He's my brother-in-law, remember. But that

200

doesn't make him any different from the rest of the pack. All he can talk about is cutting ribs, deflating lungs, and operations.'

'He said there's a chance that an operation might work . . .'

'And there's a chance that it might not.'

Maud looked through a small tear in the screen and saw the stripped and empty bed next to her own, and fell silent.

'Trevor's probably right,' Ronnie conceded grudgingly. 'An operation would be the best option if you stayed here. But you don't have to. Everyone knows that people with consumption improve if they're taken to a healthier climate with clean air. Mountain air,' he finished triumphantly.

'There's nothing but mountains around here,' she pointed out logically.

'Mountains but no clean air, the dust on the slagheaps sees to that. Coal isn't healthy, but there's no coal mining in Italy,' he began enthusiastically.

'Italy!' she exclaimed incredulously, feeling that he might as well have suggested the moon.

'Why not? I have grandparents there.' He omitted to tell her that he hadn't seen them since he was five and wasn't at all sure of the reception they'd give him if he turned up on their doorstep, let alone with a consumptive wife. 'Marry me and we'll go to Italy. I'll see to it that we're on a train before the end of the week. I'll find your father and ask him for his permission tonight . . .'

Maud knew he was talking to her because she could see his lips moving, but she could neither hear nor comprehend a word he was saying. She was too busy thinking of the pale, dark girl in the next bed. The cures she'd tried and told her about. The plans she'd been making, even up until that afternoon. Ronnie – she looked at him, seeing him in the light of a potential lover for the first time. It was the pictures come to life. True romance. Better, much better than *It Happened One Night*. His dark, rugged, brooding good looks. Italy, with a husband! For the first time since Diana had brought her back from the Infirmary she had something to think about, something to plan for other than her own funeral. She tried to sit up, then began to cough again. Her body racked by spasms, she reached out unsteadily, picked up the sputum jar and spat in it.

She sensed Ronnie looking at her, and remembered her disgust when her now dead neighbour had done the selfsame thing. Had it really only been that morning? Ashamed of her disease-ridden body, she closed her eyes, afraid to look at him lest she see something of the revulsion she felt for herself mirrored in his eyes.

'This isn't a romantic disease,' she said cuttingly. 'I'm no Greta Garbo, you're not Robert Taylor. And this,' – she lifted her pathetically thin hand and waved it close to the sickly green walls of the ward – 'isn't Camille,' she said brutally. 'People with TB die horribly, messily . . .' she fought for breath, suddenly terrified – of him – of reaching out to take what he offered in case he saw her for what she was, changed his mind and rejected her. 'They cough up shreds of lungs.' She opened out her stinking handkerchief to illustrate her words, painting the blackest possible picture of the disease, so he would hold no illusions about what she was trying to tell him.

'You're not saying anything I don't already know,' he informed her smoothly.

'How can you possibly love me – '

'I've no idea, especially when you're in this mood,' he joked.

'I don't think I love you,' she said slowly, choosing her words with care. 'To be honest, Ronnie, I've never thought of you as anything other than one of Haydn's and Will's friends. And Laura's brother, of course,' she murmured as an afterthought. 'You're so old . . .'

'Not too old for anything that matters,' he said earnestly. 'Which I hope you'll soon find out. And when you marry me – ' he refused even to think of the possibility of 'if', '– you'll learn to love me. Until that happens I have more than enough love for both of us. Besides, my parents have always told me that love comes after marriage,' he grinned wryly, wrapping his huge, thick fingers round her thin, reed-like ones. 'It must be true. Just look at them, they only saw one another twice before the wedding, and that was in front of both of their entire families. At least we've seen more of each other than that, and much more than I've seen of any of the Italian girls that Mama and Papa have been trying to marry me off to for the past few years.'

'Your parents may want you to get married, but I don't think either of them will be all that happy with the thought of you marrying a girl as sick as me.'

'What they want isn't important. Not this time. You're what I want. All you have to do is say the word. I'll speak to your father, get you out of here, marry you and take you to Italy . . .'

'You're mad.' The idea of marrying anyone, especially Ronnie Ronconi, suddenly seemed so preposterous she wondered if she were dreaming or hallucinating.

'Very possibly,' he agreed infuriatingly.

'Well I'm not mad,' she stated positively, 'and neither will I lie to you. I don't think I love you,' she said emphatically.

'I thought we'd already dealt with that point.'

'But you're offering me so much. Italy. The girls here were talking about rich people's cures in Switzerland this afternoon, and – '

'Italy and Switzerland are next door to each other, they share the same air,' he urged persuasively.

'I want to live so much,' she said fervently.

'Then live with me.'

Tears welled in the corners of her eyes. He'd seen her cry before. Stood by helplessly while she'd swallowed silent, bitter tears of pain, watched as she'd struggled with hot, fierce tears of anger. This was different. He couldn't help feeling that she was shedding her first tears of sorrow. He instinctively knew what she was thinking. He was offering her a chance to live, and all she could think of was – how long?

'We'll marry, and take whatever time we're given,' he declared practically. 'Anything has to be better than nothing, and if our marriage lasts for years instead of months, I'll just have to take my chances that you don't turn into a nagging wife like Laura, and make my life a misery.'

'That's another thing,' she fought to keep her tears in check. 'Trevor and Laura went out together for ages. They knew all there was to know about one another before they married. You don't know the first thing about me.'

'I know everything that's important.' Sensing her exhaustion, he rose from his knees and kissed her gently on the forehead. 'Right, now that's over and done with, I may as well warn you, you'll never get me on my knees again. I'll speak to your father, see about getting you out of here. Then I have to buy some train tickets.'

'My father – '

'Don't worry about a thing. I'll see to everything. You lie there, conserve your strength and concentrate on falling in love with me. If you can manage it, I'd like it to happen before next Tuesday. I aim to be away by then.'

'You still here, Mr Ronconi?' the staff nurse hissed furiously. 'I said a minute, and you've taken ten. Quick, out,' she ordered, panicking; she'd already had word that the senior night sister was on her rounds.

Ronnie smiled at Maud, and winked at the nurse.

'Do you have a day off coming to you before Tuesday? Because if you do, you can be bridesmaid,' he grinned wickedly.

'Out,' she pushed him through the door and watched him descend the stairs. She didn't return to the ward until she heard the click of the door closing behind him.

'You look happy,' she commented to Maud as she wheeled the screens away from her bed.

'I think I am.' Maud admitted as she wriggled down between the sheets.

'I can understand that. He's very good-looking, isn't he? Funny, his sister said he'd never fall for anyone. "Heart as hard as the brass in the till," that's what she said. "Might marry another café, but never a girl." But then,' the nurse couldn't help herself; for all her professional training she responded to Maud's smile with one of her own, 'what does a sister ever know about a brother? They say the harder they are, the harder they fall. You're a lucky girl,' she said quickly, glossing over Maud's illness. 'At least he owns one café, even if you're not bringing him another. And with a café, you'll never go hungry.'

'He's taking me to Italy,' Maud murmured sleepily. Excited by the prospect, she didn't give a thought to the café or the business, or what Ronnie would be giving up to take her away from the valleys. For the first time in months she was looking forward to sleeping. Tonight she wouldn't dream of wreaths, funerals and headstones in Glyntaff cemetery, but of weddings. Of floating into chapel in the centre of a cloud of white tulle, flowers in her hair, a scented bouquet in her hand, a lace veil covering her head. The only thing that had been a little misty until now was the face of her bridegroom. She thought of Ronnie's dark, handsome features, the way he'd looked at her when he told her he loved her, and she fitted him into the grey suit with the white buttonhole. She was still smiling in her sleep when the duty sister checked the ward on her rounds an hour later.

Chapter Nineteen

'You didn't have to walk me all the way home,' Jenny said as she led the way around the corner of Llantrisant Road into Factory Lane. She halted outside the six-foot-high wooden door that fitted flushly into the eight-foot wall round the back yard of the shop. 'You'll be late now for your training session in the Ruperra, and it means making a double trip. You'll have to walk down the hill and back up again later, won't you?' she asked.

'If you're serious about boxing you can't afford to give training a miss. Ever,' Eddie said gravely.

She turned her umbrella, and was preparing to lower it when she caught sight of him staring at her. She smiled, elated. Haydn might be impervious to her charms, but his brother wasn't, and that meant she wasn't wholly unattractive after all. Perhaps given time Haydn might even change his mind about her.

Eddie was aware only of the darkness – and Jenny. The light from the lamps on the main road didn't reach as far as the shadows of Factory Lane. Their beams shafted short, over streaks of navy blue, rain-filled night air, lending a faint glow to the back of Jenny's head. Her blonde hair shone like a strip of gold between her high forehead and her umbrella. If it hadn't been for the long belted mac she was wearing, she could have taken her place amongst the angels in the illustrated Life of Jesus that Maud had won as a school prize. The book he would never have willingly opened if his Uncle John Joseph hadn't thrown it contemptuously across the room, deploring it as 'Popish'. He figured that anything that annoyed his uncle had to be worth looking at.

'Do you know, you're really pretty,' he said impulsively.

'Thank you.' It wasn't up to Clark Gable standard, but she knew it was the nearest Eddie would get to uttering poetry, and the most she could expect. He couldn't stop looking at her. Her eyes were round, enormous, like those of a frightened rabbit. He fought the urge to put his arms around her, forcing himself to remember, not for the first time that evening, that she had been, and might be again, his brother's girlfriend. But even as he reminded himself, he continued to stare at her, admiring the way her nose tilted up at the end, the rounded softness of her cheeks, the inviting pout of her lips, soft, luscious – just begging to be kissed.

Something of his thoughts must have transmitted themselves to her, because before he realised she'd moved, she was standing on tiptoe before him. Lifting her chin, she kissed him gently on the spot where his mouth ended and his cheek began. The smell of her scent wafted into his nostrils. The proximity of her smooth-skinned, curvaceous body was too much – too tempting. He didn't even wait to glance behind him to ensure no one was watching, before sweeping her into his muscular arms.

Pulling her close, he kissed her hard and brutally on the lips. His bruising, insensitive touch took her breath away. Eddie had none of Haydn's finesse, or gentleness. His tongue invaded her mouth, exploring, probing, as he clamped his hand on the nape of her neck. Alarmed as much by her own feelings as by what Eddie was doing to her, she struggled to draw back. All she'd intended when she'd met Eddie in Mill Street was to be seen with him in the hope of making Haydn jealous. Perhaps exchange a highly public, flirtatious giggle with him, or a little light banter. She'd never intended things to go this far! But then she hadn't bargained on Eddie. He'd always been so quiet in the presence of girls, she'd put it down to shyness and inexperience, never suspecting such a passive exterior could conceal so much inner passion. Or how she'd feel if such a passion was unleashed on her.

She shifted position slightly, creating a small gap between them. It was just wide enough for him to manoeuvre his other hand inside her coat. Drunk with kisses, she failed to notice what he was doing until she shivered involuntarily at the cold touch of his fingers against the bare skin of her breast. She clamped her hand firmly over his.

'You mustn't!' she commanded weakly.

'Sorry,' he murmured huskily. 'Got a bit carried away there.'

'So I see.' Too embarrassed to meet his eyes she straightened her blouse and buttoned her coat. 'I always thought you spent all your time in the gym, Eddie Powell,' she said primly, striving to regain her composure. 'Wherever did you learn to kiss like that?'

He smiled, remembering one golden, drunken afternoon spent

in the bushes of Pontypridd Park with a willing, if expensive, chorus girl.

'Just because I don't wear my girlfriends on my arm like a badge, it doesn't mean I've never had any,' he said archly.

'I'd better be going.' She reached for the latch on the high wooden door.

He laid his fingers over hers and pressed down hard. The door opened inwards, and he followed her into the small back yard. It was even darker than in the lane. Black as pitch. The only relief was the faint jet gleam of glass outlining the position of the storeroom window.

'Just one more kiss,' he begged, pushing her until she was pinned against the house door and could retreat no further. His mouth closed over hers again. She felt as though he was sucking the breath from her body. His hand once more gravitated to the contours of her breast beneath her coat. He squeezed it once, before lifting her skirt and invading her bloomers. The door opened inwards into the stockroom; she didn't know how, only that she reeled blindly backwards through it, gasping for air, her nerve ends tingling, too stunned and shocked to take in the enormity of what Eddie was doing to her.

Her coat joined his on the floor. He lifted her pullover and with it her blouse and underclothes. She lay back on the boxes, where she had lain so many nights with Haydn, digging her fingernails into Eddie's back as he caressed her breasts and nipples. His fingers were replaced by his lips as his hands delved into the soft, sensitive area between her thighs.

He removed her bloomers and pulled her skirt to her waist but she was too far gone down the road of hunger and desire that he had aroused within her to protest. If they had been lying on the bandstand in Pontypridd Park, on view to the whole world, she wouldn't have cared less. She was aware only of the sensations he engendered. The thrill, the excitement, of his lovemaking. The desires he had kindled. Of wanting him to touch her naked body. Again and again and again!

He ran his hands up her sides from her thighs to her breasts and she tore her clothes off, over her head. She lay back on the boxes, stark naked before him, arms uplifted, legs spread wide, gratefully receiving the caresses and thrusts he bestowed on her, electric touches that obliterated everything, even thoughts of Haydn, from her mind.

When it was over he did not linger long. She was aware of him moving swiftly away from her in the blackness, heard the whispers of cloth rustling, and knew that he was dressing. A cold draught blew across her exposed body, the latch slipped. She opened her eyes just in time to see his shadow disappearing out into the night. He didn't even turn back to look at her. Didn't say one single word – of endearment – of anything.

An eternity passed during which she recalled Haydn's tenderness, his gentle, sensuous touch, his sweet, lingering kisses. He had always left her craving for more – much, much more. She'd always assumed that the 'more' would come with marriage.

Eddie had left her feeling weak, battered and wasted, but to her horror she realised that Eddie had given her what her body had craved for, and never got from Haydn. Pure physical passion.

But she loved Haydn. Didn't she? Of course she did. She was sure of that much. But one thing was certain now: he wouldn't want her. Not after this. She loved Haydn and had only wanted Eddie. Had wanted him enough to forget everything that Haydn had ever been to her.

Only her ridiculous pride had prevented her from going to Haydn after that stupid quarrel. She had wanted to tell him she was sorry for precipitating the argument. She had longed for a chance to make it up to him. To make him forget that she could behave childishly, jealously, over nothing. Now she realised she would never do that. What had happened between her and Eddie would prevent her; would estrange her from Haydn once and for all.

She began to pick up her clothes slowly, all the while shedding silent tears for what she had lost. A sweet first love that was now, irrevocably, consigned to her past.

There were many rooms in the Unemployment Institute in Mill Street. Large workshops where unemployed boys and men could learn carpentry and cobbling. Smaller rooms which had been handed over to the more intellectual contingent, who used them as meeting places, to talk, play chess, and remodel the world – especially Wales – along fairer, more equal, and socialist if not communist-inspired lines.

Unused to comfort in their homes, the members scarcely noticed the cold or discomfort in the rooms of the Institute. The furniture, if it could be graced with that name, was a motley collection of old chairs, sofas and scarred and broken tables that had been donated by those in the town rich enough to replace their belongings when they wore out. A few pieces showed signs of clumsy, ineffectual attempts at renovation by the boys who frequented the carpentry workshops. Those with whole, un-broken springs tended to gravitate towards what was grandly referred to as the 'Reading Room', where most of the books read were borrowed from the Pontypridd Lending Library. All the Institute had on offer was a meagre, donated store of well-thumbed magazines, dog-eared copies of Dickens and a bound edition of the complete works of Karl Marx, presented courtesy of the Miners' Union.

As Ronnie walked purposefully through the front door in the hope of finding Evan, he heard the deep, melodious tones of a choir practising somewhere at the back of the building. The sweet sounds blended uneasily with the strident barkings of a retired sergeant-major who was putting the younger element through their exercises in the gym, in the hope that the Institute team would win their next rugby match.

'Seen Evan Powell?' he asked a wizened old man whose arms were crammed with political pamphlets.

'Chess room.' The man pointed down a narrow passageway lit by a single, weak, unadorned light bulb. There was only one door at the end; once green, its paint was now dry and flaking. Half glazed with grimy, bubbled glass, it shed a brighter light into the corridor but no images of what lay within. Ronnie pushed it, and it juddered alarmingly over swollen floorboards.

A foul-smelling pall of cheap tobacco smoke hung thickly in a foggy atmosphere redolent with the unhealthy warmth of un-washed bodies packed into a confined space.

'Shut that bleeding door.' Ronnie recognised Viv Richards' voice, but he couldn't see him. He did as Viv asked, scanning the packed room for Evan Powell. He spotted him at last, at the far end of the room. If he'd been a fly he could have walked across the ceiling to get to Evan, but as it was, he stood little chance of reaching him without disturbing the entire room. So much for discretion! Every available inch of space was filled with broken chairs, men's legs and bodies.

Evan didn't see Ronnie standing by the door. His attention was fixed on a chess set laid out on an upturned packing case between him and Charlie, but he was playing in a half-hearted, desultory fashion, preoccupied with thoughts of Maud.

'And I tell you we can't allow this man to hold a meeting in our Town Hall!' A fist crashed noisily on a rickety table.

'What do you want us to do then, Dai?' Viv sniped. 'Take over the Town Hall from the Council to keep him out?'

'You're worrying over nothing, Dai. Mosley won't come to Ponty,' a skeletally thin man shouted. 'The councillors might be crache, but they know what's what. I've heard tell if he wants the place, he's going to have to pay ten times the going rate. That'll be too much, even for the likes of him.'

'Four times,' a disembodied voice corrected. 'Our May works in the council offices, and she's had it from the horse's mouth.'

'If the man wants to hold his meeting badly enough, he'll pay the asking price whatever it is,' Evan commented as he moved his rook forward two places to threaten Charlie's queen.

'I agree with Evan,' Dai shouted angrily. 'And what I'm saying is, when he comes we've got to do something about it.'

'Like what?' Viv demanded truculently. 'What the hell do you expect the likes of us to do about a man like that?'

'Infiltrate his meeting,' Dai said darkly.

'Be reasonable, man,' Evan snapped. 'You can't infiltrate a public meeting.'

'You can when you're a marked man,' Dai crowed, proud of the outlaw status that his active, paid-up membership of the Communist party conferred on him.

'Here we go again,' Viv moaned. 'Communist goodies against Fascist baddies.'

'The Communists are the only ones with the ideology, dedication and strength of purpose to oppose the Fascists. And Oswald Mosley,' Dai lectured in soapbox mode, 'is Mussolini and Hitler's henchman. You heard the lady in the last meeting same as me. Mosley will heap the same indignities on British Jews as Hitler is heaping right now on the Jews in Germany.'

'Since when have you worried about the Jews, Dai?' Viv sneered.

'They're our brothers . . .' Dai began heavily.

'They're our rich bloody brothers if you ask me,' Viv spat a gob of phlegm to the floor. 'And they only help their own, never them that needs it like us. When did you last see a Jew with the arse hanging out of his pants like it hangs out of mine?'

'That's it, Viv, bring everything down to crude basics,' Dai jeered. 'People like you have sold the working classes down the river for years. As long as you're comfortable, with enough in your pocket to put food on the table, a dress on your wife's back, coal on the fire and a pint in your belly, you're all right Jack and to hell with the rest of the world. If Hitler marched into Ponty right now and gave you a job, you'd shout "Sieg Heil" along with the rest of the poor deluded sods, wouldn't you?'

'Too bloody right. And it's not just jobs that Hitler's giving out. I've heard he's building houses, proper houses with electric light upstairs, and bathrooms for his workers. And that he intends for every man to have a car – '

'Give over, Viv,' Evan said calmly, trying to defuse the argument. 'You sound like a Mosley pamphlet.'

'It could happen here,' Viv asserted defiantly. 'It could. If enough men go to Mosley's meetings, not to scoff but to listen, it could – '

'But at what cost?'

The voice was soft-spoken and quiet, but every man in the room fell silent. It wasn't often Charlie made his opinions known, but when he did, everyone listened.

'Well I for one don't care what it bloody costs to put a wage packet in my pocket,' Viv shouted furiously.

'The Jews . . .' Dai began fervently.

'To hell with the bloody Jews,' Viv screamed.

'They're people,' Dai yelled, rising to his feet. 'Same as you and me.'

'Let the buggers suffer.'

'Jews this week, miners next, Welshmen the week after?' Charlie looked steadily at Viv. 'You've been lucky in this valley. So far you've only lost your jobs.'

Charlie returned to his chessboard and made another move.

He'd never spoken about his past. Not once, although plenty had tried to worm more out of him. He'd never volunteered anything other than the information that he came from Russia. And few apart from the well-read miners like Evan realised just how vast that country was.

Taking advantage of the silence that followed Charlie's speech, Ronnie steamrollered his way past Viv's and Dai's abandoned chairs towards Evan.

'Mr Powell.' He extended his hand first to Evan, then Charlie.

'I've never seen you in here before, Ronnie.' Evan pushed his chair away from the chest. 'Your father sacked you?'

'Not yet,' Ronnie said gravely. 'But then, although it says unemployed over the door there's a fair few like you here Mr Powell, and Charlie, who work.'

'Not nights in our own café.' Charlie lifted his feet off the rungs of a stool, and thrust the stool at Ronnie. 'Seat?'

'Thanks.' Ronnie moved the stool between Evan and Charlie's chairs. Evan looked drawn, preoccupied, and Ronnie put it down to concern over Maud. 'I've been looking for you, Mr Powell,' he began awkwardly.

'Well now you've found me, boy, what do you intend to do with me?' Evan asked, irked by the interruption of his game. Ronnie said the one thing guaranteed to gain Evan's attention.

'I've just seen Maud.'

'You've seen her!' The sun rose on the dour landscape of Evan's face. 'How is she? Was she conscious? Did she say anything? Could she talk? Is she better than she was this morning?' The questions tumbled out faster than Ronnie could answer them.

'She was conscious, she said she felt better, we talked for a little while, but she seemed tired. Very tired,' Ronnie explained hesitantly.

'Only tired?' There was a look in Evan's eye that said he was still hoping for a miracle.

'Well, she's obviously very ill.' Ronnie pulled a packet of cigarettes out of his coat pocket and offered them round.

'They told us there was no visiting on the TB ward until Sunday. How did you manage to get in when you're not even family?' Evan asked suspiciously.

'I had to deliver some eggs to the ward. A present from the

Catholic Mothers' Union.' He'd told the lie so often he was beginning to believe it himself.

'It was good of them to think of the girls,' Evan commented sincerely, 'and it was good of you to come looking for me.'

'I really need to talk to you.' Ronnie held his cigarette in the flame of the match Charlie had produced. 'It's to do with Maud and it's important. Could we go somewhere private, Mr Powell? Perhaps the back bar of the Criterion, or the Hart?'

'All right.' Evan was intrigued, but he was not the kind of man to let his curiosity show. He pushed the wooden box that held the chess figures towards Charlie. 'Coming, mate?'

Charlie correctly read the uneasy expression on Ronnie's face. 'I promised Dai a game.'

'Come over later and have a pint?'

Charlie nodded as he began to reset the figures.

It was still raining, but the fine drizzle had given way to a sudden torrential downpour.

'Do you want to wait until it eases off?' Ronnie asked, turning up the collar of his coat.

'The one thing I've learned about Ponty is that you can wait for ever for that, boy. Tell me where you're going and I'll follow.'

'The New Inn is the nearest.'

'I'd be happier with the Criterion.'

'Criterion it is. Come on, let's make a dash for it.'

Ronnie knew he'd been stupid when he saw the expression on Evan's face as he carried the tray with two full pints and two whisky chasers over to their table. The beer would have been enough. Evan would have bought him another back and that would have been the end of it. Evan could probably just about afford to buy two beers. As it was, he had set a precedent Evan couldn't afford to follow.

'Barman owes me for a dinner he never paid for,' Ronnie lied glibly, 'so these are on the house.'

'Cheers.' Evan raised his glass to the bewildered barman.

Ronnie picked up his whisky glass, swirled it briskly in his hand and downed it in one. He sensed Evan's attention fixed on him as he turned to his beer.

'I've never seen you drink like that before,' Evan commented as he sipped his own beer slowly.

'I never have, but then I've never said anything like what I'm about to say before.'

'About Maud?'

'I love her, Mr Powell, and I want to marry her,' he announced with devastating simplicity.

Maud had been shocked, but Evan was doubly so. He stared at Ronnie, his face showing absolute disbelief. 'You what?' he said incredulously.

'I want to – '

'Yes I heard you, boy,' Evan said impatiently. 'I just wasn't sure I understood you. Maud's practically on her deathbed and you come to me . . .'

'Please, Mr Powell. All I'm asking is that you hear me out.'

'I've got one question before you say another word,' Evan said sharply. 'She's barely sixteen, you're twenty-seven. Exactly how long has this been going on?'

Ronnie almost blurted out 'since last night', then realised how that could be misconstrued.

'Nothing's been going on, Mr Powell,' he stated firmly. 'And without your permission, nothing will.'

'I'm relieved to hear it.'

'When I heard that Maud had been rushed into hospital this morning, I realised how much I loved her. I couldn't bear the thought that I'd left it too late to tell her how I felt. So I talked to Trevor – '

'Trevor Lewis, the doctor. About my daughter?'

'Yes – no . . . not about her,' Ronnie explained hastily, realising the more he said, the more he was putting his foot in it. 'I asked him about the treatments for lung disease. Her name was never mentioned between us,' he lied. 'Trevor told me about operations, cutting ribcages, deflating lungs – that sort of thing. I've lived in this town all my life, Mr Powell . . .'

'So have I,' Evan pointed out drily. 'And I think you'll grant that my life's been a little longer than yours.'

'I know how many young girls die of TB,' Ronnie continued unabashed. 'Trevor admitted that the treatments don't offer a lot of hope.'

'You don't have to spell out Maud's mortality to me,' Evan said fiercely, reaching for his whisky.

'Then Trevor said something else. He said that sometimes the rich send their children to clinics in Switzerland, where they receive special treatment, breathe clean, fresh air and eat nothing but wholesome dairy food.'

'Are you suggesting that if I had enough money to send Maud to Switzerland I would hold back? Do you think for one minute that Maud would be lying in the Central Homes if I had the money to keep her out of the place?' Evan demanded heatedly. 'Do you think the thought of sending her somewhere warm and healthy hasn't crossed my mind?'

'If it has, then you know there's a chance for Maud in what I'm suggesting,' Ronnie pleaded. 'Neither I, nor my family, have the kind of money you need to send Maud to a Swiss clinic, but I could raise enough to pay for Maud's and my own fare to my grandparents' farm in Italy. The air is just as pure in northern Italy as it is in Switzerland. Probably better,' he enthused with unintentional irony, 'because there's not so many consumptives breathing it. If you give Maud and me permission to marry, I'll take her there straight after the ceremony.'

'She can barely stand being carried downstairs and you want to drag her all the way to Italy!'

'I've thought about it. She won't be any worse off than she is lying in a hospital bed. I'll ask Aldo – he has the café by the bridge – ' he explained superfluously: Evan had known Aldo since before Ronnie was born, '– to drive us to Cardiff in his car. That way we can get a through train to London. I'll book a sleeper so Maud can lie down, then I'll get a taxi to take us from the train to Tilbury docks. If I book a cabin on the boat, all Maud will have to do is rest and sleep until we reach Calais. There's plenty of trains with sleepers on crossing the continent . . .'

'Have you thought what that little lot is going to cost?'

'Not as much as I have put away in the bank,' Ronnie said with as much dignity as he could muster. 'And once we're there, there'll be no problems. My grandmother and my aunt will take care of Maud, and I'll be around to do any heavy work like lifting . . .'

'Have you discussed any of this with Maud?' Evan questioned him bluntly.

Ronnie nodded. 'Yes.'

'And what did she say?'

'What you'd expect someone as unselfish as her to say. She pointed out that if I married her, I might not have a wife for very long.' Ronnie had weighed his words carefully before speaking. He knew he'd hit home when Evan didn't come back with an immediate reply.

'What about your life here?' Evan asked finally. 'Your family, your business. You're in the middle of opening up another café, aren't you?'

'A restaurant.' Even now Ronnie couldn't allow the slip to pass. 'But there's nothing here that means as much to me as Maud's life,' he said gravely.

'Does she love you?' Evan asked shrewdly.

'At the moment she's too ill to know what she wants.'

Evan finished his pint and picked up his and Ronnie's empty glasses. He went to the bar and brought back refills. He was too preoccupied to think of whisky chasers, Ronnie noticed thankfully.

'Let's see if I've got this straight,' Evan murmured as he sat down again. 'You're telling me that you've never courted, and if I'm guessing correctly, never even kissed my daughter.'

'That's right.'

Evan held up his hand to silence Ronnie. 'Yet you say you love her enough to give up everything you have, even your family, to take her half-way round the world in the hope of finding a cure for her.'

'That's right.'

'What does your father think of all this?'

'He doesn't know about it. Yet,' Ronnie stressed. 'But he will before the night's out,' he finished confidently. He shook two cigarettes out of his packet and handed one to Evan. He looked at the older man, seeking either approbation or blunt dismissal, but Evan's face remained composed, impassive. It was impossible to read what he was thinking in the set of his features, or the expression in his eyes.

'To get down to practicalities, what are you going to live on? You've said you have money, but however much you've got put away, I'll warrant you'll run out sooner rather than later, and you can't expect your family here to keep you when you no longer work in the cafés.'

'My grandfather has a farm. It supported my father and his brothers while they were growing up. It's still supporting him, my grandmother and my aunt, and once I start working there, I'm sure I'll be able to bring in enough extra to support Maud, and me.'

'I suppose your father left Italy to get away from the good living that the farm brought in,' Evan murmured caustically.

'It'll be enough,' Ronnie said calmly, refusing to allow Evan to rile him. 'As I said, there's only my grandparents and my father's sister living there. There's no able-bodied man around the place, I'm sure they'll welcome me with open arms.'

'You're sure? You don't really know?' Evan guessed.

'They're my family. They'll welcome me.'

'And Maud?'

'She'll be my wife, and that will make her family too.'

'You've already more or less admitted she doesn't love you.'

'Maud has agreed to go with me,' Ronnie pleaded. 'All we need is your permission to marry.'

'In a Catholic church?'

Ronnie looked Evan squarely in the eye. 'No. Maud's not a Catholic and there isn't time enough for a conversion.'

'But if she lives you'll want her to convert?'

'I couldn't give a hang what she is!' Ronnie exclaimed in exasperation. 'She can be a Hindu, Muslim or Buddhist, anything as long as she's alive. All I want for Maud is what she wants for herself. And a quick wedding,' he added firmly, 'so we can leave early next week. I don't think Maud should be left in that ward a minute longer than necessary.'

'Banns have to be called wherever you get married. Even a Registry Office. And that takes three weeks . . .'

'An exception can be made if the bride is ill. I talked to the Reverend Price about it this evening, after I saw Maud.'

'You're Catholic, Maud's Chapel and you went to an Anglican priest?' Evan smiled for the first time that evening.

'I wanted advice and I could hardly go to Father O'Kelly or John Joseph Bull. Both of them would have come up with a million obstacles to put in the way of things.'

'I suppose they would have. To you it's all so simple, isn't it? You totally disregard Maud's illness, marry her and carry her off to the hills of Italy where you hope, against all medical advice, for a miraculous recovery.'

'Isn't that all Maud's got left?' Ronnie said earnestly. 'Hope? Please Mr Powell, I'm begging you, let me marry her. This could be Maud's only chance of living . . .'

'That just what I am thinking of, Ronnie. Maud's life, or rather, what she's got left of it. Let's not mince words,' he said bleakly, looking at Ronnie over the rim of his glass. 'Maud's dying.' It hurt him almost as much to say those two words as it hurt Ronnie to hear them. 'She's dying and you want me to allow you to drag her across Europe on a wild-goose chase, that will inevitably end the same way it would if she stayed here. The difference being that if she died here she'd have her family and friends around her, while if she died in Italy . . .'

'You just said it Mr Powell. "If".'

'I said if, because she's just as likely to die on the boat or the train, and then what will you do, Ronnie? Tell me, what will you do?'

'I'd bring her body home to you, Mr Powell. I'd be devastated, but at least I'd know that I'd tried everything humanly possible to save her. Could you honestly say that, if you refuse me permission to even try?'

Even stared down into his half-empty glass.

'Please, Mr Powell,' Ronnie begged. 'Please, let me at least try to save her. I love her.'

Evan looked up into Ronnie's dark, brooding eyes. 'So do I,' he said slowly. 'So do I,' he repeated thoughtfully. 'Far too much to allow her to die amongst strangers.'

219

Chapter Twenty

'You're going to get me shot, Will Powell,' Tina complained as they sneaked around the corner of Danycoedcae Road, creeping close to the damp garden walls of the houses.

'No one is going to shoot you for going roller skating with Gina, you silly girl,' he murmured, squeezing her hand.

'When I come home without her?'

'For pity's sake,' he grumbled. 'You spent long enough plotting your story. You wanted a cup of chocolate in Jenny's house, and Gina didn't. Now what could be simpler than that?'

'Nothing as long as Gina remembers the story, and Papa doesn't interrogate her until she breaks.'

'You're not living in a gangster film, Tina.'

'You don't know Papa,' she retorted briskly. 'He asks more questions than the Spanish Inquisition. And generally gets better results,' she added gloomily.

'And you worry too much.' He pulled her into the shadows. 'Any chance of seeing you after work tomorrow?'

'You don't finish on the market until ten o'clock on a Saturday night.'

'More like eleven, but a fellow can live in hope.'

'Not that much.'

'Shoni's, three o'clock Sunday?'

'What if it's raining?'

'I'll bring an umbrella.'

'Fat lot of good that will do in Shoni's.'

'All you ever do is meef,' he complained playfully. 'Meef, meef, meef.'

'What on earth is meefing?'

'You should know, you do enough of it.' He was wondering whether he dare risk a kiss, when her eyes grew alarmingly round and large.

'Holy Mother of God,' she exclaimed. 'Here comes Ronnie!

See you.' She ran round the corner, just as Ronnie thundered his Trojan to a halt outside their front door.

'Close the café early?' she asked, trying desperately to look as though she hadn't a care in the world. He gazed straight past her, completely ignoring her, then ran up the short flight of steps to their front door.

'Serve him right if he tripped over his big flat feet,' she muttered under her breath, reaching the front door just in time for him to slam it in her face.

'Hey, what about me?' she shouted irritably, turning the key and walking in behind him. He was half-way down the passage. He didn't bother to glance back and look at her, let alone apologise. She shook her umbrella outside the door, propped it in the corner on the old tin tray that her mother put there for the purpose, threw her coat over the multitude balancing on the rack, and followed Ronnie down the long flagstoned passage that led from the front to the back of the house.

The radio was blaring into the hot, steamy kitchen. Friday had been her mother's day for making Saturday's fish soup out of the heads and tails of Friday's dinner for as long as she could remember, and the smell of herrings lingered tartly in the air.

'Hello everyone,' she shouted, going to the biscuit barrel and helping herself to a home-made oatmeal crunch. Gina looked up from where she was teaching thirteen-year-old Maria and ten-year-old Stephania how to apply lipstick, and raised her eyebrows. She was dying to ask Tina if William Powell had kissed her, but knew her questions would have to wait until their sisters slept. Nine-year-old Alfredo and six-year-old Robert swept past, sword-fighting with a pair of ill-matched wooden kitchen spoons. Her mother, oblivious to the noise and chatter, smiled absently, continuing to mend a great, long tear in eight-year-old Theresa's school skirt.

'Where's Papa?' Ronnie demanded as he emerged from the washhouse. They all turned towards him, Tina and her mother both noticing a keener edge to his voice than usual.

'He's next door. He and Mr Morris are drilling a hole so they can pass a wire through the wall to set up a wireless speaker for them,' Maria explained. 'Papa thought it would be nice for them to listen to ours. After all, it's on all day.'

'Is everything all right in the café?' Mrs Ronconi shouted above the laughter that greeted Arthur Askey's latest joke. Something in the expression on Ronnie's face made her uneasy.

'Everything's fine, Mama.' He glared at the milling children. 'Everyone under sixteen to bed,' he ordered brusquely.

'Aw Ronnie!' Maria, Stephania, Theresa, Robert and Alfredo chorused in protest.

'This finishes at nine, Ronnie, that's only five minutes. Can't we hear the end of it?' Alfredo begged, knowing that where Ronnie was concerned, his pleading would hold far more weight than that of the girls.

'None of you can hear it above the din you're making,' Ronnie observed unrelentingly. 'Come on, bed. Now!' He stood over them as they trooped mutinously to the washhouse in single file. When he heard the tap running and the sounds of teeth being brushed, he left. A moment later the front door banged shut.

'The minute the show ends,' their mother warned as Alfredo poked his head around the washhouse door, letting in an ice-cold draught of air.

'Promise, Mama. Cross my heart,' Alfredo beamed.

Ronnie opened the Morris' door and walked through to their kitchen.

'It's only me Mr Morris,' he called out as he stepped into the room, which was considerably colder and less cosy than the kitchen in his house. 'Is Papa here?'

'Papa is here,' his father answered from the depths of the cupboard that filled the alcove next to the range, where he was crouched, trying to bore a hole. 'And you're just the man we want. Come here and hold this bit steady while I drill. You wouldn't believe how solid this wall is.'

'Yes I would.' Ronnie went to the cupboard and extracted the drill from his father's hand. 'You've picked the wrong place, Papa,' he smiled. 'You won't do it there, you can't see what you're doing. Here, let me. Near the ceiling will be easier.' He picked up a scarred wooden chair, positioned it on the lino near the communal wall, climbed on it and, holding the bit steady in the crack between wall and ceiling, proceeded to drill steadily. 'Get a cloth please, Papa,' he shouted, as a stream of black mortar

222

poured out of the hole he was making. Mr Morris rushed out the back and returned with a ragged pair of pants.

'I always keep the old clothes, especially the cotton underwear,' Mrs Morris wheezed from her easy chair next to the range. 'They make such good dusters.'

'Yes they do, Mrs Morris. Absorbent too,' Ronnie the knowledgeable café owner called out cheerfully. He persevered, working at a steady pace. 'Have you a drill with a longer bit?' he asked.

'I don't think so.' Mr Morris raked over the few odds and ends of tools that he kept proudly in a wooden box that his eldest son had made in woodwork class before he'd gone off to join the army.

Ronnie balanced the drill in one hand, wiped his eyes with the other, pushed forward, and almost fell off the chair.

'Steady,' his father shouted.

'We're through.'

'There, what did I tell you?' His father rubbed his hands and beamed at the old couple. 'Now all you have to do is put that speaker on top of the dresser. We'll poke the wire from it through the wall, and our Angelo can connect it when he gets back from the café.'

'It's very good of you to go to all this trouble, Mr Ronconi,' Mrs Morris gushed. 'We never thought we'd have radio in our own kitchen, did we Joe?' she smiled up at her husband.

'Never . . .'

'What are you doing out of the café?' Mr Ronconi demanded of his son, suddenly realising that he was home at a peculiar hour. 'No trouble, is there?'

'No trouble,' Ronnie replied evenly. 'Here, you don't have to wait until our Angelo gets home, Mr Morris. Pass me that wire, I'll push it through, go into our kitchen and connect it there.'

'Just in time for the evening theatre show,' Mr Ronconi smiled. 'Some of them are really good. Last week's was about a haunted room in an old house.'

'Ooh,' Mrs Morris squealed. 'Just think of it, Joe, theatre in our own back kitchen.'

Mr Ronconi looked around. Ronnie had already gone. 'I'll just go and see if Ronnie needs a hand,' he said as he backed out of the door. He could stand almost anything except being thanked for his kindness. 'When that speaker starts working, just knock on the wall. Then we'll know to leave the wires alone.' Following his son out of the door, he returned to his own kitchen where Ronnie was putting the finishing touches to a Heath Robinson conglomeration of wires at the back of the radio.

'There, that should do it,' Ronnie announced. 'Do you want to go and check?'

'I told them to knock if they could hear it.' As if to confirm his words a loud bang came from the other side of the wall.

The younger children, hands and faces washed, teeth cleaned and hair brushed, trooped out of the washhouse and stood in a line waiting for their father and mother to kiss them goodnight. Much to Robert's disgust, Ronnie patted him on the head. He adored his big brother, but he hated being patronised. Ronnie, however, was too lost in his own thoughts to notice Robert's squirmings. He was preoccupied with his parents' frequent hints that he should marry. If he'd been about to tell them that he wanted to marry one of the daughters of the Italian community he knew that his parents would have greeted the news ecstatically. He also knew that given time, and conversion to the faith, he could possibly have talked them into accepting Alma as a daughter-in-law. But not Maud. At Gina's age, she was too young. Her religion – her illness – the hint of scandal that still clung to her sister for all of Bethan's marriage to a doctor – taken separately he might have overcome one of the obstacles. Put together, they were simply too much.

When the last of the younger children had raced down the cold passage and up the stairs, he turned to Tina and Gina.

'You two going to sit there all night?'

'It's too early to go to bed,' Tina pouted. 'I'm nineteen . . .'

'And I want to talk to Papa and Mama in private,' Ronnie countered stiffly.

Tina went white. 'If you want to talk to Papa and Mama I have every right to be here,' she began haughtily.

'You, Madam, have no right to listen in . . .'

'If it's about me, I have every right to hear.'

'And what makes you think Ronnie is about to say anything concerning you?' her father enquired suspiciously.

Caught in a trap of her own making, Tina turned on her father and brother like a cornered wildcat. 'You think I'm stupid?' she asked furiously.

'Must we answer that?' Ronnie sighed wearily.

'You think I haven't seen you,' she rounded on her brother, 'sneaking around after me. You followed me tonight, didn't you? Didn't you?' she screamed. 'That's why you want to talk to Papa and Mama. Well I'm a grown woman, not a naughty little girl. I'm old enough to make up my own mind as to who I see, where I go, what I do . . .'

Terrified by the inevitable consequences of Tina's outburst, and the thunderous expression on her father's face, Gina would have sidled out of the door if she could have. But Ronnie blocked her path. She stepped back, and stood alongside her mother, who sat rooted to her chair.

'And what do you think Ronnie saw that was so terrible?' her father shouted, pushing his face very close to Tina's. 'What? Come on, tell me. What have you been doing that you don't want your own father and mother to know about?' He folded his hands inside his arms as if he couldn't trust himself to keep them off her. 'Did you, or did you not go roller skating in Mill Street with Gina?' he asked coldly. 'Or were you lying?'

'She was in Mill Street with me,' Gina dared to interrupt, gabbling hastily. 'She stopped off to have a drink of chocolate with Jenny on the way home, I didn't want to go in with them.' Gina's explanation sounded like a well-rehearsed speech at a children's school concert.

'She was home before nine, so what's the problem?'

Tina's mouth dropped open. She couldn't believe her brother Ronnie had said that.

'If roller skating with Gina and a chocolate with Jenny Griffiths was all she'd done she wouldn't have screamed at you, or be blushing the way she is. She's been out with a boy. That's it, isn't it Tina?' her father shrieked. 'You've been sneaking around with someone behind my back. The same way your sister Laura sneaked around with that, that – '

'Husband,' Ronnie broke in quietly. 'Papa – '

'Papa nothing,' Mr Ronconi raged. 'Tina, what's been going on?'

'Nothing.' Whiter than Ronnie had ever seen her before, Tina swayed on her feet.

'You've been seeing that William Powell, haven't you?' her father raged.

'No!' Tina lied defiantly.

'I don't believe you.'

'Papa, you're calling your own daughter a liar,' his wife remonstrated.

Tina's bottom lip trembled and she began to cry.

'There! There, I knew it!' Papa Ronconi began a swift ascent into one of his notorious, and amongst the younger members of his family, much feared, rages.

'All I did was walk home with him,' Tina sobbed tearfully. 'It was the first time ever. We didn't do anything wrong . . .'

'You did something wrong by speaking to him. Just look at you, just look . . .' he babbled, his voice breaking into incoherence.

'Papa I . . . I . . .'

'I forbid you. I absolutely forbid you,' Papa Ronconi's face turned purple. 'I forbid you to see that boy, and what do you do? You go sneaking behind my back, you . . . you slut!'

'Papa!' Ronnie exclaimed angrily.

'Tomorrow you pack your bags and you go to your grandmother in Bardi. She'll see you married off to a decent Italian boy within the month. I'll have no daughter of mine . . .'

Ronnie looked at Tina and jerked his head sharply towards the door.

'. . . Don't you dare leave this room!' his father screamed, beside himself with rage.

'Let her go, Papa,' Ronnie said quietly, with what seemed to Tina amazing courage. 'In a minute I'm going to give you a lot more to shout about than Tina has.'

Evan pushed his way through the crowded passage of the Graig Hotel until he reached the hatch that served as bar to the back rooms. He pulled all the money he had out of his pocket, spread it on his palm and stared at it. He had just enough for two pints, with sixpence left over for the hire of a cart tomorrow, no more. And he knew there was nothing left in the old, cracked Doulton teapot that Elizabeth kept on the top shelf in the kitchen. Throwing all sense of caution to the wind, he handed over everything except the precious sixpence to the barman.

'Bitter please, Albert.'

'Your usual?' the barman asked.

'Two pints.' Evan carried them through to the half-empty back room where Charlie was sitting staring into the fire.

'Cheers, mate.' Charlie picked up his pint and supped it slowly. He'd bought the first pint they'd drunk in the Graig, and he knew Evan had drunk a pint or two earlier, with Ronnie. One was usually Evan's limit on a weekday, so he was obviously troubled by something. But Charlie knew that if Evan wanted to talk about it, he would do so in his own good time.

Will glanced in through the door. Seeing his uncle and Charlie, he walked over to them.

'Pint?' Charlie asked, putting his hand in his pocket.

'No thanks,' Will shook his head. 'I only came in to see if anyone was about. I'm going down the gym to meet Eddie. We'll probably wait until it's time for Haydn to finish, then pick up some chips on the way home.'

'Overtime burning a hole in your pocket?' Charlie smiled.

'No.' The truth of the matter was, Will couldn't wait to tell someone he'd finally walked Tina home. And he was hoping that three heads would be better than one when it came to finding a solution to the obstacles that stood in their way: principally Papa Ronconi and Ronnie. 'Tell Di I'll see her in the shop tomorrow, Uncle Evan,' he said as he went out.

'I'll do that.' Evan went back to his pint. Charlie continued to sup his and study the flames that played between the glowing embers in the fire.

'Ronnie went into the Central Homes and saw Maud tonight,' Evan volunteered eventually.

'So he said in the club,' Charlie murmured.

'So he did.' Evan put down his pint. He screwed up his face thoughtfully. 'Damned fool!' he swore absently.

'Did he say how Maud was?' Charlie asked, wondering if Evan's black mood had been caused by a worsening in her condition.

'Conscious but no better, from what I can work out. Ronnie wants to marry her,' Evan said suddenly. He looked suspiciously at Charlie. 'You don't seem surprised.'

'I thought it might have been something like that when he came into the club looking for you.'

'She's dying,' Evan said bitterly.

'We're all dying.'

'Some sooner than others.'

'Ronnie's an intelligent man. I'm sure he knows that.'

Something in the tone of Charlie's voice made Evan look him squarely in the eye. 'You think I should let him marry her?' he demanded incredulously.

'Provided Maud wants to marry him, I can't see any objection,' Charlie said evenly. 'He's a hard worker, he has a share in two cafés, and he's busy building up a third. I would have thought that any father in the town would be proud to have him for a son-in-law.'

'The idiot wants to give up all he owns to take her to Italy.'

'Italy!' This time Charlie had the grace to look surprised.

'He thinks the air in the mountains will cure her.'

'It might,' Charlie agreed cautiously.

'Do you really think there's a chance? Trevor Lewis more or less told me that she's pretty far gone.'

'All I know is doctors aren't God. My sister had lung disease. My mother took her to live with our uncle in the Ural Mountains. She died in the end, but at least she had ten years of life she wouldn't have had if she'd stayed with us.'

Evan knew better than to question the veracity of Charlie's story.

'So you think I should let him take her?'

'That's your decision to make, not mine. All I'm saying is that sometimes it works, and sometimes it doesn't.' He shrugged his massive shoulders and finished his pint. 'And then again he must think a lot of her to want to give up his share in the cafés. Last one for the road?' Charlie held out his hand for Evan's glass. Normally Evan would have protested about the uneven rounds, but this time he handed over his glass.

'What would you do if you were Maud's father?' he asked seriously.

'If I was Maud's father,' Charlie said gravely, 'I think I'd begin by talking to Maud.'

'Giacomo please,' Ronnie's mother begged, calling him by the baptismal name that was hardly ever heard, even in his own family. She was standing in the kitchen as far as she could get from the two men. She had seen her husband angry many times, but had never been unduly perturbed. His type of anger was typical of many Italians: quick to rise, and quick to blow over – until now. This anger was different. He'd never quarrelled so vehemently with any of the children before, and for the first time since she'd met him, twenty-eight years before, she could see real and bitter pain beneath his anger.

Their eldest son was special – to both of them: the only one of their children born in Italy, in her father-in-law's farmhouse in the tiny, primitive, backwater hamlet outside Bardi. Her husband had stayed with her until the birth, then he'd left her for five long years, while he went to Wales to work in his brother's café. He'd promised to send for her the minute he made enough money to provide a comfortable home for her, and his son. But when she waved him off on the bus that left the square in Bardi, neither of them had imagined that it would take so long for him to get established.

While she'd sat and waited in her father's small spartan farmhouse, all she'd had to remind her of her young, passionate husband was her baby, and the monthly money orders he sent, which, no matter how carefully she counted them, never quite reached the figure needed to pay for her and their child's fare to Wales.

She'd cashed the orders in Bardi, spent sparingly and saved prodigiously, and in the meantime her son grew into a fine boy, and as his grandfather had said, 'old beyond his years'.

Giacomo had been born old. When the tickets to Wales finally came, it had been five-year-old Giacomo who'd helped her pack, deciding what was to go and what was to be left behind. Giacomo who'd dried her eyes when the grandparents and maiden aunt had wailed at their leaving. Giacomo who'd taken charge of their tickets, checking the train times, and pronouncing the strange place names that he'd made one of their neighbours (who'd been to Wales and returned) repeat time and again to make sure that he'd got it right. And even after they'd arrived in the two tiny rooms that were their first home, it had been Giacomo who'd helped his father mix the ice cream and stock up the handcart every morning. Giacomo who'd rushed home from school every day to wash dishes in their first café in High Street. Giacomo who'd helped her husband to make his first serious decision to borrow from their uncle to buy the second cafe on the Tumble. Giacomo who was, even now, steering the plans through for their first restaurant . . . Giacomo – always Giacomo.

She couldn't bear to see her husband and much beloved eldest son at loggerheads. The pain was vicious, cruel, almost physical.

'You want to throw up your whole life, everything we've built here,' her husband raged and ranted at Ronnie, 'for a sick girl. A dying girl!'

'I love her,' Ronnie said directly, as though those three words were enough to explain everything.

'You can't remember Bardi . . .' his father began earnestly.

'I remember Bardi,' Ronnie replied. 'Probably better than you. After all, I left it later,' he pointed out drily.

'But this girl. She's not Italian,' his mother said reasonably, as though she were afraid of her words hurting him. 'She's not even healthy, Giacomo. Listen to me, please. I had a brother who died of the lung disease, but he died after he gave it to my sister, and then she died . . .'

'Mama, please don't cry.' Ronnie wrapped his arm around his plump, diminutive mother. 'I want to get married, not die,' he smiled.

'What makes you think that Bardi is such a healthy place?' his father shouted scornfully. 'There's less money there than here. There's no work, except back-breaking farm work. The most you can make is enough food to eat. No coins to jingle in your pocket. It's poverty-stricken. In summer there's nothing but flies . . .'

'At least you can be sure of having a summer in Bardi,' Ronnie retorted.

'Surer than you can be of having food on the table,' his father taunted. 'There were times when we didn't have enough to eat. Why do you think your uncle and I left home?'

'There were a lot more of you in those days, Papa. There's only your father, mother and Aunt Theresa there now. With a young able-bodied fellow like me around the place, we'll soon produce more than enough,' Ronnie asserted forcefully.

'You?' his father ridiculed. 'You? What do you know about farming?'

'About as much as you did about the café business when you came to Wales.' He waited for his father's explosive temper to cool to the point where he could make himself heard again. 'From what I remember of farming in Bardi, the main qualities needed are hard work, brute strength, and the ability to stand foul smells.'

His father's features hardened to a stern, intractable mask. 'You go, and I cut you off with a penny. You will no longer be my son. You will not be welcome in this house. You will not darken my door again. I will give you nothing. Do you understand me? Nothing!' He spat into the fire. 'You leave this house with this girl, and to me you are dead.'

'I am sorry, Papa. I have no choice to make. I am going to marry her, and take her to Bardi.'

His mother burst into tears.

'Go ahead. Go,' his father sneered. 'What will the pair of you do for money? I know that the Powells have none . . .'

'I've worked in the business for thirteen years.'

'You've been fed and clothed. You won't see a penny more than you've already had.'

'The Trojan's in my name. I'll sell it,' Ronnie threatened. 'Even a quick sale will bring in enough for two tickets to Bardi.'

'The van belongs to the business,' his father shrieked.

'It doesn't. I bought it in my name. And I hold the logbook.' Ronnie matched his father's antagonistic glare. 'And I wasn't so dull as not to put a little aside,' he lied, wondering just how much today's takings would be. He'd have to get down to the café quick. The minute he left here.

'You, you dared to rob me? Your own father – '

'No, just took some wages.'

His father knew when he was beaten. Terrified of losing Ronnie, and having got nowhere with his bullying tactics, he tried a different approach.

'Please Ronnie, I'm asking you, begging you, please don't give up. Not now, not when everything is going so well. The new restaurant . . .'

Ronnie found this approach much harder to deal with. 'Tony knows as much as me,' he said simply.

'Tony is destined to be a priest.'

'Not the Tony I know. Ask him what he thinks of girls.'

'Girls!'

'Papa, it doesn't matter,' Ronnie said wearily. 'I didn't come

231

here to fight. I came to tell you that I will be working this weekend, after that no more. I intend to marry Maud as soon as I can. And if we can get tickets we'll be gone by Monday.'

'Then go and be damned for it!' His father turned his back on him.

'Giacomo!' His mother flung herself at him. He kissed her and helped her back into her chair, then opened the kitchen door.

'Where are you going?' his father screeched.

'To pack my clothes,' Ronnie replied. 'I presume that I can take them. They won't fit anyone else.'

'Five minutes. That's all you have, then I call the police and have you thrown out.'

Chapter Twenty-One

Tina and Gina were sitting on the edge of the double bed they shared. The three younger girls were huddled together in the other bed in the room, their eyes wide, fearful at the sounds of the argument coming from the kitchen below. Tina'd left the door open so she could listen to every word that was being said. And never in her life had she felt so much sympathy for her eldest brother.

She watched Ronnie walk upstairs. He passed the door to the girls' room as he went into the box room. It was the smallest room in the house, but until that night he'd been able to call it all his own. As the oldest child by nearly six years, his parents felt he was entitled to a room of his own, even if it was only six foot six inches by five foot.

'Ronnie.' Tina dried her eyes before she crept to the door of his room. She watched as he went to the narrow old wardrobe that scraped alongside the bottom of his small bed and lifted down the same battered cardboard suitcase he had struggled with when he had left Bardi at the age of five. He opened the wardrobe door and began packing his shirts, pants and vests, cramming them into the case anyhow, just as they fell.

'Ronnie, where are you going?' she whispered, as he picked up his one good linen skirt.

'For tonight, the café, afterwards, we'll see.'

'Ronnie, will you and Papa make up?'

'Not this time,' he smiled grimly.

'Is it true?' she ventured. 'Do you really love Maud Powell?'

'Yes,' he answered shortly. Strange, he hadn't minded talking about his feelings to Maud, Mr Powell or Trevor, but Tina was different. She was his kid sister, and he very much minded talking about his personal feelings to her.

'If you love Maud,' she swallowed hard in an effort to gain courage, 'then you must understand what I feel for Will.'

'I'm not sure I can approve of Will Powell,' he said without a

233

trace of humour. 'He's not steady enough to marry a sister of mine.'

'And Maud's too sick and too young to marry anyone,' Tina countered smartly.

'Snap.' He pushed the last of his clothes into the case and looked around. There was his alarm clock: he picked that up and dumped it on top of the clothes. Three books on the windowsill. He looked at them: there was a Bible his aunt had given him on his confirmation, a prayer book his mother had bought him one Christmas, and a western Tony had lent him.

'Give this back to Tony.' He handed Tina the western, and packed the other two books.

She clung to the book, pressing it hard against her chest. 'You're really going Ronnie, aren't you?' she asked, the enormity of what was happening just beginning to sink in.

'Oh yes.' He picked up the case and buttoned his jacket. Then he looked at her. 'I'm really going,' he said slowly.

She clung to him and began to cry again.

'Come on, no tears. Pull yourself together and help Tony, he'll be the one to make all the decisions from now on.'

'But he's going to be a priest!'

'When Papa begins to talk to you again, suggest that he tries to keep that one for Robert. He'd better not try Angelo or Alfredo. I'm afraid they're too hot-blooded. Like him.'

She heard him walk along the landing and whisper goodbyes at both the girls' and the boys' bedroom doors. Then the front door slammed. The Trojan started up. She was still standing there in the empty bedroom when her mother came up moments later. They sank on to his bed together and cried. More for themselves than for Ronnie.

Since his one brief, disastrous appearance on stage, Haydn had found his work at the Town Hall unbearable. The title 'callboy' meant a lot more than simply calling the acts to go on stage. Most of his time was spent clearing the dressing rooms of accumulated rubbish, buying evening papers, and running errands for the 'stars', collecting discarded props and making sure they were put back where they could be found for the next performance. And then, when the show was over and the performers and manager were relaxing, he and the rest of the staff under the direction of the under-manager had to comb through the rows of seats, checking them for cleanliness and things left behind.

The routine he'd so found exciting when he first worked in the Town Hall now became dull, boring and tedious in the extreme. The smell of greasepaint palled until the merest hint of it in the atmosphere made him nauseous. The sounds of the orchestra that had once set his pulse racing and foot tapping, now clattered, deafening and discordant, in his ears. Each and every day he came to loathe his work more and more, the loathing born of the realisation that there was no prospect of ever climbing as high as even the lowly ranks of the chorus. This was it! His life! All he had. All he was ever likely to have, unless he lost his job and sank into the mass of unemployed.

Dreams shattered, there were days when he could barely summon energy enough to drag himself out of bed. Ambition, aspirations, strength – all dissipated into a mood of sullen moroseness. There were no light spots, no highlights left to brighten his days. Not even Jenny. Whenever he walked past the shop he was tempted to linger, go in and find out if she'd talk to him, but fear of rejection always made him cross the road. He knew his family were beginning to look at him sideways. Not his parents – they were both too wrapped up in Maud's illness to notice anyone, or anything – but the others had observed and remarked on what William termed 'his departure from the land of the living'.

He had never found the curtailment of his social life by work so irksome. But even on those nights when he could have gone into any one of the half a dozen pubs in Pontypridd that dared to breach the strict code of licensing hours, he didn't. Occasionally he met the landlords or barmaids of the pubs he'd frequented, and they pleaded with him to return to sing, insisting that everyone was missing him. He suspected their motives, steeped in the belief that after his last fiasco people only wanted to hear him to have a good laugh at his poor performance and failed ambitions. He invariably smiled and told them he might call in later, but never did. It was easier than announcing that he'd decided to give up singing – permanently.

The first Friday night that Maud spent in hospital dragged, worse than any other. He looked around the Town Hall and tried desperately to think of a way out, both for her and himself. He was convinced that money could buy anything – even a cure for his sister – but short of robbing a bank he didn't know where to begin. If he'd studied harder in school he might have got a scholarship out of the boys' grammar school to go to university – then he remembered his father on short time and realised that even if he'd won a scholarship that had paid his fees, he wouldn't have been able to manage his living expenses. And as he was only twenty he wouldn't even be qualified yet, which meant he'd still be poverty-stricken, and of no real use to Maud at all.

'Move it, Haydn,' one of the stagehands shouted, pushing a scenery float towards him. He caught it just before it toppled on its side. Shuffling round the back curtain, they pushed it out of the way. 'Only the floor check to do and we can go home,' Fred the stagehand mumbled through his toothless gums.

Haydn stared dully at Fred's coarse, whiskery face that rarely saw a razor, noticed his broad back, curved and bowed from lifting too many heavy weights over too many years, studied his clothes, old, stained and musty smelling from lack of washing. Would this be him forty years from now? There was no one around now who could say what Fred had looked like when he'd started in the Town Hall. Perhaps he'd even wanted to go on stage, like him.

'Did you ever think about the stage, Fred?' he asked suddenly.

'You say something, Haydn?' Fred cocked his head to one side, turning his good ear towards Haydn.

'Did you ever want to go on stage, Fred?' Haydn shouted.

'Oh ay,' Fred's face split into a large, gummy grin. 'When I was a nipper, like, that's why I took a job here.'

Haydn picked up a torch from the box where they were kept between houses, slammed open the door into the auditorium, and stepped down, ready for the search. That did it. He'd have to leave. He didn't know how, or where, he only knew he had to go.

The search seemed to take three times as long as usual. By the end of it he was hot, sweaty and his hands were sticky from the discarded chewing gum, toffee wrappers and other unmentionables he'd picked up. He washed in the grimy staff toilet that never received more than a quick, cursory wipe-over; the cleaners always left it until last, knowing that the manager would never deign to enter it to check their handiwork.

He hung away his uniform jacket, bell-boy cap, collar and bow tie in the cubicle that held staff uniforms. Tying a muffler over his collarless shirt, he shrugged his arms into his own jacket and rammed his well-worn cap on his head. The night air was cold and damp, the street wet underfoot, but for the first time in days it had stopped raining.

'Haydn?'

He looked up. William and Eddie were waiting for him.

'How about a drink in the Horse and Groom?' Will grinned.

'I don't much feel like a drink.' Head down, Haydn walked on. Eddie and Will had to run to keep up with him.

'We called in Ronconi's, and Ronnie told us he'd seen Maud tonight,' Eddie burst out.

'Ronnie Ronconi?' Haydn paused in amazement.

'Apparently he delivered some eggs to the ward for the Catholic Mothers' Union,' William explained. 'He said Maud was awake, and not feeling too bad at all.'

'So you see we have got something to celebrate after all,' Eddie chirped.

'I'll celebrate the day she comes out of that place,' Haydn growled.

'Bad night?' Eddie ventured sympathetically.

'No worse than any other.'

Eddie and Will exchanged glances behind Haydn's back.

'Come on, a pint will do us all good, and it's on me,' Eddie chivvied.

'You come into money?' Haydn asked.

'In a way. I worked on Charlie's stall today.'

'And he has the makings of a fine butcher,' William added generously. 'Come on Haydn, don't be a stick-in-the-mud,' Will added his powers of persuasion to Eddie's. 'We thought if we went to the Horse and Groom we might see one of the porters, or even a nurse finishing the late shift. And you never know, they might have something to add to what Ronnie told us.'

Ashamed of his rage, Haydn nodded agreement. He'd been so wrapped up in what he saw as his own problems, he'd forgotten that Eddie and William were fond of Maud too.

The Horse and Groom, situated at the foot of the Graig hill in

High Street, was the sort of pub that only really came to life after hours. It was packed out, and Eddie had to fight his way to the bar. A chorus of voices greeted their arrival, demanding a song from Haydn. After his fifth curt refusal, he heard someone whisper that his sister was lying seriously ill in the Central Homes; after that he was left alone. He went to a quiet corner and leant his elbow on one of the standing-height marble and iron tables, the only one that was free. William looked around, searching for a familiar face. Eventually he found one.

'Glan?' he shouted. 'Just the man we want to see. Spare us a minute?' he asked, conveniently forgetting all the time he could quite cheerfully have punched Glan's head off his shoulders.

'I'll be there now.' Smelling a free pint in the air, Glan picked up his half-empty glass and pushed his way through the throng to join them.

'Have you heard how Maud is?' Will asked quietly as soon as Glan was within earshot.

'Heard she's bad,' Glan said bluntly.

'Nothing else?' Will asked hopefully.

'Just that. We brought a body down from her ward tonight. But it wasn't her. About the same age, though, and from what the nurse said, next bed.'

There was a supercilious smirk on Glan's face that Will longed to wipe off.

'Is there anyone here who works on her ward?' Haydn asked.

'Don't know of any nurses who come into this bar. A few go into the Ladies only room, but not after hours.' Glan downed most of his pint, still hoping for a free one. 'And not many porters go up to the TB ward. There's not much call for us unless there's a body that needs shifting like tonight, or a patient needs an operation. And because they operate off the wards we don't always go up for that. I'll try to find out more for you tomorrow, if you like,' he offered, pointedly twiddling his empty glass.

'I'd be grateful if you would,' Haydn replied.

'You're looking a bit down tonight,' Glan commented tactlessly.

'Anyone would, the length of time Eddie's taking to get our beer,' Will broke in quickly.

'You drinking with your brother?'

'Any reason why I shouldn't?' Haydn asked warily.

'Well, all I can say is you're more forgiving than I would be in your shoes,' Glan said airily. 'But then there's no accounting for people, and as my father says, you Powells are a strange lot.'

'What are you gabbling about?' William demanded irritably, sensing one of Glan's infamous 'stirs' coming.

'Haydn's girlfriend, of course.'

'I haven't got a girlfriend,' Haydn countered angrily, ignoring the hard look that William was giving him.

'Well you and Jenny Griffiths did go on for a long time and we all supposed – '

'Then you all supposed wrong, Glan Richards.' Haydn looked around for Eddie. All he wanted was his pint so he could drink it and get out of the pub.

'So I see. Or at least I did after I saw her wrapping herself around Eddie tonight at the top of Factory Lane. Honest to God, I thought he was going to eat her. It's just as well she took him into her back yard when she did. If she hadn't they might have both been arrested. Old Mrs Evans' eyes were nearly popping out of her head as it was. What's the betting she'll start a rumour on the Graig tomorrow that we'll see a shotgun wedding before too many months have passed?' he finished maliciously.

'Whose shotgun wedding?' Eddie lined three full pints up on the table.

'You and Jenny Griffiths.' Haydn's voice was low. Soft. 'Glan was just telling us how he'd seen the pair of you wrapped around each other at the top of Factory Lane tonight.'

Eddie looked up guiltily, and that look told Haydn everything he hadn't known, and a great deal more besides. Picking up one of the pint glasses Eddie had just placed on the table, he threw its contents full in Eddie's face.

'Haydn!' Eddie ran out of the door after him. William was half-way out of the room behind them when he remembered the beer – and Glan. He picked up both remaining glasses and drank them, one straight after the other in quick succession. Wiping his mouth with the back of his hand, he turned to Glan.

'I'll not forget this in a hurry, Glan Richards,' he said furiously, then followed his cousins.

Eddie was shouting Haydn's name as he ran up the Graig hill, beer trickling through his hair, down his face and into his clothes. He caught up with his brother outside the Temple Chapel.

'I didn't mean for it to happen,' he pleaded. 'Neither of us did. It's just that she was by herself, and I took her home – '

'She was my girlfriend.' Until that moment Haydn hadn't admitted even to himself just how much he wanted her back.

'That's just it, Haydn,' Eddie protested. 'She *was* your girl-friend. I wouldn't have taken her home if you'd still been going out with her.'

An upstairs window banged open in the terrace across the road and an irate male voice yelled, 'For Christ's sake keep it down out there! Some people have to get up in the morning.'

'She said you were through,' Eddie whispered miserably. 'I didn't go looking for her. We just bumped into one another in the roller hall in Mill Street. It was getting late and she asked me to take her home . . .'

'And you muscled in,' Haydn said furiously.

'It wasn't like that,' Eddie protested.

'Glan said you kissed her . . . and more. Did you?' he demanded savagely. 'Did you?' he repeated wildly.

Shamefaced, Eddie looked down at his boots. Haydn lashed out, catching him off guard. As Eddie fell on to the soaking wet pavement it was as much as he could do to remember that Haydn was his brother. Anyone else and he would have been up on his feet and after them before they'd gone six yards.

Ronnie moved restlessly around the café until closing time, superficially busy but in fact accomplishing very little. Customers spoke to him, told him what they wanted, paid their bills, and he managed to misunderstand at least two out of every three orders. Alma, uncertain what was going on in Ronnie's mind but fearing the worst, flounced round the tables in a foul mood. Tony and Angelo, who were working behind the counter and in the kitchen, gave both her and Ronnie as wide a berth as possible in between checking the clock. Despite the brisk trade, the evening dragged slowly for both of them until eleven-thirty, when Ronnie finally locked the door.

Turning his back on Alma, who'd already begun to pile chairs on tables and sweep the floor, he shut himself in the kitchen with an apprehensive Tony and Angelo, and told them as much about the quarrel he'd had with his father as he reasonably could without mentioning Maud's name; finally he announced that if all went well he'd be leaving Pontypridd for Bardi within the week. Ignoring their shell-shocked faces, he handed them their coats and told them to leave.

Wondering if something had happened between Ronnie and Alma, Tony tried to talk to her on his way out. But all he got for his trouble was a brusque, 'How the hell should I know what's going on with your brother?'

Ronnie saw his brothers out and pulled down the shutters. Alma finished the floor, and went to get her coat. Ronnie waylaid her on her way out.

'I'd like to talk to you,' he said quietly. She saw that he'd taken the chairs down from the table closest to the stove, and laid out two cups of coffee on it. A lump came to her throat. It was the sort of thing he'd done when they were getting to know one another, before she'd begun to go upstairs with him.

'I have to go,' she said tersely, biting her lower lip in an effort to stop herself from crying.

'Please? Just for a few minutes,' he pleaded. 'I'll drive you home afterwards.'

The spectacle of sardonic, capable and confident Ronnie, her boss and lover, quietly and softly begging her to stay and talk to him was too much. She sank down on one of the chairs and opened her handbag, rummaging blindly for a handkerchief.

'I wanted to tell you – '

'You don't have to tell me anything!' she snapped bitterly.

'But I want to, Alma. I owe you a great deal. And I know I've treated you very badly.'

'If you know, then there's no point in talking about it.'

He laid his hand gently on her arm. 'I'm sorry, Alma.' His voice was soft, sincere. 'Very, very sorry. If I'd known that I was going to fall in love with Maud Powell . . .'

'Then you do love her?'

'You were the one who told me, remember?' he murmured wryly. 'Alma, if I'd known that we were going to end up like this I wouldn't have . . . have . . .' he searched in vain for the word he wanted.

'Wouldn't have what, Ronnie?' she demanded furiously. 'Slept with me? Made me fall in love with you?'

He looked at her silently, recollecting the depth of his feelings for Maud. Knowing how devastated and broken he'd feel if it was Maud who was walking away from him.

'I wanted you to know that the last thing I intended was for you to get hurt; that I'm grateful to you. I respect you. That if there's anything you need, anything at all that I can do to help you, you only have to say the word, and I'll – '

'You'll what, Ronnie?' she cried acidly. 'Wave your magic wand and transform me into unsoiled goods? Or would it soothe your conscience to give me money, and make me feel even more like a whore than I do already?'

'What I also wanted to tell you, before you found out from someone else, is that Maud and I are to be married as soon as the ceremony can be arranged,' he said quickly, glossing over Evan Powell's refusal to give his permission. 'I spoke to Maud tonight, asked her to marry me, and she said yes.'

Alma sat white-faced and very still, but said nothing.

'As soon as we're married, we'll be leaving – '

'Leaving Pontypridd?'

'I'm taking her to Italy.'

'In God's name, why?'

When she'd screamed, 'you love Maud Powell' at Ronnie, she'd hoped against hope for a denial that she could believe. For twenty-four hours she'd lived on tenterhooks, hating herself for thinking that it could be worse. That Ronnie could have fallen in love with a girl who wasn't out of reach in the TB ward of the Graig Hospital. She'd been prepared for Ronnie to ignore her, and moon around after his sick love, but the thought that he'd leave Pontypridd had never once crossed her mind. To lose him to a girl as young and as ill as Maud Powell was torture, but the realisation that she might never see him again was purgatory.

'You'll be back,' she whispered, needing to believe it.

'No.' He looked her in the eye so there could be no misunderstanding between them. 'I'm taking Maud to Italy in the hope that she'll get well . . .'

'But she might not,' Alma blurted out thoughtlessly, loathing herself afterwards.

'And she might,' he countered sternly. 'Maud's the reason I'm going, but I won't be returning because I've burned my boats with my father. He won't have me back here.'

'But where will you go? What will you do?'

'My grandfather has a farm. We'll live on it.'

'Ronnie, think about what you're doing,' she pleaded, forgetting her fury with him for an instant, knowing just how much the business and the cafés meant to him. 'You only saw Maud Powell a few weeks ago. Your falling in love with her is like Tina falling in love with Clark Gable.'

'No,' he said abruptly, dismissing the thought: it was one he'd already considered – and rejected. 'I've known Maud Powell all my life. It just took you to make me see her in a different light, sooner rather than later. I'm sorry, Alma – ' he reached out and took her hand in his, '– I've made my choice. And my only regret is that I've caused you pain. But I promise, I'll talk to Tony, make sure you always have a job here, and in the new place. That if you want or need anything he'll help you out. I'd like to think that you and I could still be friends – '

'Friends!' She snatched her hand away, and stood up. 'Friends! Ronnie, you want it all don't you? A sweet, virginal, dying wife – and my blessing. Well you damned well can't have it. You're nothing but a selfish swine, Ronnie Ronconi. You used me . . .'

'I never meant to,' he protested.

'And you think, because you didn't mean to it will all come right. Well, it won't. I hate you! Hate you!' She swept her hand across the table, sending the coffee cups flying. They shattered against the wall and sent rivulets of coffee shooting over the floor and clean tables. 'I wish you and her dead! I wish . . . I wish I'd never set eyes on you or your bloody café.' She ran to the door and wrestled with the lock. Ronnie wisely decided against following her. Eventually she managed to wrench the door open. He watched her go with mixed feelings of shame, weariness, and relief that it was finally all over between them.

Chapter Twenty-Two

For the second night running Ronnie didn't sleep. He worked vigorously until two in the morning. The place had never been so clean. Relishing the peace and quiet, he scrubbed the kitchen tables, sink, walls and floor. The mindless labour left him free to take stock and think. He'd accomplished a great deal in one day. He'd proposed to Maud, and been accepted. He'd broken the news to his father and Alma, and suffered the worst of their rages. All that remained was to see Evan Powell again and persuade him to let Maud go. Then he could take her out of the Central Homes, marry her – and leave. It was simple. All he had to do was concentrate his energies on convincing Evan that it was the only thing to do – for Maud's sake.

When the entire café was spotless and fragrant with the smell of bleach and polish he put on his coat. He was half-way out of the door when he realised that the early hours of the morning was not the best time to make a social call.

He took off his coat and went to the big cupboard in the kitchen. Ignoring the bottles, he pulled out the ledgers and account books from the top shelf, set a kettle of water on the range to boil and made a jug of coffee. Taking the jug and the books over to the table in front of the door, he sat down and began to study. Unlike his father, he'd always been meticulous about figures: he knew to the last penny what had to be spent setting up the new restaurant, and what amount would be needed to keep it going through the first lean months when he doubted they'd cover costs. He pored over the bank books and ledgers, working out his figures carefully, checking and double-checking every balance.

He couldn't have picked a worse time to leave the business. Investing in any new venture was inevitably expensive; in a smart new restaurant, doubly so. After his father's lifetime of hard work and the thirteen years that he'd put into the business, they had a surplus of just two hundred pounds that wasn't earmarked for the new place. Deciding he couldn't take it all, he settled on half.

Picking up the chequebook he wrote out a cheque to cash. By the time he'd paid for the tickets to Bardi there wouldn't be a great deal left to begin a new life, but whatever there was would have to do. He tore the cheque out of the book, and penned a note detailing all his calculations for Tony's benefit. He smiled as he wrote. He wasn't the only one in the family who'd be getting his own way. Tony wouldn't be going into the priesthood after all. He felt sorry for Angelo, Alfredo and Robert. One of them would now undoubtedly be earmarked to bear the brunt of their father's religious ambitions.

The hands on the clock pointed to five-thirty as he locked the cupboard door on the books. He walked into the café and looked around. He'd been fifteen, Angelo's age now, when his father had borrowed money from his uncle and bought the place. Papa would never have done it if he hadn't persuaded him.

He'd spent his first full year out of school in their café in High Street, and twelve years here. He'd never known any other working life. What if his father was right? What if he couldn't adapt to farming? Pushing the unpleasant thought from his mind he opened the front door and pulled up the shutters. The sky was just beginning to lighten, there were no clouds. Perhaps it wouldn't rain today. He hoped so. Somehow it seemed like a good omen.

'You can't be serious?' Elizabeth questioned Evan sharply as he heaved himself out of bed before her for the first time in years, and pulled his trousers on over the long johns he'd slept in.

'You got any better ideas, woman?' he countered angrily.

'But Maud's sick. She's . . .'

'Dying!' Evan supplied succinctly. 'I'm going down Trevor Lewis's straight after breakfast, and I'm going to ask him to let me see Maud. If she loves Ronnie as much as he seems to love her, we'll get her out of that place today. Then we'll see about arranging a wedding.'

'But she's a child!' Elizabeth protested strongly. 'She can't possibly know what she wants, not at her age . . .'

'She's going to be a dead child very soon if something isn't done,' Evan stated bluntly. 'Ronnie's offered her a chance. Not much of one, but a chance, and if it's what Maud wants I'm not going to stand in her way.'

245

'Have you thought to ask what the Ronconis have to say about all this?'

'Knowing the Ronconis, they'll have enough to say, and all of it loud,' Evan replied sternly. 'I've told you what I'm going to do, Elizabeth. It's not up for discussion. If Maud wants to marry Ronnie Ronconi, then the sooner it's done and they're on their way to Italy the better.'

Diana heard her uncle leave his bedroom and go downstairs. She glanced at the hands on the battered, painted tin alarm clock on her chest of drawers. They pointed to twenty-past five; usually only her aunt was up at this hour. She pulled the bedclothes over her shoulder and explored her wakening body. Every bit of her was sore and aching, as though she'd been pushed through a crushing mill. She lay there, reliving last night's nightmare, watching the minutes tick slowly, inexorably past.

She heard her aunt leave her bed, pour water into her basin and wash. There were creaks and groans as Elizabeth walked over the bedroom floor. The wardrobe door opened and closed. Water ran as her aunt emptied her basin into the slop jar. The protest of bedsprings as the bedclothes were pulled back. She listened, but failed to hear Haydn's and Eddie's voices. They must have been out late, or had a pint too many, to sleep in until now.

The hands crept round to a quarter to six. Normally she would have been out of bed and dressed. Time to make a move. She sat up stiffly, thrusting her legs out from under the bedclothes. The last thing she wanted to do was excite her aunt's, or anyone else's, suspicions by doing anything out of the ordinary. Her handbag was on the chest of drawers, propped up against the toilet set Will had brought from their Uncle Huw's house. She looked at it in disgust. She had stuffed the five pounds Ben had given her into it last night. Five pounds! Ten weeks' rent and subsistence money. Would she be able to find a job in that time? Would she be able to walk around the town, holding her head up, after what Ben had done to her? What if anyone besides Wyn found out, or guessed . . .

Elizabeth's heavy step crossed the landing. She rapped her knuckles hard on the boys' door. 'Six o'clock,' she called briskly. 'Time you were up.' A muffled reply came from the room.

'Diana!' she shouted coldly without troubling herself to take another step along the landing.

'I'm dressing, aunt,' Diana lied, struggling to her feet. Needles of pain pierced her entire body, bringing with them a tidal wave of shame. She bent double and buried her head in her hands. When the spasm passed, she clung to the chest and peered into the small mirror that her brother had brought along with the toilet set. Her eyes were red-rimmed and puffy. There were enormous black shadows beneath them, and a plethora of red marks around her neck. Bruises were turning from red to black on her cheeks. There were bound to be questions. She'd just have to dream up some lie as an explanation.

She washed dully, mechanically, trying not to look down at her body, but as she rubbed her flannel over the flat of her stomach a ghastly thought crossed her mind. What if Ben had made her pregnant? What if his child was already forming inside her?

Revolted by the idea, she fell back on the bed. That would really be the ultimate horror. Just the thought of being pregnant disgusted her – but Ben . . .

'Diana!' her aunt called irritably up the stairs. Gulping in a great draught of air, she pulled herself together, finished washing, dressed and made her way unsteadily down the stairs, clinging to the banisters for support. Charlie, Eddie and William were sitting at the table. She thought it strange that she hadn't heard Eddie go downstairs, but she was in no mood to question him. They, like her, all seemed subdued.

She went out the back. The morning air was cold and fresh, even in the shelter of the small back yard. She used the *ty bach*, and washed her hands and cleaned her teeth in the washhouse.

'No breakfast today?' her aunt asked suspiciously as Diana laid her hand on the knob of the door between kitchen and passage.

'Not this morning, thank you aunt,' Diana mumbled meekly.

'Christ, what happened to you?' Will demanded, looking at his sister for the first time that morning, and seeing her bruises.

'A pile of boxes fell on top of me in the stockroom yesterday,' Diana lied quickly.

'Then I'll go down that shop and give Ben Springer a piece of my mind. He's obviously working you too hard. You look terrible,' Will said solicitously.

247

'Don't bother,' Diana insisted hastily. 'It was my fault, really. I tripped as I came down off the ladder. I'm going to call in and see Laura on the way into town. Just to check I haven't broken anything.'

'If you're not well you can't work, sis,' Will said firmly.

'I'm all right.'

'You don't look all right to me.'

'I told you, I'll check with Laura before I go in.'

'Promise?'

'I promise,' she agreed irritably.

'You turn up late again today and you're likely to lose your job,' Elizabeth carped.

'I'll walk down with you, sis.' Will gave his aunt a telling look as he rose from the table, leaving his breakfast half-eaten in front of him.

'If you're going now, you can open up, Will,' Charlie threw the keys of the stall at him. 'I'll go to the slaughterhouse and pick up another lamb.'

'And I've business to attend to this morning, as well,' Evan announced, walking in through the door in his best suit.

'I thought you left half an hour ago,' Elizabeth commented.

'I went upstairs to change after I washed.'

'So I see,' Elizabeth frowned disapprovingly.

'Do you want to come with me? If you do you might be able to talk to Maud yourself.'

'You going to see Maud?' Eddie asked eagerly.

'No he's not,' Elizabeth dismissed coldly. 'He's only going to try. And unlike him I haven't a morning to waste on a fool's errand.' Picking up the coal bucket, she walked out to the coalhouse.

'I'll walk down as far as Laura and Trevor's with you, Diana,' Evan said flatly, ignoring Elizabeth's comments. He looked at Eddie. 'Get the horse and cart out of the yard.' He tossed him his last sixpence. 'Can you do Cilfynydd on your own?'

'Of course. Have you got any pennies for the rags?'

'I forgot.'

'But it's Saturday.'

Evan brushed an imaginary speck of dust from his coat. 'You're going to have to make do with the sweets and bits and pieces we've got,' he asserted brusquely.

248

'Here.' Knowing how important pennies were on Saturdays, Charlie dug into his pocket and studied his change. 'There's two bob's worth of coppers there.'

'I'll pay you back tonight, Charlie,' Evan said stiffly.

'Fine.' Charlie pushed a whole round of black pudding into his mouth.

'Has anyone called Haydn?' Elizabeth asked as she walked back in with the bucket full of small coals.

'I'll call him on the way out. Ready Diana?'

Elizabeth washed her hands and began to clear the table. She heard Evan shout up to Haydn, and Haydn call back. She relaid a place at the table and pulled the letter that had come for him that morning out of her apron pocket. It was postmarked Brighton. She wondered just who Haydn knew in that town.

'You got time for a cuppa?' Laura asked Diana, as Evan and Trevor left the house.

'Yes.' Diana sat in Trevor's easy chair next to the stove. It faced the small window that overlooked the tiny paved back yard. Hemmed in by the washhouse wall on one side and the five-foot wall that separated Laura's yard from next door's on the other, the window did little to brighten the atmosphere of the gloomy kitchen, but like an imaginatively painted scene it lent an impression of what nature could do if it was given half a chance. At the end of the short, dark tunnel of walls there was a square of brilliant sunshine filled with a shiny-leaved, evergreen bush.

'Been busy gardening?' Diana asked.

'Got to do something to hide Trevor's rows of vegetables.' Laura glanced at the clock. It was a quarter-past seven. If Diana intended to go to work, she was late. An unheard-of phenomenon when there were forty girls for every job. Something was obviously very wrong, but Laura bided her time, carrying dishes to the washhouse, making a fresh pot of tea, all the while sneaking surreptitious glances at the bruises that Diana had insisted she'd picked up when stock had fallen on her in the shoe shop.

She might have fooled the men, but not Laura, who'd done a stint on the casualty ward of the Royal Infirmary. She'd seen too many women and children who'd been battered by their drunken menfolk. There was only one way that Diana could have acquired

249

the long marks on her neck, and it wasn't by falling stock. They were very obviously finger pressure marks, and by the width and length of them, they'd been caused by large hands. The huge, spreading bruise that was on the point of turning from deep purple to black on her chin looked as though it was the result of a blow from a fist. It must have been a heavy blow to have caused such damage, but Laura suspected that for every mark she could see there were probably ten more that she couldn't.

'Two sugars?' Laura asked, deciding that if Diana hadn't said anything by the time they were both sitting down, she would forget the training that had taught her to be tactful first and curious last, and bring the subject up herself.

'Please.'

Laura spooned sugar into both cups, stirred them, handed one to Diana and sat in the chair opposite her.

'Skiving off today, are we?' she questioned lightly.

Diana was trembling too much to carry her cup to her mouth.

'Trouble with Ben Springer?' Laura asked intuitively. Diana put her head down and nodded dumbly. 'If the stories I've heard are true, you're not the first, love, and unfortunately you probably won't be the last.'

Laura laid her cup safely on the table, and reached across to take Diana's from her shaking hands. 'Did he do this?' She put Diana's cup down, before gently touching the cut on Diana's forehead. Dissolving into sobs, Diana was incapable of answering. 'Come on, love, did he hit you?' Laura continued to probe. Alarmed by Diana's silence, she laid her fingers under Diana's chin and lifted her head so she could look into Diana's eyes. 'Did he rape you?' she asked quietly.

'Yes!' Diana's confession was harsh, guttural.

'You poor, poor love.' Laura took her into her arms.

'Laura, I didn't know where to go, who to turn to,' Diana sobbed, her hair falling over her face and getting in the way of her eyes and mouth. 'He said, he said . . . terrible things about me,' she whimpered. 'He said if I told anyone what had happened, they wouldn't believe me. And now . . . now I could have a baby. Couldn't I?' she demanded, willing Laura to say otherwise.

'Not if Trevor and I have any say in the matter.' Laura smoothed Diana's hair back, away from her forehead. 'It'll be all

250

right. You'll see, we'll sort it out, love. Don't worry. You'll be fine, there's pills you can take – '

'You don't understand,' Diana cried hysterically. 'It can't be sorted out. Not now. Not ever. What he did to me . . . what he . . . I'll never be the same again. Never!'

'Of course you will. You're still the same person.'

'No I'm not. You don't know what it was like. You weren't there. He . . . he . . .' The horror flooded over her again with renewed vigour, sparing her none of the degrading, miserable details. 'I just wish I was dead!' she moaned with a fervour that sent a chill down Laura's spine.

'We'll wait for Trevor,' Laura said insistently, struggling to conceal her panic. 'Don't worry. He'll help you. He'll know what to do.' Laura was never more grateful that she had a husband to turn to. One look at Diana made her ralise that any husband who was prepared to act as a buffer between the world and his wife would do, but in finding one as kind, gentle, loving and understanding as Trevor, she'd struck gold.

'Your breakfast is on the table,' Elizabeth said coldly to Haydn as he walked into the kitchen from the washhouse.

'I'm late,' Haydn said shortly, stating the obvious. 'I haven't time to eat.'

'You might be late, but you'll soon be ill as well if you go working all day on that stall, and all night in that . . . that place' – Elizabeth never could bring herself to say the name of the Town Hall. In the chapel's and her opinion the theatre was synonymous with all the evils of Sodom and Gomorrah – '. . . with nothing inside you. Come on now, be sensible.' She pushed towards him a bowl of thick, lumpy porridge surrounded by a moat of watery milk and topped by a gleaming cap of brown sugar.

'I told you, I don't want it,' Haydn snapped with uncommon discourtesy, for him.

'You'll be passing out half-way through the morning,' Elizabeth warned.

'More like if I eat it I'll be throwing up half-way down the Graig Hill,' he retorted vehemently.

'There's no need to be vulgar.'

'Throwing up is not vulgar.'

Elizabeth didn't know what to make of Haydn. She'd never seen him in such an aggressive mood. Deciding that it might be as well to divert his attention than argue any further about what was vulgar and what was not, she nodded towards the table.

'A letter came for you,' she said briefly.

Haydn looked at it. He could count on one hand the number of letters he'd received in his life. Sitting down in his chair he picked it up, turning it over so he could read the postmark.

'I didn't know you were acquainted with anyone in Brighton,' Elizabeth commented indifferently.

'Neither did I.'

She poured and set a cup of tea at his elbow. Hesitating for a moment, she debated whether or not to have one herself. Haydn rarely had more than one cup and there were at least three in the pot. Deciding it would be a shame to waste it, she eventually poured the second one of the morning for herself.

Forgetting his earlier assertions, Haydn absently spooned a mouthful of porridge into his mouth before attacking the envelope with his thumbnail. He ripped it open awkwardly, tearing a corner off the letter in his eagerness to read the contents.

'You should have used a knife,' Elizabeth admonished. It was not in her nature to allow an opportunity for criticism to pass unnoticed.

'Didn't see one handy.' Haydn picked up the corner and held it next to the torn sheet of paper.

'Violet notepaper,' his mother clucked disapprovingly. 'A sign of poor taste.'

Haydn didn't hear her. He was already reading the letter.

Dear Haydn,

I don't know if you remember me. I certainly remember you and the night we spent in the two-foot-nine after the show, when you and Alice entertained us all by singing 'Heart and Soul'. I'm getting together a cast for a pantomime to be performed in one of the smaller Brighton theatres. A friend of mine is putting up the money and he's given me carte blanche on the artistic side. I've already managed to book Alice Moore to play Cinderella, and when we talked about Buttons, she suggested contacting you.

If – and it is an 'if' – the show's a hit, we may tour the North

*with it in the New Year. I say 'if' because I don't want to mislead
you. All I'm offering is twelve weeks' work initially, and that isn't
much to give up a steady job like yours for.*

*I didn't want to write to you care of the Town Hall in case the
letter got lost, so Alice rang the pub and wheedled your address
out of the barmaid. If you're cross about it, be cross with us, not
the barmaid. Alice can be very persuasive when she wants to be.*

*Please give the offer some thought before turning it down as
you did with Ambrose. It's a break, as they say in this business.
Not a grand break, but if you work at it, it could lead to
something better. We start rehearsals Monday next. They last for
four weeks, and we're offering one pound ten shillings a week
during rehearsals, rising to two pounds when we open. It's not
the three pounds a week Ambrose offered you but there's no
strings attached, of the kind that Ambrose dangled, I promise.
You can live with my sister who lets out good theatrical digs at the
above address. It'll be ten shillings a week all found, and I
promise you won't find better or cheaper in Brighton. Not during
the season, and if you're careful you'll still be able to help out at
home. (Alice mentioned you had problems there.)*

*Should your answer be no, would you please reply as I'll have
to cast around for someone to replace you. If you agree, please
send a telegram, or better still turn up yourself, as soon as you
can.*

yours, and best wishes,
Patsy Duval

*P.S. Alice sends her special love, and wants me to say she hopes
you'll come.*

Haydn read the letter over slowly twice again, studying the
enormous flourishing 'D' that dwarfed the remainder of Patsy's
signature. Irritated by his silence, Elizabeth left the table and
began to fuss and fidget with the stove.

'You're now very late,' she pointed out sourly.

'The letter is from one of the head girls.' Haydn smiled for the
first time in days as he looked up at her.

'A head girl, from a school?' Elizabeth stared at him uncomprehendingly.

253

'Not a school, a chorus,' Haydn laughed.

'I didn't know they had such things.' Elizabeth frowned, tight-lipped.

'She's offered me a job for the Christmas season. In panto-mime, in Brighton.' He was unable to conceal his glee.

'Where did you say?' she demanded coldly.

'Brighton. She says I can lodge with her sister . . .'

'In what kind of a house? That's what I'd like to know. Chorus girls,' Elizabeth said scornfully, tossing her head as she picked up her cup and saucer.

'Good theatrical digs, she says.' Haydn was too excited to see or care about his mother's disapproval. All he could think of was that he'd been offered a heaven-sent opportunity to leave all his problems behind him. His job! Jenny . . . and her defection to Eddie. Thrusting the letter into his pocket, he left the table.

'I'm going to Brighton,' he announced decisively, forgetting his resolution to give up all stage and singing ambitions.

'And how long exactly is this "job" of yours going to last?' Elizabeth enquired icily. 'You said Christmas pantomime. Are you going to give up steady work here on the promise of a pantomime?'

'You don't understand, Mam.' Nothing could dampen Haydn's spirits at that moment. Not even his mother. 'It's a break. It'll lead to more work, and more. Two years and I'll be on stage in the West End, three and I'll be on the radio.' He laced on his boots. 'You'll see.'

'Stuff and nonsense,' Elizabeth dismissed the idea in annoy-ance. 'I just wonder what kind of a family I've brought up. Your father wasn't reared decently or properly, so I suppose I should excuse his rag and boning on that basis, even if it does mean I can't hold my head up straight in this town any more, but I reared you and Eddie differently. And look at the pair of you now, despite all my efforts. Eddie with all his insane ideas of making money from getting beaten to death in the boxing ring, and you wanting to go on stage. Why can't either of you concentrate on something sensible? Something that will bring in a good living – '

'It *will* bring in a good living,' Haydn snapped, hating his mother for destroying his moment of excitement. 'I'll be able to send money home, at least as much as I'm contributing now. And you won't have to feed me,' he added sourly.

'Well, all I can say is I hope that you've got enough money to get to Brighton, boy,' Elizabeth retorted coolly. 'Because if you haven't, I haven't any to give you. And that's for sure.'

Chapter Twenty-Three

'She's looking better, don't you think?' Evan ventured apprehensively, seeking confirmation from Trevor as they stood on the steps of the isolation block in the Graig Hospital.

'It's called hope,' Trevor smiled. 'Ronnie's given her something to look forward to. To be honest, I'm amazed. I never thought of him as the type to sweep a girl off her feet. Figuratively, that is,' he added as he saw the irony in the idea of sweeping a consumptive off her feet when she was already lying in a hospital bed. 'And then again, knowing Ronnie, I never imagined he'd fall in love with anyone. Like Laura I always assumed that any marriage he made would be a café merger.'

'I think Maud's still reeling from the shock.' If Evan could have afforded to send Maud to a kinder climate in the hope of effecting a cure without Ronnie coming into the equation, he would have. He had no doubts whatsoever about the depth or sincerity of Ronnie's love for Maud: the man's actions spoke volumes on that score. But Maud's feelings for Ronnie were something else. She was so bound up in the hope of finding a cure and the excitement at actually travelling to a foreign country that she hadn't given a single thought to marriage, or what it entailed, let alone what marriage to a man like Ronnie might mean.

Trevor cleared his throat uneasily. 'I'm sorry about what happened back there with Doctor John,' he apologised. 'I know you think he was being a bit hard on you.'

'I think it's a bit hard to tell a father he's going to kill his daughter if he takes her out of a hospital's care,' Evan agreed drily.

'He advised you as he thought best,' Trevor murmured, torn between the loyalty due to his immediate superior, and his personal feelings.

'Yes, well, it makes no difference in the long run,' Evan asserted philosophically. 'When it comes down to it, what Maud wants and what's best for her are the only things that matter.'

'Then you are going to take her out tomorrow.' It wasn't a question.

'I'll see Ronnie, and check if that suits him. He's the one who seems to think there's no problem with arranging weddings and journeys at short notice.'

'Knowing what Ronnie's like once he's made up his mind to do something, he'll make sure there're no problems.'

Trevor walked alongside Evan as he crossed the female exercise yard. Evan had been kicking his heels in the hospital for two long hours, barely ten minutes of which he'd actually spent with Maud. Trevor had warned him before they'd got there that Doctor John never came in before nine in the morning. It was probably just as well, because Trevor had had to draw on every ounce of influence to which his status as junior doctor entitled him, to get Evan a brief interview with Maud. Doctor John's disapproval of any break in the routine of visiting hours would have been all that the sister needed to turf Evan out.

Mind already made up about what he intended to do, Evan had then sat outside the sister's office for over an hour and a half, rehearsing again and again what he intended to say to Doctor John. In the event, he didn't have an opportunity to say half of it: his interview with the senior doctor lasted less than five minutes. Evan had never met Bethan's father-in-law before, but from a few hints that Bethan had dropped he'd had a shrewd suspicion that he wouldn't like the man. Now that the meeting had finally taken place, his suspicions had hardened into certainty.

Evan paused to allow a crocodile of pregnant girls and women to pass. Dressed in identical drab, grey-flannel work dresses, each carried a bucket of soapy water and a scrubbing brush as they walked in single file towards the door that led into the main kitchens and dining room.

'You know, I've lived on the Graig all my life, and this is the first time I've been within these walls. I suppose I just never had reason to come before, not even when Bethan worked here.'

'Count yourself fortunate,' Trevor said feelingly. 'My grandfather died in the workhouse in Cardiff. My mother took me to see him there just before he died. She really felt the disgrace of it all, but she had to put him there. My father had just been killed, and she was hard pressed to keep a roof over our heads, let alone his.'

257

'Then you understand why I've tried to steer clear of the place. Why I tried to keep Maud out of here.'

'Only too well.'

The last of the girls disappeared through the high, green-painted wooden doors, and they walked on. As they turned the corner Evan caught sight of a group of men in the yard behind the kitchens. They all had axes, and were chopping logs into fire-sized sticks under the supervision of a white-coated overseer.

'Don't believe in leaving anyone idle, do you?' Evan murmured.

'They're casuals who've opted to stay in another day. No work, no food,' Trevor explained uneasily, as he saw the supervisor berate a man for tardiness. The man was moving so slowly, the chances were that he was ill, but Trevor didn't dare interfere with the running of the workhouse. As Doctor John frequently said to him, 'If the man's ill, we'll find out soon enough. They'll bring him before us, tomorrow, or the day after.' Valuing his job, Trevor hadn't replied that tomorrow or the next day might exacerbate the man's condition – if he lived that long.

'I know why your boss is so set against me moving Maud out of here, but you haven't given me your opinion,' Evan said suddenly.

'I'm only a junior doctor . . .' Trevor began apologetically.

'You're qualified, and some would say a new degree is better than an old one.'

'And there's those who say experience counts for everything. Have you asked Andrew to come down and take a look at her?'

'I've thought of it,' Evan admitted. 'But with Bethan expecting, it didn't seem right to drag them all that way. Come on, tell me Doctor Lewis, what do you think? I promise I won't hold you to anything afterwards. Do you agree with Doctor John? Should Maud stay here until you've completed all your tests?'

'The tests will take time,' Trevor admitted reluctantly. 'There's a waiting list for the X-ray machine, not to mention the ambulance we'd need to book to ferry her to the Cottage Hospital to carry out some procedures. It could take as long as two weeks, and really all we'd have in the end is a better picture of the parts of her lungs that are diseased. We know what's wrong at the moment, we simply don't know the extent. Two weeks can be a long time in the progression of a disease, and it's more time than Ronnie needs to get her to Italy. The weather is better over there, even in winter. The mountain air might do the trick.'

'You really believe that?'

'After a few years in this place I've learned not to build up hope where there may be none,' Trevor cautioned, 'but I do know one thing.'

'What's that?'

'I've worked here six years, and in all that time I've never known anyone to walk out of that TB ward. If you want my opinion, Mr Powell, I'll give it to you, but I warn you, it's not based on scientific knowledge or study. Occasionally miracles do happen, and if strength and determination can overcome illness, Ronnie has enough for the whole ward, let alone one slip of a girl like Maud. We haven't anything better to offer her. Not really. Perhaps she'll die more slowly in here than she would at home. But that's all. She seems happy enough to go with Ronnie, and after what he's told me, I have no doubt he'll be ecstatic at the prospect of taking her. Let her go, Mr Powell. The worst that can happen is what would inevitably happen here.'

'That's more or less what I've been thinking.' Evan drew his empty pipe out of his pocket and put it in his mouth. 'I suppose I'd better go down the café and see if I can find your brother-in-law, and hope that something hasn't happened to change his mind now that Maud's set on going with him.'

'He won't have changed his mind, Mr Powell. And something tells me you won't have to look very hard for him either,' he grinned as he recognised Ronnie's van waiting outside the gates in Courthouse Street. 'Either Laura or Mrs Powell must have told him where you were.'

'Thanks for everything you've done for us, Doctor Lewis,' Evan said as he held out his calloused hand.

'Don't you think after all this you could bring yourself to call me Trevor?'

'It wouldn't be right,' Evan said gravely. 'Not a ragman and a doctor on first-name terms.'

'Sorry, Mr Horton,' Haydn apologised as he rushed up to the stall in the second-hand clothes market. The dealer had only recently moved there after a lifetime of trading out in the open.

259

'I thought I could rely on you, boy,' his boss complained in a hurt, petulant tone from behind an enormous bundle of woollen pullovers, clean, pressed and mended, that he was heaving out of a lock-up chest on to the stall. 'You know I'm getting on, and can't do things as quickly as I used to, yet you – '

'Mr Horton I'm sorry, but I've had an offer,' Haydn explained enigmatically, unable to contain his excitement.

'Well I've made you an offer. To work,' he grumbled testily. 'You'd think you'd show some gratitude after all the years I've helped you.'

'The offer is to play in a pantomime, in Brighton. I've a chance to work with professionals, in a real theatre. This could be the big break I've been looking for.'

'Ay, ay boy.' Mr Horton began to arrange the pullovers in piles on the trestles. 'I suppose it's what you've been after for a while.' He didn't even try to hide his disappointment at the prospect of losing his assistant. 'When will you be off?'

'By Monday, if I can make it.'

'That's fine. Go ahead, leave me high and dry.'

'No one's leaving you high and dry, Mr Horton,' Haydn countered. 'There's loads of boys would kill for a chance to work on this stall. My brother for one.' He might never want to see or speak to Eddie again, but family finances were family finances, after all. And he couldn't bear the thought of his parents going short when he could have done something to alleviate the situation.

'Eddie, the boxer?'

'I've only got one brother, and you know it,' Haydn smiled.

'Thought he was helping your father on the rag round.'

'The round's not going as well as it might. He could spare Wednesday, Friday and Saturday to work for you.' Haydn kept his fingers crossed behind his back. The Wednesday and Friday wouldn't be a problem, but he wasn't too sure about the Saturday, traditionally the ragman's busy day.

'He is a good strong boy,' the dealer mused thoughtfully, 'and with him around the stall, there'd be no problems with anyone trying to lift anything either. When did you say you were off?' he asked Haydn sharply.

'Monday, if I can make it.'

'Right then, he can take over on Wednesday. Tell him to be here, quarter to seven. On the dot.'

'He'll be here,' Haydn said, thinking that if his father couldn't spare Eddie, there was always Diana. Three days a week at two bob a day – always supposing that Mr Horton would pay a mere girl the same as he now paid him – was as much as she was getting in the shoe shop, and he knew she was looking for a chance to leave Ben Springer.

'That's settled then,' Mr Horton said resolutely. He hated any uncertainty especially where business was concerned. 'Your brother will take over.'

'He'll be delighted to, Mr Horton.'

'Come on then, boy, get busy. You're late, remember. Tell you what, because you've been so good to me until today, how about you take your pick of whatever you fancy at the end of the day? Three-piece suit, with waistcoat, watch pocket, the works, sports jacket, trousers and a couple of shirts. Sort of bonus.'

'That's very good of you, Mr Horton.'

'We can't let a Welsh boy go up to the English in rags, can we? It'd be like letting down Wales. And then again, you've got to look smart on stage.'

Haydn didn't have the heart to tell him that he would be wearing stage costumes. 'Thanks very much, Mr Horton,' he beamed. He would have a decent suit to travel in, and wear between shows. He still needed a suitcase, and the means to get him to Brighton, but he had two bob coming to him at the end of the day and a week's extra wages due from the Town Hall, the week in hand he'd worked when he started there. Even after handing over his lodge to his mother, he'd still be left with fourteen and six. Not enough for the fare, but something would turn up. Perhaps Charlie knew of a meat lorry going that way.

He went to the chest and lifted out the pressed and folded trousers that Mr Horton always laid out at the bottom. When he carried them over to the stall he was whistling for the first time since he'd last spoken to Jenny.

'I gave her two spoonfuls of laudanum.'

'You what?' Trevor stared in horror at his wife. 'That's a proscribed drug, it was locked in my cabinet.'

261

'So? I know where you keep the key, and I unlocked it,' Laura said defiantly. 'Don't be such a dyed-in-the-wool doctor, Trevor. I know as much about treating shock as you, and after a stint on the maternity ward I've probably had more experience of dealing with it. The girl was in a dreadful state. I wouldn't have dosed her if there was any other option. She needed help and she couldn't go to her aunt. Not with a story like that. You know what Bethan's mother can be like.'

'I know she was very good when Bethan was ill,' Trevor affirmed euphemistically, careful not to say too much. Not even Laura knew the full extent of Bethan's attempts to rid herself of an unwanted pregnancy.

'Look, the girl's ill. We've a spare bedroom. Can't she stay here for a night or two until she sorts herself out?'

'What about her family, Laura?' Trevor demurred, wary of treading on anyone's toes, especially the Powells with all that they had to contend with at the moment.

'I sent little Gwynfor next door up to Graig Avenue with a note, telling Elizabeth that Diana has delayed shock and that she shouldn't be moved for a day or two.'

'I don't know why you bother to consult me about anything,' he said testily. 'Seems to me you covered everything before even telling me about it.'

'I didn't cover everything,' she said furiously. 'I didn't make allowances for a dense, unsympathetic, heartless fool of a husband.' She wiped over a soup bowl with a clean tea towel and ladled out a bowlful of lamb stew, slamming it down on the table in front of him. Then she went to the breadboard that Angelo had shaped for her from a thick wedge of fresh pine, and sliced a chunk of coarse brown bread, practically throwing it at him.

'Before you rant and rave at me, Laura, just remember that rape is a criminal offence,' Trevor said in what Laura took to be a pompous tone. 'Diana is the principal witness to a criminal act, and as a doctor I should report it.'

'Do you think I don't know that?' Laura demanded hotly.

'If you knew it, why didn't you call the police?'

'I'll tell you why I didn't call the police,' Laura rounded on him like a cornered wildcat. 'I didn't call them because Ben Springer would deny the whole thing. He'd call Diana a whore. Say she'd wanted him to do all those despicable things that he did to her. That she enjoyed it.'

'Laura . . .'

'Don't you Laura me. You know this town as well as I do. You tell me, what chance would a young girl like Diana have against one of the commercial fathers of this town? For God's sake Trevor, her mother's in jail, she lives on the Graig, people talk. And what's the betting that when they do, all that business with Bethan will get dragged up all over again? And for what? For Ben Springer to get off scot-free and Diana to have what little remains of her reputation ruined.'

'Her uncle's a policeman – '

'A nice enough constable who has absolutely no clout when faced with the Ben Springers of this world, and you know it.'

A few months of marriage had accustomed Trevor to being on the receiving end of the rough edge of Laura's tongue, but this was somehow different. Here was an anger and emotion he hadn't seen in Laura before.

'I'm sorry Laura, I suppose I didn't think it through, and then again I didn't realise you'd taken this so hard,' he murmured, leaving the table and reaching out to her.

'You'd have taken it just as hard if you'd heard her.' Laura didn't try to stem the tears that were pouring down her cheeks. 'He did disgusting, revolting things to her, Trevor. You, thank God, probably aren't capable of imagining what. And then, when he'd finished, he wrapped her, half-naked, in her coat and put her out on the street. After pushing a five-pound note into her pocket,' she seethed. 'Wyn Rees stopped her from tearing it up.'

'Wyn . . .'

'Yes, queer Wyn,' Laura said shortly. 'He found her, and took her home with him. Made her some tea, let her have a bath in his house, and gave her his sister's clothes to wear home.'

'Good for Wyn,' Trevor said in amazement.

'You will let her stay here a couple of days?'

'If you think it will help,' he said resignedly.

'And you won't go to the police?'

'No,' he murmured. 'Though pity help me if any of this gets as far as Doctor John's ears.'

'It won't,' she assured him. 'Thank you. I do love you, you know. I don't mean to fly off the handle.'

'I know.' Sitting on a chair, he pulled her down on to his lap and kissed her. Diana's story still fresh in her mind, she shook her head and moved away.

'Not now, love. I'm still too angry.'

'With me?'

'Not you. Never with you. Well not seriously,' she qualified. 'Just all the Ben Springers of this world who think that women are there to be used, at their convenience.'

'Where the hell have you been?' Tony confronted Ronnie as he walked into the café at six o'clock on Saturday night. 'We've been rushed off our feet all day. Angelo couldn't manage the cooking. I had to take Gina off the till and put her out back, and that meant I had to cover the till as well as the counter. Tina didn't have any help with the waitressing, and we got behind . . .'

'If I were you I'd think about taking Maria out of school,' Ronnie said placidly. 'She's not doing anything constructive there, and with the new place opening in a couple of months, the sooner she starts learning the trade the better.'

'But she's only thirteen. You know Papa likes us all to stay on in school until we're fourteen. He says – '

'Papa more or less yanked me out of school when I was twelve, and I didn't visit the place very often before that.'

'That's not what Papa told me. He said you wouldn't stay in school even when he sent you.'

'I wouldn't go because I knew Papa needed me in the business. You lot ate more than the profits of the High Street place every week,' Ronnie informed him drily. 'And don't go thinking that it's easier now because we've got two places and another one opening soon. The overheads will be higher, as well as the profits, and there'll still be eleven Ronconi mouths to feed, even with me and Laura gone.'

Tony stared in amazement as, instead of going into the kitchen and changing out of his smart street jacket, Ronnie walked behind the counter, helped himself to a cup, and filled it with coffee. He looked around the cafe as he picked it up. 'Despite all your moaning you must have managed to keep everything under control, little brother,' he commented lightly. 'The place is still standing, and it seems quiet enough now.'

'Just when I'm due to finish for the day,' Tony griped.

'Shutting up shop early?' Ronnie enquired airily.

'Now you're back, I'm off to the pictures.'

'I'm not back.' Ronnie finished his coffee, and poured himself another.

'But you're here,' Tony protested.

'For the coffee, and to say goodbye. I told you last night, I've left the business. By the way, I've written out some notes for you on the new place. And I've balanced the accounts.'

'You're not coming in tomorrow?' Tony stared at his brother in disbelief.

'I most definitely am not coming in tomorrow,' Ronnie smiled. He pulled his watch chain out of his pocket and flicked through the fobs. 'This is now yours.' He extracted the key to the cupboard. 'There you are: official boss badge. You're in charge now, boy. Supremo! This is what you've been waiting for all your life.'

'Ronnie, I can't take over,' Tony remonstrated. 'I don't know enough.'

'If you don't, you've no one to blame but yourself. You've been under my feet for eighteen years. Is it my fault that you didn't keep your eyes and ears open?'

'But there's the new restaurant!'

'I've left you a challenge. If I were you I'd try to enlist Laura's help. For a woman, she's smart,' he teased. 'If you're pushed, I suggest you put Papa in here with Angelo, and let Tina manage High Street. That'll leave you free to run the new restaurant.'

'Ronnie!' Tony was talking to the counter. His brother had picked up his cup and taken it into the back room where Tina and Gina were clearing tables. Although it was after six o'clock on a Saturday neither of them had even attempted to leave. Tony felt that not only the fabric of his family but the routine of the café was falling apart.

'Is Alma coming in?' Tony interrupted Ronnie, as his brother hugged the girls, wrapping his arms around their shoulders.

'How should I know? It's up to the man in charge to know what shifts his waitresses are working.'

'Ronnie, please . . .'

Thrusting his fingers into his top pocket, Ronnie pulled out a packet of cigarettes and extended it to Tony. Tony nearly fell over: it was the first time Ronnie had recognised that he smoked, let alone offered him a cigarette.

'Now look,' Ronnie smiled patiently, 'it's really very simple. Give the customers what they want, keep them happy, treat Alma well, and mind you enter up the takings in the ledger every night. You leave it even one night and you're in dire trouble. You always think you'll remember the figures, but you don't. And that's the voice of experience talking.'

Tony tried to take in what Ronnie was saying, but he couldn't. He found it impossible to believe that Ronnie was really leaving. Ronnie who'd always been there when he'd needed him. Whenever there'd been trouble in school, or with friends, it had always been Ronnie who'd sorted it out for him. Ronnie, never Papa or Mama, because unlike their parents, Ronnie understood the Welsh systems and way of life, and he'd been the first Ronconi to cut the path and smooth the way for the others in the family.

'You'll remember to do all that?' Ronnie asked, sensing that Tony's attention had wandered.

'I think so,' Tony mumbled.

'You do know, don't you, that Papa doesn't understand the first thing about book-keeping?' Only his imminent departure from Wales could have wrested such a disloyal statement from Ronnie. 'If you get stuck, you could always write to me in Italy, but the Italian post isn't that reliable, or so Mama's always said.'

'Mama said you're marrying Maud Powell and taking her to Bardi. Is that right?' Tony finally ventured.

'That's right.' Ronnie winked at Tina and Gina, who were still hovering close. 'At four o'clock tomorrow afternoon.'

'On a Sunday? But Father O'Kelly – '

'We're marrying in St John's.'

'St John's! Ronnie, that's Church of Wales!'

'The Reverend Price did mention it,' Ronnie said flatly.

'But why?' Tony demanded urgently.

'Because I didn't want Father O'Kelly to make a lot of fuss.'

'Not the church,' Tony dismissed irritably. 'Why marry Maud Powell and all? Papa said – '

'Please don't tell me. I've a feeling that the saying "Least said soonest mended" should be applied to Papa and me at the moment. He made his views clear last night, and I don't blame him for them. If any of you want to come to the wedding, you'll be very welcome. Just don't expect any more than a short ceremony, that's all. And if you don't turn up, I'll understand why. And as Maud and I are leaving Ponty at six o'clock on Monday morning, if you're not coming, I'll say my goodbyes now.'

'Ronnie . . .'

'Look, I have to go and see Laura and Trevor. I'm taking my things.' He left the table and walked towards the staircase. 'If I were you I'd look at the accounts. Check them. And if you come up with any questions, call in Laura's on the way home. I'd appreciate a word about some promises I've made to Alma.'

Ronnie retrieved his case from the upstairs bedroom and left quickly, hugging his brothers, and kissing his sisters on their cheeks as he backed out through the door. He went to the White Hart car park to get the Trojan. As he pulled the starting handle out from under the seat, he made a mental note to hand the keys over to Tony later. There was so much to do, and so little time left to think of everything.

Chapter Twenty-Four

Laura and Trevor were eating tea when Ronnie walked in. Meat and potato pie, bread, cheese, fruit cake, and a very prettily iced sponge cake.

'Sit down.' Laura went to the dresser and lifted down another plate and a knife and fork.

Trevor looked at him inquisitively. 'Everything arranged?' he asked.

'We're marrying in St John's tomorrow at four, and leaving first thing Monday morning. Half-past seven train from Cardiff.'

'I'll take you to Cardiff in the car,' Trevor offered.

'I asked Aldo because I thought you'd be working.'

'Not so you'd notice at that time in the morning. I'll get the new junior doctor to cover for me.'

'You don't have to.'

'I know I don't have to,' Trevor said calmly. 'But you're going to be changing boats and trains enough with Maud as it is. Take a brotherly hand when it's offered. If not for your sake, then for Maud's.'

'In that case, thank you,' Ronnie said gratefully. 'There is one thing I was going to ask you.'

'Ask away.' Trevor helped himself to another spoonful of pie.

'Not you, Laura. You always were good with the café books,' he complimented his sister.

'If I remember rightly, I had no choice to be anything but. They drove me mad, particularly when I had to translate your figures into legible numbers. They're the sole reason I went into nursing,' she assured Trevor.

'Please, give Tony a hand with them if he gets stuck. And if you have time, keep an eye on him. It's not that he isn't up to taking over, it's just that he's going to need all the help he can get.'

'Even that of a mere woman like me?' Laura raised her eyebrows.

'I suggested to Tony that he puts Tina in charge of the High

Street café,' Ronnie went on, ignoring his sister's sarcasm. 'That will free Papa to take care of the Tumble and leave Tony to run the new place, but it would be better if everything stayed as it was and you took over the restaurant Laura, at least for a while,' he qualified, in deference to her status as newly married woman.

'To what do I owe this praise?' she demanded. 'You never told me I was any good when I worked in the cafés. All you ever did was whinge every time I dropped a plate, or burnt an egg.'

'Big brother's prerogative,' he grinned. 'You were good, but I wanted to make you even better. If you run the restaurant for Tony, there should be enough money left for you to get someone to help you with your housework. You'd let her work outside the house, wouldn't you?' he turned to Trevor.

'Let her?' Trevor shook his head. 'The first thing I learned as a married man is that you don't "let" your wife do, or not do anything. All capacity for choice is taken away the day you walk down the aisle. As you'll soon find out for yourself.'

'I'd like you both to be there, but I wouldn't want you to come if it means a quarrel between you and Papa, Laura. I know how unforgiving he can be.'

'Just try and stop me,' she smiled maliciously. 'I wouldn't miss the sight of you tying the knot for all the world. I only hope that Maud finds enough gumption to keep that ego of yours well and truly under control.'

'Thank you so very much, dear sister. Maud told her father that she wants Diana as a bridesmaid . . .'

'I'll ask her,' Laura said unthinkingly.

'Would you? I don't intend to go back up the Graig tonight. And I'll need a best man.' He looked hopefully at Trevor.

'What about Tony?' Trevor asked, failing to conceal his pleasure at being asked.

'I don't want to make Tony choose between me and Papa,' Ronnie said.

'In that case I'd be delighted.'

'Good, that's the wedding settled.'

'Got your tickets?'

'I went to Thomas Cook's in Cardiff this afternoon. I booked first-class seats to London. Hopefully, as it's coming from Wales, the carriage will be empty and Maud will be able to lie down. I'll get a taxi from Paddington to Tilbury . . .'

'Bethan will be annoyed if you don't give her a chance to see the blushing bride, and Andrew will be only too happy to drive you across London,' Trevor interrupted.

'Do you really think so?'

'He'll be your brother-in-law as of tomorrow. I'll telephone him.'

'It would be a help to have a car waiting,' Ronnie agreed. 'I've booked a cabin to Calais, and from there a first-class sleeper to Genoa.'

Trevor let out a long, low whistle. 'That must have cost a pretty penny for the both of you.'

'It did,' Ronnie agreed.

'And what about tomorrow night?' Laura asked.

'As Papa's thrown me out, and I presume that means the café as well as the house, I was going to ask if I could sleep here for a couple of nights.' It was more than just his father. Ronnie had developed a sudden aversion to the bedroom in the café. It held too many memories that he'd rather forget.

'Diana's in the spare room,' Trevor blurted out tactlessly.

'Diana . . .'

'Don't ask, it's a long story,' Laura interrupted. 'But if you don't mind sleeping on the parlour couch, we can put you up.'

'I'd appreciate that very much.'

'You really are going through with this, aren't you?' Laura asked abruptly as Ronnie began to eat.

'Yes,' he mumbled, his mouth full. He was hungry. Apart from his usual endless cups of coffee, he'd hardly eaten in two days.

'I find it difficult to believe. You and Maud Powell!'

'Are you going to see Mama tonight?'

'You know I always go to see Mama on a Saturday,' she said, irritated because he obviously wasn't going to entertain her by talking about him and Maud.

'Tell her and the kids the time of the wedding, and tell them when I'm leaving. But don't forget to say that I don't want them there if it will put anyone in Papa's bad books.'

'I'll explain, and better than you just did,' Laura retorted.

'I've left the accounts books and the plans for the new place with Tony.'

'I'll call in the café on Monday.'

'Thanks Laura,' he said sincerely. 'I'd hate to see all Papa's and my hard work go down the drain.'

'Don't worry, it won't. You and Papa aren't the only Ronconis blessed with brains, you know,' she said harshly, annoyed with the thick feeling that was creeping into her throat.

'I always knew that, but boy, have the rest of you given me a hard time trying to prove it.' Ronnie smiled as he reached for another piece of pie.

'Here she is!' Diana, who'd been pressganged by Laura into putting on her best face for Maud's wedding, had gone up to Graig Avenue to help Maud dress. Laura had walked up with her, taking the entire contents of the 'best' side of her wardrobe, together with her boxed wedding dress and veil just in case Maud fancied being married in white. Elizabeth had turned out her hatbox and spread the contents on Maud's bed. Gina and Tina had sneaked away from Danycoedcae Road, and turned up with a small case that nine-year-old Alfredo had smuggled out the back and over the mountain for them. It was crammed with perfumes, powders, lipsticks, and their best dresses wrapped in tissue paper.

'Look, quick, Trevor's stopping the car!' Forgetting her misery for the first time in two days, Diana called the Ronconi girls to the window. Gina and Tina leant heavily on the sash, watching as Trevor opened the door of his car. Evan stepped out of the back, then leant over and picked Maud up from the front seat. Maud protested loud enough to be heard in the bedroom, but all to no avail. Evan carried her up the steps and in through the front door, pushing past Haydn and Eddie, who were observing an uneasy, silent truce in honour of the occasion.

Diana rushed to the landing, just in time to see William plant a kiss on Maud's cheek. Without pausing for breath, Evan continued to carry Maud straight up the stairs. He deposited her, still protesting that she could walk, on to the bed.

'And you're not to walk down the stairs,' he said firmly. 'When you're ready, give me a shout and I'll carry you down.'

'She won't be ready for ages yet, Mr Powell,' Laura asserted. 'We've got to turn her into a bride.'

Maud smiled at the girls. Her mother, sensing that she wasn't wanted, muttered something about 'pressing her black brocade', and left the room. The first question Maud asked when the door was shut was, 'Where's Ronnie?'

'You told Trevor you didn't want to see him before the wedding,' Laura reminded her.

'I don't, but I still want to know where he is.'

Gina and Tina laughed, and even Diana managed a smile.

'You just keep that up Maud Powell, and you'll be all right,' Laura said seriously. 'There isn't a man born who doesn't need tabs kept on him.'

Ronnie was dressing in the bedroom that Diana had thoughtfully vacated for his use, when Trevor returned from taking Maud up to Graig Avenue.

'She's looking good,' he reported. 'Evan Powell insisted on carrying her in and out of the car, but she could have walked.'

'You really think she'll be all right?' Ronnie asked anxiously.

'For a while,' Trevor assured him, not daring to voice an opinion as to how long 'a while' could be. 'Here, do you want a hand with that collar stud?' he asked as Ronnie struggled to fasten a new starched collar to his best boiled shirt.

'No, I think I've got it. There, that's done.'

'Brandy?' Trevor asked. 'I bought a new bottle.'

'I think I could manage one.' Ronnie slipped his arms through his waistcoat sleeves without bothering to do up the buttons. Picking up his tie and jacket he checked around the room to make sure he hadn't left anything, before following Trevor downstairs.

'I've got a couple of things for you.' Trevor poured out two glasses of brandy and handed one to Ronnie as they sat either side of the kitchen stove. 'First, there's a room booked in the New Inn for you and Maud tonight. You can take her there straight after the ceremony. Everything's paid for, including dinner,' he added. 'I told them you'd want it in your room.'

'Trevor, I wasn't expecting anything like this . . .'

'It's a wedding present from Laura and me,' Trevor said quickly. 'And then, you'll be needing these.' He handed Ronnie an enormous package wrapped in brown paper. 'French letters,' he explained briefly. 'I don't know whether you'll be able to get any in Italy so I scrounged a hundred for you. Write and let me know when you're running low, but be sure to give me plenty of time to send more. The one thing you can't afford to risk with Maud is pregnancy. On top of everything else it would kill her,' he warned bluntly.

'I have no intention of . . . of sleeping with Maud,' Ronnie stammered. 'At least not in that sense,' he asserted, colouring in embarrassment.

'You might not have any intention of sleeping with her in that sense now,' Trevor said matter-of-factly, 'but now is not tonight, and Maud may have other ideas on the subject.'

'She's ill,' Ronnie said quickly.

'Not that ill. She's spent the last couple of days in hospital resting, remember. She told me only this morning she was looking forward to married life, and if at the end of the day you don't take her to bed, she'll quite rightly wonder why you bothered to go to all this trouble.'

'Then it'll be all right for me to sleep with her?' Remembering Trevor's medical qualifications, Ronnie finally subdued the qualms he had about discussing such an intimate subject with his brother-in-law.

'I've never heard of it doing anyone in Maud's condition any harm,' Trevor smiled broadly. 'And if the rumours that some of your ex-girlfriends have spread around town are to be believed, it may do her some good.'

'You shouldn't believe everything you hear.' Ronnie took the package from Trevor. 'I'll put it in my case.'

'Oh, and there's this.' Trevor held out a couple of bottles. 'Cough mixture,' he grinned. 'I've given Maud six bottles. I thought you might need a couple more for the journey. Keep them to hand.'

'Anything else?'

'I don't think so.' Trevor smiled, the devil in him enjoying Ronnie's embarrassment. 'That is, unless you'd like another brandy.'

'Life is so simple for men,' Laura grumbled. 'All they have to do is put on a clean shirt and collar, a tie and their best suits and they look fine, whereas we . . .'

'I had no decisions to make before you brought this lot,' Maud complained playfully. 'It would have been my blue satin dress, or my blue satin dress.'

'You can't get married in a dance dress,' Diana protested.

'You can if that's all you've got,' Maud contradicted.

'How about going traditional?' Laura opened the box she'd brought and pulled out the wedding dress and veil that the best dressmaker on the Graig had made for her wedding.

'Laura, I couldn't! Could I?' Maud asked, her eyes shining in delight at the thought.

'Yes you could,' Laura asserted. 'The only problem is it's going to be too big for you, which is why I went down the market and bought this off Mrs Jones last night.' She pulled out yards and yards of wide, gleaming white satin ribbon. 'I thought we could always tie the dress in at the waist, hiding the gathers under a big bow at the back. I just hope it's not going to be too uncomfortable.'

'We got you some new underclothes.' Tina and Gina thrust a paper carrier bag towards her. 'It's from all of us, even the boys,' Gina said, remembering that as they'd run out of money, Tony and Angelo, not to mention the till, had contributed more to the fund than they had.

They watched Maud open the bag. A fine, white silk petticoat and a beautiful, coffee-coloured, lace-trimmed satin nightdress spilled out.

'There's some other things in there too. Another petticoat, bloomers, silk stockings . . .' Gina blushed as she remembered all the silk stockings that Diana's mother had sold them.

'And this is for you.' Not to be outdone, Diana thrust an envelope containing five pounds at Maud. It was the five pounds Ben Springer had given her, but no one had to know that. Every time Diana touched it, she felt dirty, and used. At least Maud wouldn't know where it had come from.

'Diana, I can't take this,' Maud protested as she looked inside. 'This is all the money you've got.'

'There's bound to be things that you want that no one has thought of. Please take it,' Diana said curtly.

274

Touched by everyone's generosity Maud didn't even notice her mother standing in the doorway, a strange expression on her face.

Gina, Tina, Diana and Laura worked hard on Maud for two solid hours. They waved her hair, puffed perfumed talcum powder over her body, lightly rouged her cheeks and powdered her face, adding as the final touch before the dress went on, a lavish sprinkling of 'dabs' of Evening in Paris.

'You'd better pack Maud's things, Diana,' Laura said suddenly.

'There's no need, I'm coming back tonight.'

'No you're not,' Laura smiled. 'Ronnie has a surprise for you.'

'We're not leaving today, are we?'

'No,' Laura said mysteriously.

'Then if they're not leaving until tomorrow I think Maud should spend tonight in her own bed,' Elizabeth said quickly, as she carried a tray of biscuits and home-made lemonade into the room.

'You'll still be able to wave her off tomorrow morning.' Laura fingered a wave on Maud's forehead, sharpening its edge.

'But with the journey and everything she's going to need her rest,' Elizabeth said sharply.

'Don't worry, she'll get plenty of that.' Laura's hackles rose at the shadow Elizabeth was casting over her and Trevor's surprise, and that was without taking into account the inference that Ronnie wouldn't allow to Maud to rest.

'I would like to know where my own daughter is going . . .'

'If you come downstairs with me Mrs Powell, I'll tell you.' Laura propelled Maud's mother out of the room, leaving Diana to pack in peace. There wasn't much to stow away. The contents of two drawers and the wardrobe still left plenty of room on top of the Gladstone for the new underclothes and nightdress that the Ronconi girls had given Maud, together with her well-used sponge bag and bottles of Evening in Paris perfume and Essence of Violets.

At a quarter-past three Laura returned and helped Maud on with the dress. It was the right length but about six inches too wide everywhere. It took the combined efforts of all four girls to tie the sash to their communal satisfaction, but once the bow was finally pulled out as wide as it would go, the veil secured with combs to Maud's head, and the lace allowed to fall gently over her shoulders, the general consensus was that she was the most stunning bride that the Graig had seen since Laura had walked down the aisle with Trevor.

'Now remember,' Laura ordered as she walked around the chair that Maud was sitting on. 'Rest until it's time to go, let Diana do everything.'

'If we're going we'd better go,' Elizabeth said firmly from outside the door. Thinking that Elizabeth would want some time alone with her daughter, Laura swept everyone out of the room.

'I have something for you too.' Elizabeth took Maud's hand and folded something into it.

'Not your mother's locket, Mam, I know what it means to you.'

'It's all I have left to give you, so I'd appreciate you taking it with good grace, Maud,' Elizabeth said briskly. She kissed her daughter, grazing her cheek with chapped, dry lips.

'This wedding, and Italy. It is what you want, isn't it Maud?'

Maud looked up at her with her enormous blue eyes. 'More than anything else in the world,' she affirmed.

'That's all right then,' Elizabeth said as she walked out through the door.

Ronnie sat impatiently in the front pew of St John's church and waited. The church was strange, peculiar, unlike any he'd sat in before. It not only looked different – chilly, barren and spartan in contrast to the glitteringly gilded, image-strewn interior of the Catholic church in Treforest. It even smelt different. The sweet, lingering perfume of incense that he'd associated with prayer and God, ever since he had first been carried into a church in his mother's arms, was absent. In its place was a rank, musty odour of damp, mixed with beeswax polish and decaying flowers.

He glanced behind at the empty pews, hoping to see Trevor, not only because he felt he needed a sympathetic being next to him to lend moral support, the advent of Trevor also meant the advent of Maud in Trevor's car, and he wanted the ceremony to be over and done with as quickly as possible. He wouldn't be able to relax until the brand new gold ring he'd bought in a Cardiff jeweller's yesterday afternoon was firmly fixed on Maud Powell's finger, signalling the irrevocable change of her name to Ronconi. Once that was done, it would be too late for Evan Powell to change his mind about giving his consent to the marriage. Too late for his father to make a scene, and even too late for Maud herself to have second thoughts – a prospect that had concerned him ever since he walked away from the Graig Hospital, too worried by the ease with which she'd acceded to his proposal to be elated by his success in wooing and winning her.

He'd had so little time with her, and what he'd had, he felt he'd wasted. He hadn't told her any of the things he'd wanted to. Nothing that would make her want to be with him as urgently as he needed to be with her.

In an effort to suppress the image of Maud shaking her head and hesitating that insisted on intruding into his mind, he studied his surroundings. The plain, bare, whitewashed walls. The severe lines of the rather utility pulpit, and the unadorned wooden crucifix above it. The altar, covered by a white, gold-embroidered cloth, that looked positively empty spread with its meagre furniture of brass candlesticks and matching cross.

The Reverend Price, who unknown to Ronnie had incurred a great deal of wrath from his parishioners for agreeing to perform a marriage ceremony for an avowed Catholic and a Chapel girl, came out of the vestry, bowing and smiling at the people who'd begun to shuffle into the pews behind Ronnie. His young and astonishingly pretty wife struck up the organ – and Ronnie continued to wait. He stared at the wooden plaque that hung above the vestry door, displaying the hymn numbers for evensong. He contemplated the Reverend Price's receding hairline and attempted to divine at what point in time he would go bald; he abandoned the diversion when he realised that he might never know, as he wouldn't be there to witness the transformation.

Bardi! Did he really want to go to Bardi? He ransacked hazy, obscure, half-forgotten corners of his memory. From somewhere came an image of a farmhouse. A long, low-built, greystone building that blended into a rock-strewn, barren hillside. He remembered a stone passage running right through the house, which was cold – ice-cold on even the warmest days. People – his black-garbed, cuddly grandmother, and sharp-featured, angular grandfather – lived on one side; cows on the other. A stone pigsty in the corner of the field next to the house, a huge, fat old sow grunting and snuffling in and around the soiled straw. Vines growing against the south-facing back wall of the house, blocking the light from the few tiny windows that punctured the ancient stonework.

And inside – inside, the house was cool. He saw again his spinster aunt sweeping the dirt from the flagstoned floors out through the open door into the yard. There were rough wooden chairs and tables, so rough that if you weren't careful you picked up splinters in your hands. And everywhere the smell of garlic and strong purple onions that wafted down from the racks hoisted close to the ceiling, out of reach of the mice. The air, dark and heavy with smoke from the wood-burning stove, and the aroma of his grandfather's wine fermenting in its wooden barrels. A wine so coarse and sour that even his grandfather cut it with water from the well before he drank it.

Aunt Theresa, his father's sister, who had never married because of some great tragedy, often hinted at but never openly spoken of, spinning wool in the evening after he and his grandfather had brought the sheep down from the top fields for the night – or had it been for the summer? He simply couldn't remember any more, except the warmth. The sun, and the clean, clear air. Sun and air that Maud needed. But at what cost? Could he go back to Bardi? Live there again? Fit in? Work as a farmer?

The music changed. Red-faced, Trevor rushed up, taking his place breathlessly beside him. He turned, and saw Maud walking slowly, unsteadily down the aisle towards him. She was leaning heavily on Evan Powell's arm, her dress a fairytale princess's gleaming gown of satin, that he didn't even recognise as his sister's. Her pale, thin face was radiant beneath the lace veil. She saw him looking at her, and smiled. That smile stilled every doubt: if Bardi would give Maud a chance of life, then Bardi was what he wanted.

Chapter Twenty-Five

'Giacomo!'

'Mama, you came!' Ronnie put down the pen he'd used to sign the register in the vestry and clasped his mother's bulk in his arms. Tears poured down her cheeks on to the sleeve of his best suit.

'We all came. Even little Robert and Theresa. But not Papa.' She dabbed her eyes with a preposterously tiny square of lace-edged linen. 'He wouldn't listen to me,' she wailed. 'But then, when would he ever listen to anyone except you, Giacomo? The rest of us, we told him, we told him straight,' the borrowed Welsh colloquialism sounded strange couched in her Italian accent. 'We said we were coming, and that was an end to it. He couldn't stop us. He didn't even try,' she sobbed. 'But he wouldn't come with us, and you our eldest son . . .'

'Mama . . . Mama!' Smiling, he drew her gently round the table and put her hand in Maud's. 'Please Mama, say hello to my wife.' Mrs Ronconi wiped her eyes, clasped Maud to her ample bosom, and succumbed to another outburst. Laura looked at Trevor and rolled her eyes heavenwards.

'Everyone in our house,' she said firmly. 'For tea. You're invited too, Reverend Price, and your wife.'

'Most kind, most kind,' the Reverend Price mumbled, frantically trying to think of an excuse as to why he couldn't go. But as it was too late to walk up the hill to the vicarage and back before evensong, he didn't really have one.

'Come on, Ronnie.' Laura prodded her brother in the ribs. 'If you've finished signing your life away to Maud, you may as well get on with whatever is left to you. Lead the way.' She watched critically while Ronnie helped Maud out of the chair that the Reverend Price had thoughtfully placed in the vestry for her. 'Mr Powell, I believe you lead Mama out,' she said, briskly taking charge. 'Trevor gets the bridesmaid. Diana, where are you?' She looked around impatiently until she saw her leaning against the wall next to the outside door. 'Mrs Powell, if you don't mind walking with another woman, you can have me.' She extended her arm to Elizabeth.

'I don't mind,' Elizabeth said stiffly, in a tone that clearly said she did. But then, Laura's suggestion was just one more insult in a day that had been filled with insults and peculiarities. She dreaded having to walk into chapel that night. When the new minister and her Uncle John Joseph got to hear of this, they'd have something to say about it. Of that she was sure.

Maud clung to Ronnie's arm as the vicar opened the door for them. She gasped in amazement. She'd seen people when she'd walked down the aisle, but with eyes only for Ronnie, she hadn't realised just how many were there. She couldn't even begin to imagine how they'd all heard, when the date had only been fixed the day before. The Graig grapevine must have gone into overtime. Mr Griffiths and Jenny were there, but not his wife. Mrs Richards and Glan from next door, some of her Aunt Megan's old neighbours from Leyshon Street, their neighbours from the Avenue, the Ronconis' neighbours from Danycoedcae Road, and all the tram crews who were off duty, presumably to represent the cafe's customers.

'Just smile sweetly at everyone, and get into Trevor's car as quickly as you can,' Ronnie said quietly as he slipped his arm from Maud's and supported her round the waist.

'But Laura's only across the road,' she protested.

'I thought I just heard you promise to obey me.' He glared at her in mock anger. 'Let's start as we mean to go on. In Trevor's car, woman,' he ordered.

Ensconced in Laura's front parlour with a plate heaped high with Mrs Richards' egg sandwiches, Jenny Griffiths' sausage rolls, Tony's cream cakes, and Laura's ham and egg pie balanced in one hand, and a glass of home-made blackcurrant wine that Laura had poured her in the other, Maud watched in bewilderment as Ronnie thanked everyone for the envelope that had been presented to him by Harry Griffiths.

'It's not much,' Harry said gravely, 'but as most of us didn't know about the wedding until this morning, there wasn't time to get you anything. And then again, seeing as how you're off to Italy first thing in the morning, it's probably just as well that we didn't get you anything bulky to carry.'

Used to dealing out largesse, not receiving it, for the first time in his life Ronnie was at a loss for words. Unable to mutter more than an inadequate 'thank you', he shook the hand of everyone who'd managed to cram into Laura's tiny parlour, before his mother called them out into the kitchen for a slice of the cake she'd baked that morning in defiance of her husband's disapproving glares.

'We'll be going in five minutes, Maud.' Ronnie crouched before the chair Maud was sitting in as soon as they were alone. 'Trevor's taking us to town in his car,' he said.

'Wherever we're going, I should change.' She looked around for her case, forgetting that Trevor had left it in his car.

'No you most definitely should not, young lady,' Laura contradicted as she bustled into the room and closed the door behind her. 'Go as you are and there'll be no argument from the desk in the New Inn about wanting to see your marriage lines. Damn, I shouldn't have said. Now I've spoilt the surprise. Your boys are all hovering outside wanting to say goodbye to you Maud; you can have as long as it takes me to find Trevor.'

Eddie, William and Haydn trooped in awkwardly together. They held out a parcel.

'Charlie knocked up a fellow he knew this morning and made him open his stall,' Eddie explained, emotion making him suddenly garrulous. 'We wanted to give you something to remember us by.'

'As if I'd forget any of you!' Biting her lower lip to stop it from trembling, Maud unwrapped the brown paper parcel.

'A clock!' she exclaimed. 'It's beautiful. Really beautiful. We'll treasure it always, won't we Ronnie?' She fumbled for his hand, and he squeezed her fingers gently.

'Brass bedside clock. Real brass,' Eddie said proudly. 'And it's got a second hand. There's an alarm button on the back. That small clockface at the bottom, that's where you set the time for the bell to ring.'

Maud reached up and wrapped her arms around Eddie's neck. 'You look after yourself,' she begged. 'If you must box, please be careful. And you will write, won't you?'

'I'll try,' he murmured, screwing his cap in his hands. 'You know I've never been very good at putting things down on paper.'

'Diana and I will make him write at least once a week.' William pushed his way past Eddie, and kissed her on the cheek. 'And don't worry, I'll be behind him every fight he has,' he joked.

Haydn was the last to kiss her, and by that time her soft blue eyes were brimming with unshed tears.

'Hey,' he smiled, lifting her chin with his fingers. 'We all have to grow up and move away, that's life.' He sat on the arm of her chair and embraced her warmly. 'Tell you what, I'll give you a secret to go with,' he whispered. 'I'm leaving tomorrow morning too, for Brighton. I've finally got a job where I'll be singing on a stage, not sweeping one.'

'Haydn, are you serious?' Maud stared wide-eyed at her brother.

'I wanted you to be the first to know,' he lied, blessing Elizabeth's tight-lipped silence and forgetting the long talk he'd had with his father about the move earlier that morning.

'You're really leaving tomorrow?' Eddie and William chorused.

'Yes, and I've got you a job with Mr Horton, that's if you want it,' he said briefly to his brother. 'Sorry I couldn't get you into the Town Hall as well, but the manager knew someone. Might even have been family.'

'Your mother and father are waiting, Maud,' Laura prompted from the doorway, concerned that the boys were tiring her.

Ronnie ushered the boys out of the room, so Elizabeth and Evan could get into the parlour. It was a tight squeeze in the passageway, and some people had already spilled up the stairs and out on to the pavement.

'I've got a couple of bottles of beer in the kitchen if you fancy some, boys,' Trevor shouted from the back of the house. William followed the call like a dog to his dinner, but Eddie and Haydn hung back. Haydn held out his hand to his brother-in-law, but Eddie looked him squarely in the eye before offering his.

'Just don't ever forget one thing, Ronnie Ronconi,' he said flatly. 'That's my sister you've got there.'

'She's not just your sister any more, Eddie,' Ronnie said with a wry smile. 'She's also my wife, and you'd better be careful in the ring. I don't want anyone, not even you, upsetting her.'

*

Elizabeth kissed Maud briefly on the cheek then left the room, sensing, yet resenting, Maud's desire to be alone with her father. Evan hugged Maud, kissed her, then delved deep into the pocket of the trousers of the suit he'd had made for his own wedding.

'The Italians set great store by valuables, or so they tell me. So I want you to have this.' He pressed his father's gold pocket watch and chain into her hand. 'Keep it safe love, both the watch and the chain are real gold. I was going to knock up Arthur Faller this morning and swap them for a piece of jewellery, but then I thought, no. They're solid, safe pieces. You'll be able to sell them anywhere in the world if you need to.'

'Dad, Grandad left them to you. I can't take them off you.'

'Yes you can. It'll please me to think of you looking at them, so you must take them or you'll upset me. Take care of yourself love, and don't forget to write. Keep well.'

Ronnie, hovering in the passage, saw Maud bite her lip again, and nodded to Trevor. Two minutes later she and Ronnie were sitting in the back seat of Trevor's car, their luggage safely stowed away in the boot as they sped down the hill towards the centre of town, and the New Inn.

The house remained crowded, even after Maud and Ronnie left. Haydn stood in a corner of the kitchen, drinking a small glass of Trevor's beer and surreptitiously watching Jenny Griffiths out of the corner of his eye. Charlie had arranged a lift for him with the driver of a meat lorry who was taking a load of lambs to London. The load was leaving the slaughterhouse at five in the morning, and for all he knew, if everything worked out the way he hoped, he'd never be back in Ponty again.

Finishing his beer and leaving his glass on the table, he took his courage in both hands and walked over to where Jenny was talking to Laura and Diana.

'Hello,' he said quietly, so quietly she didn't hear him. But Laura did. Pulling Diana's sleeve, she dragged her off to the front parlour. Puzzled, Jenny looked after them, then turned and saw Haydn.

'Could I talk to you? It won't take a moment,' he murmured. Jenny glanced around the packed room. 'We could go out the back,' Haydn suggested.

She followed him through the washhouse where the Ronconi girls were clearing and stacking plates, sorting Laura's from those that had been lent by the neighbours. Haydn walked ahead of her; he didn't see the winks and nudges that Tina and Gina were giving each other, but Jenny did. He stopped at the end of the small garden, and leant on the wall.

'I can't stay long,' she said awkwardly, conscious of all the attention that was being bestowed on them from the washhouse.

'Neither can I,' he said quickly. 'I just wanted to say sorry for that stupid row we had . . .'

'Oh so do I,' the words poured out in relief. She turned to him, an emotional, intense expression on her face that made his blood run cold. Did she think he didn't know about her and Eddie?

'Please let me finish what I want to say.' He looked away from her over the scrubby clumps of brown and moss-green grass towards the top of the mountain. 'I wanted to tell you,' he was talking quickly. Too quickly. 'I wanted to tell you that I'm leaving,' he said finally.

'Leaving?' she stared at him in bewilderment.

'Early tomorrow morning.' He was determined to keep speaking so there would be no awkward silences between them. 'I've been offered a job in Brighton.'

'In Brighton,' she echoed uncomprehendingly.

'Yes.' Her repetition of his words was beginning to irritate him. She sounded like a bad chorus echoing a lead singer. 'I'll be there until the end of the pantomime season, and with luck, the job might lead to another. It's what I've always wanted.'

'But you'll be back, home I mean, for weekends?' she asserted wretchedly.

'No,' he said briefly, still refusing to look at her. 'I won't be back.' He finally turned to face her. 'Hopefully, not ever. I just wanted to tell you myself before one of the others did. And of course I want to say goodbye.' He extended his hand to her intending her to shake it, but she clung to his fingers as though they were a lifeline. 'And I wanted to wish you and Eddie luck,' he added cruelly. He pulled his hand from hers and walked quickly away, leaving her feeling totally bereft.

'Well Signora Ronconi, what do you think?' Ronnie laid Maud

down gently on the huge double bed and looked around the room. It appeared vast, and incredibily beautiful to Maud's eyes, just like a Hollywood bedroom. The walls were hung in gold brocade paper, the windows and bed draped in rich blue satin, edged with deep, crunchy ruffles of thick lace. The furniture was old, Victorian, and dark oak, but she could forgive the old-fashioned look of the bedroom suite because the room was large enough to take the pieces and still leave enough space to walk around in.

'Bathroom's out in the corridor, first door on the left,' Ronnie smiled. 'So you can have a bath whenever you like. There's electric light' – he switched on the two bedside lights as though to prove it – 'and there's even a radio.'

'It's wonderful. Ronnie you shouldn't have,' she said, suddenly remembering practicalities like money. Ronnie had never discussed finances with her, and she wondered if he knew that all she had in the world was her bank book with three pounds in it, and the five pounds Diana had given her.

'This room is a wedding present from Trevor and Laura. They said they didn't want to give us anything we'd have to carry to Italy.' He began to empty his pockets on the dressing table as the bellboy came upstairs with his suitcase and Maud's Gladstone. Picking out sixpence from his loose change, he threw it to the boy, who caught it with a grin on his face.

'Thank you, sir. I hope you'll both be very happy, sir.' He gave Maud, who was lying on the bed in her wedding dress and veil, a quick, shy look, before Ronnie closed and locked the door behind him.

'Tell me, Mrs Ronconi,' Ronnie sat on the bed next to her, 'are we going to be very happy?'

'Yes,' she said decisively. 'Most definitely yes.' She lifted her hands to her head and began to fiddle with the veil.

'Here, I'll help you with that.' He gently disentangled the lace and head-dress from her hair.

'I hate to sound like a spoilsport, but I think you should get into bed. We've got a busy few days ahead of us. I don't know why it should, but travelling wears you out. Particularly a journey as far as Italy.'

'I don't know about bed, but I think I would like to get out of this dress before I crease it any more than it is now.'

'Do you want some help, or can you manage?'

'I can manage,' she said quickly, blushing at the implication of what he'd said. There were some aspects of marriage she was going to have difficulty growing accustomed to.

'In that case I'll go downstairs and get the dinner menus so we can order well in advance,' he said tactfully, pulling his pocket watch out of his waistcoat. The chain felt strange, too light without the keys to the café and van that he'd handed over to Tony.

'We're eating dinner here?'

'Evening dinner. Trevor and Laura paid for that too, and asked if we could have it in our room. Here – ' he carried her Gladstone over to the corner, 'I'll put your sponge-bag next to the sink.'

'There's a sink?' she looked around blankly.

'Behind the dressing screen.' He pointed to a large silk-covered Edwardian screen in the corner. 'Promise you won't faint if I leave you alone.'

'Promise.'

As soon as Ronnie left, Maud unbuttoned the row of mother-of-pearl buttons that fastened the front of the dress. Standing rather unsteadily next to the bed, she stepped out of the dress, found a clothes hanger in the wardrobe and hung the dress away, before going to the sink to clean her teeth and wash her face. Clinging to the sink for support, she reapplied her lipstick and powdered her nose. Then she looked in her Gladstone: the nightdress and jacket that Tina and Gina had given her was on top. She slipped them on over her underclothes, dabbed a generous amount of Evening in Paris on her throat and wrists, combed her hair, and checked her reflection in the mirror. Her face was ashen, but she knew that rouge would only make it look worse. Pinching her cheeks in an effort to impart some colour, she made her way back to the bed. She stared at it for a moment, smoothing the creases from where she'd lain. Then she looked around. There was a chair beneath the window that looked out over Taff Street. She sat in it, arranging the folds of the nightdress skirt gracefully round her thin legs. There was a knock at the door, and she shouted, 'Come in', expecting Ronnie, but it was the bellboy again.

'Champagne, Madam, with Doctor and Mrs Lewis's compliments. Where shall I put it?'

'Where do you usually put it?' Maud asked, trying to look as though this wasn't the first time she'd been in a hotel room.

'On the table, Madam.' He carried the silver bucket over to a small table that stood in a corner close to her. Pulling the bottle from the bucket, he proceeded to open it.

'Please don't.' Maud sat back in the chair and smiled. She had never been so happy. 'I'd like to wait for my husband.' The word had never sounded so sweet to her ears before.

'Jenny, if you're going home I'll walk you,' Eddie offered.

'Haydn talked to me,' she said miserably.

'I know,' Eddie replied abruptly. 'He talked to me too,' he almost added for the first time in three days, but thought better of it. 'Look, it's a fine, dry afternoon. If you don't want to walk through the house and face everyone again, we could go over the back wall and across the Graig mountain.' He made the suggestion as much for his own sake as hers. The idea of avoiding everyone, especially the Ronconi girls and Glan Richards, was extremely appealing in the light of the row between him and Haydn, which had now become far too public for comfort.

'Would you help me over the wall?' she asked, thinking of her best heeled shoes, and silk stockings.

'Yes,' he agreed flatly.

He lifted her unceremoniously on top of the wall, scrambled over it himself, then lifted her down the other side.

'I'm sorry,' she murmured. 'I realise that you and Haydn must have had a row . . .'

'We did,' he said shortly, not wanting to talk about it. 'But it doesn't matter. Not now.'

'Yes it does,' she insisted, wallowing in self-pity. 'I shouldn't have asked you to take me home that night, and I shouldn't have . . . shouldn't have . . .' she ceased her stammerings when she realised exactly what she had allowed Eddie to do to her, and only two nights ago. She lowered her crimson face and stared disconsolately at the ground.

'If I remember right it wasn't only you that made the moves.' He was walking along the mountainside aimlessly, not really knowing, or caring, what direction he was heading in.

'Do you think Haydn is going away because of me?' she ventured.

'Don't kid or flatter yourself. Haydn's going away because that's what Haydn wants to do. You don't come into it. He's been mooning after a career on stage for years, you should know that.'

'Then you think he'd go, even if we were still going strong?'

'I don't doubt it,' he said with more conviction than he felt.

'But to do it now this way, with no warning . . .'

'Now is when he had the offer,' Eddie pointed out logically. But Jenny didn't want logic. She wanted Haydn to suffer, just as she was suffering. 'It's probably all for the best,' Eddie continued practically. 'If you and he had still been together, he might have felt that he shouldn't go, but he probably would have just the same. This way he can start off on the stage without feeling guilty about anything.'

'I suppose you're right,' she conceded reluctantly. 'It's just that . . . that . . .'

'Look, Jenny,' Eddie said brusquely. 'I know you feel bad at the moment, but you're not the only one. I feel terrible too, and we can't undo what's done. Perhaps we could go out together one night. A walk maybe, or to the park.' He deliberately steered clear of anything that cost money. It would be a while before he paid Charlie back for his share of the clock.

'I don't know,' she murmured. All she knew was she wanted Haydn. And she'd never have him again.

'You know I like you,' Eddie persisted.

'I know,' she said miserably. 'The problem is, at the moment I don't like myself very much. I wouldn't be fit company for anyone.'

'As you please,' he said gruffly. He wasn't one to beg or chase a girl. 'Let me know if you change your mind.'

It was quiet in the New Inn. Quiet and peaceful. Maud had drunk a glass of Champagne before her dinner, one with it, and one afterwards. And that, along with the potent cough mixture Trevor had prescribed for her, had made her ridiculously happy, light-headed, and pleased with herself. The remains of the meal had been cleared away, and she'd had her bath. Dressed in her brand new nightdress (this time without her underclothes) she was half

288

lying, half sitting in bed sipping the fourth glass of Champagne that Ronnie had poured for her.

He was sitting in a chair that he'd pulled against the bed so he could be close to her. His jacket was in the wardrobe. He'd unbuttoned his waistcoat, and taken off his starched collar. His tie was hanging loosely around his neck and she could see the paisley pattern on his braces. She'd never seen Ronnie without a collar and tie on before, and the state of his undress carried with it an air of intimacy and excitement. Although as she'd seen her father and brothers without their collars on often enough, she couldn't have explained the peculiar feeling.

'Eight o'clock,' he murmured, putting the tickets he'd been studying back into his wallet. 'I asked them to give us a call at five so it's probably a good idea for you to get to sleep.'

'Not you?'

'I thought I might go for a walk.'

'To the café?' she enquired intuitively. 'On your honeymoon night? Don't you think everyone will think it a little strange, or worse still, me boring?'

'You boring? Never.' He picked up her hand from the bedcover and kissed her palm. 'I just feel restless.' He rose from the chair and stretched theatrically.

'I've got a cure for restlessness. Come here,' she demanded, patting the bed beside her.

'I will later. There's a couple of things I ought to talk over with Tony . . .'

'You did nothing but talk things over with Tony in Laura's,' she insisted. 'Come here!'

'I can see you're going to be a bully.' He sat beside her on the bed and cradled her in his arms.

'Laura said I should start as I mean to go on.'

'Laura! My God, you haven't been taking advice from my sister, have you?' he exclaimed in mock horror.

'How long did you say it's going to take us to get to Bardi?' Maud asked, wrapping her arms round his waist. Now she had him, she had no intention of letting him go.

'Tomorrow night, we'll be in London. Tuesday morning in France, then we have two days and nights on the train . . .'

'Then shouldn't we make the most of the time we have now?'

'Maud, you're ill.'

'Not that ill. Please, come to bed.' He could feel her trembling. Not just her hands, but her whole body.

'I'll have a bath, then I'll be back.' He opened his case and took out his sponge-bag, a bundle of clothes, and the packet Trevor had given him.

'Promise you won't go to the café?'

With his collar hanging over the back of his chair and his coat in the wardrobe, the question was faintly ridiculous. 'What café?' he asked blankly.

It had been years since Ronnie had worn anything in bed. As a child he had worn woollen nightshirts that his mother had stitched from the back and front of his grandfather's worn-out working shirts, but worried about Maud's sensitivity he had bought a brand new pair of pyjamas for himself in Cardiff along with the wedding ring.

When he returned to the bedroom, all the lights were out except the electric lights either side of the bed.

'I'll set the alarm clock that the boys gave us.'

'You've asked them to call us,' she reminded.

'So I did.' He dumped his sponge-bag and clothes on the chair, then closed the door and turned the key. 'Just in case someone mixes up our room with theirs in the dark,' he murmured.

It was ridiculous. He was behaving as if he was the inexperienced virgin, not Maud. All the women he'd known, all the evenings he and Alma had spent upstairs in the café, and he was the nervous one. He laughed suddenly, without warning.

'What's funny?' she asked.

'I was just wondering why I feel nervous, then I realised it's because I've never gone to bed with my wife before.'

Remembering Alma, and all the rumours Tina had spread about Ronnie's love life, Maud remained tactfully silent. He climbed into the bed, moving between the sheets until he lay alongside her. Sliding his arm beneath her shoulders, he pulled her head down on to his chest.

'I love you, Mrs Ronconi,' he murmured softly, ruffling her hair as he wrapped his other arm around her. She crept as close to him as she could. He could feel her skin scorching his beneath the thin layer of silk that she was wearing. He fought to keep control of himself, but innocently, apparently oblivious to the havoc she was creating within him, she snuggled close, clinging to him like a limpet.

'I never did like sleeping alone,' she murmured. 'It's good to know I won't have to again.'

'Oh yes? And how many other men have you slept with?' he teased.

'No men, silly. Only Bethan. I missed her when she went away.'

'You'll see her tomorrow,' he said without thinking, unintentionally spoiling the surprise he'd meant to give her.

'See her?' Maud asked excitedly.

'Trevor telephoned Andrew and arranged for him to pick us up from the train.'

'Did I ever tell you you're wonderful?'

'I already know, thank you. Tell me again and I might get big-headed.'

'I'm sorry,' she murmured.

'For what?'

'For dragging you away from your family and your cafés. I don't think your mother will ever forgive me.'

'Mama's forgiven you already.'

'Be honest, you would never even have thought of returning to Italy if it wasn't for me.'

'Yes I would,' he lied stoutly.

'Tony told me about your plans for the new restaurant, and the cafés, and how they'll find it impossible to manage without you.'

'No one's indispensable. And it's just as well we're leaving, because if we stayed you'd find out what a dreadful whiner and complainer Tony is.' He hugged her tight. There didn't seem to be any flesh on her bones at all.

'Ronnie I'm sorry . . .'

'Will you stop apologising?,' He kissed her forehead.

'I know I'm not very beautiful . . .'

'What are you on about?'

'I'm skinny and white, and ill, but I promise you, it won't always be this way. Would it help if I took my nightdress off?' she blurted out shyly, finally finding the courage to say what was uppermost in her mind.

'We've got a long journey tomorrow.' She was so frail he was truly terrified of hurting her, despite Trevor's approval.

291

'You married me,' she protested. 'I think I'm entitled to find out what being married really means. Laura said – '

'Laura always has said rather too much.'

She kissed him on the cheek, mindful of what Trevor had told her about passing tuberculosis on by mouth contact. Then she moved away from him and took off her jacket. He pulled her gently back down beside him.

'How about we take time to get to know one another first?' he murmured. Slowly, ever so slowly, he ran his fingers lightly down her arms. He was able to circle even her upper arms with his thumb and forefinger. Her bones felt so thin, so fragile, he was afraid that if he grasped her too firmly, he'd snap them.

Just as slowly, but more timidly, she responded. Somehow the buttons on his pyjama jacket came undone, and he rolled on to his side, pulling her down beside him, carefully keeping his weight on the bed, lest he crush her.

She kissed his bare chest, running her fingers through the thick mat of black curly hair on his chest and arms.

'You don't know what you're doing to me,' he whispered hoarsely. Sliding his hands down, he ran them upwards from her knees to her thighs, lifting her nightdress to her waist. Shifting slightly, he slipped his fingers between her legs, gently, tenderly, caressing and arousing her.

Despite Bethan's talks to her while she'd been growing up, the first touch brought hot flushes of embarrassment and shame to Maud's cheeks, but they lingered only as long as it took for new and wonderful sensations to erupt into life. Lifting her with one hand, Ronnie gently peeled off her nightdress with the other.

She heard the whisper of silk as it fell to the floor. Moments later, it was joined by the soft thud of cotton as his pyjama jacket fell close to it.

All feelings of naivety, shyness and inexperience dissipated as Ronnie continued to kiss and caress every inch of her. He kicked off his trousers, and she shuddered as the full length of his naked body came into contact with hers. He eased her on top of him.

'Ronnie, please,' she begged. There was a fire between her thighs that she had never experienced before. He rose to meet her until the fire was quenched by pain. She cried out, and he held her gently, while withdrawing quietly away from her.

'No, please. Don't move,' she panted breathlessly. 'Please . . .'

Still entwined, they rolled over until he was above her, resting his weight on his elbows. She moved beneath him, and for the first time he forgot her fragility, her sickness, losing himself wholeheartedly in her pleasure as well as his own.

It wasn't until afterwards, a long while afterwards when she was sleeping beside him, that he realised his face was wet with tears. The first tears he could remember shedding, and they were of sheer joy and happiness.

Chapter Twenty-Six

The customary Sunday night card game in the back room of Ronconi's café had a strangely funereal air about it. Eddie was conspicuous by his absence, and when Alma, during one of her rare moments of conversation, dared to enquire after him, Haydn almost bit her head off before William muttered something about him going down to clean up the gym.

Outwardly it seemed much the same as any other Sunday night, but as none of the Ronconi girls or Diana had come down, Alma was very conscious that it was different, because it was Ronnie's wedding day. And that consciousness burnt into her heart and mind with all the destructive force of a branding iron.

Haydn, William, Tony, Angelo and Charlie took turns to shuffle and deal the playing cards, but they did it in a mechanical, desultory fashion as though they had no interest in the outcome. And after witnessing some of the physical altercations that had taken place following the more disputed results on other evenings, Alma found the whole situation strained, and unreal. Even Tony's rather hit-and-miss attempts to play mine host in the way Ronnie had, grated on her delicate nerves. She'd already made up her mind that no one could take Ronnie's place: not in the café, not in the town, not with his family – and especially not in her heart.

She was very glad when the hands on the clock finally turned to eleven and Tony gave the order to clear up.

'Pity we can't have a drink to celebrate your good fortune,' William said mournfully to Haydn. 'That is, unless we manage to knock up the Horse and Groom.'

'They won't open up on a Sunday,' Charlie commented as he left the table. 'If they tried the magistrates would throw the book at them.'

'I suppose they would. Damned shame a man can't do what he wants in his own town because of the licensing laws. Harry Griffiths once told me that he could get a drink any time he wanted in France.'

'That's because he was there when there was a war on.' Tony picked up the chairs and began to stack them on the tables.

'No, you can drink in Europe any time you want to,' Charlie contradicted.

'Right, we'll all go to Europe,' William said gleefully.

'I didn't say they were giving it away for nothing, Will,' Charlie said seriously. 'You still have to pay.'

'Then we won't all go to Europe. Not this week anyway.'

'Nex week then?' Haydn smiled as he picked up a heavy tray loaded with their dirty cups and carried it out to the kitchen. Alma was there, dumping crockery into the overflowing bowl of warm, soapy water that Angelo had mixed to do the dishes.

'Off tomorrow then?' she asked.

'Yes.'

'You coming, Haydn?' William and Charlie shouted from the front.

'Thought I'd walk up to the gym and meet Eddie.'

William made a thumbs-up sign to Charlie. The estrangement between the brothers had upset both of them.

'In that case, we'll see you back in Graig Avenue,' Charlie replied diplomatically.

Alma untied her apron and hung it on the back of the door.

'Your brother trains at the Ruperra, doesn't he?' she asked.

'Yes. Why?'

'Can I walk along with you? I live in Morgan Street and it's on the way,' she explained awkwardly. 'I don't like walking through town on my own at this hour. Ronnie used to run me home in the Trojan, but Tony's not used to driving it, and anyway I don't like to ask him. Not after . . . after . . .'

'I'd be delighted to have your company,' he said, rescuing her from her embarrassment.

'As long as it's not taking you out of your way.'

'As you just said, Morgan Street's on a direct line to the Ruperra, or almost direct,' he qualified. He went into the café, picked up his new jacket from the back of a chair and followed her out.

'Nice night for a honeymoon,' he said unthinkingly, gazing up at the star-studded sky, which for once was cold, clear and dry.

'Yes it is,' she answered abruptly.

'I'm sorry,' he apologised. 'That was a stupid thing to say after you and Ronnie – '

'We weren't anything special to one another,' she interrupted.

'Yes, well, there's plenty of other fish in the sea, or so everyone's been telling me since Jenny and I split up.'

'I don't think I want to meet any other fish,' she replied sourly. 'Not for quite a while.'

'I know how you feel.'

By tacit agreement they kept to the right-hand side of the road, not crossing over until they'd passed the New Inn, but as they headed towards Gwilym Evans' shop, Alma couldn't resist looking back to see if there was a light on in any of the hotel bedrooms that faced Taff Street or Market Square. All were dark, and she had a sudden, heart-stopping, very real image of Ronnie and Maud lying side by side in a comfortable, luxurious bed. At that moment all she wanted to do was hurt him. As deeply and as irrevocably as he had hurt her.

'The quickest way to Morgan Street is to go past the YMCA isn't it?' Haydn asked, interrupting her illogical, vengeful thoughts as they drew close to the empty Fairfield.

'Yes.' She looked at his fair hair and finely chiselled features. 'Happy to be leaving tomorrow?' she asked.

'Hopefully it will turn into the break I've always wanted,' he replied carefully.

'I wish you well.' She couldn't help wondering what he'd do if it didn't work out for him in Brighton, now that his jobs in the Town Hall and on Horton's stall were filled.

'Thank you.' They entered the network of small streets and alleyways behind the town.

'This is it.' She paused outside a tiny two-up two-down. 'Would you like to come in for a cup of tea? I don't know why I do it after working in a café all evening, but I always make myself a fresh pot when I get home.'

'I'd like to, but I might miss Eddie. Thanks for the offer, Alma, and I hope all goes well with you too.'

He extended his hand, she took it, and lunged close to him. Her lips, warm and wet, were on his, her hands around his neck. 'My mother always goes to bed early,' she whispered in his ear. 'There won't be anyone downstairs, and I always find this time of night so lonely, don't you?' She opened the door. Taking his hand she led him unprotestingly down a dark passage into the back kitchen. 'Stay there,' she ordered.

He stood in the doorway while she fumbled with a box of safety matches close to the stove. Moments later the soft glow of an oil lamp filled the room. 'We can't afford to put electricity in,' she apologised. 'Or lino on the floor.'

He looked down involuntarily. The floor was bare flagstones, scrubbed almost white. A brightly coloured rag rug had been laid down in front of the stone sink, and there were multicoloured patchwork curtains at the window, but the furniture was old and rickety: the kind of stuff that Bown's sold off for three pennies a piece in their junk pile.

'It's not much, but it's home,' she said defiantly. 'My dad was killed in the pit when I was five, and my mam had a hard job bringing me up. When she went blind four years ago, it was almost the last straw.'

'I'm sorry. I had no idea . . .'

'It doesn't matter. Not now.' She regretted telling him as much as she had. The last thing she needed – or wanted – was charity. 'Ronnie promised me the head waitress job in the new restaurant,' she said proudly, 'and Tony said tonight it's still mine if I want it. And until it opens I've enough work to keep me going.'

They were standing close to one another, so close that when she reached out to pick up the kettle from the range her fingers brushed across his arm. The effect was electrifying, and not only on him. Alma had always recognised that her relationship with Ronnie had been primarily a physical one. At the outset she'd acquiesced to his demands because she'd believed submission to be the way to hold him. Later, when he'd aroused passions she'd only dreamt existed, she'd enjoyed and looked forward to their lovemaking much more than she'd ever hinted to Ronnie. And since the night she'd quarrelled with Ronnie over Maud, no man had touched her – until now.

Dropping the kettle on to the table, she laid her hand on the back of Haydn's neck, pulled him close and kissed him again. After the kiss outside, Haydn had been waiting for her to make another move. But it all felt strange – wrong, somehow. The cooking smells in her hair from the café. Her body more angular, and thinner than Jenny's. Even her kisses – soft, experienced, passionate – were different from Jenny's. But once her small breasts pushed against his chest, and her thighs pressed against his, he lost all thoughts of Jenny.

He didn't come to his senses until she moved away from him. 'We shouldn't be doing this,' he murmured huskily, looking into her eyes. 'I'm not Ronnie . . .'

'You wouldn't be here if you were,' she said caustically.

'Alma, this isn't fair on you . . .' He looked around for his hat, forgetting that he hadn't even taken it from his head.

'It's perfectly fair,' she said clearly. 'You're not Ronnie, and I'm not Jenny. But there's no law that says two lonely people can't share just one night.'

'It might be different if I wasn't going away tomorrow.'

'I asked you to take me home because you are leaving. No ties, no apologies. No regrets.'

She unbuttoned the front of her dress and let it fall to the floor, baring herself to him as she had never done for Ronnie, not even stopping to think why. Her clothes fell in a heap at her feet. She kicked them aside and walked to him, wrapping her arms around him. He ran his hands over her body, caressing her, kissing her.

Slowly they sank to the rug on the floor. She reached up behind her and pulled down a cushion from the only easy chair. Putting it beneath her head, she drew him on top of her, easing his arms out of his coat as she did so.

As their lovemaking progressed from tentative caresses to rougher, more urgent movements, he forgot about the strange scent and the unaccustomed feel of Alma's body beneath his. He was back in Harry Griffiths' storeroom in the shop on the Graig, and it was Jenny's face, not Alma's, that floated in his mind's eye as he thrust himself satisfyingly inside her. Just as it was Ronnie's face that occupied her thoughts as she surrendered herself to her physical needs.

Ben Springer drank in the Ruperra for many reasons: it was within easy walking distance of both his shop and his house at the 'smart' end of Berw Road; it had a rough, masculine atmosphere generated by the boxers who frequented the gym at the back of the pub and who very occasionally drank a glass of orange juice in the bar; and finally because the landlord, like him, enjoyed a game of cards and a glass of whisky. A common liking that had led to the setting up of a Sunday night private card school for the exclusive use of the landlord's favoured cronies, Ben amongst them. He was a popular member, not least because he was in business and solvent and never grumbled about putting in the ten-shilling stake that the landlord insisted on.

The boys who frequented the gym had often seen him leaving on a Saturday night, followed by the landlord's directive, 'Seven tomorrow all right for you Ben?' They cast envious glances at his made-to-measure clothes, his staggering gait, the result of at least five beers and whisky chasers, and whispered stories to one another in which the ten-shilling stake multiplied in magnificence until it reached as many pounds.

The gym, like the pub, was closed on a Sunday. Eddie generally cleaned it on a Sunday afternoon, but that Sunday he didn't even begin until early evening because of Maud's wedding. When Ben left at midnight, Eddie was still there, shadow boxing in the ring, lost in glorious fantasies of cheering crowds and Lonsdale belts, the door of the gym bolted and barred behind him.

Ben was always the last to leave the pub, even on a Sunday. As he paused to light a cigarette outside the door, the landlord dimmed the lights behind him. He set his face away from town towards the White Bridge on a route that he'd walked more times than he could remember. Half-way along the road was a pretty clearing of grass sprinkled with trees, where children played and old people sat in summer. On a cold winter's night it was dark and shadowy, and one of the street lamps had failed, plunging a fair proportion of his path into blinding blackness. He quickened his step, and as he did so someone tapped him on the shoulder.

The last thing on his mind was the 'bit of fun' he'd had with his erstwhile assistant. He wasn't sure what to expect. Someone who owed him money from the shoe club who was looking for more time to pay? Or, more hopefully, someone who wanted to order a special pair of shoes? He turned, straight into a closed fist.

Before he had time to shout, or defend himself, a second punch jerked his false teeth out of his mouth and on to the pavement. They fell on to the dry stone with a dull clink, then smashed into five pieces. A third punch knocked him off his feet, then a well aimed kick between his legs sent agonising, torturous pains shooting through his body. He vomited once, twice. The pains came again. Then mercifully the blackness intensified, numbing and finally blotting out the pain.

Wyn Rees walked quickly across Berw Road. He glanced over his shoulder: the street was empty. Standing close to the wall that overlooked the river he tossed a bundle as far as he could. The throw was well aimed: the bundle sank in the centre of the flowing water. He had no fears that it would rise again. He'd weighted it too well. His dead grandfather's overcoat that no one would miss was firmly wrapped round the same grandfather's steel toe-capped boots, and the stone that he'd used to put out the streetlight. He stopped just once, close to the chapel opposite the Ruperra. He had to rub his feet. The boots had been a size too small, and they'd pinched his feet.

He breathed a sigh of relief when he saw the light still on in the gym, but he had trouble getting Eddie to answer the door.

'Saw the light on,' he said, flinching as an expression of distaste curled Eddie's top lip when he saw who'd knocked him up. 'I left my wallet here last night.'

'Black one. There's nothing in it,' Eddie said flatly.

'Yes there is.' He followed Eddie into the office, took it off the desk and flipped open the secret pocket folded cleverly into the back panel. 'If you were a pickpocket you would have missed ten bob there.'

'Good job I'm not a pickpocket then.' Uneasy in Wyn's company and anxious to be shot of him, Eddie led the way to the door.

'By the way,' Wyn said casually. 'Your cousin Diana lives with you doesn't she?'

'She does,' Eddie answered shortly.

'Tell her there's a job going in one of our shops if she wants it. Starting tomorrow morning at seven. Twelve and six a week.'

'How do you know she's looking for a job?' Eddie asked suspiciously.

'She came in and asked.'

Eddie remembered Diana's job hunting. It was like her to leave no stone unturned. Even with a queer.

'You'd better warn her though, she'll be on her own. My sister will only be able to give her a hand for the first day or so. My Dad's had a funny turn, and the neighbours will help out for a while, but Myrtle really wants to take care of him herself. Doctor says his working days are over, so the job's permanent.'

'I'm sorry to hear that about your Dad.' Eddie was. Rees the sweets was a part of every Graig kid's heritage. 'But thanks for thinking of our Di. She'll be chuffed to beans. She wasn't very happy in Springer's.'

'I know. That's why I thought of her. But warn her it's until eight at night. Six days a week.'

Eddie opened the front door. Wyn Rees might be a queer, but there were plenty of others besides Di looking for work. He'd have the pick of the crop at those wages. Perhaps Di had reformed him. Perhaps he fancied her. He decided to have a word with William on the subject; after all, Diana was his sister.

'Bye Wyn,' Eddie said as he saw him out. 'And thanks again for thinking of Diana. She'll be there. Seven tomorrow?'

'High Street shop.'

Huw Griffiths ran past them as they stood talking on the doorstep. 'Seen anything, boys?' he panted, his face ruddy with exertion.

'No, why?' Wyn asked innocently.

'Man beaten up, on Berw Road. Bad by the sound of it. See you.'

'See you,' Wyn shouted. Things had worked out better than he'd hoped. He knew the way a copper's mind worked. No criminal waited around to be spotted near the scene of crime.

'Tired?' Trevor asked Laura as he folded back the sheets on his side of their bed.

'Depends on what you mean by tired.' She turned to face him, her head resting on the pillow.

'I'm whacked. Today seems to have lasted forever. Particularly the last two hours. I never thought I'd get your mother out of the car. She just wanted to talk . . .'

'And cry. She's just lost her eldest son, remember.'

'To marriage and Italy, not the scaffold.' He walked to the door and switched off the light. Using what little light percolated through the thick curtains from the street lamp outside their window to manoeuvre by, he struggled to the bed. 'Damn,' he cursed loudly.

'Stub your toe on the bed leg again?' Laura asked with irritating superiority.

'Your flaming fault for buying a bed with splayed legs.'

'It looks nice.'

'It bloody well hurts.' He sat on the bed and rubbed his stinging foot.

'I'd kiss it better if it was any other part of you.'

'Promises, promises.' He lay beside her and wrapped his arms round her shoulders.

'Trevor?'

'Mmm,' he murmured as he nuzzled her neck.

'Would you mind if I took over the setting up of the new restaurant, as Ronnie suggested?'

'No, of course not.'

'There's no "of course" about it,' she insisted peevishly.

'Why not?' he enquired innocently, still kissing her neck.

'Because every husband wants his wife at home, looking after him and his children . . .'

'Laura, please . . .'

'Not Laura please!' she exclaimed irritably. 'Every other man I know would object to his wife going out to work.'

'Do you, or do you not want to run the restaurant?' He moved away from her, sat up and crossed his arms.

'Yes,' she snapped defiantly.

'Well there you are then,' he said in a patient, long-suffering tone of voice. 'I don't see what this stupid argument is about.'

'This "stupid argument", as you put it, is about you minding.'

'But I don't,' he protested helplessly.

He reached out to her and she turned her back on him. He wrapped himself around her. Burying his head in the nape of her neck beneath her hair, he whispered, 'What's the matter, sweetheart? You afraid of failing if Ronnie's ideas and figures don't add up to success?'

Furious with him for being able to read her so clearly, she retorted, 'That and – ' She bit her lip and clammed her mouth shut.

'And what?' he pressed.

'And because I want a baby.'

'Laura, we've only been married a couple of months. There's plenty of time. Believe me, one day we'll have so many babies you'll be cursing me,' he said lightly.

'You don't understand.' She turned and clung to him. 'Sometimes I'm just so afraid of everything. Of having children. Of not having children. Of making a pig's ear out of the restaurant without Ronnie around to tell me to do things differently.'

'You poor, poor darling.' He kissed her on the mouth.

'I hate you doing that when I want to be angry,' she murmured.

'Then don't be.' He pulled at her nightdress and she sat up, lifting it over her head.

Slowly, tenderly, sure of her love and her response, he caressed her body with his own.

'Is the phone going to start ringing?' she muttered.

'Not tonight. I've told everyone in Pontypridd they're not allowed to be ill.'

'Then take off your pyjama bottoms, the knot's digging an extra navel in me.'

'Can't you be a little more romantic?' he grumbled playfully, as he kicked them off, and out from the bedclothes.

'Give me Clark Gable and a mansion and I'll show you romance.'

'I've been thinking . . .'

'Don't, not now,' she pleaded.

Trevor had been more than thinking; he'd been making serious plans, and wasn't about to be put off now that he'd begun to tell her about them.

'Speaking of mansions, you know that money we've put away to buy a house?'

'You've found a mansion on offer for a hundred and twenty pounds?'

'We did have a hundred and twenty pounds,' he cautioned.

'You've spent it?'

He could feel her temper kindling.

'The hotel and the dinner for Maud and Ronnie cost me five.'

'That's all right.'

'And Maud's medicine and some other things I got, like the beer, the sherry and a few odds and ends for Ronnie came to another five.'

'I've got five brothers. Make a habit of this and we'll never get a house.'

'I thought, as you're intent on spending the next couple of months working towards the opening of the new restaurant, you won't have much time to think of moving house.'

'I'll have all the time that's needed,' she began hotly. 'You needn't worry, you won't suffer . . .'

'I know I won't, sweetheart,' he said evenly, irritating her simply by refusing to allow his temper to rise to meet hers. 'It's just that in a year or two we'll have all the time in the world to think of buying a house, and if I'm lucky enough to get that senior's position – '

'You don't get it, and the hospital board will have to deal with me.'

'I'm sure they're all trembling in their beds this very minute at the thought,' he said, not entirely flippantly. 'Soon you'll have an income from the restaurant, I'll be earning more money, but in the meantime there's now. We have just over a hundred pounds in the bank. How about after you set the new place up, and it's running smoothly, we go on holiday?'

'You mean take a chalet in Porthcawl or somewhere like that?' she said doubtfully.

'I mean let's take a boat and train to Italy,' he said quickly. 'I've always wanted to see Rome, Venice and Florence, and I thought you'd like to see the village your parents came from.'

'And you'd like to see Maud?' she suggested shrewdly.

'She may need a doctor in six months.'

'Is that all you give her?' she demanded, fear crawling down her spine.

'How about it, Laura?' he asked, ignoring her question. 'This may be our last chance to travel. Once you start running the café, and the babies start coming, which they will, I promise you, we won't have time to even think of ourselves, let alone go away together. Just consider it for a moment. Only the two of us – no patients, no family, no neighbours to bother us for a whole month. I know it will put back the house, but we'd see a new country, or two,' he added thoughtfully. 'We'd have to travel through France, and we could either do the Italian cities first and then go to Bardi, or go to Bardi first. Wouldn't you like to meet your grandparents?'

'Yes, yes I would.' She kissed the tip of his nose. 'It's funny, I've never really thought about them much, not even when Ronnie used to talk about them. He said Papa's father is short. I can't imagine that. And my grandmother is immensely fat.' She suddenly burst out laughing. 'You know what they say? You should always look at a woman's mother before you marry her. Be warned. Hearing about my grandmother and looking at my mother you could end up with a mountain for a wife.'

'I'd still love you.'

She closed her eyes and imagined the warm, bright yellow Italian sun, and deep blue summer skies that her father and Ronnie had described so often on cold, wet, Welsh winter nights. The old, low-built farmhouse. The fields dotted with sheep and cows. The spire of the church in the village. But as she dwelt on happy thoughts of what was to come, Trevor was thinking darker thoughts. His mind's eye was preoccupied with an Italian cemetery, and a British Christian name preceding an Italian surname carved on a foreign marble headstone.

Chapter Twenty-Seven

The call came at quarter-past one. Laura swore, wriggled down under the blankets and pulled the pillow over her head. Trevor took his clothes downstairs and dressed in front of the kitchen stove. He drove quickly to the Cottage Hospital, waving to the policemen he passed. They all knew him and his car. Which was more than Ben Springer did. He'd come round in a white antiseptic room to see a young, tall, thin doctor bending over him. All he knew was that he felt blissfully numb from the waist down.

'Soon have you right as rain, Mr Springer,' Trevor reassured him as he dripped chloroform on to a gauze mask.

Ben Springer didn't find out until after the operation exactly what the young doctor had meant by 'right as rain'. He screamed, shouted, ranted, raved, and threatened legal action, but all to no avail. Everyone who'd seen him that night, including the policemen and nurses, said that the course of action taken by young Doctor Lewis was the only one possible under the circumstances. Doctor Lewis had undoubtedly saved Mr Springer's life. If Mr Springer thought that the loss of his manhood was too great a price to pay, then that was unfortunate.

Trevor didn't mind putting up with Ben Springer's screams and insults – not when he saw the smile dawn on Laura's face when he woke her to tell her about Ben's misfortune. And as she said, 'Terrible place, Ponty, after dark. But who'd have thought something like that could happen at the Berw Road end of town?'

Diana was up at half-past four to see Haydn off. She kissed him goodbye as he went out through the front door with his father, who'd offered to walk down the hill with him. Just as she turned to make her way back up the stairs, Eddie thundered out of Charlie's room and down the passage, muffler flying, boots in hand.

'They gone?' he demanded.

'Two minutes ago,' she said in astonishment. 'Why?'

'Want to catch him up.' Knees bent, Eddie pulled on his boots as he ran but didn't stop to tie the laces. He raced out of the door, and she heard him shouting down the street.

'What's all that din?' Elizabeth stood at the top of the stairs, a thick, ugly knitted shawl thrown round her nightdress. 'We'll have the neighbours complaining.'

'Eddie wanted to say goodbye to Haydn,' Diana explained as she returned to her room.

'I thought we'd dispensed with all that nonsense last night,' Elizabeth muttered tersely. 'Well now I'm up, I suppose I'd better stay up.'

Diana heard her aunt pouring out her washing water as she returned to her own, now cold bed. She lay there in the semi-darkness, creating images to fit the shadows cast on her walls by the street light, her mind preoccupied with her worthlessness. Where could she go, and what could she do? She had no job. No family other than William, and he could do very well without her. Maud had needed her, but now she had Ronnie. Even her place in this house was dependent on her uncle's charity, and he wouldn't be in a position to keep her once her savings ran out, no matter how much he might want to. That left the agency in Mill Street and another skivvy's job which would barely bring in enough to keep her, let alone put anything aside towards the time when her mother would come out of prison. And she didn't even have the prospect of marriage to look forward to. No man would ever look at her the way Ronnie Ronconi had looked at Maud yesterday. She would never be able to wear white, never . . . but then, did it matter? After what Ben Springer had done to her, she wouldn't be able to face marriage – to anyone.

Wrapping her head in her arms, she cried. Hot burning tears of shame, misery and despondency. Later – she'd get up later and pack. She may as well give in and leave for service today, while she still had her five pounds in the Post Office.

'Haydn?' Eddie caught up with his brother and father as they reached the Graig Hotel.

'Where's the fire, boy?' his father demanded.

'No fire, just wanted to say goodbye to Haydn.' Eddie held out his hand. Haydn looked at it for a moment, then he gripped it.

'Good luck, Haydn. All the best. I mean it.'

'I know you do.' Haydn shook his brother's hand firmly.

'I'm sorry for everything.' His father stood back mystified, not understanding what Eddie was talking about.

'If it hadn't been you it would have been someone else.' Haydn clasped his brother's neck. 'Take care in that boxing ring.'

'And you take care living with the English.'

'Nothing but goodbyes lately,' their father muttered miserably. 'First Bethan, then Maud, now you . . .'

'Just think of all the places you'll be able to visit,' Haydn said on a cheerful note as he released Eddie.

Eddie bent down to tie his shoelaces. When he straightened up Evan and Haydn had been swallowed up by the darkness. But at least he and Haydn hadn't parted with bad blood between them. He was glad of that. And he smiled as he remembered the good thing he'd almost forgotten in his rush to see Haydn. He had something to tell Diana.

His mother was raking the hot ashes from the stove when he went back into the house.

'Eddie Powell, just look at the state of your bootlaces,' she grumbled as he walked into the kitchen. 'You've been running down the road with them undone. You could have broken your neck. As it is they're frayed to ribbons, good for nothing . . .'

'Diana up yet?' he asked, helping himself to a cold leftover pikelet from a plate in the pantry.

'No.' Elizabeth looked at the clock. 'And seeing as how it's only a quarter to five she doesn't need to be up. That's if she's still got a job in Springer's to get up for.'

Eddie kept his secret to himself. It didn't seem right somehow for his mother to know about Diana's good fortune before she did. He went into Charlie and William's room to collect the clothes he'd carried downstairs the night he and Haydn had quarrelled. William would be pleased to see him move back upstairs. It had been a tight squeeze, two of them in a single bed.

Elizabeth had breakfast waiting on the table when Evan returned from town. Charlie, William and Eddie were eating, but there was no sign of Diana.

'He got off all right then?' Elizabeth asked.

'Ay, he did,' Evan assured her.

'I'd be happier if I knew more about where he was going.'

'He knows the people, and he seems to think he'll be all right.'

'He's only a boy.'

'A sensible one,' Evan said firmly.

'I'm going to call Diana again.' Eddie left his seat.

'Sit down and finish the food on your plate,' Elizabeth ordered. 'I don't know what's wrong with you this morning. You're like a cat on hot bricks.'

'I've a message for her.' He pulled the door open and bumped into Diana, who happened to walk in just as he tried to walk out. She was wearing her best dark green costume, and cream blouse.

'And may I ask where you're off to, young lady?' Elizabeth asked.

'New job,' Eddie smiled.

'New job?' Diana looked at him blankly.

'Wyn Rees called round the gym late last night. His father's been taken bad, and he asked if you could take over the High Street shop for him. His sister'll help you today and tomorrow, but then you'll be on your own. Twelve and six a week because it'll be long hours. Seven until eight at night, and you'll be responsible for everything.' Diana sat down rather suddenly. 'He said you'd know all about it, because he told you what was expected when you went round asking him if he had anything going in the shops.'

'He did?'

'That's a darned sight better than Springer's any day, love,' Evan said. 'I never was very happy with you working there.'

'No.' She looked at her aunt. 'I'll be able to pay my way now, Aunt Elizabeth,' she said proudly. 'Seven and six. The same as William and Charlie.'

'Well, seeing as how Bethan and Maud have both gone, and you know how to make yourself useful around the house, supposing we keep it to four shillings on the understanding you help out. Especially on Sundays. Now that Uncle John Joseph's on his own, he needs all the help I can give him.' Evan stared at his wife in amazement as Diana stammered her thanks. 'And you may as well move your things into Maud's room. No sense in leaving a big room like that empty. You can have the box room, William, and that means you can have a room to yourself, Mr Raschenko.'

309

'Thank you, Mrs Powell,' he said, winking at Diana.

'Mrs Powell, Diana?' Laura walked into the kitchen. 'I'm sorry for calling so early,' she apologised.

'Not at all. Sit down. I'll pour you a cup of tea,' Elizabeth offered stiffly, smoothing over her apron.

'Please don't put yourself out, Mrs Powell. I can't stop. I'm on my way up to Mama's. I want to see Tony before he starts in the café, and I rather hoped to have a word with Diana beforehand if I could.' Laura was bubbling with suppressed excitement. 'If you'd like to walk me to the door, Diana. It won't take a minute.'

Completely bewildered, Diana followed Laura out through the door and into the freezing cold passage. The door slammed behind them. Two minutes later there was a huge shriek.

'What on earth . . .' Eddie was half-way out of his chair when William pulled him down. 'I've no idea what it's all about, but they won't want you there,' he pronounced knowledgeably, used to Diana's ways. 'Probably some stupid girl rubbish or other,' he added, hurt that Laura hadn't let him in on the secret.

'Seems to me that's the first time I've heard that girl laugh since she's come home,' Evan commented, looking sideways at his wife as he bit into his toast and dripping.

'It's five to six, I'd better see if Trevor's arrived.' Ronnie took one more look around at the room he'd begun his married life in, before kissing Maud.

'Not on the lips,' she admonished, sinking back against the cushions of her chair.

'As I'm sleeping with you, woman, it's time I got used to your germs.' Maud had insisted on getting up at four to have another bath and wash her hair. He'd helped her dry it, and it now framed her face, soft, fluffy and curly.

'Promise me something?' he asked as he picked up their bags.

'What?' she smiled.

'Don't wave your hair again. I like it just the way it is.'

'Frizzy?'

'Soft, like an angel's.' He dropped her Gladstone so he could run his fingers through it again. 'I also think it would look better long.'

'Long hair isn't fashionable.'

'It is in Italy,' he hazarded a guess.

'Then seeing as how you asked nicely, I might let it grow.'

He picked up the case again. Laura's wedding dress and veil were on the bed, where he'd laid them earlier. 'I'll bring Trevor up to take down the dress,' he said, 'and you – ' he pointed a warning finger at her, '– will not move from that chair until I lift you out.'

Maud smiled impishly.

'I mean it.'

'I'm terrified.'

'So you should be.'

He left the room, whistling happily as he ran down the magnificent wide staircase.

'Bridegroom looks happy,' Trevor grinned from the foyer.

'Bridegroom is happy. Very happy,' Ronnie beamed.

'Your chariot awaits, and someone who wants to talk to you. I picked him up half-way down the Graig hill.'

Ronnie looked behind Trevor and saw his father hovering in the doorway holding his mother's fox fur coat.

'I'll put the cases in the car,' Trevor said as he took them from Ronnie.

Ronnie walked warily towards his father and extended his hand. He'd feared a rebuff, but his father took it.

'Twenty years I've been wanting to send this to your grandfather, but there's always been something. Another café to open, or worries about it getting lost in the post, or one of you needing something . . .' He folded a fifty-pound note into Ronnie's palm. 'It's for your grandfather,' he repeated sternly as though Ronnie was likely to misunderstand him. 'To buy a white suit and a good horse. All his life he's wanted a white suit and a good horse. And I promised when I left home that I would buy them for him. And this', he gave Ronnie another twenty pounds, 'is for your grandmother and Aunt Theresa to buy new Sunday clothes. You mind you tell them what it's for.'

'I will, Papa, but the business won't stand this money being taken out . . .'

'You're not the only one who knows how to put a little by,' his father admonished. 'And this is for you.' He gave him one more fifty-pound note. 'There won't be enough food put away on the farm to feed two extra mouths until the crops come in. And I won't have your grandparents and aunt giving you their rations.'

311

'Papa – '

'Maud!'

Ronnie heard the shock in Trevor's voice and looked behind him. Maud was clinging to the elegantly carved mahogany banisters as she walked slowly down the stairs.

'Please don't be angry,' she laughed as Ronnie rushed to her side. 'I wanted to see if I could do it. And I have!' she announced triumphantly, allowing him to help her as she reached the last step.

'I told you . . .'

'I know.'

'This is your wife?' his father asked, although he'd known Maud since the day she was born.

'Yes Papa.'

'This is for you.' He thrust the fur coat at her. 'Don't thank me, it's none of my doing, it's Ronnie's mother's, and I wouldn't let her come this morning to give it to you herself. Couldn't stand any more of her fussing and crying. She won't wear it, not here where it rains all the time. And it can get cold in Italy in winter.'

'Mr Ronconi, I can't take this,' Maud gasped.

'None of my doing. Just you see that she wears it, Ronnie. Looks like she needs something to keep her bones warm. There's no flesh on them to do the job.'

'Yes Papa,' he choked back his laughter as he helped Maud into the coat.

'I've got the wedding dress and veil.' Trevor ran down the stairs with them in his arms. 'If there's nothing else we should be on our way.'

'There's nothing else.' Weighing up the austere expression on Mr Ronconi's face, and balancing it against the twinkle in his eye, Maud stepped towards him and ventured a hug. He kissed the top of her head, then propelled her gently back to Ronnie.

'I've an idea. Why don't you come to Cardiff with us, Mr Ronconi?' Trevor asked. 'You can keep me awake on the way back. I had a night call,' he explained.

'As if I can spare the time to stand on railway platforms, when this good-for-nothing son of mine leaves me to run the business on my own. Who's going to open the cafés in the morning now? That's what I'd like to know.'

'Goodbye Papa,' Ronnie lifted his hand again, but his father clasped him by the shoulders and kissed him on both cheeks.

'You think you could have found a healthy one,' he grumbled as Trevor helped Maud to the car.

'She's the one I want, Papa.'

'Then you'd better make her healthy.'

'I'll try.'

Ronnie stood on the steps of the New Inn and watched as his father walked away without a backward glance.

'Laura put a rug and a pillow there for you, Maud,' Trevor called from the driving seat as Ronnie finally climbed into the back of the car with her. 'She wants you to take them on the train with you.' He had to repeat himself twice before Maud and Ronnie answered. They were engrossed in watching the bowed, solitary figure of his father as he made his way through the litter-strewn streets towards the Tumble.

Andrew John stood, arms folded loosely over the barrier in Paddington Station, watching the tides of people as they flowed from the Swansea train. He kept a close eye on those leaving the third- and second-class carriages, searching for a glimpse of Ronnie's dark, slicked-back hair, or Maud's blonde curls.

'Doctor John?' Ronnie stood before him, dressed in a good winter-weight overcoat and expensive trilby.

'Ronnie?' Andrew shook his hand enthusiastically.

'It's very good of you to meet us.'

'Not at all. After all, we are brothers-in-law now.'

'So everyone in Pontypridd keeps reminding me.'

'Where's Maud?' Andrew looked over Ronnie's shoulder for the pert, pretty blonde who'd teased him in Graig Avenue when he'd gone there with Bethan.

'She's still in the carriage, I thought it best for her to stay there until I knew where your car was.'

'It's over there,' Andrew waved his hand to the left. 'When I showed them my bag and told them I was waiting to pick up a semi-invalid they let me park it by the taxi ranks.'

'I'll get the porter.' Ronnie disappeared into the crowd, re-emerging moments later with Maud in his arms and a porter in tow. Andrew rushed to open the car doors. Ronnie deposited

Maud tenderly on the back seat before walking around to help Andrew stack the cases in the boot.

'The boat sails at eleven tonight,' he murmured, heaving his suitcase next to Maud's Gladstone.

'So Trevor told me.' Andrew slammed the boot shut. 'Bethan has a meal waiting. She wanted to come, but I wouldn't let her. Not in her condition in this crush, but she's desperate to see you.'

'Me or Maud?' Ronnie smiled.

'Both.' Andrew delved under the front seat for the starting handle. As soon as the car purred into life he removed it quickly and dived into the front seat.

'Nice car,' Ronnie commented from the back seat where he'd sat next to Maud before Andrew'd had a chance to greet Bethan's sister.

'Nice of you to say so, but it's not mine,' Andrew replied as he pushed the car into gear. 'I borrowed it off my brother-in-law.'

'Sorry.'

'So am I,' Andrew replied drily as he pulled slowly out of the station and up into the light of the street. 'If it was mine, it would mean that I was doing better than I am.'

'This is London!' Maud cried out excitedly, staring round-eyed in wonder at the façades of terraces that were even longer, larger and grander than the ones she'd seen in Cardiff.

'This is London!' Andrew steered carefully around a taxi and a bus; as he pulled up at a junction he looked in the mirror and smiled at his sister-in-law. The smile died on his lips. Maud had pulled back the thick blanket and fur coat that Ronnie had wrapped round her when he had carried her from the train to the car, and was sitting forward, poised on the edge of her seat, holding Ronnie's hand. The sight of her thin, almost skeletal figure reminded him of the line, 'The skull beneath the skin', and it took no imagination on his part to place Maud amongst the cadavers that the first-year students in the hospital practised on. Realising that Ronnie was watching him, he pulled the wheel sharply to the left, and concentrated on his driving.

'Bethan's so looking forward to seeing you, and getting all the gossip from home.'

'There's lots,' Maud pronounced with an air of bright animation that belied her outward appearance of wan, sickly fragility. 'But I've no intention of telling you any of it in advance.'

314

'Same old Maud,' Andrew gave a rather forced laugh. 'Tell me Ronnie, do you think you'll succeed in turning her into a subservient wife?'

'A wife, yes,' Ronnie caught Maud's hand and pressed it to his lips. 'Subservient, never.'

'Beth, this is lovely. Really lovely.' Maud lay back on Bethan and Andrew's bed, watching as Bethan sat on her dressing-table stool and combed her hair.

'You like the flat then?' Bethan was horror-struck by Maud's appearance, but well schooled by her mother in the art of concealing her feelings, she kept her shock hidden. They heard the sound of male laughter coming from the living room, accompanied by the clinking of ice dropping into whisky glasses. Maud laid her hand on Bethan's.

'You're really happy, aren't you?'

'Ecstatic!' Bethan smiled, patting her enormous stomach proudly.

'I do envy you. I hope Ronnie and I have a dozen.'

'I suggest you get well first.'

'I intend to. So does Ronnie, and he always seems to get his own way.'

'With you around, he won't be doing that for long.'

She washed her hands in the bathroom, and went into the kitchen. Maud followed her and sat on one of the up-to-the-minute, art deco beechwood chairs that Andrew had bought in Barker's in Kensington.

'And you,' Bethan asked, looking her sister in the eye. 'Are you happy with Ronnie?'

'Yes. He's wonderful. I never thought of marrying him before he asked me. Well, he always seemed so much older than me. But he's terribly good-looking, and . . . and . . .'

'He swept you off your feet?'

'Something like that,' Maud answered shyly. Bethan gave her sister a hug before she began to dish out the food. It was obvious to anyone who looked that Maud was in the first flush of love – or infatuation. For both Ronnie's and Maud's sake she hoped it was the former, and of the kind that would last. With what lay ahead, they'd both need it.

315

*

'I've found you a porter, he'll take your cases to your cabin, and I had a word with a customs officer. He's promised to see you and Maud through as quickly as he can. I've also managed to get a chair. God knows how old it is, but it should hold Maud's weight until you've wheeled her to the cabin. You've got your tickets and everything?'

'Everything being our marriage certificate and my original Italian passport. There wasn't time to see to anything else. But it should be enough. Thank you for a lovely evening and for driving us here.' Ronnie shook Andrew's hand. 'Shall we see if we can prise those two apart?' He nodded to the car where Bethan and Maud were still locked in conversation.

Andrew and Bethan watched as Ronnie, porter in his wake, wheeled Maud into the customs hall.

'She's dying, isn't she?' Bethan asked, clinging to her husband.

'She has advanced tuberculosis, yes,' he admitted, 'but Ronnie is doing all he can. And if she doesn't live, it won't be for the want of him trying. He's taking her to the best place. Italy has a wonderful climate. Not too hot, not too cold. Dry, warm, clean air. It just might work.'

'And it might not.' She lifted the collar of her coat around her neck and shivered. The air was chill, with a hint of snow in it. He put his arm tenderly round her shoulders.

'If sheer bloody-mindedness counts for anything in effecting a cure, then Ronnie will have Maud fit, well and working in the fields by the end of the summer,' he pronounced resolutely. He slipped his fingers beneath her chin and lifted her face to his. 'How about we go home to bed?' he murmured huskily, suddenly very grateful for all his blessings.

Chapter Twenty-Eight

The crossing was a nightmare. The steward gleefully told Ronnie as he emptied Maud's sick bowls down the toilet that he hadn't seen a rougher one in thirty years. And the whole time Maud tossed and turned uncomplainingly in her narrow bunk, Ronnie crouched on his knees beside her, spongeing her feverish face with tepid water and holding empty bowls to her mouth. He had to take the coats that he'd hung on the door and fold them on to the bunk he didn't have time to sleep in, as their alarming swaying from side to side began to affect him too.

He had cause to remember his glib words to Evan many times over during the course of that interminable crossing: 'I'll get a cabin with a berth, then all Maud has to do is sleep until Calais.' No one slept. Not Maud. Not him, and none of the other passengers if the noises coming from the corridors were anything to go by. And the nightmare didn't end with the docking of the ship.

Calais was still shrouded in grey misty night when he wheeled Maud off the ship. He peered in the direction that a blue-coated official pointed him in, and just about managed to make out the wavering lights of the customs sheds that punctuated the darkness ahead. The French excise officers were neither as sympathetic nor as understanding as the ones Andrew had spoken to in Tilbury. They shouted at him in harsh guttural French, which they repeated loudly, syllable for syllable, even when he shrugged his shoulders and spoke to them in English and Italian. They made no allowances for Maud's weakness, insisting that she leave the wheelchair so they could search the folds of the fur coat and blankets, and when Ronnie tried to help her back into the chair when they'd completed their search, he discovered to his fury that someone had taken it. He supported Maud as best he could, while the officers rummaged through her Gladstone and fingered her clothes. All he could do was stand by incensed, watching helplessly as they heaped the silk underwear his sisters had bought

Maud on to their rough wooden tables, and opened the packet of contraceptives Trevor had given him. Long before the search was finished Maud fainted, the dead weight of her head lolling weakly against his shoulder.

Eventually the officials moved on to their next victim, leaving him, and an unconscious Maud, to repack their own bags. Fortunately an elderly British couple came to his assistance, the husband going in search of porters while the wife packed for him.

Even then it seemed to take an eternity of shouting, arguing and bad-tempered exchanges before he managed to leave the customs shed. Tipping the porter with an English ten-shilling note, the lowest coinage he had, he persuaded the fellow to follow him to the trains. There, only after ten harassed minutes, they managed to locate the carriage that was to take them to Genoa. The Italian steward helped him get Maud aboard, stowed away their suitcases in the stateroom he had booked, pulled down their beds, and offered to heat up some soup for Maud who had still not recovered from her faint.

Pathetically grateful for the steward's kindness, help and blessedly familiar language, Ronnie gave him a pound, promising the man more if he would help him care for Maud on the journey. As soon as they were alone, Ronnie undressed her and put her between the stiff, starched sheets on the makeshift bed. She lay there like a wax doll, white, silent and just as lifeless.

She came round as dawn was breaking over the horizon of the French countryside. Pushing aside the chicken soup Ronnie tried to feed her, she insisted on sitting up and looking at everything; exclaiming at the red-roofed, greystone French farmhouses, similar yet different from the ones in Wales. The flat country, the level patchwork of fields, the towns, so strange, peculiar and foreign after Pontypridd. Afraid of missing anything, her eyes darted in their sockets as she tried to assimilate all that could be seen from the window. She found something to wonder over with every mile they passed: a windmill, a French peasant woman driving a donkey, a man wearing a beret . . . When she began to cough Ronnie fed her three spoonfuls instead of the usual single spoonful of mixture in the hope that it would induce her to rest, but if anything it had the opposite effect. Bright-eyed, feverish, she point-blank refused to lie down.

The steward brought them a meal when Ronnie declined to visit the dining car. Ronnie laid the trays over their knees on the bed. Sitting next to Maud, he tried to force her to eat, slipping morsels of chicken and potato into her mouth as she continued to stare in wonder at her first foreign country. He stayed with her even after the steward removed the trays, propping her against him, holding her while her skin grew first warm, then uncomfortably hot, until it burned his chest through the thick linen of his shirt.

He tried to listen to her enthusiastic cries and make suitable comments, but his mind was elsewhere. Evan had posed the question of what he would do if Maud died on the journey. Had Evan had a premonition of sorts? Had his own stubborn streak set Maud on a course that was going to end here, in this carriage?

By nightfall she was delirious. Mindful of Ronnie's large tip and the promise of extra money, the steward produced iced water, soup, and more pillows at regular intervals. Ronnie did what little he could, and sat holding Maud's hand as her colour heightened and her eyes grew wild.

That night they stopped to take on coal. The steward disappeared, reappearing an hour later with a doctor, who shook his head and gave Ronnie a bottle of laudanum in exchange for an English pound note. Ronnie had no compunction about using it, hoping that the drug would finally compel Maud to rest.

When the train began to move, he lay beside her. As the next dawn broke the steward looked into their room, but he did not raise their blinds, figuring that sleep was better medicine than chicken soup for both the sick young signora and her exhausted husband.

When Maud finally woke again the sun was high, and Ronnie's eyes were open as he lay, fully dressed, beside her. She smiled, and he breathed again: the smile was one of recognition, not delirium.

Somewhere on that interminable train journey, Maud's infatuation with Ronnie died. She found it impossible to remain infatuated with a man who sat beside her in shirt-sleeves, braces and no collar, with two days' growth of black stubble covering his cheeks, feeding her while she lay in bed as weak and helpless as a baby. He washed her, changed her, dressed her in clean clothes, and while he cared for her generously, selflessly, and more tenderly than any nurse the image of the tall, dark, sardonically handsome Ronnie, always dressed immaculately in clean jacket, boiled shirt and stiff white collar as he cracked acidic jokes in the café was replaced by a weary, grey-faced exhausted Ronnie who winced every time she coughed. And as infatuation died, so it was supplanted by a sounder emotion, rooted firmly in his caring, obsessive passion for her.

She forced herself to eat when he spooned food into her mouth, even though she felt food would choke her. She smiled at him, and held his hand, because they were the only ways open to her in which to show her gratitude. But he was too busy nurturing the flame of life that flickered weakly inside her to notice the change. All he knew was that she was mercifully quieter.

'Genoa, Signor!'

Although he had dressed Maud and repacked their suitcases in preparation for reaching the town, Ronnie had been dreading the end of the rail journey. It meant having to leave the steward's care and the security of the bedded stateroom that had enabled him to care for Maud with at least the rudiments of comfort to hand.

'I'll find you a porter, Signor,' The steward offered.

'And a taxi,' Ronnie pleaded, slipping him two more pounds. 'I need to get to the Bardi bus. But first I need to change my English money for Italian lire . . .'

'Signor, all the buses leave outside the station. May I make a suggestion? My cousin's wife runs a small *pensione* here. You can leave your wife with her while you change your money and find your bus.'

'I'll do that.' Ronnie grasped eagerly at the idea of finding another bed for Maud to lie in.

The steward returned with a porter and handed Ronnie a small heap of coins.

'You paid me much too much, Signor,' he said gravely. 'I have already tipped the porter and told him where to take you. Good luck to you and your wife.'

Ronnie shook the man's hand appreciatively. Picking up Maud, he stepped off the train into an icy blast.

'Italian winds are just as bloody freezing as Welsh ones,' he muttered as he gritted his teeth and followed the porter.

'Did you say something?' Maud mumbled sleepily. After the excitement of the the journey through France and the attack it had precipitated, Ronnie was taking no chances. There'd been more than a spoonful of laudanum in the coffee he'd fed her after their last meal.

It was six o'clock in the evening. The square was full of people hurrying home from work. A sprinkling of travellers lingered in the cafés waiting for their buses and trains. A few steps and he found himself in the small lodging house. The room the proprietress showed him to actually overlooked the square. It was clean, and the woman friendly. If Maud's condition was bringing them sympathy and good service, he certainly wasn't too proud to accept it. He put Maud to bed, and left after asking the woman to keep an eye on her. He had no choice. They needed Italian money, and he h to find out about buses to Bardi.

'The day after tomorrow!'

'They only go once a week, Signor. Bardi is not a popular place. Every market day, one bus comes in and one goes out. It will leave at noon.'

The market bus. He had a sudden memory of that bus. Packed with gnarled old countrywomen laden with chickens and geese, the whole shrieking every time the ancient, battered vehicle jerked over pot-holes that speckled the unmade roads, like currants in Welsh cakes.

'There's no other way? A car, perhaps?'

'A car! To Bardi? No, Signor.' The driver laughed at his naivety.

There was nothing for it. He returned to the *pensione*, lay next to Maud on the bed and waited. Perhaps it was just as well she could rest before the worst part of their journey began. And their landlady proved as kind as she was friendly, doing their washing for them and bringing rich minestrone soups and omelettes to their room to tempt Maud's non-existent appetite.

The Signora had a cousin who knew the driver. At her injunction he kept seats for Ronnie and Maud close to the front of the bus, where they could receive some benefit from the warmth of the engine. They needed it. The Signora's husband carried their cases on board, and Ronnie carried Maud.

The journey from Genoa to Bardi was every bit as hellish as Ronnie had feared. They bumped and rocked their way painfully over dirt roads, stopping at every out of the way hamlet and farmstead, and all he could do was hold Maud suspended on his lap and hope that the cheeses and live chickens stowed overhead on the string racks next to their suitcases wouldn't fall on to their heads.

They eventually reached the square in Bardi at five in the afternoon, and even Ronnie was cold, tired and exhausted. He left Maud slumped in her seat and carried the suitcases off first, then he went back for her. He stood feeling totally lost and bewildered in the darkening square, holding a sick and barely conscious Maud in his arms.

He couldn't remember anything. Not even the road out of the town to his grandfather's farm.

'You look as though you need help, Signor.' The man was old, bent and grey. A busybody. A blessed busybody who might know everyone in the village – and outside.

'I need to get to Signor Ronconi's house,' Ronnie blurted out urgently, worried about the darkness and the rapidly dropping temperature. 'My wife is sick.'

The man studied him thoughtfully in the lamplight.

'You are related to Signor Ronconi, perhaps?'

'His grandson.'

'Ah, now I see, you are Giacomo's son?'

'I am Giacomo too.'

'Come, we will go to Mama Conti. She will look after you, please follow me.' The man led the way to a large house on the edge of the square. Trusting to fate to look after their cases, Ronnie followed him. Mama Conti, a large and warm-hearted Italian housewife, asked no questions – at first. She opened her door, took them in, sat Maud by the fire and spoonfed her minestrone soup – which Ronnie was beginning to think was the Italian cure for all ills.

Bit by bit he told his story, and a boy was dispatched to the

322

square to pick up their cases. An ox was found which would draw a wheel-less sled to his grandparent's farm, both to carry their luggage and bring news of their arrival, and later, much later, when they were both fed and rested and after much discussion as to the best way of conveying Maud there, they were allowed to leave with a guide who promised to show Ronnie the way to their new home. He carried Maud. It seemed the easiest solution to the problem. Too weak to sit on a horse, even if one could be found, and far too delicate to withstand the bumping of the local sleds, the only solution seemed to lie in Ronnie's strong arms.

He had been warned it was eight kilometres. He had remembered it as five, but when he finally saw the oil lamp flickering in his grandfather's kitchen window he would have believed anyone who had told him it was twelve.

Maud was taken from him, and carried upstairs by his aunt and a neighbour who had been summoned to help. His grandparents embraced him, sat him by the fire in the only chair that boasted both a cushioned seat and back and fed him minestrone soup and wine that was so raw it hurt his throat. They asked only one question: 'Are you here to stay?'

When he said yes, they nodded and smiled so broadly he felt that he really had come home.

Maud was sunk deeply into a fluffy feather bed that had enveloped itself around her. She felt warm, cosy, sheltered and very, very comfortable. She opened her eyes. The first thing she saw was her own arm, encased in the sleeve of an unfamiliar linen nightdress, the wrist ornamented by thick, crunchy cotton lace. She looked up. A candle flickered on a pine chest next to the bed she was lying in. Two brown faces looked down at her, both smiling, one old and wrinkled, the other impossibly ancient. There was a single moment of blind, urgent panic.

'Ronnie?' she called out weakly.

'I'm here.' His hand grasped hers, strong and reassuring.

'Ronnie, don't leave me,' she pleaded.

'Not now darling,' he murmured. 'Not ever.'

323

Epilogue

It had been a glorious summer, and the weather showed no sign of abating even in late September. The harvest had been a rich and golden one. The vines had never been as full, nor the grapes as sweet. Ronnie had even suggested to his grandfather that for once the wine might not need watering down. The sheep grazed, bald and contented, on dried grass that was already hay on the lower slopes of the valley. The cattle chewed on a sweeter cud nearer the stream and the farmhouse. The sow suckled her thirteen piglets, and even the runt that Aunt Theresa had taken to feeding wrapped in a shawl in the farmhouse kitchen was doing well enough to warrant a prognosis of continued life rather than a sticky end as a glazed suckling pig for Sunday dinner.

The animals lazed in the sties and the fields, Aunt Theresa and grandmother spun wool as they sat on the wooden kitchen chairs that grandfather had carried outside for them, and held their noses as they watched Ronnie carry buckets in and out of the stone tank beneath the farmhouse.

There'd been so many things he had forgotten about Bardi, he reflected, choking on raw sewage fumes as he lowered himself and his buckets into the murky depths of the cesspit. Not least the ritual, twice-yearly emptying out of the huge stone waste pit beneath the house.

The animals in the barn rested their hooves on a slatted stone floor. The slats were carefully spaced, close enough to allow the hoofs a firm grip, but not too close to obstruct the animal waste from falling into the tank. It didn't help that the waste from the farmhouse drained into the same pit from chutes that led out of the kitchen sink and outhouse.

He carried his buckets to another tank, two fields away, built conveniently close to the vegetable plot. Stopping to breathe in clean air for a moment, he doused his hands in a horse trough before picking up his wooden buckets again. The walk back and forward across the fields he enjoyed; it was the short descent into the pit that was unpleasant. Only this time, he noted with satisfaction, the job was done. He was hard pushed to fill both buckets.

'Dear God, I never expected to see Ronnie Ronconi, the immaculate Ronnie, dressed in work dungarees and up to his eyes in . . .'

'You don't have to say the word.' Ronnie struggled out of the pit. Putting down his buckets, he extended his hand.

'I'd rather not, if you don't mind,' Trevor shook his head.

'Coward,' Ronnie smiled. They walked together across the fields. Trevor watched while Ronnie emptied the buckets and washed them in the wooden trough, before tipping it out on its side.

'Shouldn't you have stepped in there?' Trevor asked gravely.

'I've a better place lined up,' Ronnie grinned. A set of perfect white teeth gleamed through the grime on his face. He walked on down to the stream. Trevor followed. Ronnie stepped straight into the cold water, still wearing his grandfather's old working dungarees. He scrubbed the worst of the filth from them with sand, then, taking them off, he scrubbed himself with a crude wooden brush and bar of strong carbolic soap that he'd had the foresight to place on the bank before he began his job.

'Looks like you've done this before,' Trevor commented, squatting on his heels.

'Second time this summer. Did you and Laura have a good journey?'

'No. And as you've done it yourself, how can you even ask?' Ronnie lay down, full length in the stream, and allowed the water to rinse off the soapsuds.

'By the time we reached Bardi – '

'You were tired, hot and hungry. And as the last straw, you found you had no other choice but to walk here.' Ronnie left the water and pulled a pair of rough black cotton trousers over his slim, soaking flanks.

'Aren't you going to dry yourself?'

'No need to in this heat.' He picked up an unevenly woven linen shirt, and a leather belt.

'How on earth did you manage with Maud, when you reached here?' Trevor asked.

'That was difficult.' Ronnie's face fell serious. 'She was so done in by the time we got to Bardi, she was barely conscious. I met one of my grandfather's friends. He had a sled – '

'Don't tell me,' Trevor groaned. 'One of those wonderful contraptions pulled by an ox, with no wheels, that bumps over every lump in the road.'

'Good God, man, don't tell me you and Laura tried to sit on it?'

'For about five minutes.' He watched Ronnie tuck his shirt into his trousers and pull the leather belt tightly around his waist. 'You've lost weight,' he said critically.

'I could afford to,' Ronnie said carelessly. 'Those sleds are all right for luggage.'

'That's what we ended up using it for.'

Ronnie picked up his filthy overalls. Wrapping them in a bundle and grabbing the soap and brush, he began to walk up the hill, back towards the farmhouse. 'I carried Maud here,' he said quietly.

'She must have been exhausted.'

'Half dead might be a better description,' Ronnie told him. They reached the top of the hill. Trevor was panting from the heat and the unaccustomed exertion, but Ronnie was as fresh as if he'd just left his bed.

'As I said, I carried Maud here. It's only about four miles.'

'Dear God, Ronnie, weren't you tired yourself? I could barely drag myself up the hills to here. The thought of carrying Laura as well . . .'

'Maud's lighter than Laura,' Ronnie pointed out. 'And by that time I'd seen enough to jog my memory. I remembered enough of my grandmother and my aunt to be sure of our welcome. I wasn't disappointed. My grandmother had already stripped, cleaned and made up the biggest bed, in the best bedroom, for Maud. Not that they wanted me to share it with her,' he complained drily. 'Between them, Aunt Theresa and my grandmother elbowed me very nicely out of the way. They must have been bored out of their minds before we turned up, because judging by the amount of time they spent nursing Maud they couldn't have had anything to do before. They spoonfed her the best spaghetti, the freshest vegetables, the richest cream. They stayed with her day and night, pouring weird concoctions of herbal teas down her throat. They talked to her, sang to her – not that poor Maud understood a single word they were saying – and I couldn't swear to it, but in my opinion I think they even resorted to casting a spell or two.'

Ronnie looked to the back of the house where his grandfather had carried out three more chairs and a small table. The older women had put away their spinning, and a bottle of his aunt's strawberry wine stood on the table together with four glasses. Maud, still thin, but more robust than she had been in Wales, was sitting engrossed in conversation with Laura.

'You had a chance to examine her before you came looking for me?' Ronnie asked Trevor.

'Only a third of her right lung is functioning, and her left is badly scarred, you do know that?'

'The local doctor told me she'll never be strong.'

'He's right,' Trevor agreed flatly. 'And if you're asking for my opinion I think a return to Wales would be as good as a death sentence for her.'

'Who wants to go back to Wales?'

'You're happy here?' Trevor asked incredulously, staring at the primitive farmhouse, and Ronnie's rough clothes.

'Blissfully,' Ronnie laughed. Maud looked up, saw Ronnie and smiled. He smiled back, and Trevor saw everything.

'Good God, she's now as besotted with you as you were with her!' he exclaimed.

'Of course. Did you doubt my ability to make her fall in love with me?' Ronnie slapped his brother-in-law soundly on the back. 'Come on, I'm still waiting for you to tell me what you think of Maud's progress.'

'Considering she's only been here a few months, it's incredible. She might not be strong, might never be strong, but the disease is no longer active. Provided she takes things quietly – '

'As if my aunt will allow her to do anything else,' Ronnie interrupted.

'It's a complete and utter miracle.'

'No, not a miracle.'

'Then what?' Trevor asked.

'Just my wife.' Ronnie went to the well and pulled up a rope. Attached to the end of it was a bottle of his grandfather's rough wine.

'It's not best brandy, but I guarantee you won't have tasted anything like it before,' he warned, handing the cool bottle to Trevor after pulling the cork with his teeth and taking a deep and satisfying draught himself.

'What are we drinking to?' Trevor asked.

'Life, health and happiness.'

Trevor looked across at Laura, remembered the secret she had told him that morning, and saw the bloom it had already brought to her cheeks.

'I must be the luckiest man alive,' he murmured as he put the bottle to his lips.

Ronnie walked towards his wife, smiling, thinking of what they had to look forward to that night once they were closeted in the privacy of their bedroom.

'You're wrong,' he said firmly, taking the bottle from a coughing, spluttering Trevor. 'If there's such a thing as a luckiest man alive, I'm it.'